ICEBERGS

ICEBERGS

REBECCA JOHNS

BLOOMSBURY

For Elizabeth M. and Arthur Currie Johns
and Carol and Richard Johns

First published in Great Britain 2007

Bloomsbury Publishing Plc
36 Soho Square
London W1D 3QY

ISBN 978 0 7475 7800 0

A CIP catalogue record for this book is available from the British Library.

Typeset by Hewer Text UK Ltd, Edinburgh
Printed in Great Britain by Clays Ltd, St Ives plc

Bloomsbury Publishing, London, New York and Berlin

10 9 8 7 6 5 4 3 2 1

The paper this book is printed on is certified by the © Forest Stewardship
Council 1996 A.C. (FSC). It is ancient-forest friendly. The printer holds
FSC chain of custody SGS-COC-2061

FSC
Mixed Sources
Product group from well-managed
forests and other controlled sources
Cert no. SGS-COC-2061
www.fsc.org
© 1996 Forest Stewardship Council

www.bloomsbury.com

. . . is the shipwrack then a harvest, does tempest carry the grain for thee?

—Gerard Manley Hopkins,
"The Wreck of the Deutschland"

CIRCLING THE WRECK

1944

ONE

Already the Liberator's starboard engines were dead, the port engines windmilling and starting to smoke. Below the plane was the coast of Labrador—low black mountains and snow-covered woods, the silver sea—and Walt Dunmore, the wireless air gunner, was wondering what it would be like to die. He hoped it would be quick. He hoped he would not be afraid. But then the pilot yelled back for Walt to transfer fuel to the remaining engines, anything to keep them up as long as possible, and Walt tore off his gloves and did what he was told and tried not to think so much.

They sank down and down. From the nose Alister Clark, the navigator, barked their position into the com. Walt sent the SOS, but the wireless and the radio were transmitting nothing but static. He hit the key, hoped for the best. Down the bomb bay catwalk the Polish tail gunner, Josef Dusza, was coming toward him. The narrow metal span was not wide enough for both feet at once, and Dusza had to hold on to keep his balance. Beneath him, around the edges of the bomb bay doors, came light from the clouds and snow and ice that were driving them down. Dusza smiled a little, the lines around his mouth deepening, and he shook his head and laughed, inaudible over the noise of the engines.

How clear the world looked from this angle, and in a minute now it would be over.

For the last three hours, coming back from Iceland, they had realized they were in trouble, the storm thickening and closing in, creeping into the open places on the Lib, filling the plane with mist and cold wind. They were heading back to Newfoundland, but three hours from home they got the news that the landing field at Gander was closed because of the weather. They were told to head farther north, to Goose Bay, Labrador, a long trip in the best of conditions. They crept up over the Strait of Belle

Isle, the Liberator's starboard engines icing up and dying in succession, first number four, then number three, announced by the sudden calm over the wing. The pilot fiddled with the fuel, the speed, backfired the engines, anything to try to keep the port engines running, and it was all he could do to keep her level, to keep her up and out of the water.

But here was land at last and reason to hope still. They could set down. They could be safe. It happened that way sometimes. The pilot yelled, "Not yet! Not yet!"

Engine two sputtered and whined, and the plane listed to starboard, tossing the men around. They bumped into sharp edges, the metal skeleton of the plane. Books, maps, oxygen cans, hoses, and loose ammo hurled through the tight spaces. Walt slammed against the fuselage, cold metal against his back, the greasy smell of gas on his hands. Under them, the sound of trees breaking. He heard Dusza say, "Oh, my God." But no one spoke after that.

When they hit and the plane tore in half, Walt felt a sudden change in pressure and saw light as the tail end of the plane ripped free and fell away, and Dusza was pulled out, and then Walt himself, losing his grip on gravity, arms grabbing air, feet out behind him, sucked out in the pressure of the wind, loose and alone and sailing through the sky, an animal with no thought or instinct but fear. The ground coming up fast, stone and earth and trees, and cold wind, stinging snow in his teeth, and then falling, a memory of making cannonballs in a lake when he was young, tucking up and making himself as small as possible, too small and unimportant to die. Down, down, then impact, scratches of ice along his face, and sudden cold, and no air, and black.

In his half-sleep, in the blackness, he was cold. He must have been thrown clear of the wreck into a snowbank. He was surprised at how deep it was. He reached up and scooped wet snow off his face and spat it out of his mouth. So cold that it burned. His hands were burning. His gloves were lost, so he clamped his hands underneath his armpits to keep them warm. Pushing out with his elbows, he could feel there was snow all around him, in a very small space. He couldn't get any purchase in the softness. His limbs shook. Fear clawed at his back, and it was all he could do to keep from thrashing around, trying to break free. Snow crumbled in on him, sliding like gravel, and he didn't know which way was up, which way was out, which direction to dig. He might be buried head down, like a baby waiting to be born. He could be sideways. There was no way to know.

The flight suit covered everything, kept him dry if not warm, but his hands and face were exposed. He was dressed for the inside of the plane—the flight suit hooked up to the plane's electrical systems for heat—not the inside of a snowbank. This was a deep freeze, a subarctic winter. Walt knew he was in trouble if he stayed where he was, and he was in trouble if he tried to dig out. The snow was dry and powdery as sand, filling what air there was with a dusting of glitter. He felt the first stirrings of panic, a fine edge of fear. He would die here, curled up in a ball. He would suffocate. No one would ever know where he was. He thought of his mother, at home in Sudbury, hoping he would be found. His wife, Dottie. He knew what that kind of waiting was like. He didn't want his family to feel that for his sake.

He yelled out, "I'm here!" But the sound was so muffled, he was sure the others couldn't hear him.

Urgency came over him. His brother Bill had died in a storm like this, in a cold like this, long ago when Walt was still a boy. Bill had been out with their father, surveying the mining country in northern Ontario, when a sudden blizzard whitened the air. Bill had gotten lost looking for firewood. Walt remembered his father telling how they had found Bill curled into a ball in a snowbank, snow drifted over his face and in his mouth and the corners of his eyes. He said the mortician had had to break all his brother's bones to straighten him out enough to put him in a coffin. He recalled the look on his father's face when he told the family what had happened, his mother's stony silence, and he knew that more had been broken beyond repair in that blizzard than bones.

Tears on his face, sliding down, panic tears. Even though he was alone, he hated them and couldn't stop them, and he shook and wiped them away, and they kept falling, sliding down his face and off his chin, and his face was cold where they slid past. They slid *down*, in the direction of gravity, toward his shoes.

The air was somewhere up there, above his head, if he could reach it.

He would. He started digging. He knelt in his little space and dug and dug until his hole started filling with snow, caving in around him. His fingers quickly went numb. Each space he cleared around his face ended up in a pile around his feet. It was hard work. His skin grew hot. Snow slipped into the cuffs of his flight suit. He dug, and his breath came fast, though he tried to hold it. The harder he tried to hold it, the harder he breathed, his body taking over, instinct threatening the air supply. Inside his little tunnel, his limited vision started to go gray, go black with little sparkles of stars, and he gasped. He was deeper than he had thought. The snow above him slid around loose and kept threatening to fall in on him and cover him again. Then his hand broke through, and he felt a rush of cold air on his freezing fingers and pushed the snow aside, and there was cold air on his face, and he took it in like a drowning fish, and he coughed and coughed until he thought he would choke.

He grabbed hold of a nearby bush and pulled himself out of the snowbank. He looked around at the crash site, at what was left. Snow was still falling, and the sky was low and threatening, the storm not letting up. Smoking pieces of the Liberator were lying everywhere in a little clearing surrounded by scrub spruce and balsam and paper birch. The clearing was barely the size of a town lot, and the Lib had come down on the edge of it, sweeping a path of broken trunks and branches, some as big around as a man. The pale yellow hearts of the trees were exposed here and there. The woods parted enough that the snow had room to blow around, had drifted in places, peaks and valleys like dunes, but the crash had left streaks of black oil and smoke on the otherwise perfectly white, undisturbed surface.

It was midday, but Walt knew the light wouldn't last much longer, not this deep in winter, not this far north.

The trees held up their dark branches. They grew at an incline, a lean in their trunks, because the land around him was hillier than he'd thought from the air, low hills that sloped down toward the distant, invisible sea. The sky was so low and gray that the landscape looked like a photograph, colors bleached out of everything. There was a ringing silence in his ears, like the shadow of sound when it disappears too quickly, and for a minute he worried he had gone deaf. But then a blast of wind swept through, and the trees bent hard under its onslaught, and he heard the whistling of air through the waving branches.

The exposed skin of his hands and face was burning in the cold. The snow came down with a soft hum, or maybe it was the ringing in his ears. A rabbit track, bounding, and something larger: moose, maybe, or caribou. The tracks led away from the grove, as if the animals had felt the disaster descending upon them and gone running.

He shouted out, "I'm here! I'm over here!" His voice felt furry thick and strange in his throat, but there was no answer, and none of the boys was in sight.

Determination, then, and what needed to be done. A list formed in his mind. Find the others. Build a fire. Build a shelter. Find something to eat. Signal to the rescue planes. He was satisfied to see how much needed to be done. He wouldn't panic.

He took a step, feeling the snow sink under him. He wobbled, his knees untrustworthy still, likely to buckle. But he was all right and he could breathe now and he had lived through it, he had lived through it, and there were still men missing and maybe hurt and work to be done, and he'd be damned if he wouldn't keep moving and be glad he still could. Other than the cold and the ringing in his ears, he wasn't hurt at all. He held on to the tree trunks and made his slow way around the wreck, stopping to look in the craters made by pieces of plane and tree, looking for anything that might be useful, anything that might be salvaged, anyone still alive. "Hello?" he called again, but no one answered.

He rubbed his hands together. He stuffed them under his armpits to warm them and wished he had left his gloves on when Len Ingalls, the pilot, had called back and told him to switch the fuel-line feed before they hit.

They had been returning from a convoy escort to Southampton with a partial crew and had been told to put in to the Canadian base in Iceland for a two-day furlough. Some of the boys went into the officers' club for a drink, but when Walt had a moment alone he bought souvenirs in Reykjavík for his wife and later soaked in a mineral blue pool of hot water until his skin steamed like cooked mussels. He had never felt so warm, even in such a cold place, and the minerals made the water so dense that it held him up, high in the water. He felt light and buoyant as wind. There at the far reaches he felt like a new man, as if he could go back to the war for another week, another month.

Walt had joined up back in 1940 with his younger brother, Harry, signing up for a wireless air gunner slot. Harry had ended up as a navigator in Ferry Command, shuttling supplies across to Great Britain, planes new-minted and shiny, stripped of their guns but full of troops and food and bullets. Walt was glad that his brother had joined the Royal Canadian Air Force too, because it meant that once in a while they crossed paths, and Harry, who was better at writing letters, would send word home to their mother that they were both all right.

Walt had been raring to go, like most of the other fellows, but not for the same reasons. He didn't believe so much in all that king and country business. He was eager to get out of Canada, see what else there was in the world. He could be stationed in Britain, Italy, Africa. Later Burma, Australia, the South Pacific. Countless places he had heard about, in schoolbooks and encyclopedias, but never thought he would have a chance to see. Suddenly it was not only possible, but noble. The right thing to do. Work had been scarce before the war started, so Walt figured he could learn some new skills in the service, something to take with him back into regular life once the war was over. Maybe he would go to work for Canadian Pacific or Western Union. Maybe he would work on the railways. He could even go to the States. For the time being, the military was as good a way to make a living as any. He did see new places. He had learned new things.

Wireless air gunners were two for one: He had learned to work the wireless and, later, the .50-caliber Browning turret guns, their barrels sticking out of the cone of the turret like the antennae of some warrior beetle. In the air over Ontario, with a group of other recruits, he had taken his turn at the gun behind a Fairy Battle trailing a target drogue and peppered it with red-colored bullets for target practice. Part of his training had included taking the Browning apart and putting it back together blindfolded, because in the air, during ops, you wouldn't be able to turn on your lights, not if you didn't want the enemy to see you. He liked the feel of the metal parts, the click when you slid the bolster home. He had learned to recognize planes from a long ways away, Allied or Axis: Sunderland Flying Boats, Cansos, Lancasters, Flying Fortresses, the swift wooden Mosquitoes, as well as German Arados, Stuka dive bombers, and Junkers, so he would know when to shoot and when to wave as they passed.

But it was the wireless Walt really excelled at and loved. There was a music to Morse code, a quality that could be discerned only by listening. Each word had its own inflection, its unique pattern, and everyone had his own style. The new kids were the easiest to pick out: They still had the painfully slow, methodical rhythm of someone trying to remember the exact pattern of the letters and numbers, a five-year-old banging on a piano. A good wireless operator could get out maybe twenty, twenty-five words a minute. Walt had got up to thirty words a minute, a feat that in certain moments he let himself be more than a little proud of, hitting the key fast, hearing the words go out to the world.

He had flown over Greenland, Iceland, places that from the air hardly seemed like land at all. Rock and ice. He had flown enough miles to circle the globe eleven times. Running between Newfoundland, Labrador, Great Britain, or Ireland—it got harder and harder to tell, sometimes, where they were going and where they had been. In the summer there was too much daylight, in the winter too little. Boredom and cold usually set in at about the same time. There wasn't much in the way of talking that anyone could do over the monstrous roar of the engines, the tin-can shudder of sound inside the plane, unless you cluttered the com with lots of chitchat. There was the cold and the noise and the boredom, the cramped spaces, the endless, usually empty ocean, the gray fog and the clouds blurring the line between sea and sky, and the days and nights passed one by one.

On the ground it was a different story. At Gander the boys knew how to have a good time, and they got drunk and sang bawdy songs and joked about the Women's Division girls, waited for their weekends down to St. John's, their leaves to go home to their families. On days when the weather was warm, they'd play baseball against the Americans, who had their own compound on the other side of the base, hitting dingers into the birch woods. He liked Len, the tight-lipped pilot, who had been a crop duster before the war, not least because he didn't take foolish risks with the plane and the men inside. He was fond of Arch Dawson, the co-pilot, who had a wife in Ottawa and a sweetheart in Ireland and made each man swear to destroy the Irish girl's letters if anything happened to him. And he liked Josef Dusza, who had learned English by listening to the other fellows over the com. Walt had known him for more than two years before he found out Dusza's mother rarely went out anymore because people thought her accent was German and she was afraid of what people would say. Dusza was no-bullshit. When the younger boys started moaning that they hadn't been assigned to the bomber units in Britain or the dogfighters, Dusza was the guy who told them to be grateful they got to spend the war freezing their asses off over the North Atlantic, dying of boredom, instead of swimming through a sky full of Messerschmitts.

Walt was close to all the guys, but none more than Alister Clark, the navigator. He'd grown up in southern Ontario, not far from Walt's wife, Dottie, and once or twice when they'd had leave at the same time, they'd gone home together, sharing a bench on the train and falling against each other in their sleep. Al was a smiling man, a proponent of a brand of gallows humor that kept the whole crew in stitches. But he was serious about navigating. Something about measuring time and distance by the stars loosened his tongue, and he could sit over his beer for hours and tell Walt how to take a measurement with a sextant and how with a watch and a knowledge of the stars you could find your way anywhere on earth. He had learned to navigate on his back in a small round room with a map of the sky tattooed on the ceiling. The instructors spun the ceiling the way the sky would spin at night, and Al was told to name the constellations. Ursa Minor, Orion, Cassiopeia, beautiful names for such cold-looking pinpricks of light. Take a reading and find your position. One fixed point in space, a map of the sky, a watch, and a compass, and he could say, *You are here. I am here.*

Walt and Al crewed together often, sometimes for months at a time, all missions over the North Atlantic, long sweeps of empty ocean, looking for U-boat wolf packs. Back and forth across the Atlantic, in daylight, at night, as wide-open and impenetrable as outer space and nearly as thinly populated, Walt at the wireless listening for the *dit-dit-dit* of humanity out there in the blackness. The Liberator not a Flying Fortress, but a desert island, a tin drum banging out the existence of life: *We are here.*

They knew the U-boats were out there, looking, too, for ships to bring down. U-boats were fast on the surface but had to slow down underwater, which made it hard for them to catch Allied convoys, so the North Atlantic Squadron was there, if not to sink the subs, which was nearly impossible, then at least to make them submerge and hide until the planes had passed overhead and the convoys could get through in one piece. The Liberators would fly out, turn, and circle back to catch the submarines breeching, the Nazis thinking the danger had passed. Walt and Al had crewed together on a bunch of Libs. Sometimes they got shot up pretty badly, lost engines, and took flak from the subs' deck guns, and later he would find holes in the fuselage big enough to put his fist through.

In the fall they had taken on a U-boat, coming down from ten thousand feet into little deadly clouds of flak. Walt had manned the upper turret, let the lead boat have it with both guns, and took out two of the deck gunners. Ingalls circled around again. When they opened their bomb bay doors and released the last of the depth charges, the blossoms shot up into the air like geysers. The sub started to go down. Walt had expected men to pile out into rubber boats and push off and drift out into the North Atlantic as the vessel sank underneath them, but the boat sank so fast that no one appeared on the surface, and when it went down there was only an oil slick over the water and a bouquet of small dark bubbles rising to the surface to show where it had been.

Sometimes there were bodies in the water. Sometimes they swept down low, skimming the surface of the ocean to have a look, and Walt could see the frozen faces of men—German or Allied, who could tell?—bobbing in the ocean like human icebergs, held up by the futile buoyancy of their life vests; and usually after that no one spoke for a while. Walt knew there was no point in bailing out over the North Atlantic. He kept his Mae West stowed and hoped the plane blew up, if it came to that. The boys told him he was tempting fate, but he knew what he wanted and what he didn't want, and what he didn't want was to fall asleep with his eyes open, turned up toward a perpetual view of the gray sky.

But it was weather, not flak from the wolf packs, that had brought them down over Labrador. The town was in front of them, the Goose Bay air base ahead of them somewhere in the storm. Ingalls shouting to Clark about the distance left to Goose. Out the blister, Walt could see nothing but fog and wind. They lost altitude fast, the Liberator tilting dangerously to the side as Ingalls struggled to keep it up and keep it going forward, through the cold January air, toward the rocky coast. Then the sound of numbers one and two whining under the weight of the plane, the boots slicked over with ice.

Walt had looked out the window under the wing; suddenly there was land, not water, underneath them, low mountains, scrub trees, snow. Then he was afraid enough to hope.

He heard Dawson on the horn, shouting over the noise to Ingalls through his throat mike. "The lake or the trees," he said. "What you think?"

"Trees," Ingalls shouted. "Ice won't hold us."

The plane sank down, and out the window Walt could see the crowns of trees whipping by, and then the sound of metal tearing, and then Josef Dusza, coming toward him, was gone.

Walt went slowly around the wreck. The snow was very deep, almost as deep as Walt was tall, and he knew if he went in again, he might not get back out. He slowly crossed the parts that looked deepest, testing each step, trying to hurry without hurrying, but still he sank in every few steps, one leg or both, and had to pull himself out again. He took a step, waited. Another, waited. At this rate it would take months to find the others.

He took another step, and the snow gave way under him. He went in up to his waist, and his arms went out to break his fall or he might have gone in farther. He was sure he would be stuck for good until he was able to pack a little snow down and pull himself carefully out of the hole and stand on top of the thin crust that covered the snowbank.

"Hello?" he called.

The snow kept falling. His legs shook underneath him, and even though he held on to the slender trunks of young trees as he went through the woods, he sank up to his knees with every step. He was still optimistic about Al and Dusza and the others, still hoping to find them not too banged up. The gray air had darkened with smoke. There were holes in the snow, pockmarks like an acne-scarred face where bits of burning metal had been flung. Walt checked them out one by one. He saw from a distance a large hole, something deep, and he crept toward it carefully, slowly, though he wanted to run. When he peeked inside, his hands shaking, he saw that it held the upper turret, big around as a pickle barrel and cold to the touch. Not a man at all. Walt blew out a fierce breath of air. The look of surprise on Dusza's face when the fuselage ripped open and he went sailing out, and Walt tried to remember if in the confusion he had seen Dusza go out clean or if he had hit something on his way out. The sound of tearing metal, and a rush of air, and Dusza went through the hole first.

The look of surprise, then Dusza's head jerking forward. The look and then blood. What had he hit? Walt went through the same hole, went through too quickly to see what was around him. A feeling rose in his gut that finding the tail gunner would not be much use to either of them.

The plane had split in the middle, right at its weakest point—the bomb bay—and the tail had torn loose and separated from the rest of the plane. Walt walked toward the spot where he could see it lying on its side. It had skidded down a low slope, leaving behind a long, scooped-out snow trail slicked over with grease and soot and strewn with metal parts. He followed the trail back up, amazed at how far he had been thrown from the wreck, and walked around, listening, looking for footprints or any sign of the four other men who had been in the plane. But there were no footprints in the snow except his own.

"Anyone hurt?"

There was no answer. Of course there was no answer. Walt walked around the open space for the rear turret gun, touching the metal. Every inch was bent and crumpled, no longer resembling anything solid or useful, the once smooth skin of the plane collapsed to show the seams and ribs underneath. No one was there. No one had been in that part of the plane when they hit.

Pieces of the skin of the plane and the bomb bay doors were scattered around the clearing. The nose lay farther up the slope, so he trudged back up, grabbing tree branches, careful not to fall in. He would have given anything for snowshoes. The front end of the Lib looked almost as bad as the back end. It had rolled in the crash and ended upside down, the flight deck and cockpit underneath, the small nav compartment on top. The nose looked like a fish on ice, its tail gone, its silver scales growing dull. He picked his way through the debris and circled round until he could see the hole he and Dusza had been thrown through when the Lib ripped apart. He stooped down, looked inside, his snow-glazed eyes taking a moment to adjust to the dark. The inside looked worse than the outside. Everything was bent, everything thrown around and tossed aside and useless, bullets and hoses and headsets, so vital in the air, nothing but scrap on the ground. Loose cables and wires hung down across the hole he'd come out. He felt sick, looking at them.

"Hello?" he called, still hopeful he would find someone alive.

From inside, a voice: "Here," it said. "In here."

He couldn't see inside, but the voice kept him moving forward in the half-light. A banging noise, someone tapping on the inside of the fuselage. As he got closer he could see it was Al Clark, trapped in the nav compartment under the front wheel, which had collapsed in on him in the crash. The nav compartment under the flight deck was a tight squeeze in the best of conditions, a tunnel of sharp metal and plywood and the large front wheel spinning slowly with the motion of the plane; but now, turned upside down, it was nothing but a little cave, a mess of metal and rubber and hoses. Light came in through the nose blister, dimly.

"I'm here," Al said, and gave a grin, but his face was white. "I think I need some help," he said. Blood was oozing out from Al's shoulder, from underneath the metal arm that attached the wheel to the plane, staining rust the snow that had come in through the holes in the fuselage. "This isn't as comfortable as it looks," he said.

Walt crawled through the debris to take a closer look at Al's shoulder. "You're bleeding pretty good there."

"I noticed," Al said. "What about the others?"

"I don't know. You're the first one I've found."

"What luck." Al laughed, but there was no mirth in it. "I think Len and Arch may have had it."

"Don't worry about them right now. Let's get this off you first." Walt stooped and looked hard at Al's shoulder and tried to move the wheel, but it was too heavy, and Walt's hands were too cold. He couldn't see well what was underneath, where the damage was to Al's shoulder, but from the amount of blood he imagined it was bad enough. "Stay here."

"Sure," he said. His breath was hard. "Nowhere to be right now, anyway."

Walt squeezed out of the nav compartment and pawed through the wreckage of the flight deck, looking for a fire ax. Because the plane had landed upside down, nothing was where it should have been. He finally found one near the fuel pumps he had manned just before the crash but had some trouble wrapping his hands around the handle. When he got back inside the nav compartment, he found a small section to attack and was able to manage a few swings—not great, but they were enough—and then he was able to lift off the piece of metal and rubber that had pinned Al's arm down. He wrapped Al's shoulder with a torn piece of parachute, trying not to make the pain any worse, but the blood started seeping through immediately. If the wound had been in a different spot, he would have put a tourniquet on it, but right there at the top of the shoulder there was nowhere to tie one. Walt pressed the fabric into the flesh, and Al used his good arm to hold it there.

Walt tucked his hands back under his armpits, but the fingers flapped numbly. He should start a fire—they would need a fire soon—but the boys took precedence, the boys were in trouble.

"What happened?" Al asked.

"Had to dig myself out of a snowbank. You all right?"

"Cold as a witch's tit."

"Me too." He looked at the bandage, already soaked through. "I think I should wrap you up a little tighter there. We need to stop that blood."

Walt took off the first bandage and tried again. This time he wrapped it tight, despite the noises Al made. "Son of a bitch," Al said. "That hurts."

"Sorry," Walt said. He tied it off, then bound Al's arm tight to his body to keep him from moving it.

He still looked pretty pale. Walt looked around one more time for his gloves, but they weren't on the flight deck by the radio where he had left them. They could have flown out in the crash, been anywhere.

Al made a sound as if he were choking, bringing Walt's attention back around. "What's wrong?" he said, but Al was laughing, a nervous, high-pitched sound.

"Don't be so goddamned serious," Al said. "You're starting to make me worry." There was fear in his eyes, a tremble in his chin. He was shivering, shock or pain or relief, maybe a little bit of everything.

Walt pulled a parachute out of its pack and wrapped it tightly around Al, as if wrapping a child. "Don't get too comfy," he said.

He backed out of the tight nav compartment and bent down to see inside the flight deck, where he had always sat tending to the radio and the wireless, and then crawled forward to the cockpit. The cockpit windows had been smashed in, and when the plane landed upside down it had filled with snow. It was a very small space to begin with, and with the snow Walt couldn't see Len or Arch at all. He started digging again, hoping they made it out, hoping maybe they'd been thrown out like him. His hands were very numb, but he kept digging. He dug until he touched something solid—a hand, cold and dead, and he couldn't tell to whom it belonged. He dug more, uncovering another hand, a face. Len and Arch were still strapped in their seats. They had suffocated in all that snow.

When he knew they were dead, Walt felt around the cockpit for their gloves. In the darkness he shoved aside papers and pieces of broken Plexiglas and metal bits. But there were no gloves. They could have been anywhere, even back in Iceland, for all the good they would do him.

He stood up and looked back into the nav compartment. Al's pale face looking out at him was a relief.

"No?" Al asked.

"No."

Walt left Len and Arch where they were for now. He couldn't do anything that would help them. But Al was alive, and he was alive, and maybe Dusza if he could find him, and for now that would have to be enough. They would get through this. They would not be afraid. Not yet.

"Stay here," he said.

Al called back, "If you're going out, would you pick me up a pack of cigarettes?"

Walt crawled back outside the wreck and into the snow. He began his

slow, careful circle back around the rest of the wreck. He still couldn't
see where Dusza had landed. He called out again to the trees, the wind.
But the only answer seemed to be the wind shaking clumps of snow out
of the branches. A soft *whump*, and branch after branch cleared. The wind
was picking up, and night was coming on. He had better get started on
that list.

He didn't like this darkness. It came on too early, in the middle of the
afternoon, as it did in all the places where they flew, the far northern
reaches of the globe. It was a thick midwinter dark that he never really got
used to. It didn't get dark like this in Sudbury, where he had grown up,
which had the paved roads and electric lights of a boom mining town, had
had them for years. It didn't get dark like this in Essex County, where his
wife lived without him, across the river from Detroit, lighting up the night
sky like a new Jerusalem. He walked a little faster, was a little less careful.
Whatever it was he needed to do, he would have to do it fast, before the
dark came on and he couldn't see three steps in front of him.

Search planes would be dispatched when they didn't turn up. They
might be found. They might not. Sometimes Libs went down and were
never heard from again. In October, not long after the battle with the U-
boat, a plane transporting twenty-four men from Gander for a weekend
furlough had gone missing and had never been found. They had been
heading for Mont-Joli and in bad weather had been told to turn for
Montreal, and that was the last anyone heard from them. Surely they were
dead. Surely if anyone had lived, they would have been found somehow.

He found Dusza, finally, stuck upside down in a tree on the other side of
the clearing, not far from where Walt had landed. Caught by the foot from
a tangle of low branches, Dusza swayed back and forth whenever a blast of
air shook the tree, the fingers brushing the snow, scraping out faint, dusty-
looking lines, as if trying to write a message.

There was a great deal of blood, more than Walt would have thought
possible. He bent down and tipped Dusza's head back to look for signs of
life, still hoping a little, hoping beyond hope, but when he touched it the
head leaned over a little too far to one side, came off the shoulders like
removing a cap from a bottle. An unnatural angle. The cables he had seen
in the fuselage had, in fact, taken his friend's head near clean off, and only a

thin flap of skin held it on. Walt snatched his hand back in surprise. He stepped away and closed his eyes. At least it was fast. At least it wasn't me. Jesus H. Christ, it could have been me.

He pulled his friend down and covered him with the rest of the parachute. He wrapped him up tight, as if to protect him from the cold. Dusza wasn't wearing gloves, either.

There were things to be done, gloves or no gloves. He went looking for anything he might be able to use as a signal. He spread one big red-and-white parachute across the snow and pinned it down with metal cans of fuel and part of the heavy machine gun he had manned the day they took on the Nazi sub. Then he went back inside the plane to look for food and medical packs and whatever he could use for blankets and shelter.

Al asked, "Did you find him?"

"Yeah."

Al nodded and let his chin fall forward onto his chest. He looked tired.

Walt focused on the dark inside the plane, the growing dark and the things that were still left inside, things that might be useful if they were going to be stuck out here all night. Surely someone would come looking for them before long, maybe were already looking. Surely it wouldn't be more than a night out in the bush; but it was wartime, and they were coming back from Iceland, and there was a lot of ground to cover in Labrador, a lot of heavily wooded ground and places with no roads and no people. A lot of empty space between Goose and Gander.

How close he had come. If he had been the one who had been closer to the hole, what might have happened? It was pure dumb luck that Dusza had gone out the hole first and Walt himself after, that the other had died and he had lived. Josef went first, and Josef lay under the parachute, and Josef was minus one head, and there was nothing to be done about it. Walt pressed his cold hands against the cold metal of the plane, held himself up, took in gulps of air, felt himself on the edge of a gulf of gratefulness and shock and fear and longing. He stepped away from it. There was no time to be afraid.

His hands were very pale, and he was starting to lose feeling in them. He would need to warm them soon, or it would be too late. Looking for dry wood seemed to take an eternity, but soon he had a small fire going outside the nose. It was so cold that the smoke wouldn't rise. When he put his hands over it, he could feel the pain in his palms as they started to warm, but the fingertips were still numb. Not a good sign. He should have a pail of warm water. He should have a pair of gloves, while he was wishing for things. But night was coming on, and he needed to built a shelter, and there was no one else to do it.

The inside of the plane wouldn't do. The empty bomb bay was a crumpled heap, though the doors, designed to break away on impact, might come in handy. The flight deck and cockpit were too small, too destroyed, and the tail section too far away to drag Al to, especially in snow that deep. Walt decided to build the shelter outside, under one of the wings, not far from the fire. There he tamped down the snow, slogging until he was wet with sweat under his flight suit. Then he dragged out extra parachutes and sheepskins the crew had brought from Iceland—presents for wives and girlfriends—flight suits, any kind of cloth at all. He made a pile under the one remaining wing on top of some balsam boughs and topped it all with some aviation maps. Then he threw a parachute over the whole works, held up by the wing of the plane. Inside, the light was red through the fabric. It was a good temporary shelter, enough to get them out of the wind, at least, and there was the fire. He helped Al out from under the flight deck. The snow was still falling, and the dark came on a little at a time, gray getting grayer, until night came on as a darker shade of gray, a curtain that closed all around them.

When they were both in the shelter, they huddled close under the pile of blankets and sheepskins, looking like a couple of native chieftains with their skins around them. He took another look at Al's shoulder, carefully unwrapping the pieces of parachute material. The blood had clotted but started to leak out again as soon as the bandage came away. He held up a match to it to try to see a little better, but when he saw the gray white bone in the heart of the wound, he knew why Al was making so many bad jokes. He took the first-aid kit he'd found and bandaged his friend back up properly this time. When he was done Al held the arm close to his body as if cradling a child. Walt was so close that he could feel his friend's breath on his own cheek. It smelled like the pea soup they'd had for lunch, which seemed years ago.

"How are those hands of yours?" Al asked.

"Blocks of ice."

"Here." Al reached out in the dark until the fingers of his good arm touched Walt's icy cold ones. He took them in his good hand and rubbed hard.

"Jesus!" Walt said. "That hurts."

"It's supposed to hurt. Rub snow on them—that should help."

"It doesn't," Walt said. "That's an old wives' tale."

"How do you know?"

"This isn't California. Didn't you ever get frostbite before?"

"No," Al said. "We actually had *heat* in the winters." He took off his left glove and gave it to Walt. "Take this."

"I can't. You need them. It's not your fault I lost my gloves."

"It's all right. I'm keeping the other."

Walt would have argued, but he was starting to fear for his hands. When he yanked on the glove, his fingers felt dead. He didn't dare warm them now—if they refroze afterward, he could lose both hands.

"What do you figure we hit?" Al asked.

"Tree," Walt said. "A big one."

"Rip off the tail?"

"Yeah."

"Talk about luck."

When Walt was old enough, he had gone to work with his father like his brother Bill. He still remembered how his mother had frowned when he said he wasn't going back to school that fall after grade eight because Papa had said he could learn the business, and anyway the family could use the money. "We don't need it as badly as all that," she had said, and later he had heard his parents arguing long into the night. But the next week he left with his father for the woods in the north country and tried to pretend he wasn't afraid, but he was a little, an apprehension that bordered on excitement, growing out of the pit of his belly and making everything seem clear and new and bright.

Mine surveying was usually done in winter, when the ground was hard, because it was easier to drill that way. There were precious few roads in those parts, certainly none that were paved. He and his father and the rest of the team of men and animals shuffled north by dogsled and snowshoes, following the lakes and streams, frozen over like a long white path through the woods. When they came to the area they were to survey, they cleared a space and staked their tents and then spent a day or two building a great wooden ceiling of boards over the entire camp, a roof that went from tree to tree to tree, and in the center of that they cut a hole for a massive fire that lit the whole place like an electric lamp. Under that ceiling, for the weeks they lived at the camp, the fire warmed everything and melted the snow down so far that the grass underfoot became visible. In time, the grass started to turn green, even though outside the camp it was still winter.

Under that shelter Walt spent his first winter as a surveyor's assistant, staking chains and holding targets so his father could take accurate measures. He liked living in the woods. There was a quiet to it that wasn't easy to come by at home with a house full of kids, and his father was a different man there, too. In the woods his quietness was less like anger, more like determination, more like strength.

When the job was done he snowshoed home with his father, but the house he'd grown up in was different, and Walt was never sure afterward if it was where he belonged. When he got his pay he was even more eager to leave again, get out of the house and back to the woods, and he began to understand why his father was gone so often and so long, because there was always work in those days, and always money to be made for those willing to make it, and always the call of the woods and the north and the falling snow, where a man could feel in charge of his own life. For years he followed his father into the woods, staking claims and laying out mines for cobalt and copper, nickel and asbestos, following boom to boom to boom for men who would become rich on the things they could pull out of the stony earth. Walt learned the business from his father, how to mark and measure, how to live on what you could build and break and kill, and until the depression worsened, he found it wasn't such a bad way to live. Like his father, he never really went home again, because whenever he was there, he was always thinking about the next time he could leave. Until the war broke out and he left for good, worrying his poor mother, who had never wanted anything but to have her whole family at home under one roof.

He told Alister Clark this as they lay together under the shelter of boughs and blankets, and Al whistled and said he was glad that if he was stranded in the bush with anyone, it was with Walt, and then they thought about the bodies lying still inside the plane and were quiet again for a while.

Under the blankets, it was close and warmed by the body heat of the two men, like the inside of a winter barn full of gamy animals. They lay together, back to back, and through the flight suit Walt could feel Al shiver, that deep, bone-crushing shivering that started in the bowels and worked its way out through the skin. He had known that shivering himself many times out in the woods with his father. He rolled over to face the back of Al's head and wrapped his arms around the other man to warm him up.

"I don't know why," Al said.

"It's all right. It'll stop in a minute."

Inside the plane, they were used to tight spaces and the discomfort of too much togetherness, as Ingalls had called it, but this was a different place, and a different kind of togetherness, and a different kind of warmth. Walt brushed against the wound in Al's shoulder and felt him stiffen, felt the sticky blood on his fingers. He could smell Al's sweat and the mineral smell of the blood. Slowly his arms and legs warmed, and his face, and Walt was never so glad not to be alone in his whole life.

There they were in the middle of the bush, at the very edge of the continent, their place unknown. When had he ever been so unsure of where he was or which way was the way to safety? It made his skin itch. He had a compass, but that worked only when a man was sure of where he was to begin with. Al wasn't in any shape to travel anyway, and without snowshoes or a dog team Walt would have very little luck slogging through the bush. He thought of all that wilderness around them, the trees and snow and hills, the sea, and himself and Al small as drops of rain in the ocean, smaller even, and wondered how on earth they would ever be found.

He dozed a little, woke, and felt the stirrings of panic. The blankets were heavy, then heavier, then leaden. He felt he might smother under the weight, and an uncomfortable, unfamiliar feeling came over him. Even though he knew the blankets were going to keep him alive that night, it was all he could do to sit still, to breathe in and out, to not let himself imagine the snow piling up on top of the blankets, snow closing in around his face and his breath smothering him, and the panic rising up in him that he would never be found, that there was no one out there who knew where he was or how to get to him, and he would lose his breath out here in the wilderness and freeze solid and never be found. At times it was all he could do to sit still and not lift the edge of the blankets, to not let the cold air underneath.

Just a breath. He just needed a breath. He stuck his face out and felt the cold like a wall, and it went all through him, and he wished he could get rid of the smothering feeling. Beside him, he heard Al lift the blankets and spit into the cold. The spit crackled and froze in midair, a small explosion.

"Guess I'm holding it tonight," Al said.

"Guess so."

They huddled under the blankets and tried to get warm. The wind picked up the edge of a parachute, whipped it around like a dog with a rag, and Walt reached out of the blankets for a minute, grabbed it, and sat on the edge to keep it still.

"Think our wives have their telegrams yet?" Al asked.

Walt wished Al hadn't brought that up. He didn't want to think about Dottie, back in Ontario. No—he wouldn't think about her, not now. He could get through this if he didn't have to think about his wife or his mother. "Maybe not yet. Maybe tomorrow."

He had never met Al's wife, but he knew Adele lived in Windsor with Al's mother. Al and Adele had known each other since childhood. He knew she'd just had a baby, a little girl, and that Al was sick about not being home with them then, that he'd been trying to get leave for months with no luck.

"You think they know where we are?" Al asked.

"They know we're out here." He was silent for a minute, thinking. "How far do you figure we are?"

"I'm guessing twenty miles. Did you send the SOS?"

"I did, but the wireless was out of commission. Couldn't get a signal in, so I doubt I got one out. But they'll find us. Len put us down in a good spot."

They were silent then, the air close under the pile of blankets, thinking of Dusza out in the snow, and Dawson and Ingalls. In the morning, Walt would have to find somewhere to put them. In the morning, he would look for supplies and the portable radio and maybe make a signal fire away from the wreck. In the morning, hopefully, they would still be there to be rescued.

The dark was heavy, oppressive, and complete. Walt couldn't see Al's face, just a few inches away. When he looked out from under the covers, he could feel, but not see, the trees ringing the grove like an occupying army, and he felt how small the fire was, throwing the barest circle of light around them, a perimeter they dared not cross. The sky bent down and covered them, thick and cold and damp. He could hear the branches bending, breaking, and he felt very small in his own skin, as if he might shrink away and disappear.

He said, "They'll come for us in the morning."

Above them the snow whirled down, and the two of them huddled close for warmth as the wind rose up and howled.

His last trip home, Walt and Dottie had sat in the kitchen after dinner, by the coal stove, and had a beer. The radio played low, the volume barely above a whisper. His mother-in-law, Jean, called from the front room, her voice so thick with brogue that he had trouble understanding her. "I put a warming pan in the sheets, so don't forget to take it out before you go to bed," she said.

"I will," Dottie said. "We'll go up in a minute."

"And turn off that radio. Your father doesn't like it on when he's trying to sleep. Dottie, you ken?"

"All right, Mother."

When Jean's shape disappeared from the kitchen doorway, Dottie stood up and turned off the radio. She sat down again, her hand feeling for his until she found it. Her own was cold and damp from the bottle of beer. She said, "Mother wants everything to be perfect for you. She spent all week cleaning, you know."

"She doesn't have to do that."

"She likes to. She thinks you'll come more often if she makes you comfortable."

"You know I come whenever I have leave."

"I know. I tell her, but I think she doesn't listen to me."

The kitchen was white and very bright, and the dark windows showed their faces back to them. A long line of yellow light spilled out into the hallway, toward the front room where Jean was bunking down for the night on the chesterfield. It was late February, and a week of dry skies and a hard, bright cold had driven everyone indoors. They were all making one another slightly crazy. Cabin fever.

Jean called out, "Walt. I put those shirts on the bed." She paused in the doorway. "Good night, then."

"Good night, Mother," Dottie answered.

"Good night," said Walt.

These small domestications seemed like something from another world. He didn't like Jean or Dottie waiting on him, or doing his laundry, or making the bed, or drawing him a bath. He was used to doing things for himself. Dottie said they enjoyed it, that this was how she and her mother showed their pleasure at Walt's visits, but it made him uncomfortable. He felt as though he were trespassing on Jack's good graces, that the old man wanted him somewhere else, was fed up with the intrusion. When Walt went to sleep up in Dottie's room, the room she had lived in since she was a child, he felt that everything he did and said and thought was amplified and transmitted through the walls and the floors to everyone in the house, as if he were committing some grave sin under the noses of everyone there, though he wasn't sure what it was.

It seemed there was no place he could go, really, to clear his head: When he was away, he couldn't stop thinking of home, of Dottie, of Ontario, of places where the war was far away and he could rest. But when he was back home with his wife on her parents' farm, his mind was always on the war, on who was taking his place on missions, at the radio, in the upper turret with a 360-degree view of the whole world and all the danger in it.

The home he'd known when he was small was his mother's boardinghouse in Sudbury. He had shared a bed with his brother Harry when he was young, until Bill died, and then he got to sleep in Bill's old bed, a pleasure he had felt guilty about for some time. When he started working for his father, "home" usually meant a one-room cabin in the woods, which he and his father and the crew would build at the beginning of any big job with help from the mining company or the timber company, or else a tent, set up for a few days and moved at will, under the trees in the dark woods, where rabbits and skunk and sometimes moose or bobcat were the only neighbors. He did what his father told him, carefully staking out lengths of chain to measure each hundred loops, each sixty-six feet, and that way they measured and marked timber claims, mines, townships, road routes. He rolled up the chain when the job was done, kept the equipment neat as a pin during and between jobs. He learned how to build with wood and nails, with logs and pegs, the home that he lived in himself, and he thought that was a skill worth having.

After the war broke out and he was sent to Newfoundland, he lived in the barracks on the Canadian side of the base with four other fellows, including Al Clark, in dark plain little rooms, bags and footlockers stowed under the beds until it was time to go. There was always someone disappearing and someone else taking his place. But they didn't spend much time in the barracks. They ate in the mess during mealtimes; they saw films at the drafty little theater on base. In the spring the birches were like ghosts out the windows, and in the winter the snow and wind and fog closed in around the airfield and made it feel like the only place left on earth. In the boxy wooden barracks they slept like dead men, and when they weren't sleeping they talked. They talked about the war, and where the subs were being spotted, and who had bought it on his last mission, and why the COs gave them a hard time for any dishes they broke in the mess when the Americans could break as many as they liked, and what kinds of cars they would buy when the war was over. They talked about what they would do when they got home. But home had changed—it wasn't the boardinghouse in Sudbury anymore, it was the farm by the Lake Erie shore. He was a guest in his father-in-law's house; he lived there because his wife lived there.

He had promised Dottie it wouldn't always be that way. Someday things would be back to normal. They would have a house and a family and everything else. She wrote, "When?" and he always wrote back, "Soon." But he didn't know. When his tour was over. When the war was over.

In the kitchen, Dottie was saying how her mother had bragged to the neighbors about Walt, her son-in-law, the war hero.

"I wish she wouldn't do that. She knows that's not true."

"Who says it's not true?"

"I do." He finished the last of his beer and put the bottle on the table. The liquid landed heavy in his stomach.

Dottie said, "She's so happy you're here, she doesn't even want me to help with the chores."

"You don't need to change your routine on account of me."

"I don't," she said. She picked up her beer and took a long drink, swished the liquid around in the bottom of the bottle. He had the feeling he had hurt her in some way, and he didn't know how.

Dottie, his wife, a thought still hard to fathom. He should have been changed in some way since the wedding, almost a year ago. He did feel like a man with responsibilities, a man making plans, but sometimes those plans seemed a million years away, a million miles. Maybe if he had been there every day since. Maybe if they'd had a real honeymoon instead of a weekend. Maybe if they had their own house, their own home, instead of this limbo, Dottie still living with her parents, Walt still living like a bachelor among his friends at Gander, flying around the world with everything he owned in one bag slung over his shoulder, pub nights in towns whose names he couldn't remember. It was not any kind of life he had envisioned for himself, and yet even more difficult to imagine was that someday it might end.

He said, "What are you thinking?"

But then her father was at the door, clearing his throat. "Going to bed now," he said. "Got an early morning tomorrow."

They heard his steps going down the hall and into his room. He was still wearing his boots. Through the wooden walls, they heard him take them off one by one and drop them on the floor. The bedsprings creaked, but the light stayed on. They could see it through the kitchen door. The light

27

stayed on until Dottie stood and said they should go up, too—the command unspoken but understood that it was time they all got to bed, even guests. When Dottie and Walt turned off the kitchen light and started up the stairs, Walt saw the light go off under the crack in his father-in-law's bedroom door. His mother-in-law was already asleep on the chesterfield in the front room, her feet up on the arm, because it was too small even for her. Normally she slept up in Dottie's room, in Jimmy's old bed. She looked uncomfortable. He didn't like her having to move on his account, but there was no getting around it. She couldn't share a room with the two of them, and it had been a very long time since she'd shared one with her own husband.

Walt usually didn't sleep well at his father-in-law's, and that night was no different. He found it easier to sleep in the rattletrap insides of the Liberator than in the velvet silence in Dottie's bedroom, under the eaves in the old farmhouse on her father's rented farm. There were birds building nests in the attic; Walt heard them fluttering, calling to one another as if lost. That night he was afraid to touch her. He was sure that either her mother or her father would hear. But more than that, he had trouble clearing his head, trying to think about something other than the war, trying to be glad he was home. Also, Dottie snored like a bear. She snored all that night, sometimes so loudly that she woke herself. Once she rolled over and poked Walt in the ribs, but he was already awake. "Walt," she said. "You're snoring again." Then she turned over and went back to sleep.

Christ, she was beautiful. And didn't know it, and that made her more so. There was a hunch to her shoulders that he'd seen tall girls get, trying to disguise their height, and the way she blushed if he looked at her too long, or too carefully, and barked at him to knock it off. There were times when he'd been afraid he might try to climb inside her skin, those visits, those few days, here and there, when he could get away from the war long enough to come see her. After the wedding it was even worse, once he did learn to climb inside her skin and sleep with her snoring against the back of his shoulder, the sour sticky smell of her morning breath. So what if they had the most temporary of housing, the most unorthodox married life imaginable? Not enough days, not enough of anything, and he carried her back with him every time he left, often in the form of some silky thing of hers, some underthing he slipped in his bag when she wasn't looking, a stocking or a slip.

In the morning, the air grew hot as the sun crossed the faded floor-boards, and he waited for Dottie to wake up. Her heavy snoring had lightened to a soft buzz, the sound he had come to know she made before waking. He let her sleep. Her mother usually let them sleep until well into the late part of the morning. It embarrassed Walt. What did she think they were doing up there, anyway?

He looked around her room, at her clothes and furniture and things. In some ways it was still a little girl's room, still harbored the remnants of Dottie's childhood. *Anne of Green Gables* on the dresser, a grouping of seashells she'd kept from her childhood in Scotland. A photograph of her as a young girl, holding up a kitten for the camera, was stuck in the frame of the mirror. The furniture was old, the dresser and bed scuffed around the legs from years of childhood knockings-about, greasy with years of polishing. He touched the photo, picked it up, and read on the back: "May 1929."

Her father called up the stairs. "Dot!" Jack Farquhar shouted. "Time to get up!" Dottie shook herself, threw off the covers, and stood up, eyes still closed, a suddenness to her movements that spoke of instinct under command. He recognized those motions from his years in the military, doing as he was ordered.

He asked if she'd gotten a good night's sleep, and she said no, as a matter of fact, she hadn't, her face as puffy and white as the pillow she'd slept on. But she dressed quickly and went downstairs, leaving Walt alone in the bedroom, lounging in the bed that was too large for one person, too small for two, in his pajama bottoms and warm as the house heated up for the day. He felt both the urge to stay and the urge to go. After a minute, he got up and dressed and went downstairs.

In the afternoon, Jack asked for some help nailing down some shingles on the barn roof that had shaken loose in a recent storm. He wouldn't have asked, Jack said, except that it was unusual for him to have male help so close by these days. Walt said he would. The weather was still clear but warming. Jack had cleared the roof the day before, so it was dry by the time Walt climbed the ladder. With a hammer and nails he felt like a useful person, not an extra body taking up space and eating his father-in-law's food.

He'd always gotten along with Jack Farquhar well enough. The old man was no saint; he ordered his wife and daughters around more than Walt liked, but he'd known men who were worse about it, who got physical, thought that was their right. Dottie had hinted at her father's indiscretions but had never come right out and said what she knew. It bothered her something tremendous, so he didn't push. It was none of his business. Jack was good with those vegetables, though. He grew cucumbers like no one Walt had ever known, and lettuces and onions. Anything he stuck in the ground came up like weeds, and though he didn't own the farm, he'd told Walt that he was talking to the landlord about buying the place, and Walt thought he'd do it, too. He was a determined old cuss. Walt respected him, even if he didn't like him much. Respect would do for both of them.

That day it seemed Jack had more on his mind than roofing. He handed Walt some fresh shingles and stepped onto the roof. His pipe hung out of his shirt pocket and almost fell out when he leaned over. "Nice day, for February," he said, straightening up. "Awful nice to get out of the house."

"It is."

"Gets darn close in there."

"You're right about that." Walt picked up one of the bad shingles and pulled it free. It was old, beaten up by the weather, and, Walt guessed, probably should have been replaced long ago. The old man was tight with his money. Walt threw the tile off the roof and went on to the next one.

"I wanted to pick your brain about something," Jack said.

Walt ripped off another shingle, the nails squealing. "All right, then. Go ahead."

"You're a married man. You married my daughter. But she's still living here in my house."

With a flick of his wrist, Walt sent the shingle sailing toward the ground. "Yes."

"I take care of her. I take care of her and everyone who lives here."

Walt stopped pulling at the shingles. "You know there's a housing shortage."

Jack Farquhar pulled up another shingle. "True, true. Not your fault. But what I'm saying is we don't have room or money for a little one running around. Not while the war is on."

"That's none of your business."

Jack took a fresh shingle and, lifting one of the old ones, nailed it into place. When he dropped the old one back down, they overlapped perfectly. Only the difference in color (one new, one sun faded) showed where the repair was. "It is while she's living here."

For a minute Walt thought the old man could go to hell, finish his roof by himself. He looked out at the land all around and realized how different the world looked from this little bit of height. He could see his brother-in-law's farm down the road—where Dottie's sister, Bella, lived with her husband and their little girl—and the steeple of the church poking up from behind a line of elms. Behind him, the blue green lake divided the earth from the sky. He was embarrassed for both of them, the conversation, the day—he wanted it over with.

"You understand what I'm saying," Jack said.

"Yes." Walt picked up his hammer and a new shingle. "I understand."

It took them all afternoon to finish, working side by side in silence. After supper, Walt went up early to their room and sat in the dark while Dottie finished the dishes with her mother. Downstairs he could hear Jack listening to the radio, the war news. Walt picked up his bag and put in his folded shirts, his socks and underwear, his pants and shoes, so he would be all ready to leave in the morning, first thing.

The day after the crash, the sun came up and backlit the mountains, the shadows in between shrinking little by little until only the north side of each ridge stayed in darkness, but the cold took longer to retreat from the grove where the Liberator lay in pieces. The sky was a relentless blue, and the glare from the snow was so hard that Walt had to narrow his eyes to slits to sit up and take a look around. When he did, all he could say was, "What a mess."

He hadn't slept, not really. The wind and noise and strangeness of the place had left him too uncomfortable, and anyway he had to tend the fire. It had gotten colder than he had thought it would, and his hands had never warmed as much as he thought they should. This was not Ontario. It wasn't even Canada. He had lain awake all night, drifting and letting his mind sift through plans. The storm had buried more of the plane overnight, covering the smallest pieces of metal, drifting inside the hollow sections, making it hard to find things they would need. The snow was dangerously deep now, drifting against trees and bushes and boulders. He would need to find the portable radio; he would need food and supplies. He would need to melt some snow for water. He would need to climb out from under the blankets and parachutes and get on with the business of surviving until he and Al were found.

Under the blankets Al seemed tired and pale, more than the day before, and gray around the edges, but Walt supposed he might not look so good himself. The two of them kept under the blankets as much as possible for the warmth, discussing what to do. It was still dark under there, and close, and Walt could feel Al's breath on his face, wet with the smell of the hardtack and the salty cubes of bully-beef he'd chewed up for breakfast. Walt felt again that rising fear that he might smother. He remembered being pinned inside the snowbank as if it were a coffin, and how the air had changed colors as his oxygen ran out, and how it felt to think that he could die there and never be found.

He clambered out and stood up. Seeing was going to be a problem— the sun was brutal where it hit the snow. He would be useless with snow blindness; the pain and the days it took to heal were more than they could afford. But he couldn't use his hands to make the goggles he would need, so he had Al tie a piece of red parachute material over his face to cut the glare and the wind.

He went around the wreck, carefully holding on to the trunks of the trees, looking for anything, now that it was daylight, that they could use to survive; but the blowing snow had covered the smaller pieces of the wreck, and he'd already salvaged what he could from the bigger pieces. He knew now that he would have to leave Dusza and Ingalls and Dawson where they were inside the plane and out in the snow; he should have buried them earlier, before the bitter cold night had turned his hands completely useless. But it couldn't be helped. He tried not to think about them; he tried not to walk past the places where they lay, the places where they died. When help came they would take them home anyway; they wouldn't leave them out here in the middle of nowhere. When help came they would manage all right.

He didn't find the Gibson Girl, the portable radio that would let Goose Bay know two of them were still alive, somewhere between Goose and the ends of the earth. They had a compass. They had very little food and not enough warmth. They had two bad injuries between them, dangerous injuries getting worse by the hour, and only a few hours' worth of daylight in any case even if they could get up and walk out of the bush. For now, Walt knew, their best bet was to stay with the wreck, but the question, after a while, would go from When will they come? to How long will we wait here for them to find us?

The skies were empty. Once Walt swore he heard a two-engine plane, maybe a Canso, in the distance. Out here the war felt very far away, as if it were happening in a different time. The shadows between the hills shifted and began to spread again. He wished someone would come. The fire helped, and there was the parachute he had spread the night before, but that was already half buried in the snow. If help did come, would anyone even be able to find them? Labrador was just a lonely empire outpost on the edge of the sea. Walt longed to go home again. He could hardly think for wanting to go home. But no—he would control his fear. He would go home. They would both go home, not die out here, not in this wilderness.

For so long he had never liked staying in one place. He had never understood why his mother stayed in Sudbury when she could have moved to Toronto, for instance, when his father's business took them there. She had refused to leave. She stayed home with her church group and her boardinghouse and the neighbor lady who talked to her across the backyard fence. Papa had been gone for months before he had a chance to come home again. Walt hadn't understood at the time why she would object when he, at fourteen, eager to put his restless limbs to the road, wanted to join up with his father's surveying business and head out to the woods. But now he felt he understood his mother's stubborn refusal to leave home. It was her corner of the world—everywhere else she would be a stranger.

When he came back to the shelter, Al was awake and staring into the fire, wrapped in a parachute with a sheepskin thrown over his shoulders. Al asked about the Gibson Girl, but when Walt said he hadn't been able to find it, he closed his eyes, swayed a little.

Walt said they should try to make snowshoes out of tree branches, a trick he had learned from his brother Bill, who had liked to do a little ice fishing even in the worst weather.

"Where on earth did you grow up, Dunmore?"

"Out in the bush," Walt said. "You have to learn these things."

"Your part of Canada must be bushier than most." Al lay as still as he could, trying to keep from shifting his weight, which brought new blood to the surface of the bandage on his shoulder. He joked that together they made only one useful man.

Walt smiled. He wanted to keep on about the snowshoes, but there was another, more immediate problem that Walt was starting to face: He needed to relieve himself, and because he couldn't pinch his fingers together anymore, there was no way to get his zipper down. He walked around to the other side of the plane to fumble with it where Al couldn't see, but it was no use. After a few desperate minutes, he came back around the fuselage and asked Al to help him, and though Al turned away when Walt was finally able to manage a piss, Walt felt his face burn when he had to ask his friend, a second time, to help him tuck himself in and zip up. He looked away while Al did what he had to do.

"At least *that* part of you isn't frozen yet," Al said. "Don't want Dottie to have to complain to the government."

"You don't think she'd get war widows' pay?"

"Not a chance."

They sat near the fire and warmed up. Walt put his feet toward the flames; they were dry and snug in their boots, but he wasn't taking any chances. He held his hands over the fire, close and then closer, but he couldn't feel it. He wouldn't be able to work the wireless if he didn't have his hands. He wouldn't be able to make a living when the war was over.

Then a slow thought, rising up: For him, the war *was* over. If he lost the use of his hands, he would be going home.

Dottie must have got word of the crash by now. The telegram would come, and the Canadian Pacific man would get into his car and drive out to the house, through the town and its little shops, its neat squares of houses, out into the countryside near the Lake Erie shore, past the farm where Bella lived with her husband, out to the little farm Dottie's parents rented, pull up to the house into the snow-packed drive, and knock on the door. He would hand over his envelope and leave as quickly as possible and not turn around to see the look on Dottie's face when she read the telegram.

What would she be thinking now? She must be guessing that he was dead. Eleven months since he'd seen her. But he wouldn't think about her. It wouldn't help either one of them now.

Al seemed to get weaker as the day wore on. Sometimes he seemed to go to sleep, his head falling forward on his chest; then he would jerk awake and look around with a kind of greenish light in his eyes, a distant look, as if he could see things that were invisible. Walt let him sleep as much as he wanted. The bandage on his shoulder was brown and thick; he must have lost a good deal of blood. At one point, he sat up and said, "Didn't we say we were going to make snowshoes?"

"I don't think snowshoes are going to do us much good."

"Hey," Al said, "I'll walk out of here yet."

"I know you will. I just don't want you walking off and leaving me here to freeze." Walt looked and saw Al's face, firelit and pink on the cheeks, an unnatural glow that gave him the look of a Kewpie doll, but there was a frightening glaze to his eyes. They had eaten their midday ration; there was nothing to do but wait.

"What should I do?" Al asked. "Tell me what I need to do."

"Help me," Walt said. "My hands aren't working so well."

"They haven't warmed yet?" Al asked, and took off his single glove to feel Walt's frozen fingers.

Walt peeled off his own glove with his teeth and unwrapped the other hand from the strips of cloth he'd wound around it. Underneath the skin was whitish blue, with a slow creeping border of red that was moving down the length of each finger as the day wore on. "Good as dead."

"You'll need a doctor."

Walt shook his head. "I think we both need a doctor."

"Never one around when you need one."

"That's the truth."

Al closed his eyes. He seemed to have something he wanted to say, but Walt didn't want him to say it, didn't want to hear it.

"All right, we'll make snowshoes," Walt said. "Here's what you do."

So, using some green branches and parachute cord, Al and Walt slowly pieced together four snowshoes. They used their feet to brace the pieces and what little use they still had in their hands. Al's were stiff but functional, especially the healthy arm, and he seemed to perk up a little as he worked.

The snowshoes were square and awkward, and Walt's left one was strung a little loose, but really they were pretty good homemade—they would do. Al helped him tie them on. He stood up and marched off into the snow, the long awkward strides needed for snowshoeing, but for the first time he felt some hope. He could walk, finally—they might still get out of there alive. "Stay here," he said. "I'll be right back."

"Where you going?" Al said.

Walt called back, "I'm writing my name in the snow."

It was a short hike to the lake, and the snow was too deep, and afterward he was dead tired, but the SOS Walt stamped out in the deep snow covering the lake in his homemade snowshoes would be visible from the air, to let any planes flying overhead know that men were down, were alive in the wilderness, there at the edge of the earth: *We are here.*

TWO

The baby was crying, a note that lifted and fell. Dottie had left her niece on the porch for a moment, just long enough to go inside and fix a bottle and get a sandwich for herself from the icebox. But Janice had rocked herself over trying to climb out of her cradle and landed face first on the boards, chubby limbs splayed. It wasn't far to fall, maybe four or five inches, but she bumped her head, a little red knob on the hairline that Dottie felt when she picked her up, and she knew her sister would see it and ask what had happened.

Dottie bounced her niece on one hip, tried to feed her the bottle, but Janice's disconsolate crying dissolved into sobbing hiccups, and Dottie thought, Well, I would cry, too, if I had a goose egg in the middle of my forehead.

How would she explain this to Bella? The first time her sister had left her alone with the baby. Dottie had said she would take care of everything, that Bella should get done what she needed to in Windsor, the baby would be fine. An afternoon of playing with her niece, pretending this was her house, her baby. A good baby, an easy afternoon.

She had been glad to get out for a little, away from the frayed edge of worry that covered everything in Daddy's house. Mother was waiting for a letter from Dottie's brother, Jimmy—not listed with the dead or wounded after the occupation of Sicily, but not heard from since—her eyes searching the road for black cars. Escape from Daddy, too, complaining that the American reports virtually ignored the importance of the Canadians in Italy, that they might as well have been invisible, and when Dottie looked in the paper she saw he had repeated, almost word for word, that morning's editorial.

Daddy made her promise to pick him up a pouch of tobacco if she was going over to Ed and Bella's, then thumped his pipe on the post that held up the porch roof, spilling wet brown mash on the porch, and watched to see what she would do. She said, "You waiting for the maid?" Left the mess where it landed, started her march toward her brother-in-law's farm, but even before her back was turned she knew she would sweep it up when she got home, when he wasn't looking.

Nearly two years married and still living at home. Three times since the wedding she had seen Walt; three times he had come by train and stayed with her in her old room in Daddy's house. Walt wrote from Iceland, England, Newfoundland. Told her about flying missions over the North Atlantic, shooting at submarines, about dead men frozen in the sea, looking up toward the sky, toward help that would never come in time. Dottie didn't want to see the things he saw; she didn't want him to write such things to her, because she saw the faces when she closed her eyes.

She gave Janice her bottle and listened to the hiccups fade as the baby sucked down the milk. She would have to think of a good story to tell her sister about the goose egg.

Movement in the corner of her eye: Someone was there. Bobby Wisniewski, the American, standing on the other side of her sister's bed of pink geraniums, looking up at her. He was dirty with sweat and the stink of the afternoon's work, his overalls brown with muck from the new well he was digging behind the milkhouse. His hands, though, had been washed, as if he were expecting something.

"Bobby," she said.

"Mrs. Dunmore."

Had he seen the baby fall? He might tell Bella, maybe not maliciously, maybe in passing. Maybe Ed. An uncomfortable feeling ran up and down her back.

"You spying on me?"

"Done anything worth spying on?"

Maybe he would not mention it. He thought he was being clever, grinning at her. He said, "You got to watch 'em every minute. They get that mind of their own pretty early on."

An expert on babies, him. "I know that."

He looked at the plate on her chair, the sandwich. "Mind if I join you?"

"Eh?"

"No kitchen in my little room. I usually eat with the family."

She knew the part about no kitchen, but she also knew he normally ate upstairs by himself: Bella said he wasn't very sociable at mealtimes, that he took a plate and the paper and went to his room. She wondered why he would lie. She handed Janice her bottle and asked him to keep an eye on her for a minute while she went in to fix another sandwich. His laughing eyes. She was glad to go inside in the cool and get away from him for a minute.

Five months now, was that right? Since he moved into the little room over the tractor garage. She had helped Bella clean up the space before he moved in; they cleared out old birdcages and bits of broken harness and empty feed bags, swept out the leavings of mice and small birds, a dusting of pale pigeon feathers. They had scrubbed the walls and floors and the one window until everything was clean as could be, then struggled with the single bed up the narrow stairs, the old highboy with the one short leg. When they were done it was a nice, clean, small room, bright with white paint except where it peeled in a few spots. It was perfectly fine for hired help, a place to sleep at night that was warm and dry. Good enough for pigeons, good enough for anyone.

He had come over looking for farmwork in Amherstburg or Harrow and ended up picking tobacco for Ed Mackie in exchange for room and board over the tractor garage and a little bit of money. People in town still talked about the time he said, "They can grow tobacco in Canada?" as proof that most Americans thought the Arctic Circle started at the border. A whisper that he was hiding from the draft, that he couldn't go home again because he would be arrested, but she knew that was ridiculous; Ed said he had a medical exemption on account of a bad knee, that people should know better than to listen to rumors and should spend their time on something more productive than opening their fool mouths.

Dottie hadn't thought much about him at all. One of a string of farmhands who worked over at the Mackies', but unlike the teamsters he lived there full-time and pretty much kept to himself. His solitary nature seemed only to add to his appeal to the other girls in town, like Dottie's best friend, Peggy Mason, who licked her lips wickedly whenever his name came up. "Wouldn't Pop die?" she'd say, sighing, and Dottie would give her an elbow as though she were chastising a kid sister who knew better.

She had talked to him a few times. He had been there for Victoria Day, one of half a dozen extra faces around the table who sat and talked to Ed and Daddy about chores and crops and horses and never said anything to Dottie or the other women other than "please" and "thank you" when she filled their plates. He was easy enough to pass by in those big groups, especially when there was so much work to do in the kitchen to help Bella and Mother get the food on the table, and afterward with the cleaning up, and by the time everything was put away the men were drifting back out toward the door to finish the evening chores, always chores, even on holidays, because Ed said the animals had never heard of Queen Victoria and wouldn't give a shit if they had. So she didn't know him that well. So there was a first time for everything.

Dottie got out the bread and meat and a jug of tea and made another lunch. Bobby Wisniewski, the American, living by himself above her sister's tractor garage with no family, no home that anyone knew of. What did he do up there in that room, at night, when the work was done and he was by himself? No kind of life.

She brought out tea, glasses, another plate, some cookies Bella had made the day before. He finished his sandwich and attacked the cold tea, pouring a glass and gulping it down, then pouring himself another and one for her, too. She said, "You'll make yourself sick, drinking so fast."

"Maybe. Then I'd have to take the rest of the day off, wouldn't I? I'm sure Ed would understand."

He bit a cookie in half, then complimented her baking. "Thank you," she said, watching him eat. Quick, fluttery movements, like a bird's, a sense of nervousness that made her watch almost everything he did. Not like a man, at least not the ones she knew, certainly not like Ed Mackie or Walt or the boys she had been to school with. Not like Daddy. His hair, bleached white blond from a summer working out of doors, stuck up in all directions, as if he had recently passed a hand through it. He had nice man's hands, large and callused with work, each finger ending in a crescent moon of white. The back of the right hand was marked with a fading blue black tattoo, a cross with its long end pointing upward, at the swelling of his arm. He grinned at her, his two front teeth turned in toward each other.

Janice dropped her bottle on the floor, a stream of milk shooting from the nipple into the air. He picked up the bottle and the baby, swung her over his lap, and popped the bottle into her mouth. A strange thing, watching a man she hardly knew feed her little niece, her round red mouth sucking down the milk, her hands curling contentedly in the air, her eyes never leaving his face. Bobby looking right back at her. He said, "Is that what you were after?" Janice smiled around the nipple and grabbed the bottle with both hands.

She never knew before how beautiful that could be, a man who was perfectly happy to feed a baby and not give it a second thought, not hand it over at the first chance to the woman nearest, a man with a baby smiling into his face and him smiling back. He tickled her round belly, and she laughed, showing her milk teeth.

She said, "You seem to have a way with her."

"I like kids. Want to have a bunch of them someday."

"Really? I wouldn't think that. Most people seem to think of babies as a burden. Something troublesome and unavoidable."

"There's one way to avoid 'em."

She laughed. "You're right about that."

A line of dust coming up the road, trailing a red truck: Ed and Bella back from Windsor. Dottie stood and took the baby from him. She smoothed back Janice's fuzz of hair, looked in her eyes. She seemed fine, but the goose egg was red and angry on her forehead. Dottie sighed and said, "What am I going to tell your mother?"

"She tripped. She tried to stand up and tripped," Bobby said. "Nothing you did wrong. You were watching her the whole time." His face was mild and perfectly serious, though while she stood there deciding whether or not to believe him, the faintest hint of a grin creased the corners of his mouth. "Don't worry. I won't tell."

A blind date, Peggy's idea, company for a couple of boys home on furlough from bombing and gunnery school, the first time Mother agreed to let her go into Windsor. Peggy didn't say how she knew the boys; for all Dottie understood, maybe she didn't very well. Peggy had been allowed to date in high school and was fearless around boys, a trait that made Mother sigh whenever Dottie mentioned her name at home. Dottie was eighteen that year and learning how much fun it was taking risks.

Dottie had never dated much. The only boy Daddy had ever approved of was Bert Mason, Peggy's older brother, whose idea of a fun date was having Dottie stand and watch while he tinkered around with his car. That had lasted until the war broke out and he was off to England. Bert wrote her a few times, then stopped. After a few months abroad, he cabled his parents that he had married an English girl. Dottie got the feeling she was expected to be disappointed by this, but she wasn't. A few times she and Peggy had gone to the dances in town, and she even danced with a few boys, soldiers even, but no one special.

They got dressed at Peggy's house. Dottie wore green organza, summertime, something old of Bella's. She borrowed a pair of shiny heels from Peggy that squeezed her feet so the skin rose up a little, like fermenting dough, but they complemented her dress. Peggy did her hair, swept it up off her face and neck, tied it behind. As the Ford pulled up with the two boys inside, she felt about ten feet tall and full of hot air, as if she might explode.

Peggy introduced them. Dottie, Walt. Walt, Dottie.

Instead of going to the dance, they turned south and parked the Ford on the banks of Lake Erie, left the radio turned up louder than Dottie thought was wise, and walked down the steep steps to the rocky lakeshore. Dottie didn't like Peggy's date, a tall fellow she had seen only from the back, mostly because he hadn't said hello when Peggy introduced them. She wasn't too sure about Walt, either. He was good-looking enough, handsome in a kind of rough way, but he hadn't said anything other than "hello" in the car. When he helped her out of the car, and she stood up straight next to him for the first time, she realized she was taller by several inches. It was the heels—her perspective was off.

A stiff breeze came over the water and blew Dottie's dress flat against her. The shore was dotted with the glittering carcasses of alewives turning pink in the last light as the sun sank, a smell of dead fish coming off the lake. Someone had brought a bottle of gin. They passed it around for a while and then put its fat end into the lake water to keep it cold.

Peggy and her date walked down the beach, disappeared. Dottie frowned as she watched them; she didn't like Peggy leaving her there alone with this strange man. Benny Goodman was on the radio, faint from where the car was parked. Walt asked her to dance. He had to tilt his head up to get a good look at her. She put her hand on his shoulder and took the smallest steps she could.

He looked at her feet and scowled. "Those shoes are too small for you. You should take them off."

"Who asked you?"

"Suit yourself. They're not my feet."

She leaned down and unbuckled the shoes, pulled them off, and tossed them in the sand, out of the way.

He was a klutzy dancer, but at least she didn't tower over him anymore. He led her around in the faint light, circles that got smaller and smaller rather than bigger. Somewhere in the growing dark she could hear Peggy and her date laughing, a sound that stiffened her back. Walt hardly spoke; she wondered if he was counting his steps. Benny Goodman was playing "Sentimental Journey."

"My favorite," she told him.

"I wouldn't have thought. I'd have pegged you for Glenn Miller."

"You shouldn't peg anyone before you know 'em."

He looked over her shoulder at the lake and the land and sky, and she heard him blow out a skeptical breath. "It would be pretty here if it weren't so flat. Too flat for my taste."

"You're sure full of opinions."

"I'm from up north. More woody up there, and hilly. You can't see the sky so much. You don't feel so small. Here you can see the whole sky from one end of the earth to the other. It's too big for one person."

"It's good farmland. The best in Canada."

"I know that. I'm just saying."

His hand on her waist was the only spot on her that was warm in the lake breeze. He had taken off his wool dress jacket and airman's hat and stood there with his white shirtsleeves rolled up, his black shoes dusted

43

with sand. She thought about the feel of sand in his shoes. One side of his mouth turned up as if he weren't quite ready to smile at her yet. Under her bare feet she felt a rough assembly of stones, the coarse lake sand brown as tobacco spit in the daytime but cool and white in the dark. For a minute they didn't say anything. Dottie thought about the road north, into the woods, into places where there were wolves and bears and Indian settlements and where the ground stayed partly frozen all summer. Places where the sky didn't press down so much, places not boxed in by bodies of water, places that weren't trapped. She wondered what his home was like.

The moon started to rise over their heads, throwing long shadows on the ground.

She said, "I would like to see that sometime. The woods. I'll bet it's pretty."

He tilted his head to look at her. They had danced in circles, smaller and smaller, until they were completely still.

She started walking into town to see if Bobby was there. Not every day. Not so often that anyone would really notice. Only when she thought she could: She told Mother she would check for a letter from Jimmy or stop by Peggy Mason's for a visit. Always some excuse, just real enough. No one would notice. Not Mother or Daddy or Bobby himself, or anyone else. She went because she wanted to, because she could, because no one knew the warm thoughts she was thinking and said, *Grow up*. A burr of pleasure stung her that this part of her life did not yet have to be over, as long as no one knew.

That afternoon the half-moon was up, a grin in the middle of the cloudless sky. Here was golden yellow light on the stumps of wheat stalks, and drying tall grass, and the September end of a long, droughty summer. Here was the ditch where Queen Anne's lace grew tall as a man; here the dark stain where the yellow cat had been killed a month earlier. Each landmark on the road was a step that should not be taken, a place she should turn back. The edge of town on the horizon was dark with trees and houses. Dust on her legs and arms and face, coating her flat shoes, up the back of her dress, where an itchy bead of sweat slid slowly down and then soaked into the cloth at her waist. A cool breeze up from the Lake

Erie shore straightened the air for a minute, lifting the hair off her neck, then died.

Bobby wasn't often alone in town. If Ed Mackie came with him, they'd run their errands, pick up wire to mend fences or feed for the milking goats, and be off again. But sometimes Ed would send him alone to fetch paint or wood, feed, groceries, chewing tobacco. If he did come alone, Bobby would sometimes stop in at the Masons' restaurant for a piece of rhubarb pie and coffee and sit at the counter for a visit with whoever else might stop in.

If he did come alone, if he found himself sitting at the counter of the restaurant, it might be that he turned and spoke to her, if she was the one sitting there.

She reached the edge of town at the Livermores' brown brick house. A humid heat was clinging, leaving her damp under the arms and generally wilted by the warmth of the day, but her feet kept going. Mrs. Livermore waved from the garden and offered a glass of lemonade. "Can't, thanks," she said, stopping her feet just long enough to be polite. "Daddy's got me running around." And Mrs. Livermore nodded with a knowing look and went back to clipping her bushes.

Feet tired, and now she was thirsty. She kept moving forward. Marveling at herself, searching out the American on one of the hottest days of the year when she should have been weeding the garden. Marveling at the momentum she built up that kept her feet going forward, the want in her. Wanting to be like the other girls her age.

The restaurant was shaded and cool, fans blowing at the counter. He was already there, talking to Peggy Mason, who worked afternoons behind the counter because her father owned the place. Peggy leaning over to listen to something he had to say, laughing. Here were shades of the child Peggy used to be, the tomboy Dottie had known until they were thirteen, the year Daddy made Dottie stay home to help Mother care for the vegetable garden and the cows, saying she could learn whatever else she needed at home. Peggy went to the town school after that. A flare of jealousy remembering Peggy's high school graduation party, a modest affair with a little chicken and potato salad and homemade cake; but suddenly her friend had seemed more glamorous, more grown up in her heels and her hair piled up. As she greeted her guests that day, Peggy tipped her head to one side, as if she knew the secrets of the universe. Dottie had wished that Bella had waited another three years to marry Ed Mackie, or that Mother had stood up for her, or that she'd had the courage to stand up to her father herself.

Again Peggy with the tip of the head, the knowing look. This time for Bobby Wisniewski.

He caught Dottie's eye and grinned, showing his crooked teeth, and gave her the farmer's chin nod she saw so often from her father and brother and brother-in-law, raising the eyebrows, a gesture so familiar that usually she didn't notice, but from him it annoyed her, a feeling that boiled over and stuck in her lower jaw and wouldn't go away. The gesture or the fact he was sitting there, with Peggy, free as you please. She could see the mud caking the bottom of his boots as he tipped back his head to swallow what was left in his glass of lemonade. He stood up as Dottie sat down.

"Bobby."

"Mrs. Dunmore."

Leaving already. She felt stung. "Don't go on my account," she said, lifting the hair off her neck, looking across at the front door of the restaurant instead of at him.

"I wasn't," he said, and gave her a teasing smile. "Wouldn't want to make you angry. You might drop me on my head."

"I don't know what you're talking about," she said. Damn it all. She knew she couldn't trust him.

He grinned again, handing his glass back to Peggy and thanking her for the drink. "I'll leave you ladies to your gossip." On his way to the door, he passed Dottie too closely, brushing against her and managing a little squeeze of a couple of her fingers. She held her breath. He turned back to Peggy and said Ed Mackie would have his behind if he didn't get back soon with the salt blocks for the horses. He raised his chin again at Dottie and thumped out in his boots.

A bold move, that. Peggy might have seen. The idea of it, in broad daylight, and when he had just been drinking Peggy's lemonade and keeping her company. A delicious fear swelled cold over the hot day.

"I see he's starting to fit in," Peggy said. "Must be learning his manners from those goats. Almost knocked you over." A slow smile spread over her face like honey. "He can knock me down anytime."

"Hush! Someone will hear you."

"I hope so. I hope someone tells him I said so, or one of these days I might tell him myself." Peggy went back into the kitchen to fetch a clean glass for Dottie. She hadn't seen, Dottie was sure of it.

Bobby's glass was on the counter, still sweating. She picked it up and ran her thumb through the beads of condensation, erasing the marks his hands had left there. She could still feel the place where his hand had squeezed hers, a little heat and sweat exchanged quick as daylight, a couple of fingerprints passed back and forth.

When Peggy banged opened the kitchen door, Dottie dropped the glass on the floor, shattering it into emerald shards. She bent over, scooping up the bits carefully with her hands and gathering them in her skirt. "I'm so sorry, Peg. Don't know what I was thinking."

Peggy told her not to worry, that she would get the broom. She gave Dottie a wicked stare, checked to see who else might be listening. Peggy said, "Too bad it broke. I was going to keep it as a souvenir."

"Don't be ridiculous."

On the front porch, Walt had taken her hand in the dark and stroked a knuckle with his thumb. Cleared his voice a couple of times. If he had something to say, she wished he would come out and say it. Something caught in his throat, maybe. She knew what he wanted; he had been hinting around for days but wouldn't come out with it.

His awkwardness was something that both frustrated her and filled her with a deep tenderness that made her want to kiss the top of his hair, like a little boy, protect him, take away all the things that were making him fearful. And she wanted to say, "For God's sake, say what's on your mind." He was shy and gruff and a little klutzy, as she had noted that first time they danced on the Lake Erie shore, but he kissed her as though he knew what kissing meant, holding her face with both hands as if it were a treasure, as if wanting to soak her in, and she thought she liked it, and him, better than almost anything in the world.

He cleared his throat again, stroked the little hairs on the back of her hand, and his voice in the dark was disembodied, almost ghostly. He said, "I can talk about love the same as anyone. Except with me, you know I mean it. I'm not going to fool around with your heart."

She knew he was telling the truth.

On the dark porch, Walt was just a voice, rich and gravelly, the syllables knocking together in his throat before they found her ears. Crickets were coming out for the summer, and a night with no moon, only some faint stars and the orange glow of Detroit and Windsor in the northwest. The house was dark behind them, heavy and sleeping, the porch light turned off to keep the bugs away. Two chairs on Daddy's porch, and Mother waiting inside in the dark with the front window open, probably listening to every word, holding her breath. Gravely he talked about the future— that she wouldn't have to live in Daddy's house forever, that there would be places they would go together, have a house in Windsor or Toronto or even Vancouver if she wanted, and the future washed over her, taking shape as it reared up into the form of major events and markers, buoys on the ocean to show form and distance—here the wedding, here the purchase of a house, here the first child (a girl), here the second (a boy), and vacations by the sea. He talked about love, about how he'd never met anyone in his life who made him think he'd ever want to get married until the night he met her, prickly and stubborn and beautiful as a purple thistle. She thought she should be bothered by the comparison, except she wasn't—she thought it was lovely, or maybe it was the way he said it. Waves of the future kept washing up on the shore in her mind, and she could almost see each piece of furniture, breathe the new-baby smell of each child as he described them, see old age float over them both like gray foam, a beautiful old age with grandkids and retirement in Florida and tennis lessons, not a hardscrabble life and wearing down and getting thick around the middle, the way Mother had done. Eventually the images piled up inside her like a raft she was constructing, until she floated above each wave of plans and rode them out to sea, toward a shining objective that seemed more like destiny than choice.

"What do you think?" he said.

She knew, but she wanted to hear him say it. "About what? Getting married? Is that what you're trying to say?"

"Well, yes."

Say it. Say it properly.

"You know I love you. You know you're everything I want."

Eight times he'd come from the bombing and gunnery school to see her since that first night. There were dances, lunches in town or an afternoon picture, a day or two here or there; once there was nearly a week. At first his friend Pete came with him and they stayed with his family in town. They would double-date with Peggy and Pete, especially because Pete had a car he kept at his mother's. But later, after Peggy told Pete she'd started seeing a pilot from Alberta, Walt started coming alone. He had charmed Mother so completely by then that she made up the chesterfield in the front room for him and fixed him breakfast in the morning, and even Daddy had to admit that Walt was a hell of a good guy. Mother sighed and said that he looks so handsome in his uniform, and he's so polite, and he's not a farmer, and Daddy had dumped his pipe into the ash can and said, "Well, there had to be something wrong with 'im."

The last time he came to visit, he kept Daddy busy for hours with tales of operations over the North Atlantic, and Daddy sat enthralled, smoking three pipes' worth of tobacco, drinking the tea that Mother poured over and over and eating her shortbread, and Walt thanked her each time and said he'd rarely had such a treat. Later, after Mother and Daddy headed for bed, he took Dottie by the arm and whispered, "I'd never have you wait on me the way your mother waits on your dad, I promise you that," and she had gone to sleep with a smile on her lips, because he saw the way things were.

She liked his company. She liked his smell, and the feel of his shoulder under her hands when they danced, and the way his eyes tilted to the side when he wanted to look at her, and how he always asked her what she was thinking, as if she were a mystery he was trying to solve. Every time he said he was coming to visit, she thought she might burst from having to wait. She liked waiting for him on the train platform, liked having someone to wait for, like the other girls. She liked it when people stopped her in town, friends from her school days, friends from church or acquaintances of Mother and Daddy, and asked her how Walt was doing and when she'd last heard from him. She liked feeling that she, too, was in the middle of things, that she wasn't just living on her parents' farm but waiting for something important to happen.

She had answered his letters in pages and pages she wrote about farm life, asked questions about what he was doing in flight school, given details of people he didn't know or had met only once or twice. He wrote her about flight training and the boys in his outfit and where he thought he would get stationed eventually, and the things he learned about Morse code and navigating by instrument and by stars, and how to draw maps and measure latitude and longitude, and how to tell where you were by the time it took to get from *here* to *there*. She'd never met anyone so interesting, and with the war on, all her feelings popped like oil that had been heated too long, giving ordinary life a frightening intensity she hadn't known before. At first she signed her letters "Best," or "Take care," but she was deeply flattered when he started calling her "Benny," as if the name were part of a secret language they had invented. Then she started signing "Love," and he signed "Love," and that was how love progressed in written signs, until when she saw him again he kissed her in greeting on the platform of the train station, and she blushed and then realized that was what she had been waiting for all along, a public acknowledgment, an outward sign, and love lodged itself in her ribs and became real there, real as her flesh and bones.

His voice was still on the porch, his face barely visible in the dim starlight. She realized he was waiting. She realized that he would wait as long as she wanted.

She did love him. She would.

She said, "All right."

She saw the back of Bobby's head in church on Sunday, sitting next to Peggy in his one good white shirt and clean pants, his skin red and raw from working on the harvest, getting the crop in before the weather turned cold. She saw a white half-moon under the hairline from where the barber had shaved the back of his neck, and she felt sick to her stomach, a lilt to the side that might have been the heat, when she realized she had been looking forward to seeing him there. That she had been waiting to see him. That she could hardly look at anything else except the white stripe on the back of his newly shorn neck.

She had walked to church alone, as usual. Mother and Daddy and Bella and Jimmy were still Catholic, but Dottie had changed to the Anglican church when she married Walt. The pews were nearly full, so Dottie decided to sit with Peggy up front. On that short walk up the aisle of the church, she felt as though she'd been flayed open and the bloody tint of her inner colors displayed for the world to see. But Peggy smiled at her over Bobby's shoulder when she sat down. On the far end of the pew, Peggy's parents nodded hello. The four of them sitting in a row like family, as if they did this every weekend. Maybe he had been coming around to Peggy's house or the restaurant or any one of a number of places where he might safely graft himself onto Peggy's family under her father's watchful eye. Dottie felt as if she were trespassing, looking in someone's living room window when the curtains were open at night.

The sanctuary of the church was plain, white, and as hollow sounding as the inside of a guitar. The windows were open to let in the smoky October air stirring outside, and out of the corner of her eye, Dottie saw Peggy dab at her face with a handkerchief. Bobby was in between them. He said hello but did not look at her. When the service started he uncrossed his legs, casual enough, but then he pressed his knee into her leg, insistent, unmistakable. She dropped her head and worried who might notice, that Peggy might see. But then she knew that he had come to church that day to see her, not Peg, that all the days he'd spent chatting with her friend, all the times she'd come upon the two of them together, he had been looking for Dottie as much as she had been looking for him.

The inside crooks of her knees were damp. She pressed them together the way Bella had taught her when she was starting school. "Otherwise, the boys will look up your skirt."

"Will they?" Dottie couldn't imagine why anyone would want to do such a thing.

Daddy had taken them to school that first day to introduce them to the teacher. Dottie was six and had never been to school before. Mother had said she could wait to start school until they joined Daddy in Ontario, where he had been living for four years without them, working on the farms in Ontario and saving up enough money to send for them. But Jimmy and Bella had been to school in Scotland and were nervous about starting in a new place. So Daddy drove the three of them to the brick one-room Colchester School and herded them out of the truck. In those days, Dottie was afraid of her father. She hadn't remembered him from when she was small as anything more than a photograph and a promise of something to come. Daddy was too tall, too gray in his suspenders, and had thick, dark glasses like a mask over his face. She didn't like the heat from his pipe or the fact that he liked to tease her with it, threatening to burn her hand against the bowl, and even though Mother said he wouldn't really, that he was only joking with her to make her squeal and run away, she was never quite certain that he wouldn't.

At school the children playing outside watched them, not stopping to stare but not ignoring them, either, as if Dottie and her brother and sister were too dangerous to look at head-on. Dottie stayed close to Bella. She walked past and tried not to look as if she were looking, because Mother said it wasn't polite to stare. They didn't look that different. They didn't look the way she thought Canadian children would look when she thought of them back home. She had imagined them all tall and blond like children in picture books, blue eyed, smooth skinned, identical; but some had black hair, some were red haired and speckled, and there was one little boy playing ball whose skin was as dark as wet earth. Bella had to poke her to get her to stop staring. It was their voices that were strange. She heard them calling to one another and thought how different they sounded: flat, as if they were talking out of their noses. She didn't think she would ever get used to it.

As they went past them, Dottie heard one boy call out, "Farquhar! Farquhar!" She wondered how he could know their last name already when he hadn't met them yet. He came running toward them. He was almost as tall as Bella and had the reddest red hair Dottie had ever seen. When he got closer Dottie heard he was saying *Mister* Farquhar. He was calling out to Daddy, and Dottie felt strange knowing that Daddy had lived here in Canada four years without them, for most of her life, and already knew everyone in town, even this strange boy with his strange flat accent calling out to her father from across the school yard.

The boy came running right up to Daddy, so close that Dottie took a step back. "Mr. Farquhar," he said again.

Daddy looked down and patted the boy on the head. "How are you, Malcolm?" he said. Dottie felt a stab of jealousy, and she wanted to punch the boy and send him into the dirt.

"I didn't know you were coming today," the boy said.

"These are my children," Daddy said, putting a hand on Dottie's shoulder. She smiled broadly. "I thought it was high time I signed them up. Show them the ropes, now?"

"Yes, sir."

"I knew I could depend on you." He steered Dottie toward the schoolhouse. She turned to look, and the boy was still there, watching them.

Inside it was too dark and smelled dirty, like coal smoke, and the floorboards creaked. The teacher was nice enough, but she had the same nasal accent the children did, and Dottie said, "What?" twice before Daddy grabbed the top part of her arm hard and said, "Say hello back to the teacher. Don't be rude."

Dottie whispered, "Hello."

Bella seemed sullen and impatient. Jimmy looked as if he might cry. His upper lip was quivering, so Dottie turned away quick before he made her cry, too. She didn't want Daddy to leave her there. He signed Dottie up for grade one and Jimmy and Bella for grades three and six, but Dottie was relieved to find out they would all be in the same schoolroom together. It made her feel better to know that Bella was there, that if she couldn't stay at home, at least she could be with Bella.

Then Daddy left them there and drove off in the truck, and the three of them were in their seats when the teacher called in the other children for the day. Dottie felt naked as the other kids marched in and filed past her where she sat in the front row. That Malcolm bumped into her desk as he passed her and knocked her pencils to the floor. She had to stand up and walk around the desk to pick them up.

"Malcolm," said the teacher, "apologize to our new student. Apologize to Dottie."

"Sorry," he blurted from somewhere behind her. She blushed all the way down her neck and into the top of her dress.

At lunch Dottie sat on the grass near Bella, who had already made friends with one of the grade seven girls. Though Bella said she didn't mind if Dottie stayed, she spent the whole lunch hour talking to her new friend and teaching the big girls the song they'd sung at home for skipping ropes: "Raspberry, strawberry, blackcurrant jam, tell me the name of your young man." At home in Scotland Dottie would have played with them, too, but in this new place she was afraid of the big girls. Jimmy decided to try his hand at some game with a large rubber ball that the boys were playing outside, so Dottie ate alone, trying not to be seen. Malcolm saw her. He marched up to where she sat in the grass and said, "I know your father. He comes over to my house all the time. He eats dinner there."

"No, he doesn't. He eats dinner at home with us."

"Maybe sometimes he does. Sometimes he still comes over to my house. He likes my mother's ham. He used to come over every night before you came here."

"He likes my mother's cooking the best. Better than anything. So he won't be coming to your house for dinner anymore."

"He will," Malcolm said, and he put his face very close to Dottie's and smiled. Dottie could smell the hard-boiled eggs he had eaten for lunch. "I'll bet he'll even be there tonight. You just watch."

"He won't. He doesn't need to eat with *strangers*."

"We're not strangers," Malcolm said. "Yes, you *are*," said Dottie as he walked away.

He followed her home that day. She walked behind Jimmy and Bella, each of whom had a new friend, and Malcolm followed behind her, out into the wet roads fringed with damp grass. Dottie hunched into her coat and tried to walk faster, but he kept up. She could hear his shoes crunching the gravel behind her. She walked faster, but he sped up until he was behind her, and she could almost feel his hot breath on her hair, and she cringed, and he grabbed her and turned her around and kissed her on the mouth. She pushed him away and wiped her face. "You make me sick," she said.

He laughed at her and took a step closer. She stepped back, and he took another step toward her. She stepped back again, and he laughed. He said, "He's been coming for years and years. He likes it at my house. He likes my house better than yours."

"He's *my* father."

Malcolm laughed. "Maybe he won't be anymore." He turned around and ran back in the direction he had come.

Dottie turned away—she didn't want to see him with his hateful red hair ever again. She ran to catch up with Jimmy and Bella, and though she knew she was too big for it anymore, she grabbed her sister's hand. Bella held it almost without noticing, still talking to her new friend, but Dottie felt better knowing Bella was there—she knew that Malcolm wouldn't dare say those things in front of the older children.

At home she did her schoolwork and answered Mother's questions about the first day. Did she like the teacher? Yes. Did she like the books, and the school, and the studying? Yes, so far. Did she like the other children? Not sure. Not sure. She thought of hateful red hair and a high, nasally voice saying Daddy wasn't her father anymore. She had wanted to say, *You can't stop being someone's child, someone's daughter, someone's father.* But when it came to Daddy, she wasn't sure. Maybe you could.

"Dottie," Mother said, "I'm speaking to you."

Dottie said, "There's a dark-skinned boy at school. I never saw anyone with such black skin before. Where do you suppose he comes from?"

From her place by the potbellied stove, Bella said, "His family is from America. They were escaped slaves."

And Dottie asked, "What's a slave?" But Mother said it was time to help with the supper, and she could finish her books later.

At supper that night, there was an empty place at the table. Dottie asked where Daddy went. Mother said, "He had to run into town." Dottie ate her dinner and went to bed and listened for the sound of his feet on the floor downstairs. She sat up with the covers over her knees like a tent and waited for his voice in the hall downstairs, but she fell asleep before he came home.

She watched him carefully after that, always asking where he was going, when he was coming back. Sometimes he said he was going to town to pick up some feed, to see a neighbor. Mostly, though, he didn't answer her at all. He would step off the porch and walk down the road or drive off in his truck, the sound of the motor fading with the distance.

In the heat of the church, as the last song was ending, the place where her leg touched Bobby's was damp with perspiration, and when it was time to leave she was sorry, wanted it to last a little longer. But Peggy was waiting, so Dottie and Bobby stood and shuffled slowly down the aisle. She was guilty and thrilled. She almost wished she were still Catholic, so she would have something to confess.

The hollow inside of the building thrummed with after-church voices, commenting on the sermon, the music, the other churchgoers, the latest news about the war. Behind her, Dottie heard Bobby say, "So, Mrs. Dunmore, heard from that husband of yours lately?"

"He's coming home on furlough this winter. Couple of weeks, maybe."

"When was the last time he was home?"

"February."

"You must miss him."

Peggy chimed in, "Of course she misses him." When Dottie turned around, Peggy was smiling, hands on hips, still the risk taker, the saucy girl, the one who had it all. Dottie felt sorry for her.

"Of course I miss him," Dottie said. "I married him, didn't I?"

She was glad when they reached the door and went outside, a bubble of fresh air bursting against her face. The three of them squinted and shaded their eyes from the sudden glare, and in the bright fall sunlight Bobby's hair was white. Dottie kissed Peggy good-bye, thinking, She doesn't know. She doesn't know a thing.

The monsignor had refused to marry them. He said, first of all, that she had known Walt only four months—which was true—but he also said that there were plenty of Catholic boys around if she was that interested in getting married. She didn't have to knit her life together with an Anglican, a king worshiper, just because he was the first to ask her.

Mother cried that day when Dottie came home and said she would never set foot in another Roman Catholic church if the pope himself dragged her there. Mother said it wasn't right, getting married without the sacrament, that if she waited a little, the monsignor might change his mind. But Walt talked to the Anglican priest, who said he would perform the ceremony any time they were ready. Dottie was grateful for that, Walt taking charge of things and not taking no for an answer, his practical and businesslike handling of the whole matter, calming Mother, calming his own mother, whom Dottie had never met and who couldn't leave the boardinghouse. He said, "No sense waiting when we know what we want," and she felt the sureness of the decisions they'd made propping her up like the foundation of a new house. They were ready—two weeks later, she signed on the dotted line.

Peggy was a bridesmaid, in pink satin and smart little hat with a net veil. She cried in the church when Dottie said "love and cherish." Bella was matron of honor. Her brother, Jimmy, home on leave, stood up with Walt as best man and even seemed to enjoy it, looking like Daddy in his younger days. Peggy's father took the three girls from the house to the church himself in his big car so they wouldn't have to walk over. Daddy stiff in his white shirt, open at the collar, and Mother in her best hat with the little veil, a black suit, not appropriate for a wedding, but it was her only good dress.

Their honeymoon night under Daddy's roof. They had talked about a hotel in Windsor or even Detroit, but Walt had to report back two days later, and it seemed like a waste of money. That night Mother slept downstairs on the chesterfield to give them some privacy, but Daddy said he wouldn't be turned out of his own bed and slept in his room that night right under her own. In the morning, when she came downstairs to help Mother fix breakfast, his eyes were hard and bright and they followed her from the door to the stove where the bacon was already frying. He said, "Had a good time, did you?" and she burned so hot that she had to go out on the porch and sit for a minute before she could finish cooking breakfast.

Walt left the next day. They drove him to the station, Mother wringing her hands on the platform, Daddy waiting in the truck with the engine running. Dottie let herself cry a little. Walt said, "Love you, Benny. I'll write when I get there."

When he got on the train and rode away, Mother turned back toward the car with her purse in her hand, tucking away a handkerchief. She said, "Benny? What kind of a name is that for a man to have for his wife?"

Dottie made her niece a dress, blue with white polka dots and a matching hat. Took it over herself in the afternoon, wrapped in paper and tied with baling twine, down the road to the Mackies', even though there was the rest of the mending to do before Daddy got home, his shirts and a pair of pants with a rip in the crotch. It could wait. She went to Bella's instead, despite a gray fall drizzle that misted over everything. She wrapped her coat around herself and buttoned the little package with the dress inside in case it rained any harder.

At the house she knocked and found her sister not at home, maybe into town for something, maybe the post. Ed's red pickup was gone, too. She let herself into the house and left the package on the kitchen table, wrote on it with pencil, "Bell— Came by to drop this off, but you were gone. Love, Dot." The empty house was cool, silent without the baby, strange to her. It had been a refuge for her ever since Bella got married seven years before, but she had never been there alone, without even the baby. It seemed like a different place, as if it could have belonged to anyone, yet she felt her sister's presence in the cleanliness of things, the order of the china statues on the mantelpiece, the dishes drying on the rack by the sink. Dottie could lie in any of the beds, could take anything out of the drawers or cupboards. She felt herself trespassing on her sister's life, her sister's silent spaces, and had a glimpse of how lonely the place must have been during those years she had lived here with Ed, before the baby came, all those breakfasts and dinners and suppers for Ed and all those farmhands, and Ed's father when he was still alive, and the washing and cleaning all by herself, and she realized her sister had taken on the same kind of life Mother had. She felt the compromises her sister had made in marrying a man like Ed Mackie, the give-and-take of it, and it was strange to think of her sister as a married woman. Herself as a married woman—unimaginable. As if it had happened to someone else, a different life.

She and Bella had been close once. Bella was like a second mother, the one who did not scold (at least not as often), the one she told everything to, even things she never told Peggy, the one into whose bed she crawled when she was afraid at night. Bella was the quiet one, the one who rarely got into trouble, the one who kept the peace between Jimmy and Dottie, and even between Mother and Daddy, on days when things turned bad. When the shouting started, Bella would quietly ask to speak to one or the other of them somewhere else and so put herself in the middle of their anger, making it seem a smaller thing, less ugly, less hard. But Bella had married Ed when Dottie was still in school, and though she moved just down the road to the Mackie place, Daddy's house had been so different since she'd gone that it was hard to believe she had been there at all. It was after Bella got married that Mother moved upstairs to the children's room, sleeping in the empty spot next to Dottie, and then later, when the war started, in Jimmy's abandoned bed. It was a preference Dottie could hardly blame her for.

In the yard, Dottie stooped to pet the barn cats that came up to see if she had a little food. A coolness coming in, and the smell of drying tobacco from the shed, fall starting to come on hard. A ripping deluge started to fall, white hailstones bouncing off the pavement, so she ran for the barn, pulled aside the doors, and went in to get out of the weather.

A soft nickering as she came in, a deep brown shade. The horses greeted her with a *whoosh* of their wet breaths, and she reached in to touch one old mare on her whiskered muzzle. The mare lipped at her hands in return. In the humid darkness of the barn, she saw rows of pink and gray white noses sticking out between the bars, the horses curious about who was there. A smell of creosote on the slats of the stalls so the horses wouldn't chew the wood, corn dust, clean straw laid that morning. From somewhere down the aisle, she heard the stallion urinate insistently in his stall and stamp his feet in frustration that he had to stand around in it after.

The hail pattered on the tin roof in waves of sound, first soft, then more demanding. Now she was stuck. The cats ran in out of the weather, too, rubbing around her ankles and mewling for food. Outside in the puddles around the drive floated the Chinese geese Ed favored as watchdogs, happy for any body of water, no matter how small. Their wings were clipped; they would never know Lake Erie was less than a mile away.

She looked out the other end of the barn to see if there was anyone moving in the fields, in the milkhouse. No Bobby. No Ed, no Bella. No teamsters. Farms were lonely places when no one was there. Maybe because of the animals, all expectation and dependence, useful each in turn, but only if someone was there to make them so. No wonder Ed and Bella needed so many farmhands—so much life in their care, so much growing, so much dirt and piss and blood and water to put together, take apart, harvest, and store.

The middle of the day, and no one was on the farm. Maybe they went to town. Maybe Bobby was with Peggy at her father's lunch counter. She pictured Peggy's turned-up smile and hoped not.

Well, he wasn't here. It couldn't be helped; she couldn't make him be here if he wasn't. She thought for a minute of walking out to the tractor barn and climbing the stairs and having a look around his little room for clues—to what? To the tricks of his heart, to his past, his future, hers? Disappointment settled on her back, and relief climbed on with it, so when the rain let up she started out of the darkness of the barn to head home.

He was standing in the doorway of the tractor barn, waiting out the storm, same as she had been. Arms folded, that maddening grin on his face that grew bigger when he saw that she saw him. Gravel and hail crunched under her feet as she crossed the drive between the barns. She would go up and say hello and go home, and she would mend Daddy's pants, and that would be the rest of her day.

His tan was still red dark, and she could see the white skin under the edge of his shirt where it was rolled up. Pale hair, pale eyes. "Dottie," he said. "Fancy meeting you here."

She folded her arms. "I don't see why. You live here."

She realized that they were completely alone. She walked to the door of the tractor barn and leaned on it, trying to think of what to say.

"Taking the afternoon off?" she said.

"Not really. Just waiting out the rain. Gets a little close upstairs."

She tried not to think of it, his little room, him alone in it. What did she know about him, really? What did she know for certain that she hadn't made up in her own mind, alone at night in her room in Daddy's house? Six months on Ed Mackie's farm, and he hardly had any friends, no one in town he talked to about himself, certainly not to the silent Ed, who didn't talk of anything that wasn't related to farmwork. Most of what she knew came from Bella. He was from Missouri. Maybe he was from Missouri— he also said he'd lived in Ohio for a while. Once or twice he had a letter from a woman with the same last name in Ohio, Bella told her, though it might as well be from a mother or sister as a wife. He was maybe a year or two older than Dottie, certainly not past twenty-four. Had not left Canada that anyone knew, not a single visit home, not for any reason. He could be a fugitive from the law, a murderer. He could be a deserter from the army. He was anything she wanted him to be.

She jumped; he was behind her. His hands on her shoulders, up under her hair, on her neck, and he turned her around and kissed her full on the mouth before she had time to ask what the hell he thought he was doing. Soft, cold lips, and wet. She could smell his damp stinging smell, and his hands on her skin were cold from the rain. She was glad. Her hands around his back, and everything different from Walt. He was taller, for one, taller than she was, and thinner, and she liked his thinness, the ribs under her fingers prominent enough to count. It seemed the right thing, only natural, and about time.

He pushed her toward the wall of the barn, and she stepped back with him as if dancing, until the wall was at her back. She breathed in everything about him as quickly as she could, as if her breath might stop at any second. He pulled at her coat, his hands underneath the fabric, warm, and her fingers tightened around him. She tipped her head back and saw the rafters of the tractor barn, the beams covered with pigeon feathers and gray white droppings, and the birds themselves roosting there, looking down at her with hard, small eyes like flecks of coal. The light coming in from the open doors was gray and wet. She closed her eyes and decided not to think. A car drove past on the road, the spin and knock of gravel under rubber tires, and Bobby's mouth was on her neck, his saliva wet and cold, and his hands were fumbling with her skirt, under it, trying to pull it up. Suddenly she was freezing. She thought she might freeze to death.

She put both hands up and pushed him away, pushed herself, rather, away from him.

He grinned. Said he knew what she was thinking. And he was right; shame burned her face, because she had not been so secret, not so clever, and if he knew, then someone else might, too: Mother or Bella or Daddy. Not as clever as she thought she was, and her belly went cold thinking that someone might have seen, might tell Walt. Walt, who had stroked her fingers with his clumsy hands and given her something to dream about other than a life on Daddy's farm. It had seemed a small thing at first to risk, a husband away overseas whom she had seen exactly three times since the wedding, nine months ago the last time, and herself stuck in Daddy's house. It had seemed a small thing, something she was willing to risk, but only as long as no one knew.

She tried to walk past him. He put up his arm to block her path, leaned against the door. "No one's here," he said. "No reason to leave."

"There is, and you know it." She tried to push his arm out of the way, but he grabbed her by the wrist. She could not move. Another wave of coldness, and she wished she had had enough sense to stay home. She said, "I know where Ed keeps his shotgun." He smiled and dropped her wrist. Still too close, still too much. His smile infuriated her. Go, just go. So she stepped out into the weather, away from him.

Dottie had seen her father in town. Mother took the two girls there to buy new shoes for school and pick up a letter at the post office. Dottie sat at the front window and pressed her face against the glass, watching her breath fog it while her mother waited for the postmaster. Aunt Liebie writing from Scotland. Bella looking the other way, talking to one of the older girls from school.

She saw Malcolm and Malcolm's mother in the front seat of Daddy's truck. They were parked across the street, in front of the dress shop, and as she stood looking he came out of the shop with a package, handed it inside the truck, walked around to the driver's side, and got in.

They looked like a family. That was the thing she couldn't get over. The woman in the car wore her hat askew, but under that her hair was red like Malcolm's, though hennaed, maybe, not like Mother's white hair. She was pretty. Malcolm on the front seat between them. Dottie thought if she didn't know better, she would guess they belonged together. That it was she and her mother and her family who had interrupted the scheme of things, not the other way around.

Mother behind her. "Dot," she said, "time to go."

Dottie took her mother's hand, wouldn't let her leave. She didn't want either Bella or Mother to see what was happening outside. She would protect them. "What did Aunt Liebie say?" she said. "Read us the letter."

"Not here," Mother said. "You know that."

She turned around and breathed on the window, wrote her name with her finger. Bella tsked. "What did you do that for?" she said, wiping off the letters with her sleeve. "The postman will have to wash his windows now because of you."

Mother buttoned her coat. "That's enough from the two of you," she said. "Let's go home." Dottie was about to stop them, but the truck was gone: Daddy had driven his other family home.

She didn't say anything when Daddy came home that night, too late for dinner, washed in the sink, and sat down with his pipe and the newspaper. She wouldn't say anything to upset Mother. But she sat across from him in her chair and did her schoolwork and watched him and thought, I saw you. I know what you've been doing.

CANADIAN PACIFIC TELEGRAPHS
10 Jan 1944
Mrs. W. G. Dunmore

Regret to inform you that your husband Warrant Officer Walter George Dunmore is missing after flying operations stop Any further information received will be communicated to you stop Please accept my sincere sympathy in your great anxiety stop Kindly acknowledge by telegram collect.

Co. Capt. 4 Overseas

After the telegram came, Peggy took the afternoon off and Bella came over with the baby. The light never quite turned up full on the day. The inside of the house was dusky and quiet, voices kept down so everyone could hear the radio crackling and hissing in the corner. Dottie sat on the floor with the skirt of her dress pulled around her knees, Peggy on the chesterfield behind her, pulling Dottie's hair back gently and letting it down again in a pattern that was steady and soothing and familiar. Mother made cream tea, and when she brought it in and set it on the table, Dottie could see she had been crying in the kitchen. She wiped her face and disappeared again, saying she forgot the spoons. Dottie looked down at her hands in her lap, at Mother's pink-glass lamp that stood lit in the window and threw a rosy glow over the gray light and the faces of the women in the room. She looked at the yellow screen over the radio speaker, the dust on top and her own fingerprints in it. She heard the voice coming through from miles away and wondered how long he'd been missing, what she herself had been doing the moment his plane went down, exactly when that was, and she felt she should have known somehow the moment it happened, but she didn't.

Once he had told her that if she heard he went down over water, that would be it for him and she should go on and have a nice life. Because the water was freezing and he never put on his life preserver. No point in putting off the inevitable, he said. Sometimes, he told her, flying north from Iceland, he had seen the Northern Lights come down, pinks and purples and greens. "It's the strangest thing, seeing how beautiful the world can be, and then the next morning we're strafing submarine convoys," he'd said.

Walt was the wireless operator. It was his job to keep in touch with the world outside the plane's fragile metal skin. He would let them know. He would let her know. If they had found land at all, he would find a way to let her know.

The radio crackled and hissed, and the report came in about a missing Liberator, and the walls of the room seemed to stretch and hold their breath to listen.

The radio said the plane went down, but not where. The pilot had radioed that they lost two of their four engines on the flight out of Reykjavík, that they had tried to make for the coast. No one had seen them go down, over neither the sea nor the Labrador coastline, but there was no reason to believe they were dead. Rescue parties were being dispatched to search. The radio said there was still reason to hope.

The afternoon started to shift down to a darker shade of gray, as if it might snow, and Peggy said she should get going. Her parents would be worried. Bella, too, left a little while later because she had to get supper on the table, but she would be back in the morning, and when they embraced to say good-bye she held on a little too long.

Dottie sat by the radio, waiting for more news and doing the mending that had piled up. Mother was weeping in the kitchen. Once in a while she would stop her washing and stand nervously in the doorway and listen. Dottie wished she would keep to the kitchen if she was going to go on like that. But even Daddy would come in for a few minutes to warm his feet and listen. Whenever her hands paused over the mending, when she held the needle still in the air as she listened to the radio, he told her she didn't have to do all that, he would get Mother to do it. "You've got other things to worry about just now," he said.

Dottie didn't look up at him, didn't want to see the expression on his face. "I like to do it. I need something to keep me busy," she said, and he let it drop. He spent a lot more time in the parlor listening to the radio than he usually did, and chores out in the barn were going undone. The sound of Mother's weeping from the other room made her grateful to sit in Daddy's long silences.

Dottie got out her atlas and ran her fingers over every inch of the map, every little town, every inlet and lake and bay, but there was so little land, and so much water, so much blue covering everything. Exactly how are you supposed to know when the old life ends and the new one begins? How do you choose one, standing on the border between then and now?

It was her own fault. She had taken everything for granted, and her life had suddenly steered off the familiar road.

She went out to the porch to get some air. Winter bitter now, a dust of snow, the cold seeping into her bones and making her stand up straight again. She saw Bobby on the road, walking slowly by the house, his white blond hair sticking up in all directions and his collar up against the wind. He looked at her, and she crossed her arms as if to ward him away, to warn him not to come any closer, and he saw her hard stare, her hard eyes, and kept walking.

THREE

On the third day in the bush, when Walt lifted the blankets and looked out at the world, Al wasn't there: The blankets, where he should have been, were cold, and one of the pairs of snowshoes was missing. A deep, dragging track led away from camp and out into the bush. The grove seemed very still, the trees sunk deep into the drifts. The air was sucked dry, the cold having burned all the moisture out of it. Every sound was magnified: the snap of frozen branches breaking off, snow blowing across the field, rattling and stinging like sand, the constant ringing in Walt's ears. He felt again that he was alone out there, completely alone, a feeling he didn't like one bit. Robinson Crusoe on his snowbound island, at the edge of a cold and inhospitable sea.

He stood up and tied on his snowshoes with difficulty, followed Al's trail into the woods and up an incline, afraid at every step that it might stop abruptly, that there Alister Clark would be lying in the snow. The trail wound away from camp and up the base of a large hill. The trees here were firs, spruce mostly, their branches weighed down heavy with loads of snow.

He was out of breath and warm from the exercise when he saw Al standing on a little rise, looking out at the surface of the lake, which was covered in snow like spilled sugar. Al didn't turn when Walt came up behind him. He stood leaning against a tree, holding his right arm with his left, keeping it close. There was blood on the bandage.

"Nice job you did there," he said. "Damn nice signal. Too bad no one's seen it."

"What are you doing out here?"

"I wanted to look," Al said. "I wanted to stand up and take a walk." He looked back over his shoulder and gave an anemic laugh. "A walk. Isn't that the dumbest thing you ever heard?"

"It might be."

Al was shaking still. He looked as though he might shake himself right into the ground. "I wanted to get up," he said. "I started to think I was never going to get up again."

"You did it, though," Walt said. "You could walk all the way home if you made up your mind to."

"I could," Al said. "I could if I wanted."

They stood and stared out at the bright blanket. There seemed to be nothing to say. "We should go back," said Walt. "You must be freezing."

"I am, but so what. So are you."

"All the same."

Al turned and Walt saw the change in his face, the mask of bravery dropped. He leaned on Walt's shoulder, and together they made a slow march back toward the wreck. Halfway there and Al was out of breath. "Heh," he said, and smiled at Walt. "You might end up dragging me all the way back."

"You want to rest?"

"No. Keep going."

"Just for a minute, maybe."

"No," Al said, and took another step.

Back in camp, Walt stoked the fire and put Al next to it, wrapping him in the blankets and giving him the last of the food. He knew he would probably wish tomorrow, or the next day at the latest, that he hadn't, but at such a time there was no point in quibbling. "Is there any coffee left?" Al asked, and Walt said no and wished he hadn't drunk the last of it before starting off that morning. Al's eyes were dull and greenish. He said, "We should make a plan. We should make a sled or something and leave in the morning."

"I think that's a good idea," Walt said. "We can't wait for them to find us forever."

"You show me how and I'll do it," Al said.

"I will. I think I know how."

"Okay," Al said. He sank deeper in his blankets. "You get the wood and show me. We'll leave in the morning. We'll send them back for the others when we get there."

"Good idea."

He closed his eyes. "Do you know the way?"

"I do," Walt said. "Of course I do."

Day hunched down into dark, and in a little while Al seemed to sleep. In their shelter of birch and spruce boughs and parachute silk, his skin seemed translucent in the firelight when Walt could see it, as if everything inside him were trying to be visible. Once he awakened and complained about being cold in his hands and feet, so Walt curled up tight next to him under the blankets, tucking his friend into the hollow at the center of his body. Something about Al smelled sickly sweet, as if he were starting to rot, and this turned Walt's stomach when he realized it was coming from Al's shoulder.

Walt's hands were heavily bandaged by then with strips of parachute material and some cotton they'd found in the first-aid kit, but underneath they had swelled bluish white, frozen hard, deep down in the skin. Blisters formed on his palms and down to his wrists, but those didn't worry him as much as the white blocks of ice at the ends of his fingers, the parts that didn't hurt anymore because they were dead. He could no longer use his hands for anything.

Instead of sleeping, he lay on his side with his friend tucked up inside him like a child in the womb. He listened for Al's breathing, at first hot and rank, then shallow and shallower, then ragged. Whenever that hot, panicky feeling came over him, whenever he felt he couldn't sit still another minute under the blankets, he willed himself still one more minute to stay and keep Al warm, keep him company.

Underneath the blankets it was even colder than it had been, and the light from the fire didn't penetrate, so it seemed darker, too. Once or twice he heard something crackle in the distance, like the sound of footsteps, and he sat up, the cold deep and dense, and shouted, "Hello? Anybody there?" Deer, maybe, or moose. There he was, calling out to wild animals. He must be getting loopy.

Next to him, Al stirred. "I'm cold."

"I know. I am, too."

It had been a long time since he'd lived out of doors. Not this far north, though, and never alone. His father had always been there to tell him what to do, how to build a shelter, how to make snow goggles, how to walk in snowshoes, how to stake a line of chain or find a post in the snow. His father would have handled things better, made a better shelter, found a way to get home. His father would have figured out a way to help Al somehow.

The fire threw out a meager but sheltering circle of light, a weird edge to the flames, beating against the air as if being torn away by some invisible hand. Eventually the wood burned down to coals, and Walt dozed a little, on and off, dreaming. Once he thought he heard a plane, close and getting closer, but when he sat up and listened, there was only the wind in the trees.

He closed his eyes. He dreamed he was in the Liberator again, the roar of the engines, the popping of the machine guns, and in his dream something exploded, and for a moment he thought he had gone deaf. A terrifying thought. He shook himself awake and listened to the silence around him, the soft sound of falling snow, and realized that it was so quiet suddenly because Al had stopped breathing.

Dark was full on, the wind was coming up, and when Walt stuck his face out from underneath the blankets, he could feel how far the temperature had dropped since the sun went down. Unless Walt wanted to freeze to death, Al would have to spend the night under the blankets. Walt stayed curled around him until the body got cold. Then he slid away, inch by inch, until no part of them was touching any longer.

He remembered a high cold day, a scrim of thin clouds under the plane like an iced-up lake. There had been nothing out there all morning. Either the subs had gone deep or they weren't there. Nine hours out and seven to go. He was bouncing off the walls. He had had his dinner and slept for a while and read all his magazines and letters twice and thought he might lose his mind.

He had seen the dark shape in the water from his blister at the top of the plane, the shadow below the surface huge, moving fast, and alone. He shouted up to Ingalls that there was a target below, and when the pilot took her down Walt saw more shapes in the water, other dark forces under the surface, a whole U-boat wolf pack. When Ingalls turned the plane to take a look, Walt opened up with the top turret gun and sprayed the water. He saw the white foam pop up where the bullets hit, and then there was blood in the water. Someone was yelling over the horn; Ingalls was shouting, and Arch was laughing so hard that he couldn't speak, but Al sounded mad enough to spit nails. "You stupid ass," he shouted into the com. "What do you think you're doing?"

Walt looked again; the whale turned on its side, its fins breaking the water, and its muscular tail, and the shadow that had looked so massive was reduced. The whale flapped its tail, weakly, and blood kept seeping out into the ocean. The other whales in the pod sent spray into the air from their blowholes. Walt felt ridiculous. "It was a mistake."

"You bet it was a mistake," Al said. His expression didn't change, and for a second there Walt thought they might have more than words. "What a stupid thing to do. What a jackass thing to do."

"It wasn't on purpose."

"Of course not. That would have required some thought."

"Come on," said Ingalls. "It was an honest mistake. I almost thought it was a U-boat myself there for a minute."

"Damn," Al said, shaking his head and turning away. "Damn it all." Ingalls took the plane higher, and they turned again around the dying whale and flew away. From his perch high above, Walt watched the spot of blood in the water diminish and disappear until it was absorbed back into the sea.

In the morning he wrapped Al in a parachute and dragged him inside the fuselage, where he at least wouldn't get buried in the snow. It was slow going trying to keep the ends of the parachute under his arms and move forward at the same time. He couldn't make snow goggles without Al's help, or even tie on the piece of parachute he'd used before, and in the few minutes he was outside, the sun coming off the snow was hard on his eyes. When he got inside the plane he stepped on something he couldn't see in the dark, something that clanged against the metal fuselage and made a dull ringing noise around the grove. His vision cleared a little, but everything inside the plane looked small and useless. Arch and Len were still buried in the cockpit where they had died. Frost had formed on everything, and snow had blown in from the place where the nose blister had broken, drifting into every corner of the little space. He tried not to look at the dead men, but they were the only other human forms visible, and his eyes went to them immediately and could hardly look away. He stripped off Al's glove, the remaining one of the pair they had split between them. It wouldn't fit on his bandaged hand, so he put it in his pocket in case he did decide to try to hike out of the bush toward Goose in the homemade snowshoes. Then he covered Al back up and picked his way back outside the plane, squinting to ward off the glare. The grove where they had landed felt more silent, more desolate, than ever before.

The tent he had built wheezed in the wind, its sides expanding and contracting as if gulping air, the seams fraying in places. In front of its mouth, the little fire smoked. A square of tramped space between the tent, the fire, the open fuselage, and the spot he and Al had picked for the lavatory was surrounded on all sides by snow as high as Walt's shoulder, and he felt trapped there, caged in. He couldn't stay. He had to get out of there. He would have to get the snowshoes on again somehow. He went back inside the tent, out of the glare, to save his eyesight. His eyes were burning and watering, and he knew if he waited much longer, they, like his hands, would do him no good at all.

The tent seemed very small, and he couldn't get comfortable. His hands seemed to hurt more when there was no one to talk to. Stifled in the tent, he would crawl out to sit near the fire; but then after a few minutes his eyes would hurt and he would have to go in again, scooping up a little snow to press against his eyes to ward off the pain. Eventually he stopped going outside. He would have to control himself. He would have to learn to sit still.

In the middle of the afternoon, as he was gathering items in the tent that he planned to take with him the next morning, he heard a plane overhead, a twin-engine from the sound of it, and he scrambled to where Al had stashed the flare gun their first night. It took both hands to lift it, and he couldn't crawl out of the tent with it in his hands, so he tucked it under his chin. He ran outside to fire it off. The plane was high and off to the west, traveling in a straight line, not circling, so he knew he had to move fast if they were going to see the flare. But then he had to unwrap his hands to pull the trigger, and it took some maneuvering for him to get his swollen and blistered fingers inside the trigger, and he held the gun with both hands over his head and tried to squeeze off a shot. But he couldn't do it. The sound of the plane's engines, which a moment before had been clear and distinct, faded behind the mountains.

He dropped the gun in the snow. He pushed down despair. No. No one would be coming. He would have to do the job himself—that was all there was to it. No one was going to come out of the woods like magic and save him.

He picked out a spot in the dark woods, a place of shadows between the trees, and decided that was a promising direction. He shaded his eyes and looked at it a moment. He thought, That's the way I'll go. That way. North-northwest. That has got to be the way to Goose Bay.

In the morning he gathered some supplies, extra clothes, parachutes for blankets, picking them up by pressing his palms together, but he couldn't tie any kind of a bundle. He decided to drag the parachute behind him like a sledge, tucking the ends underneath his armpits. It would be slow going, but who knew how long he might be out there, even if he went in the right direction?

He pulled out the snowshoes Al had made, the triangle of boughs and parachute cord, and pressed down into the middle of one to feel the tension in it. It had a lot of give. They would have to carry his weight, all of it, and keep him from falling through the snow, and he wasn't sure they would, at least not for as long as it might take him to walk out of there. He was not a big man, not as tall as some, but square and solid. He decided to take both pairs for when the first one failed. Snow blindness was another issue. The woods were dark mostly, he saw, but already his eyes were aching, both from the squint and from the glare. He would need the strip of red parachute over his eyes if he was going to make it at all. The red parachute and the snowshoes.

In the shelter he sat on the ground and tried to tie them on, pinching the cords between his wrapped hands, but he couldn't grab hold well enough to tie them. He decided to unwrap his hands and give it a try, pulling off the bandages with his teeth. He tried wiggling his fingers. His hands hurt like hell, but he couldn't get the fingers to move. They were dead down to the first joint for certain and maybe all the way to the roots. He pressed them to his face and felt how solid and hard they were, how deep the cold went into the flesh. They were blocks of ice. He couldn't maneuver them around the cords, couldn't pinch the cords between his fingers and tie them around his legs and feet. Without Al to help him, there was no way to manage the laces, and in the deep snow, without snowshoes, he would never make it. He would fall in a drift and not be able to climb out. It would take weeks to move in snow that deep without the shoes. He would starve to death before he ever got near Goose Bay.

So much to live for, and no way to live. So much to go home to, and no way to get there. Why the hell had he survived the crash, he thought, just to die out here of starvation and frostbite?

He kicked the snowshoe against the fuselage of the plane. The noise rang sharp in the air of the crash site. The fragile construction of string and sticks shattered under the impact. Watching it fly apart was satisfying somehow, and he kicked another and destroyed it, and then another, and then the last. When he was done, there was nothing left but a pile of sticks and cord, as useless as if they'd never been made into anything at all.

Well. That was the end of that.

He built the fire back up and got ready to spend another day in the snow, another night. He threw the sticks from the snowshoes into the fire, but they were green and smoked a little. He crawled back inside the shelter on his hands and knees and wrapped a sheepskin around his shoulders, scooping up a little snow to press against his aching, watering eyes. The inside of the tent looked darker than it had before, almost as if night were falling again. Frostbit and snow-blind and alone.

He heard a branch snap outside, and a soft sound of snow compressing, a noise he hadn't heard in a long time. Someone was walking around the campsite. "Hello!" said a man's voice. Walt sat up so quickly that he pushed off with his hands and was rewarded with a jolt of pain that went all the way up his arm.

A head appeared through the opening in the tent. "You all right?"

When the pain stopped, Walt opened his eyes as far as they would go. "My God," he said. "Am I glad to see you."

"It's a wonder you can see anything at all," the man said. His face was deeply lined and kindly, the best face Walt had ever seen. A pair of snow goggles sat on the top of his head where he'd pushed them up, and his skin was reddened by wind and sun except for the places the goggles had covered. He said he had been checking his trap lines down by a nearby stream, beaver traps by a big beaver house, when he heard some kind of banging noises. He walked in the direction of the noise until he saw the pieces of the plane and footsteps in the snow, and then he heard a shout and found his way to the tent.

"Lucky I found you, son," he said. "Looks like you've been here a few days."

"I have," Walt said. "My crew is dead. Four men. They're all out in the plane. The last one died overnight."

The man examined the bandages, looked Walt up and down. "You hurt?" he said.

"I'm working on some pretty bad frostbite."

He unwrapped Walt's hands. "I've seen better," he said. He asked if he thought Walt could walk on out of there. Walt said he might have been able to, but the banging noise the man heard was the sound of him destroying the homemade snowshoes.

The trapper would go for help. It was a two-day trip to Goose when the snow was this deep, one day to his trapper's tilt where the dogs were and another to town, but he would go hard and fast. He gave Walt some fish he'd caught earlier in the day and a little coffee in a tin can, patted him on the shoulder, and said he'd be back as quick as he could. Walt stood at the mouth of the tent and watched the man snowshoe away from the crash site, his long rolling strides, how he picked up speed as he moved across the crust of snow like Jesus walking on water. He disappeared into the trees, in the direction Walt had picked out himself, north-northwest.

He skewered the fish and put them over the fire. The ice crystals on their skin crackled and steamed, burning off into the cold air. The smell of them came off strong. There were other animals out there, too, with strong senses of smell, and he watched for them in case they came out of the woods looking for food.

That night it was colder without Al for company, and darker. He thought he heard things out in the clearing, things moving, but he couldn't be sure it wasn't the buzzing in his ears. He thought of the dead men in the snow and didn't sleep at all that night, wondering when the trapper would come back for him.

Late one night, not long after the wedding, he and Dottie had slipped out of the house and gone down to Mackie's beach, the shore off his brother-in-law's farm, and gone swimming in the cold water of Lake Erie. It was his idea. August, and neither of them could sleep in the heat of the upstairs room. Dottie had been afraid to go in. Out of her clothes, in the faintest starlight, she had the translucence of icicles. He had never seen her afraid of anything before. "What's the matter?" he asked.

"Don't go out too far. I don't like it when it gets deep."

"All right," he said.

His balls shivered up tight into his guts as soon as he plunged into the water, his skin prickling like a dead goose's, but after a minute he realized it was warmer under the water than above it. He walked out a little farther, out to where he could stand with the water up to his collarbone. The surf was light and gentle, but he could feel currents around his feet.

"I'm not coming in," she said. She was standing on the rocks with the water lapping at her ankles.

"It's safe," he said. "It's perfectly fine."

She stepped down into the lake. Her breasts floated on top of the water, swaying as she walked toward him. The water on her shoulders shone back faintly. She found him, pressed up against him. She was shivering. Walt looked around to make sure no one was there, but as far as he could tell, they were alone. She bent her knees and shrank down a little in the water until their eyes were at the same height, and under the water she wrapped her thighs around his waist and her hands around the back of his neck. He held her up. The surface reflected the light of only the brightest stars, and the electric lamps of tankers off in the distance, and kept their movements hidden even from each other.

After a minute she said she was cold and was going in. He didn't follow her at first, and in the dark, after a few feet, she disappeared. The water rippled toward him to show where she'd passed, and he worried that she might have slipped on the stones and gone under. He looked ahead to where he thought she should be, but she didn't appear. He started walking forward through the water, but it was slow going, like trying to run in a dream, and the rocks under the water were hard and slick. It was so dark that he couldn't see the shore, but he felt the land pulling at him like some primordial desire, the current slurring around his ankles, and under that a deeper pulling, out toward the lake. She'd been caught in the undertow. He'd heard about such things from people who swam in the ocean, the way the water grabbed at a person and pulled them under, and even the best swimmers were hard-pressed to get loose of it. He called out her name, turning around again and again, until he heard, distant, her voice answering. He turned back toward the shore. He saw a faint outline there of her star white skin. She said, "You lost?" and started back up the path. He waded out of the lake and put on his clothes, which stuck to his back, carrying his shoes so he wouldn't get sand in them, and followed her footsteps in the dark. At the top of the cliff he bent to put his shoes on. She was waiting for him.

The next morning he was spotted by an American DC-3. He heard the engines whine overhead and shaded his eyes to look. The plane was right overhead, circling. He waved, and the pilot dipped his wing to acknowledge they had seen him. There was no room for the plane to land in the clearing. The cargo door was open, and from inside someone waved back. A load of wooden boxes came tumbling out, falling hard toward the earth. Then their olive green parachutes opened, caught, and floated down toward the ground like so many drab flowers.

One by one Walt opened them, using his arms and legs and a piece of metal to pry them apart. Parkas, sleeping bags, food, real snowshoes, enough for five people. An avalanche of food and equipment that came too late for anyone except him. A bounty. Always like the Americans to have too much of everything.

It was too soon for the trapper to have made it back to town. He had been spotted twice, rescued twice. A joke. Someone must be joking.

They would be coming. Between the plane and the trapper, someone would come and find him. He knew now, for certain, he would lose at least his fingers and possibly both his hands when he got back to base. He wouldn't be able to work the wireless. He would be sent home. He would probably get a military pension, but a man has to work, has to find something to do, and there might be children to take care of, and he would be damned if he was going to live in Jack's house forever. He wished he had been able to go to college. A man who's been to college doesn't need to worry so much about his hands. He can work with his head. A man who hasn't been to college relies on his hands for everything.

He wondered what Dottie would think when she saw. If she would touch them with her soft hands, if she could rub them back to life. He remembered the night he asked her to marry him, stroking her hands in the dark. There was a part of him, too, that wondered if it was worth the risk, sending men out into the bush, risking more lives for his sake.

But the other part of him said, Don't be stupid; it's time to go home. That was the part that spoke the loudest when he heard the engines overhead.

They were coming. He had been found. Today, maybe, or tomorrow, depending on how far.

FOUR

The story was in the paper, a single column, a thin pillar of words holding up the edge of the page. Dottie read it sitting at the restaurant counter. Peggy poured coffee for the two of them and read over Dottie's shoulder. The article didn't tell Dottie anything about the crash itself that she hadn't learned on the radio: bad weather, out of radio contact, five men aboard, search planes dispatched. What it did say was that one of the crew was from Windsor, something she had forgotten until she saw it in writing. A quote from the crewman's wife, Mrs. Clark, said that she would not give up hope that her husband was coming home. Walt's name was listed below that, and the name of the town, and her own name—the Mrs. in front of Dunmore. She realized that nearly everyone in town, maybe everyone she knew in the world, would see the article. She handed the paper to Peggy. She noticed that the cups and plates were rattling, the liquid inside trembling, and she realized she was jiggling her leg, that it was shaking the whole counter.

When she finished reading, Peggy crinkled the page between her fingers and refolded it. "Nobody sent a reporter to talk to you," she said. She poured cream in her coffee from a tin pitcher, splashing a little on the countertop. The spoon clinked hard on the sides of the cup.

"No," said Dottie. "And I'm glad of it." She couldn't imagine talking to a reporter. She didn't know what on earth she would say.

Bella and Peggy had come and sat with her for the past two days. She hadn't left the house at all, not even to the barn to do chores. She sat in the front room and listened to the radio. Couldn't eat. The thought of food made her ill. Bella and Peggy and Mother had all tried to say something that would offer her a little comfort, but Dottie had sat staring at a point in the distance, wishing they would stop talking.

She had left early that morning, glad to be out of the house. Daddy drove her into town, since he was going anyway, errands to run, and he'd pick her up on his way home. Dottie wondered if he really did have to go into town or if he'd just said that, and then she decided it didn't matter. They left together after the morning chores. He helped her into the cab of the truck, holding her elbow while she climbed up, letting her put her weight on his arm until she was in. They rode together in silence, Daddy taking care in the snow that was deep and still drifting. He said he would come back in an hour and wait outside for her. Or he might come in for a piece of coconut cake if she wasn't done yet. She asked if he had anything special he needed done that day, and he said no. She thought he might reach out and pat her hand, but he didn't. He waited until she stepped out of the truck and shut the door and then pulled away.

Peggy was saying, "The paper could have sent someone. It's not even an hour to drive out here."

Dottie read the headline again: FIVE MEN MISSING IN NEWFIE CRASH. She said, "It's not a contest."

The restaurant was hot, the windows glazed with frost on the outside, steam on the inside. Dottie smelled coffee and beef stew, raisin pie, canned beans. A few bachelor farmers had come in for an early lunch. Peggy's father came out of his office in back, carrying a load of ceramic cups and, under one arm, a stack of clean white cloth napkins, folded in quarters like maps. He looked startled to see Dottie drinking coffee and sitting at the counter, and she watched him compose his face. So this is what it will be like as a widow.

Mr. Mason put down his burden and walked to where the counter split in two, came around to her seat, and pulled her into a damp hug. Dottie wasn't ready for it; her arm was pinned awkwardly between them; a tuft of his gray hair tickled her nose. "I'm so sorry," he said. The day she was married, she had dressed at his house because it was closer to the church. When she'd come out of Peggy's room, he'd kissed her cheek and said she was a beautiful bride and Walt was a lucky man. She remembered thinking it was a fatherly thing to say, the kind her own father had never uttered. Daddy, she'd noticed, had endured the day with a strange, embarrassed look, as if the ceremony had something to do with him, and he didn't say a thing of importance to her at all.

"Mr. Mason," she said. "So good to see you."

He let her go but kept one hand on her shoulder. "Peggy's mother and I are hoping that your young man will come home to you safe."

"I know," she said. "Thank you."

"The paper said they might have gone down on land," he said.

"I haven't heard anything new."

The farmers at their tables, singly and in groups of two or three, were watching the exchange, listening. Some of them she recognized. There was Mr. Spears and Mr. Dupres, acquaintances of her father's; Mrs. Spears was a church friend of Mother's. She saw the desire to speak on a face or two and realized they all knew who she was, had heard what had happened, maybe read it in the paper, maybe passed it around the restaurant that morning before she came in. The talk of the town. She knew it was big news, national bulletins going out, rescue planes dispatched. One of their own, except that he was theirs only because he was hers; only her claim on him had brought him into their circle, her marriage, her life, but it was more than that now—public property. The thought that people were speaking about her, asking one another questions about her, about Walt, was unbearable. They didn't know him, didn't know her, didn't know anything about what she was thinking and feeling.

Mr. Spears and Mr. Dupres stood up, walked over, and held out their hands for her to shake, one at a time. Offered their best wishes. Mr. Spears said Mrs. Spears had gone over that morning to call on her and her mother, but since she clearly wasn't at home, he'd wish her the best for both of them. Mr. Dupres, who always spoke at the top of his voice, boomed, "I'm sure Walt is safe. I'm sure he'll come home soon." He was so loud that everyone in the restaurant turned around to look, stared a moment, and then politely turned back to their food. Dottie felt her leg jiggling again and willed it to be still. Peggy came out of the kitchen with plates of beef for the two men, who gave Dottie the familiar nod with their chins and met their food at the table.

She watched the window for Daddy, who was running late. Each car that went past the restaurant left a new layer of slush along the sidewalk, but Daddy's green truck didn't materialize. It had been a mistake to come into town. As intolerable as the house had felt, as much as she'd grown to dread the sound of the radio in the living room, the news announcer's rolling, elegant male voice, the crackle of time and distance clouding the signal, it was better than feeling the eyes of everyone in the room connected to her like gravity. The door, the window, the snow outside, the steam inside. She waited. He had to come.

Peggy said, "He'll be here in a little bit. He told me he was coming in today."

She wasn't talking about Daddy. Behind her, the farmers' knives clinked on the ceramic plates. Mr. Dupres spoke loudly of the need to buy a tractor instead of horses to work his land and how he could finally afford one because the government was buying all his crops for the war. Peggy's father took an empty soup pot into the back and put it in the sink. Peggy poured herself another cup of coffee and asked if Dottie wanted any more.

"No. If I have any more, I'll start dancing on the tables."

"We wouldn't want that," Peggy said. "Might give these farmers the wrong impression."

She put more coffee on. The smell of the ground beans was as rich and dark as earth. Peggy was a beautiful girl, Dottie thought. Nice shape, long legs, petite, always with the nicest clothes, the nicest shoes, those upturned lips she always outlined in the brightest red. Well, why wouldn't he? She pressed her napkin into a drop of coffee that had spilled on the counter.

"Do you remember," Peggy said, turning back to her, "the time Bert and Jimmy went diving in the river for whiskey?"

The two boys had been friends even longer than Peggy and Dottie. Equal amounts of trouble, it seemed: Jimmy was always goading Peggy's brother into doing foolish things, and Bert would get them both in deeper by complying. One day, Jimmy decided they would go diving for one of the many cases of liquor that had gone overboard into the river between the States and Canada back in the Prohibition days. Bert said he didn't think they could hold their breath long enough to find the bottom of the river. Jimmy might have been all of sixteen then, seventeen for Bert, the girls both fifteen. Jimmy said he bet he could even if Bert couldn't, the river wasn't that deep in spots, so at dusk they took out a small rowboat, on a Sunday when they knew the boat traffic would be light, and rowed out to a spot they'd heard about from some school friends. The girls watched from the bank, telling the boys they were crazy and imploring them to be careful.

The boys put down a makeshift anchor, a block of concrete tied to a rope. Dottie and Peggy shaded their eyes and watched. Dottie told Jimmy before they pushed off that if he drowned, she wasn't coming out to save him; he said he would take his chances. The boys took turns: Jimmy went first, stripping off his shirt and diving over the side of the boat. He surfaced and held on to the side, saying something to Bert the girls couldn't hear. Then he took in a great breath and slipped under the water, leaving a set of rings that grew slowly outward. Her brother was a thin, sly thing in those days, a fish that jumped once and was gone. Bert leaned over and looked down into the murky water, and Dottie counted along in her head: thirty, thirty-one, thirty-two. Jimmy surfaced, gasping and shaking the water off his head. Then Bert went, repeating the steps. Dottie counted again: twenty-eight seconds. They took turns this way, one holding on to the boat, the other diving, for twenty minutes, until one of them came up at last with a brown bottle, dirt crusted, from the river bottom, and then they dove again and again, excited, came up with seven or eight more.

They put them in the rowboat and headed back to shore, whooping that they had enough to drink and a little extra to sell. The four of them had sat on the riverbank that night and drunk out of one of the bottles. Dottie took her first sips and coughed when the liquid burned her throat. She didn't know why, but she had expected it to taste like the river, green and fishy, like the things that lived in the water. The boys laughed and thumped her on the back, called her a lightweight, but she remembered thinking it was a good day anyway, the river water, the strong taste of liquor rattling her teeth, the stars, the smiling boys. Most of all the feeling that they owned the world, that everything was open to them.

"I never told you," Peggy said, "but I had the worst thing for Jimmy in those days. He was so handsome." She ran a rag under the tap at the sink and wiped the counter up and down, in slow circles. She had forgotten to wring out the rag; it left crescent puddles drying on the countertop. "When you started dating Bert, I thought we might double, but by then Jimmy was seeing Sue Livermore."

"I knew," Dottie said. "I wanted to warn you off, but I didn't know how serious they were at first."

"Well," Peggy said, "maybe it was for the best."

"Maybe it was."

They sat and drank their coffee and didn't say much else. Peggy served people who came in; once she brushed Dottie's elbow as she passed, and after that Dottie kept her arms closer in. Eventually Daddy's truck appeared out the window, the rumble of the bad muffler, smoke clouding the street. She put on her coat and leaned in to kiss Peggy good-bye, a quick peck on her pink cheek. She slipped quickly out the door before Daddy decided to come in for that piece of cake.

The cold air dried the dampness on her face; it had been hotter in the restaurant than she'd thought. Daddy waited in the car and put the engine in gear when she came out.

She looked up and down the street at the shops where people were coming and going. She didn't see him. She tried not to think about the day in church when he'd pressed his knee into hers and held it there. She tried not to think of his hands up under her skirt, the way she'd pulled him toward her as if it were the most natural thing in the world, how she'd let herself become the thing she had always despised, even if it was only for a moment. She looked at the people coming and going, the post office, the restaurant, cars driving up and down the street, but she didn't see what she was looking for anywhere.

Dottie hadn't wanted to go to Canada. She had wanted to stay home, in Scotland, in the stone house by the burn with Mrs. Norris next door who kept a pony for her to ride, and the nest of spotted kittens that had been born in the shed. She wanted to stay with her grandmother Farquhar, Aunt Liebie, and her cousins, Betty and John, who had taught her to climb the tree in their yard. She begged her mother to let her stay behind for a little while. But Mother said the family needed to stay together, even if it meant leaving the only home a body had ever known. Dottie suspected that her mother didn't really mean what she said. There was a kind of steel in her mother then that made Dottie a little afraid, as if Mother were shoring herself up against an oncoming storm.

Dottie watched her mother pack. In the big wooden trunk she stowed away the portrait of Granny Craig, the good silver wedding spoons, the fancy teapot, the christening gown in which Bella and Jimmy and Dottie had been baptized. She watched her mother give away all the furniture, some to Grandmother Farquhar, some to Mrs. Norris, some to Mrs. Pirie and Aunt Liebie. She scrubbed the house one last time and gave away the mops and buckets. She cooked one more time and gave away the dishes, the pots and pans. "We'll have to get new when we get there," she said, and that was all there was to be done about that.

She helped each of the children pack a small bag of clothes, let them each take one favorite thing, and then gave away everything else. Dottie's best Sunday dress and her old doll, the one she'd had since she was little, went to her cousin Betty, who was seven but still shorter than Dottie. Jimmy's school uniform went to cousin John. Bella wasn't asked to give anything away, since what she outgrew could still fit Dottie one day, and she didn't keep toys anymore at the grown-up age of eleven.

After Mother was done packing, the day before they were due to leave, the house was empty and hollow. She'd left the curtains up and a single pan on the stove for their last breakfast, but other than that and their small pile of luggage near the door, the house was wiped clean. She said they'd sleep in their blankets on the floor that night, that it would be like olden days when people used to sleep out under the stars, and though she smiled when she said it, Dottie could see the tears in her eyes.

It was hard to sleep on the floor. She couldn't get comfortable on her front or her back, and Bella kept stealing the covers. Dottie rolled onto her stomach, pulled her pillow up under her chin, and tucked her arms around. She looked around at the empty house under the light of the single lamp on top of Mother's trunk. The clean white curtains looked like ghosts at the edge of each window. She felt small and afraid. In the kitchen she could hear her mother fussing with the breakfast items. Then her mother came out of the kitchen, picked up the lamp, and walked around the room to each curtain. A ripping sound, and she moved on to the next one. Another ripping sound. Her mother tore the hems out of each curtain in the front room, and then again in each bedroom, and then, finally, the lone window in the kitchen. When she was done the hems of the curtains flapped loose, ragged, threads hanging off their corners. Her mother came into the front room, folded her own blanket, and blew out the candle. The curtains moved slightly in the thin whisper of wind that came in through the old, crooked window frames, billowing out like the sails on an old-fashioned ship. Dottie lay awake a long time, thinking about what it would be like to sail across the ocean in a ship and wondering why her mother had torn every curtain in the house when she had worked so hard on making it clean for whoever moved in after them.

The next morning after breakfast Dottie rode the pony one last time, with Mrs. Norris holding on to the bridle, and petted the kittens and scratched the mother cat under the chin. She cried all the way to the train station in Aberdeen, because Mother wouldn't let her put one of the kittens in her little carpetbag. She thought about running away, getting a job cleaning houses, earning enough money for a ticket home again, and if she promised to be good and help with the chores, maybe someone would let her stay.

She stopped going into town. Instead of sitting at the restaurant counter, she asked her mother what mending there was to do, went out with her father in the morning for the eggs. Bella came over and sat with her, the sisters mute, never touching or looking each other in the eye, as if looking at each other would undo the knitting together of hope and waiting. Instead they watched the baby playing on the floor, the liveliness of her small head and hands and mouth an affirmation, the only thing Dottie would allow herself to feel. "She's getting so big."

"Walt will hardly recognize her."

"You're right about that."

Dottie felt a surge of gratitude toward her sister and again wished Bella had never married Ed Mackie and moved down the road and, while she was wishing, that she herself was still small and the two of them were curled around each other in their bed upstairs, where they could sleep all night the heavy, damp sleep of children who may not be safe but don't yet know it.

At home in Scotland, when they were small, they had played school. Bella was the teacher. Jimmy and Dottie were her pupils, and after Jimmy started school and no longer thought of it as a game, Dottie enjoyed the thrill of having her sister to herself those hours down by the burn in the spring when the water was high. Bella's full and benevolent attention was like joy, like Christmas, when Dottie was four. Bella had taught her to spell her own name, the well-fed D, the shocked O, the two T's sharing the same crossbeam, like the pillar posts of a house, then the skinny I, and the clawlike E at the end. Bella drew them out herself and then gave Dottie the pencil, led her hands over the letters, tracing until the letters started to look like something she could recognize as sounds, and the sounds went together to make a word, and the word she recognized was herself. That she could be a word was something that had never occurred to her before, and after she knew it, she was not satisfied until she could write them all, herself, Bella, Jimmy, Mother, even Daddy, their first and last names in her shaky handwriting. She put the papers on the wall above her bed, watching them whenever she lay in bed and couldn't sleep, thrilling at the mystery of words, how the shape of the letters and the sounds of people's names seemed to fit them somehow, more than clothes or shoes, more than how they might wear their hair: the fingerprint of a person in the name, the written name, and it was Bella who had shown this to her, Bella who had known it all along.

Bella touched her arm. Dottie picked up the baby and pressed her face to the ginger curls, breathing in her baby smell, although Janice squirmed under the sudden onslaught of affection and wanted to get down.

Mother paused in the doorway and listened: Churchill's speech from last night, his accent stiff as meringue. "Is Peggy coming by today?"

"No," said Dottie. The house was still, listening.

Dottie asked if Bella needed help at home, someone to watch Janice while she made supper, and Bella said, "No. I can manage." Putting on the baby's coat, she looked up at Dottie. "Well, maybe I could use a hand. It might be nice for a change."

"I'll get my coat."

Outside on the road, the cold wind blew her hair across her face and across the baby in her arms. The stars were hidden. The deep snow went into the tops of her boots, and her sister's house down the road was dark, a floating hulk on a white sea, and she swam toward it as if she were drowning.

On the fifth day, already tired of the way her thoughts kept returning to the same place, Dottie had an operator look up Mrs. Clark's number, but when she called no one answered. She hung up and thought maybe it was for the best. She didn't know what she would say to the woman. She didn't really want to meet her. It was an obligation of place and circumstances: If she lived farther away, she would not feel the need to call.

The second time, Mrs. Clark answered the phone. She invited Dottie into town at once. "No one knows what I'm feeling more than you," she said. Her voice was low and rich, and Dottie pictured an older woman, in her thirties, maybe, with children in school and her own housekeeping to look after, or perhaps no children at all, one of those career women in stylish clothes who walked to work and brought a lunch pail like a man. When Dottie hung up the phone, she wondered why on earth she had agreed to go.

Over breakfast, Daddy said she could borrow the truck. "I don't need it today anyway," he said.

He scraped up egg yolk with a piece of toast, leaving a runny yellow smear on the plate, then pushed back from the table, lit his pipe, and went into the front room. Dottie helped her mother clear the dishes. Then she dressed, taking a little more care than usual, and took the truck into the city. She used up the last of her gas ration for the drive, following the highway until she could see the outskirts of Windsor, a city of brick and stone, of factories churning out personnel carriers and plane engines and other machinery needed for the war. Windsor seemed too big for ordinary people; she could see the top of the bridge and the taller buildings of Detroit in the distance, across the river. But it felt good to get out of the house, to have someplace to go.

She followed the directions Mrs. Clark had given her and stopped at the house. It was made of brick and seemed very large, as big as the Livermores'. The porch light was on, faint and yellow and pointless in the daylight. There were net curtains behind the window and a plant on a table in the window.

She thought about turning around and going home. But then the curtains twitched as if someone had been standing behind them. Parking the truck in front of the house, she wished she had a nicer car, something black and shiny and without wooden slats nailed up along the sides. She picked up the coffee cake, went up the walk, and knocked at the door. She smoothed her free hand over her hair, remembering she had meant to put on more lipstick before she got out of the truck, and she thought of going back but decided it was ridiculous.

The woman who opened the door was younger and more plainly dressed than Dottie had expected, maybe a year or two older than Dottie, in a dress that looked homemade and shoes chosen clearly for comfort rather than style. There was an elfin quality to her features, tiny eyes, tiny nose, and tiny bow-shaped pink lips pinched together in the middle of a round face. Her straight blond hair was cut very plainly and made her features seem even smaller, more delicate, like a doll's. But when she spoke, she had that same rich voice Dottie had heard on the phone.

"I'm so glad you could come."

It was the voice that threw her off: It didn't seem to belong to her, as if she had borrowed it. All in all, she was a mousy little thing. A beaten-down look to her, as if life had been disappointing her since long before her husband went missing.

Dottie went inside and took off her coat. She was glad for the coffee cake in her hands; it gave her something to do with them. Mrs. Clark put it aside carefully and embraced Dottie freely and with emotion, a gesture even Dottie's own mother was reluctant to make. Dottie patted Mrs. Clark on the back. Her hair smelled like lily of the valley and was very fine, like a child's. When she let go, Dottie took a step back. It occurred to her that if Mrs. Clark had read the paper, she could have rung Dottie, too, but she hadn't.

"I feel like now that you're here," Mrs. Clark said, "it might still turn out all right."

Dottie followed her into the front room and stood in the middle of the carpet, unsure whether to sit. The house was neat as new laundry, the smell of floor cleaner betraying how recently the housekeeping had been finished. Not a speck of dust on anything. Everything looked slightly old-fashioned but expensive, the furniture bought maybe twenty or thirty years before, golden oak and plenty of polish on it, too, enough that Dottie was sure she'd leave a fingerprint if she touched it. "Have you heard anything new?" she asked.

"No." Dottie noticed the radio was off, a feat she had not been able to manage all week. Turning it off, even to go to bed, would be an acknowl-edgment of hopelessness.

Mrs. Clark went into the kitchen with the coffee cake and came out again.

"Would you like coffee or tea?"

"Tea," Dottie said. "Thank you."

Upstairs, someone was walking around. Floorboards in a rhythmic movement, step-step-step. Dottie waited, but no one came down the stairs. What kind of person would not come down and greet a guest? Mrs. Clark did not seem to notice. She returned to the kitchen and came back with two small yellow teacups shaped like tulip heads opened partly to the sun, porcelain thin as two sheets of paper. Dottie held her cup and admired the way the lavender flowers painted on the side went down into the heart of the cup as well. She guessed Mrs. Clark had them from her own mother and said so, but the other woman replied, "No. The cups aren't mine. My mother didn't leave me anything." Dottie noted the past tense.

Mrs. Clark sat in an armchair and pressed back into it. For a moment Dottie was afraid she might cry.

"I'm sorry," Dottie said.

"That's quite all right."

Mrs. Clark picked at her dress and offered Dottie cream and sugar. She had plump hands with unpainted nails, a plain gold ring that was barely a wire. Dottie couldn't put it together—the richness of the house contrasted with the plainness of Mrs. Clark, the teacups that she used but that didn't belong to her, the footsteps upstairs of someone who was not her mother but who wouldn't come down and be counted among the living.

Mrs. Clark stayed in her chair, so Dottie sat across from her in a matching armchair and sank so far down, she wondered if she would be able to get out again. There were footsteps upstairs again and the sound of a door shutting. Maybe she lived with ghosts. Maybe it was her father. She still thought it was odd that the person did not come down, whoever it was, but there was no telling about other people's families.

On top of an upright piano in the corner was a portrait photo of a young man in an airman's uniform, smiling broadly. His eyes crinkled in the corners, and his lips parted slightly, as if he were about to speak. With some effort, Dottie got up and took a closer look. "Is this him?"

"It is."

Again, Dottie had a sense of things being strangely off-kilter. The crinkle in his eyes seemed too mischievous, as if he were in on some private joke. He didn't seem to be the kind of man who would have been interested in Adele Clark. But then, like doesn't always speak to like.

Mrs. Clark came and stood next to her. She brushed against Dottie's sleeve. She was not much taller than her own mother, a tiny thing. Dottie had always envied small women, but Mrs. Clark filled her with love and pity, as if she were a child.

"It's strange," Dottie said, "that we never met before."

"I suppose so. I wish it had been under better circumstances."

"Yes. Me too."

Tucked in the corner of the picture frame was a snapshot taken in front of an airplane, nine men in uniform, including the man in the larger photo, and there on the left was Walt, smiling. He looked as if he were laughing. The picture surprised her. She wondered what Walt was laughing at. It seemed odd that this stranger had a picture of her husband. Walt never sent her snapshots. He didn't have a camera.

Mrs. Clark pulled out the snapshot and handed it to Dottie. "He's in the picture?"

"Here."

"Ah, yes," said the other woman. "Very handsome."

"He is. Yours too."

"Yes, he is," said Mrs. Clark. She put the snapshot back in the corner of the frame and set the frame on the piano.

There was a definite weight in the room of the things they wanted to say but could not, and a solidarity that Dottie had felt with no one else since the news of the crash. Mrs. Clark met her gaze. The elfin features seemed glazed by a mask of emotion, and the longer Dottie looked, the more the mask seemed to fall away. Dottie was seized by a desire to be honest for a change and say things that would mean something. "The military will send word," she said.

"I can't bear to listen to the news reports anymore, or read the papers."

"No law that says you have to."

She wanted to embrace the other woman as she had been embraced when she first came in the house. But she had never done such a thing in her life and didn't know how to start.

Beside her, next to the chesterfield, Dottie noticed a baby asleep in a crib, a fist in its mouth, a fine mass of dark hair covering its head and the edges of its face, a small swirl on each cheek. "Oh, I didn't even know."

She bent down and took a closer look. The baby had the reddish face, the wrinkles and exhaustion, of both the very old and the brand new. The baby was probably less than a month old.

"Boy or girl?"

"Girl."

"She's beautiful. Your first?"

"Yes."

"What's her name?"

"Caroline."

"I like that. It suits her."

"Thank you." Mrs. Clark worried the hem of her dress, the apron over it, then picked it up and wiped her face with it once and then again.

Dottie picked up her hand and held it, this woman who was a stranger to her. She didn't know anything about her; she could be anyone. Her hand was small and rough, as if she'd done too many dishes. The question Dottie had had on her mind since seeing Mrs. Clark's name in the paper wouldn't pass her lips: What will you do if he doesn't come home?

Mrs. Clark pressed Dottie's hand to her cheek. The hand was cool, but the cheek was very warm. "I'm glad you called," she said. "It's good to have someone to talk to."

"I'm glad I called, too," Dottie said, and then realized she was. She felt a surge of affection for the woman. There was the coffee cake, another passing of the teacups, milk and sugar, and in all those small movements Mrs. Clark looked still like a child, naked and vulnerable, trusting, unprotected from so much that must have happened to her already.

The day shrank toward evening; the baby slept, woke, had a bottle, and slept again. The two women spoke in low voices about what each of their husbands had told them about the other's, what they might expect over the next few days, what they would do when the men were found and came home again. Neither spoke about alternatives. By the time Dottie left, they were on a first-name basis. Adele and Dottie. They made plans to meet again as soon as Dottie could get her next ration of gasoline and to speak again the next day by telephone.

"If you need anything," Dottie said, "you just ring. I can be here in about an hour." She was looking at the stairs, the way they turned there at the top and disappeared into the second level.

"I will," Adele said.

Adele saw her off at the door and kissed her cheek, a gesture that already seemed natural. But, driving away, Dottie felt vaguely as if she had neglected to do something important, as if in leaving Adele alone in that house with her baby girl and the ominous forces unseen above their heads, she had failed a crucial test. She drove back out to Daddy's farm, careful of the deep ruts in the snow, and the dark, and stray animals that might run out across the road.

CANADIAN PACIFIC TELEGRAPHS
20 Jan 1944
Mrs. W. G. Dunmore

Dear Benny
Am out of the bush today and fine stop Expect mail soon.
W. O. Dunmore W. G. Halifax

This was where the *Titanic* sank, Jimmy told her, two miles deep on the ocean floor. That it hit an iceberg and went down and took its passengers with it. "Almost all of 'em, little quinies, too." He bared his teeth as if glad about it, and Bella told him to be quiet and stop scaring Dottie; she was too little to understand that he was teasing. He pinched her when Bella wasn't looking and stood up on the railing, and Bella pulled him back down by his belt loops, because if he fell over, she said, no one was going to jump in after him.

The sea was blue and dark. She looked down into the depths for the great ship with a gaping hole in its side and floating around it the pale forms of the little girls who had died when it sank. In her mind they looked like dolls, their hair fanned out around their still cold faces, their eyes wide-open and staring up at her. But all she saw was the side of the *Melita* slicing the water in two and the white spray that splashed the black sides of the ship as it chugged toward Québec City.

She turned away. A man in uniform stepped in front of the clouds, her view of the sky. He took out a brass instrument that looked like a sailboat and pointed it at some unknown place in the sky, the sun maybe. He fiddled with it and then took out a watch and a piece of paper and scribbled something down. "What's that man doing?" she asked.

"Measuring our position," Jimmy said. "Latitude and longitude."

"How do you know?" she said.

"Daddy told me. When he used to go out on the fishing boats, that was how they knew where they were going."

Dottie was unconvinced. Her brother was only a couple of years older; what did he know? Daddy had been in Canada nearly four years without them, earning enough money for their train fare to Glasgow, their passage to Québec City. Gone so long she could hardly remember what he looked like, just that he was tall and thin like a scarecrow and smelled like pipe tobacco and wanted to be obeyed *now*, not later, or else. She was scared at the thought of Daddy, what he would be like now, and wouldn't have minded if the boat trip took another year.

Mother said they were going to Canada to start a better life, that there was nothing in Scotland but too much hard work and too little getting ahead. Mother was full of hope; her face shone with it. She trusted Daddy, believed in him, enough to stay behind in Scotland until he sent for them, raising the kids by herself and taking care of her old mother, too, until she

93

died. Mother trusted Daddy with her whole life, her whole future, every chance of happiness, and that trust was propelling them forward across the sea.

Bella shooed them belowdecks. "Tea now," she said. "Mother's waiting. She won't want Daddy to think she's been starving us."

Dottie shuffled her feet, not wanting to go back below where it was hot and stuffy and there were too many people, not all of whom were nice. She looked out again at the dark ocean and saw a speck in the distance, a spot of white on the horizon, a bright place her eyes went to right away because it should not have been there. An iceberg. She was about to shout to Jimmy that there it was, that they were going to hit it and all drown, but the navigator had seen it, too, and was watching it, and would steer the ship away from danger. They would go around it, and they would be safe. She followed her brother down into the belly of the ship.

FIVE

Dottie met him at the train station in her father's old farm truck. March, deep in winter still, a wet snow on the ground and still falling, covering everything like a bandage. Walt waited in the cab with the heater blasting while Dottie brushed off the windows with a broom. The dark inside cleared, and his wife's face became visible with each sweep of the bristles, only to obscure again as the heavy flakes dropped onto the glass one by one. His hands were restless and naked, red and sore and very noticeable without the gauze he had worn on them for weeks. On the train he had kept them in his pockets to keep people from staring. He brushed them back and forth across his lap as if that would be any help, and when he knew it wasn't he crammed them underneath his armpits to keep the warmth up and the pain down.

Finally Dottie tossed the broom into the bed of the truck and climbed into the cab beside him, shaking flakes of snow out of her brown hair and onto her shoulders, where it melted into the fabric of her good coat and stained it dark. Her face was thin and drawn, and she wore a new pair of black-rimmed glasses he didn't remember her having the last time he'd been home on leave. She was too dressed up for the day, her hair piled up carefully in front and curled down in back, red lipstick in a shade that made her look even younger and paler than she was, wispy, like a little girl playing dress-up. Her legs underneath the hem of her skirt were purple red and raw from being outside in the wind, because she had worn too light a coat for the occasion, too dressed up for such a cold and miserable day. Between them on the cab seat lay his duffel bag, and in it was everything he currently owned in the world, including his medical discharge, crammed in the guts of a rolled pair of socks.

"When did you get those glasses?"

"Last April, not long after you left last time. I thought I wrote you that."

"Maybe you did. Maybe I forgot." He leaned against the door of the truck like a crutch. "They suit you, though."

"I'm glad you think so."

She needed both hands to drive the truck, one for the steering wheel and one for the shifter, so he did not try to take one of them and hold it. He kept his hands where they were, one under each armpit, arms across his chest like a shield. The wipers swept a ridge of wet snow off the glass and piled it up on each side of the windshield, where it half melted and froze again and compacted. Dottie turned out of the station lot and onto the street, following the red taillights of the car in front of her, trying to keep to the ruts it made in the road so she wouldn't slip off and into a ditch.

Dottie glanced over at him, shyly, and then back to the road. Her hands dropped down to the bottom half of the steering wheel, close to her lap. "Mother's been cooking for two days," she said. "She thawed a pork roast, so I hope you're hungry."

"I hope she didn't go to too much trouble." Outside the windows, the landscape rolled out flat as pie dough. The dark wet trees planted in windrows sagged toward the ground under the heavy weight of the snow. Sometimes by the side of the road there were tracks, rabbit and skunk, leading back toward a small patch of woods.

"Bella and Ed are coming, too," she said. "Everyone's anxious to see you."

He pulled his hands out from his armpits and settled them in his lap, feeling the skin stretch and settle. The tips of his finger nubs were still purple with scarring. He remembered how painful his palms had been when they first were thawed at the station in Goose in a pot of warm water, how he had ground his teeth and sweated while the skin of his hands came back to life, but the ends of the fingers had stayed dull and dead. The doctors had taken off the dead ends and sewed the skin closed again. He had lost most of the last two fingers of his right hand and all of the last three fingers on his left. Both thumbs had lost the first joint only. The nurses made him do exercises for the skin and the tendons that were left, said he might still have limited use of his hands. He might still be able to work. They said he was lucky.

He rubbed at them to try to dull the pain. In the cold, the foreshortened ends of his finger bones burned, as if they were still freezing, as if the last thing his severed nerves had felt were still trapped there, as if it would always be trapped there at the ghostly tips of his missing fingers, and he would continue to freeze, day and night, for the rest of his life. "There won't be a lot of company, will there? Because I'm awfully beat."

At a bend in the road the tires skidded on a thick cushion of snow, and Walt felt the truck slide in the direction its weight carried it instead of the direction Dottie turned the wheel, and for a moment the road lurched in the wrong direction. The ditch seemed a likely place for them to end up, and how on earth would he and Dottie manage to get the truck out if they got stuck, him with his ruined hands and her in her ridiculously inappropriate clothing? But then Dottie steered into the skid, and the truck righted its direction and kept going. Dottie eased up on the gas, continuing toward her father's farm on the Lake Erie shore.

"That was a nice bit of driving," he said.

Her knuckles on the wheel were one shade off white. "We'll be there in a minute," she said, and after that she kept both eyes on the road.

The nurses had sent the telegram for him when he arrived at the hospital in Halifax. He tried picturing her face when she received it, what she might have said, or felt, when it arrived and she opened the envelope and saw that he was safe. He felt stuck in that hospital bed in Nova Scotia, covered up to his neck in a white sheet, blushing in front of the pretty Canadian Women's Army Corps nurse as he told her to address it to "Benny" and having to explain to the nurse what it meant.

The house on the Lake Erie shore looked exactly the same as when he'd last left it, sagging porch shored up on one end with cinder blocks, his mother-in-law's lacy curtains yellowing behind the front windows, a large pink-glass lamp covered with painted roses standing mute and dim behind the front windows. A line of dark spots near the front porch showed where his father-in-law, Jack, had dumped the wet mash from inside his pipe. The curtains in the front window moved, and Walt knew they had been spotted.

The door opened, and the family stepped onto the porch, women and men both, the whole of the family except for his brother-in-law, Jimmy, who was still in Italy. Walt opened the door and slid down from the cab, his hands stuffed in his pockets. Dottie came around to his side of the truck and picked up his duffel off the cab seat. She was about to carry it herself, heavy as it was. "I can do it," he said, but it came out more harshly than he'd meant. He took the bag from her. By the way she turned her head, he could tell she was hurt. Together they slogged through the snow and up the porch stairs to where the family was waiting to welcome him home.

They greeted him in a flurry of hugs and laughing. Janice hung back a bit, hiding behind her mother's skirt. In the length of her arms and legs he could see exactly how long he had been away; she had been a tiny infant, swaddled and screaming, the last time he had seen her. Jean pulled Walt hard toward her, so that he had to take a few shuffling steps to keep his balance, and pressed him to her large, shelflike bosom. Walt could feel her breath on his neck as she told him, in her accent thick and nearly impenetrable, how glad she was he was home and out of the fighting at last, and how she had cried for him and for her daughter when she heard that his plane had been lost, and how it was only the Lord's will that he alone had been rescued from the snow and come home to them. Walt felt his back stiffen, and he tried to straighten up, but Jean was a strong woman for someone so little, and so wrung with emotion, and she wouldn't let him go.

"Mother," Dottie said. "Please."

"Jean," said Jack, bluish pipe smoke rising from his mouth up to the porch roof, "that's enough now. You'll embarrass him." Jean straightened up and let him go, wiping off her face and smiling wetly.

Welcome home, welcome home, they all said. They rubbed their arms and slowly shifted their weight toward the open door of the house. Every other time he had come to this house, he had known that eventually he would be leaving again, in a few days, maybe a week. The open door of the house showed a dark room inside, a single lamp lit to ward off the gloom of the day, but he could smell supper waiting, and his stomach moaned in pleasure at the thought of it, so loud that he was sure they all heard.

They stood around, waiting, maybe, to see what Walt would do, what he would say on his first day as a civilian, as a true member of the family.

"Let's not all stand here letting the warm air out of the house," he said finally. They stood back and let him go in first.

Dottie led him into the hot-bright kitchen, where the table was already set with the Christmas-and-Easter cloth, extra chairs brought in from the front room crowded around the table. She pointed the way to the best of these, the deepest and most comfortable, and pulled it out for him. They were still watching, still waiting to see what he would do or say, and he felt a portentous weight to his every gesture and movement. He sat back against the chair cushions. "Well," he said, "I'm damn glad to be home."

The men smiled, but Dottie nodded at the baby. "Walter," she said. A warning. He had forgotten Janice was there, that's all.

Dinner was hot and good, but the space around the table was cramped, with little in the way of elbow room. He seemed to have more trouble with the knife and fork than he'd had at the hospital, where the tin utensils weren't so heavy. He dropped his knife on the floor four or five times, the handle tumbling out of his grip, before Dottie pulled over his plate and cut his meat for him herself. Most of the family turned away politely, but Walt, with his eyes closed, could feel Jack Farquhar watching the whole exchange, sucking calmly on his pipe. Walt felt very warm all of a sudden, as though he needed some air. When Dottie pushed his plate back over, the pork roast cut into bite-size pieces as she would have done for the baby, Walt picked up his fork once again and, pinching the stem of it tightly between the nub of his thumb and his palm, stabbed a piece of meat and brought it slowly, trembling, to his lips. His fingers, still healing, were on fire, but he put the piece of meat in his mouth, chewed, swallowed, and took another piece.

"Delicious," he told his wife and his mother-in-law, who both beamed. "Thank you. You shouldn't have gone to so much trouble, but it sure is nice to have a meal at home."

After supper was finished, Ed and Bella took Janice home, claiming chores that needed to be done. Ed patted his shoulder and said he was glad Walt got back in one piece. One piece more or less.

Dark was coming on, and the snow falling and the low gray sky made it seem even darker, and Dottie waited for Ed's truck to make it back out of the driveway and into the road before she shut the door. She turned out all the lights in the front room except for the pink rose lamp in the window, bathing the room in a bloody glow, and she went back into the kitchen to help her mother clean up.

Jack sat on one side of the lamp and turned on the radio. The news was all about the war in Europe. Walt, standing in the hallway and unsure if he should go in the kitchen and help or sit in the front room with his father-in-law, looked back and forth a few times before Jack said, "Have a sit." He offered Walt a smoke. Walt said no thanks, he'd never started, so they sat in silence and listened to the news from the war. The radio announcer's voice filling the room kept them from having to talk to each other, which suited Walt just fine.

The newspapers had called him a "sole survivor." He had thought a long time, both in the hospital and on the trip home on the train, about what he would say when he wrote to the families of his friends. There was nothing that would be enough.

The radio announcers were dutifully patriotic, talking about the superior forces amassed against Germany, but he felt a kind of sudden, deep despair take over him, a sick sinking feeling that constricted his chest, something he had never felt in all those nights over the Atlantic, the nights after the crash, bitter nights in the bush, and waking up in the hospital with his hands bandaged and useless. He stood quickly, because he was sure for a second it would overtake him. The sweet, heavy smell of pipe smoke was thick in the room. He stood and realized he had nowhere to go. The little house was warm and already as crowded as it could be. Jean's blankets and pillow were set to one side of the chesterfield; she would be sleeping there permanently now that he was back.

He felt a rage and a fear and a loss that he'd never felt, and if he hadn't heard Dottie's voice in the other room, speaking low to her mother, he was sure he would have walked out the door and kept walking, in any direction.

He didn't notice, at first, that Jack was asking him how long the doctors said before he was fully recovered and could go back to work.

"I don't know," he said. "They told me it's different for everyone." He sat down again.

"What do you think you'll do, then?"

"I'm not really sure," he said. "I've thought about it, but there doesn't seem to be a lot of options. Maybe go back to building, or surveying, if I can find something. I don't know a lot about what's available around here."

"Well," Jack said. "You'll find something." From behind his glasses, he looked mild. "You'll get back on your feet, and you'll figure it out," he said. "Until then you can stay here as long as you want."

"Thanks," Walt said. Old bugger, I know what you're thinking. He rubbed his hands together. The tight feeling in his chest was still there. He didn't know what was wrong with him, but he had never felt this way, and he didn't like it one bit. For the first time he noticed how small the front room seemed, smaller than it had when he'd been there before, the walls closer together, the ceiling lower, or maybe it was the winter dark and the weather outside that made it seem so. There was frost on the inside of the windows, and a rolled rag under the front door kept the cold from coming in over the threshold.

Dottie came in, wiping her hands on the apron she'd thrown over her good dress. "You must be tired," she said, standing behind Walt's chair and touching his shoulders. He was still in his uniform. He didn't have much else to wear.

"I am tired," he said. He stood and stretched. "I think I might head up to bed."

"That's a good idea," Jack said. "We do get up early around here." He stuck out his hand for Walt to shake, and he took it. Jack's thin, bony fingers closed around what was left of his own.

"Good night, then. Glad you made it back," Jack said.

Dottie led him upstairs and shut the door to the bedroom behind her. She helped him undress and wash up for bed, crawl into the cold sheets in the room under the eaves that she'd once shared with both her brother and her sister, later her mother, now the two of them. When he lay in bed waiting for her to come in, he felt how low the ceiling was, how small the room, and he wondered if he would be able to live here. The despair in his chest was pulling him down to some hole in the earth, where he was small and cold and alone.

Dottie shut off the light and climbed in next to him. He could feel her cold feet on his legs under the blankets, warming slowly. He reached over and pulled her toward him, and she slid lower on the mattress, tucking her head under his chin; in bed she was not so much taller than him. His hands on her shoulders. He ran his hands over her shoulder blades, down to the small of her back, lower. Their bodies warmed the air under the covers. Dottie said, "Are you sure that's a good idea? You're still healing."

He wanted to say, *It's the best idea I ever had*, but he couldn't manage to speak at all.

She rolled over with her back to him and tucked herself up next to him, her spine curving into the space between his chin and his knees, and he had to shake his head to move the little strands of her hair out of his mouth. She pushed up close to him. Sighed, said, "I'm glad you're home." He slid one hand down to her hip and rested it there, and didn't push, and after a few minutes he could feel her breathing slow and quiet, and in another minute she was asleep. When he thought he could move without disturbing her, he took his hand away and rolled over, staring at the darkness coming in through the curtains, showing the blanket of snow outside the window, fresh and new fallen, untouched.

It had taken two days for the dogsled teams to get him back to Goose. Eight men had come out in all, the trapper who had found him, some locals, some Americans who'd been sent from Maine. Five sleds, one for each of the men, the living and the dead. They'd been looking for them since the first night, they said, and come so close a couple of times that it was only dumb bad luck he hadn't been spotted sooner.

They told him the SOS in the snow had been what led the American DC-3 to him at last, the one he'd stomped out with the homemade snowshoes he would later destroy.

He rode in on the dogsleds under the trapper's heavy furs, beaver and fox, and the motion lulled him into a light and fitful sleep, and he was warmer than he ever remembered being, except for the place where he left a spot for his breath, because he couldn't stand to have the furs over his mouth. The other sleds followed behind, and the men who'd come out with the teams were quiet, thinking about their cargo.

At the air base at Goose, the doctor who looked at his hands said he needed to be shipped to the hospital at Halifax right away. Walt protested that one more day couldn't make that much difference, that he needed to be there when services were said for his friends, but the military doctor wouldn't budge. Walt asked for a minute alone. The doctor hemmed, but the CO, a quiet, authoritative man whom Walt liked immediately, said an airman who'd been through so much could be given a little leeway, and he told the doctor to take a cigarette break and escorted Walt down to the morgue himself.

The morgue was painted green, a color Walt never liked, and the strong chemical smell and the deep quiet made him pause for a moment at the threshold. The others were still wrapped in their red-and-white parachutes, vaguely festive, like candy canes, and laid out on metal tables. The CO said he could take as much time as he needed and left.

Walt unwrapped them, their arms and legs, but left the faces covered. He already knew what they looked like under there.

He went through their pockets, slowly because his hands were aching, and each touch brought up new pain. He found the Irish girl's letters in Arch's jacket pocket, four of them folded together carefully. He would write to her, tell her what happened, so at least she wouldn't always wonder. In the opposite pocket were the letters from Arch's wife, and Walt took those, too. Len had an American liberty-head dollar, a good-luck piece from his mother. Dusza had a scrap of paper with something written on it in Polish, or maybe German, that Walt couldn't read and a letter with a Polish postmark that was so old and faded, he must have carried it around for years, since before the war started.

In Al's pocket he found a picture of Adele. She was young, pretty, pale, and freckled, standing against a white building with peeling paint that he first thought was a house or a store until he saw the sign over the door: THE VICTORIA INN. Her hair was dark and curling, falling on her shoulders, and she was squinting; the sun was in her eyes. She gave a wry and impatient look to the camera, as if she were both enjoying it and waiting for it to be over. A long shadow fell toward her from across the street, the shape of someone out of the frame. In a tiny hand on the back was written: "All my love."

He knew he would have to see her when he returned to Ontario. How she would look when he met her and told her how Al died, not the official version but the true one, because there were things that needed to be said, and he was the only one left to say them.

He put his friends' things in his pocket and wrapped the bodies back up in their parachute wrappings. He felt he should say something, but he knew it would have been for himself, not for them, so he went out silently and shut the door.

The next morning, after Dottie and her mother left to run a couple of errands in town, he decided to go outside and get a bit of air, even walk down the road a little. It might be what he needed. He dressed and retrieved his shoes from their hiding place in the closet, put on a warm pair of socks and tied the laces carefully, pinching the ends between the first joint of his thumb and his palm the way the nurses had shown him. He got out his coat from the closet near the front door and put that on as well. But when he tried to wrap his hand around the slick metal doorknob, he found he could not. A simple gesture, something he had taken for granted all his life, and he couldn't even do that much.

He flung out his arm, smashing the pink-glass lamp that sat on the table by the window. The heavy glass top tipped over and fell, shattering on the floor of the front room and sending pink shards across the wooden floor. A few large pieces showed where the floral pattern of the lamp had once been, but it was gone, destroyed. The bottom part of the lamp was still intact, lying on its side on the table where he had knocked it over, but the shade on top was ruined, and even the clear hurricane that had been underneath was cracked and starry where it had hit the tabletop.

Breathless with the force of his own anger, Walt stood and looked at the mess he'd made. There was no hiding it, but the least he could do was clean it up. He went back into the kitchen and found where Jean kept the broom and dustpan, and holding the broom between both hands, he managed to get up most of the bigger pieces. He couldn't work the broom and dustpan both and ended picking up each small piece with his hands. Sometimes the glass points raised blood to the surface. It was slow work, and at any moment he expected his father-in-law to come in the house and catch him in the middle of his surreptitious cleanup effort, but he must have been far out in the fields or the barn, because Walt got every piece of glass off the floor and into the garbage. He righted what was left of the lamp and thought about what he would say to his mother-in-law when she returned, how he would explain himself. There was nothing to say except "I'm sorry," and he was. He couldn't believe his own foolishness. All that rage, and there he was still in the same fix.

He tried the door handle again. He pushed his palm against the smooth metal of the knob and, feeling the friction created there, turned the handle slowly until the latch gave. The door swung open, a free and clear view of the outside world, and Walt stepped onto the porch.

The snow from the day before was already melting. Up north, where he had grown up, winter might keep until late April or even May. He walked out to the road, stuffed his hands in his pockets to keep them warm, and turned in the direction of the lake. He remembered coming this way with Dottie in those months when they first met, when he used to come down from bombing and gunnery school with his friend Pete in Pete's car, going to dances and looking to meet pretty girls. He had driven this road the night he first met her, riding in the back of Pete's car down to the lake. Warm weather, and then he hadn't needed a jacket. They had walked down the rocky edge of the land toward the tumbled stones that littered the lakeshore. Reluctantly, he had asked her to dance. He hadn't felt comfortable in his feet, so he'd circled her around and around on the sand, and he remembered thinking, Who is this girl, and how did I end up here with her?

He followed the snow ruts in the road to keep his footing as he walked. The lake came into view over the tops of the trees, like a mirage at first, as if it were rising up over the shore. Low and gray as the sky, and calm, and no wind. When he came closer, when he reached the edge of the land, he walked down the steps to the icy shore once again, the rocks white and ice covered, some cracked with frost, like something from another age. In the summer, with Dottie, he had taken off his shoes and felt how cool the sand was on his hot feet.

His hands were cold, and he rubbed them against his legs. He should turn around and go back, but he didn't want to. The water was frozen over a good way out from shore, but in the far distance there was still open water, and he could see a ship moving through it and waves in the distance that had little ice floes on them. He wondered when he'd decided to feel so sorry for himself. Whenever it was, he wished he could have that moment back.

He turned around and walked back to the farm, his head down against a wind that was starting to come up. The farmhouse came into view, and it looked so small in the middle of all that snow, the barn sagging like a swaybacked horse. The road ran past it and curved away from the lake, back toward town. He stood a minute and then went inside the house.

That night he apologized to Jean over and over, said he would get her a new lamp, but she told him not to worry about it, it could happen to anyone.

Dottie pulled down a residential street, stopped her father's truck at the curb, and turned off the ignition. "There it is," she said, nodding toward one of the houses. "I told her we'd be here by three, so we're a little early."

"We left too soon."

"She won't hold it against you."

"I don't like being early. Maybe we should drive around a little or get some coffee."

"Don't be ridiculous. We're already here."

She got out of the truck and went around to the other side to open the door and let him out. He didn't like that Dottie had to drive him to see Adele Clark. He didn't want her to be there when he made his visit, but necessity had made a passenger of him. He felt a sense of responsibility, and because of this he hadn't told Dottie about the photograph in his pocket, or the letters he'd written with the help of the nurse in Halifax to Arch's Irish girl or his wife, or Len Ingalls's wife in Manitoba, or Josef Dusza's mother at home in Toronto, still afraid to go out of her house. These were his burdens alone. Giving voice to them would have diminished them, made them only the mundane loose ends left to tie up after the bodies were buried, like hanging up the clothes you wore to the funeral.

"Maybe I should have worn my uniform," he said.

"You look fine." Dottie stood in the snow, waiting. "Are you coming or not?" He slid down out of the cab, shut the door, and followed her up to the house.

The woman who answered the door was not the woman in the photograph.

Mrs. Clark was small and plain, with the smooth, unblemished skin of a child and a pleading in her eyes that he understood immediately. Her dark blond hair was cut straight, as if she'd done it herself, and rather short, like a schoolgirl's, which made her age even harder to determine. The woman in the photo was dark and freckled, smiling, with a broad, flat face and uneven teeth. This was not the same woman at all.

Mrs. Clark glanced at Dottie and turned immediately back to Walt.

"We're early," Dottie said, stepping past the small woman into the house. Mrs. Clark greeted Dottie with a kiss on her cheek, a brushing together of their faces. He had known Dottie and Mrs. Clark had become close, but it still surprised him. For a moment, the woman looked behind her to the inside of the house. Walt touched the picture in the breast pocket of his shirt and then took his hand away quickly. He took off his coat and held it awkwardly under one arm until Al's wife took it from him and hung it up in the hall closet.

"Thank you for coming," she said.

"I'm sorry. We didn't mean to be so early." Dottie was already picking up the baby. He hadn't even heard her cry. The house seemed large and empty, except for the sound of footfalls moving around upstairs.

"You're not at all," said Mrs. Clark.

"Is there someone up there?" Walt asked.

"My mother-in-law. She's ill."

"I'm sorry."

"She hasn't quite been herself since we had the news."

"I imagine not."

Dottie swayed back and forth with the baby and said, "It's all right, little quinie. You're all right now. Walter, come see Caroline."

He came in the room but could not make himself touch the baby. She was small and red and screaming. After a minute, Dottie whisked her into the kitchen for a bottle with a familiarity that startled him, and he and Mrs. Clark were alone.

The house was dark, as if his eyes could no longer adjust to indoor light, and she asked after his health and he said he was doing all right, fine, in fact, better than he had any right to expect. He had meant to come here and return the photograph to her, but that was now impossible, and everything he had been thinking he might say when he met her was unimaginable. He felt he should have something to give her, something to bring, and without the photograph to give her he was loose and deflated. He tucked his ruined hands under the crook of each arm so she would not have to stare at them.

He could see she would have questions for him. She brought tea and some cake, and he picked up the spoon and poured in the sugar, the cream. He drank his tea. In the other room, Dottie spoke to the baby in a low voice, her words a kind of lullaby. He was aware of Adele Clark studying him, and it reminded him of the hospital in Halifax when the student nurses came in to help change the dressings on his hands.

Finally, she said, "Alister always spoke of you fondly."

"And you."

"You've had a rough time of it."

"Not as much as you, I'm sure."

The acknowledgment brought tears to her eyes, a light glistening. He saw why Al had married her, what it was that his friend had seen in her, a desire to keep her from harm, a protectiveness toward her that was both more, and less, than what he felt toward Dottie. She was nervous and fragile where Dottie was strong willed, resilient. Adele's posture, her whole being, asked things of him that he was not sure he could give: reassurance, determination, strength. Her hands clamped and unclamped around the hem of her dress. He was surprised to realize that she had been dreading this visit as much as, if not more than, he had.

"How are your hands?" she asked.

"Better. They get better every day."

"That's good." She drank her tea in slow, small sips, as if she did not like the taste and were only being polite, and he knew she was gathering herself up for questions, taking into her what strength she could from the walls, the floor. "Do they still hurt?"

"Often, yes. I have some trouble with them. I have to do exercises so the tendons don't atrophy. It's bloody painful. Excuse me. It's painful."

"That's all right."

She would want to know how Alister died, what were the things he said at the end, but there was nothing, he saw now, that would give her any comfort. There was nothing Al had done or said in the bush that would mean anything to her. She would not understand what it had been like there in the cold and the deep snow and the loneliness. He wished he had never come to Al's house, that he had written Adele a letter the way he had for the others and could compose himself on paper, write several drafts if that was required. If she had questions, she could write back and he would have time to think, to be careful. She unsettled him. She reminded him of a bird he'd once seen being put together in his uncle's taxidermy shop when he was young—sort of stretched, as if her insides were thin balsa wood and only her skin was holding her up. If he touched her, she might collapse in a heap of wood and feathers.

"Do you expect to be able to work again?" she asked.

"Maybe yes. Soon."

"That's good."

She was crying, not in any obvious way and not hiding it, either, just facing him with the wetness on her face as if it were the most ordinary thing in the world. Her tears were unnerving. He decided to say very little. He meant to say as little as possible so he would not harm her any further. He had never been the kind of man who kept secrets, but now he saw that he would—he would never speak the whole truth to her, not if he knew her the rest of his life.

"I never saw it like this. I never thought it would end up like this," she said.

"Me neither," he said. "No one does."

She wiped at her face, forced a smile. "Why is that? Why do people expect to be happy?"

"I don't know," he said.

Walt drained his tea, set down the cup. His red fingers seemed monstrous on the delicate porcelain. She picked up the teapot and poured them two more cups, but the lump of sugar in the bottom of his tea took too long to dissolve, leaving the last mouthful too sweet by half. He couldn't drink it.

He did not stand up when the train slowed and finally rolled to a stop at the station. The rest of the boys took their gear and stood and stretched and were glad for their furlough, to get away from the war for a few weeks, a few days, but Walt could see Dottie from his seat by the window and was afraid to get up. He could watch her from where he was standing and she would never know. From the shadow of the train, from the *before* in this before-and-after moment, he could watch her, and in that moment of anticipation everything could still be the way he wanted. He was fearful that something in his face would let her know how afraid he really was.

The snow was falling in soft, heavy clumps. He hid his hands in his pockets. All in all, he had been lucky.

Dottie was waiting for him on the platform, and Walt held his breath: More than a year since he'd seen her, the war driven so far between them that he'd forgotten what she looked like. Yet here she was, a moment before she saw him, her hips crooked the way they did when she was impatient. Things would go back to the way they had been, or would be better than they had been, because their senses had been heightened, and both of them would be more aware of their surroundings. So much of life left to chance, more than he ever thought. A near miss; but even near misses leave a wake, an invisible breath that moves through the air.

He would give her anything she wanted, children, a house, every hidden part of himself. There would be no more nights in the wilderness, no more cold over the ocean, no more drifting over invisible borders that seemed to change every day. The door opened, and he stepped off the train and into the snow.

THE SUMMER OF LOVE
1967

SIX

The old man was there, and he was asking to see *The Reader's Guide to Periodical Literature*. It was on the shelf near Caroline's feet, and she would have to bend over to reach it, and that was the whole point. The other librarians had found somewhere else to be, the way they always did when the old man came in. He was harmless but unpleasant to be around, mostly because of his deafness and his bad breath—she had to bend close to speak to him, and the smell could be hard to bear. But really he was lonely. She couldn't make herself ignore him. He would come into the library to ask her for something off a high shelf, which meant she had to stand on a step stool and let him leer at her from behind, or something from down low so she had to bend forward. Usually she was circumspect about these requests and would adjust her posture modestly, but when he came in that day and she was the only one standing behind the reference desk and he asked to see the *Reader's Guide*, she said all right, and when she leaned forward to reach it, the pale green paper cover bent at the corners and soft with use, the old man had a clear shot down the front of her blouse.

It was so brief that she could almost pretend it had been an accident. She straightened up and handed him the book across the desk. "Good," he said. "Beautiful."

He was grinning at her. She could see his brown teeth, tobacco stained, behind his stretched lips. "You're welcome," she said. The old man took the book and disappeared.

It was July in Chicago, hot, and fans whirred on windowsills all over the library, blowing in the smell of ozone and exhaust, blowing out the smell of book mold and dust. Outside, the sky was hazy and dull. Planes lined up for approach to O'Hare, so low that Caroline could read the names painted on their sides. A large white-and-blue Pan Am plane sank slowly overhead and passed out of sight. She tried to guess where it was coming from. London, Paris. Maybe Shanghai, Saigon. She wondered about the people who would be on such a flight, what they might have seen and done or were going to do.

When he was gone the other librarians came out front, and her friend Judy said she didn't know how Caroline could stand to talk to him, and why didn't she find somewhere else to be, like everyone else? "He's *sick*."

"He's just lonely."

"I wouldn't like him looking at me like that," she said. "Chester the Molester."

"He's always here by himself. I don't think he has any family," Caroline said. No harm done. It cost her nothing, or at least nothing she wasn't willing to part with.

"It's still a disgusting thing for him to do."

Caroline wanted to say that neither of them was going to change the old man at this time in his life and there was no point in arguing about it. Sometimes she wanted to say, You just have to give people what they need to get by. But that wasn't really true, or not the whole truth—she had liked it, a little bit. His eyes on her.

The old man came back with the book—he hadn't really wanted it, it was just an excuse—and Judy melted back into the fiction stacks, leaving Caroline there by herself once more. He thanked her again and handed her the book. When she took it from him, she let herself touch the skin on the tips of his fingers. It was soft and delicate as a girl's.

"Beautiful," he said.

Afterward she thought of Sam, if he would have been ashamed of her. He had a way of making her feel ridiculous, not because he was cruel but exactly the opposite, because he was kind, and his kindness could have a slight undercurrent of disapproval. He forgave her improprieties, her public kisses and pinches. She had wanted to build a private humor between the two of them, an effort that he found either silly or childish or both, but he never lashed out, never shouted. Instead, he simply pretended it hadn't happened. "Oh," he'd say in that impossibly mild way of his, "I know you didn't mean it." But sometimes, really, she did. Her mother's judgment of all this had been that Caroline was heartless, that she didn't care about Sam at all. He's too good for you, her mother said, because her mother thought the sun rose and set on the Dunmores, and Caroline would tell her, Well, then, why don't *you* marry him?

In California it was the Summer of Love, but in the middle of the country it was just summer. Sam had left Chicago in December, quitting school and enlisting in the army in the middle of his third year of college. She was still surprised by how quickly everything had happened, how he had signed the papers, taken his physical, and reported for induction, how soon he was swept away from her, toward something she did not entirely understand or agree with. After he was gone, she worked and went to classes and had coffee in the afternoons with Dottie. She wrote him about work and school and her mother's latest illness, how the doctor had privately pulled Caroline aside and asked had she ever thought of having her mother committed? Not forever, just until she was a little better. There were things they could do for her mother in an institution she could never manage at home. But her mother needed her. She wrote of how terrifying that thought was to her, having her mother taken away. She wrote how much she hated the thought of being alone. "I hope you are making friends down there, but don't forget me too soon," she wrote, or "I think I will die between now and the time you can come home." She could imagine him reading the letters, saying to himself, She doesn't really mean that. You don't really mean you'll *die*, Caroline, he would say. He forgave her exaggerations, her fears, even when she didn't actually think she needed to be forgiven. She wondered if that was a sense all men had, that the things women said and did always needed to be forgiven.

There had been others before him, of course, good-looking, polite boys from well-off Catholic school families. They came from Lincolnwood, Evanston, Park Ridge, towns with glamorous-sounding names where the neighbors were doctors and judges and engineers and the women kept house during the day because they could. Caroline and her mother, on the other hand, lived in the city, on the shabby edge of a respectable German neighborhood of small identical bungalows and two-flats. The buildings were all so similar that when they first moved there, when Caroline was ten, she had trouble telling them apart. Later she began to notice the differences, how in the windows along her block small dogs barked behind glass, and in places the neighbors had tacked up bedsheets in place of curtains, and laundry hung between buildings or on top of roofs. At the better end of the neighborhood, Dottie and Walt's end, the houses were newer, blond brick ramblers with junipers under the front windows coaxed into interesting shapes, cones or animals. They had birdbaths and clean white curtains and doorbells that worked. At Caroline's end, the buildings were drafty and cramped and full of faulty wiring. The next Great Chicago Fire, her mother sometimes said, was just one bad lightbulb away. She complained that Mr. Hartman, the landlord, was too miserly to put in modern electrical. Mr. Hartman lived in the upstairs apartment because he said it was a lot quieter up there, not having people walking over your head all day and all night. He never seemed to consider that he was the one up there walking over their heads, he and his fat, sourfaced wife stalking back and forth and making the floorboards groan. Sometimes Caroline could hear their voices, their shouts and trumpeting. Like living underneath a herd of elephants, her mother said.

Although no visitors ever came over except for the Dunmores or sometimes Mr. and Mrs. Hartman, Caroline's mother always prided herself on keeping a neat house, scrupulously neat, even bare, no fussy knickknacks on the credenza to collect dust, no paintings or pictures on the walls except of Caroline's father, whose military portrait hung next to the front door, staring mildly out at the vacuum cleaner salesman or the occasional Girl Scout. The furniture may be old, her mother would say, but the flat was clean. If anyone looked in the cupboards or the closets, she wouldn't see a speck of dust on the tops of the soup cans, not a bit of dandruff on the shoulders of a dress. No water droplets were allowed to dry on the sink in the bathroom. Caroline's mother took to housework the way other women took to religion: penitential, gleaming. Her mother never looked as alive as she did when she was scrubbing a floor on her hands and knees, the rag clutched in her hands and the skin on her kneecaps red, bits of hair matted to her head by droplets of sweat. But no matter how hard her mother worked, the bottom floor of the two-flat had an air of slow decay, of exposure to the elements.

Caroline had never let her dates inside the house when they came to pick her up. She always waited at the window until they pulled up and then met them at the door. She didn't want them to see the inside of the house or talk to her mother, who still said "Ilinoise" instead of Illinois and "youse" instead of *you*, holdovers from her country childhood in Ontario that always made Caroline cringe. She told herself she was protecting her mother from those boys, their ironies and judgments. They did not go to school on scholarship, did not get their school lunches for free from the diocese, did not have to worry about where they would go to college or how to pay for it. They were like visitors from a foreign country, with expectations that her mother wouldn't recognize and couldn't meet.

Away from home, Caroline could give the impression that she belonged among them. She was dark haired like her father, but she had her mother's fair skin and pale gray eyes and plump figure. She had developed breasts by the time she was ten, long before the other girls. She made her own clothes, but they were always flattering, Vogue patterns done so carefully on the machine in her mother's bedroom that they looked store-bought, and when the girls at school asked, she said she got them at Field's. Every year on Caroline's birthday, Dottie bought her one good pair of fashionable shoes, because that was always the one thing she wanted that her mother couldn't or wouldn't buy. Dottie said every girl should have one nice pair of shoes. Her mother, on the other hand, would purse her lips together at the sight of those expensive oxfords or sandals, saying how nice it must be to be the belle of the ball and how the worthless boys Caroline dated weren't interested in her shoes. Watch yourself, her mother had said. It's so easy for girls to get in trouble. "I won't even remember your name then," she said. "I won't even see you if you pass me on the street." Her mother would fold her arms over her bosom and say, What boy will want you after that? No one. No one at all. Damaged goods.

Her mother didn't know anything about those boys. None of them had ever said more than "hello" and "good-bye" to her. They were mostly older boys who liked surfer music and foreign cars. They took her to movies and concerts, expensive dinners in restaurants where she couldn't pronounce the menu items. As a group, they were reckless when away from the healthy familiar confines of home and school, and she had been reckless with them, egging them on when they raced their cars down the lakeshore or sneaking into nightclubs with them for a drink, not caring if they got caught or not. Before they dropped her off at home, she would let them slip their hands under her sweater or over her blouse. She liked the attention they gave her, the way their eyes went soft with gratitude when she unhooked her bra. It never lasted long. They weren't serious, and she didn't take them seriously, those first boys with their Beatles hair and their expensive cars and their careless laughter. Still, Sam had been jealous of them. He said they were all the same—pretty boys and pretenders.

She had always known how he'd felt, even when they were children. She could see the weight of it in his shoulders. After she and her mother had moved to the States, down the street from Walt and Dottie and Sam and Charley, he had found reasons to sit with her at holidays, Sunday dinners with his parents. He never had to say, because that kind of longing was too heavy for one person. It increased until it placed itself in the hands of its object, forcing her to carry it, too, a little. Even when he had girlfriends, she always knew he would give up any one of them if she asked him to, so she was careful with him in those days, kind.

Charley noticed, too, and teased Sam about it. He was especially merciless if Caroline was around. On weekends when the three of them would go to a movie or a dance, Caroline driving because she had her own car, Charley would be in the backseat making rude noises and complaining about his brother's moony face, his silences. "Look at that puss," he'd say. "Have you ever met anyone who could suck so much of the fun out of life?" If Caroline laughed at the things Charley said, it only made Sam more miserable. She couldn't help feeling a little sorry for him, the way he made himself suffer. His thoughtfulness and seriousness made him sensitive to the lack of such things in others—in Charley, in Caroline herself. The fact that she could not return his affection was a source of constant pain. She always said he was the closest thing to a brother she had, the best person she had ever known. He told her that was not what a man wanted to hear.

Sam and Charley looked alike in that they both had Dottie's dark chestnut hair, the same pale, almost delicate skin, the wide, sensual mouths, Walt's narrow green brown eyes. But Charley, two years younger, was a couple of inches shorter than Sam and a bit thinner; also, he was vain of his thinness and the lines where his wiry muscles showed through his skin. Sam was tall like their mother and broad in the shoulders and chest like his father, but with his quiet, serious manner, he could seem shy, even aloof. Charley was more outgoing. He was a favorite among the girls in high school, even girls her own age, because he always winked and joked and made outrageous claims, like the time he told one girl he was on the Olympic track team and held the world record in the 400-meter dash, or another that he was really a Russian spy with a wife and two kids back home in Stalingrad. The girls, as they always did, had believed him. He spoke so insistently, with such conviction, that it was hard not to.

As boys they'd fought like animals, the way she'd noticed with brothers who are close in age, and because Sam was bigger he usually won any outright fistfight or wrestling match, but Charley could be sneaky. He could cheat at games without anyone but Sam noticing, get his brother in trouble for things that happened at school, goad Sam into stunts he would never have tried otherwise, like drag-racing their father's car down Lake Shore Drive or slipping whiskey into a school dance. There was a competitive spirit between the brothers that made Caroline feel like the referee at an invisible game of tag, one or the other of them always looking for an advantage. In games of war—in capture-the-flag, in football—they would go at each other with genuine violence, with hatred. Sam would land a blow, using his size and age to his advantage, and Charley would take it personally, cry foul, and throw himself on his brother, crying and tearing with his hands, his teeth. Their friends, other neighborhood boys, would slip away at moments like these, leaving the two brothers howling and bloody on the sidewalk, embarrassed for them and unwilling to be witnesses to the carnage.

One night, late, Charley had talked Sam into a game of chicken on the railroad tracks behind their house, daring his brother to face down the Soo Line locomotive. They had gone to a movie earlier in the night, something awful and pointless. Got bored, left early. They walked home along the tracks. When the lights of the train started coming closer, Caroline had slid off the tracks into the grass on the side, but Charley and Sam kept walking.

"Don't you dare jump off," Charley said. "Let the conductor see the whites of your eyes first."

Caroline had stood below the tracks, begging them to come down. "This isn't funny," she'd said. "Someone could get killed."

But with Charley watching, Sam didn't move, wouldn't budge. She watched his shadow on the tracks until the lights of the train were nearly on him, and only then did he leap out of the way and roll down the grassy embankment. Afterward he'd stood up and stalked away, not speaking to either of them, as if he'd been forced to stand on the tracks against his will and held them both responsible.

Yet there were also times when they were thoughtful of each other. Charley admired his brother's ability in sports, went to all of Sam's football games, and practiced with him after school. Sam was the one who taught Charley to drive a car, weekends in the parking lot at the high school, in their father's green-and-white Chevy Bel-Air, patient as a monk. Often they did these small kindnesses without even seeming to be aware of them, and Caroline would watch them and wonder what it would have been like to have a brother, a sister. More than simply Caroline and her mother, alone together.

Her mother would have days when she hardly got out of bed, days when she couldn't stop crying. She would find a new job only to quit after a few months, a year. It was always over some slight, real or imagined. Instead of going to work, her mother would spend her days in her robe and slippers, sitting up at the kitchen table until all hours. For days she would barely speak to anyone, and then suddenly she would lose her temper over some small thing, the housework or the laundry, something at which Caroline had evidently failed. She would cry that Caroline's thoughtlessness was killing her and lock herself in her room for hours.

Caroline would come home from work and try to slip in the house unnoticed so she would not upset her mother. Other times Caroline would look at her mother sitting at the table in her robe and think, How pathetic, how embarrassing. She would berate her for not making more of an effort. "You're supposed to be the parent here," she'd say. "You don't even want to try." She would not let up until they were both in tears. Afterward she would be ashamed and beg her mother's forgiveness, and sometimes Adele would forgive her and sometimes not.

Sometimes she would come out of it long enough to start a project like the laundry or the shopping, but not long enough to finish. She would leave things half-done lying around the house. Hours later, when she got home from work, Caroline would find evidence of her halfhearted projects: the dishes sitting in cold dishwater, the dress hanging in pieces on the sewing machine, the vacuum cleaner lying in the middle of the living room floor, still running, while her mother was in the other room asleep. The doctor said it wasn't her mother's fault. He prescribed sleeping pills that would help for a while, but as soon as her mother started to feel a little better, she would stop taking the pills, saying she didn't need them. "I'm fine," she'd say. As soon as her mother stopped the pills, she would be up all night baking or watching television and napping on the couch during the day. The idea that she wouldn't have trouble sleeping if she took her pills never seemed to occur to her. I'm fine, she would say, just leave me be.

Not long before Caroline graduated high school, her mother quit her latest job at a doctor's office over on Lawrence because the doctor's wife had not invited Adele to her son's wedding—an unforgivable offense. The bills started to pile up. "You have to find another job, Mother," Caroline said. "We're going to be out on the street."

Her mother told her not to be so dramatic, that she would look for another job once Caroline was away at college. "I don't want to waste our last months together rotting in some office," she said. The little bit of savings they had left from Caroline's grandmother ran out. Caroline started paying the electric, the gas, the mortgage, her mother's medical expenses. Someone had to.

In all this it was leaving she thought of most, getting away. Although she was a good student and had won a partial scholarship to a small college in Belle Plaine, there wasn't enough money to pay for the rest of her tuition, so she took a second job waitressing in the evenings to save up extra. Even so, she had to dip into her college fund to pay the bills, putting off school another semester and another. She could only imagine the subjects she would study, the time for books and art and literature, the things she would know when she was done. She piled up hopes for a new life. Sometimes Dottie gave her a little money, five or ten dollars, and she used it to buy herself sheets and towels, a coffeepot, a hot plate, and each of these she packed into a small box and set aside in her closet, one purchase a month, perhaps, rationing them out. It was exciting, this planning of the future. Some days she could barely sit for anticipation and would have to get up to wander around the house, or out into the yard, listening for the sounds of the trains going out of the city. Her mother, on the other hand, seemed to take it all as a personal affront. She would come into Caroline's room, sit on the edge of the bed, sigh, and go out again.

Dottie told her not to let her mother make her feel guilty for wanting to leave. She would look in on Adele while Caroline was gone. Her mother wouldn't be alone. "You've earned the right to live your own life," Dottie said, rubbing Caroline's hands in hers the way she always did when she was trying to be helpful. "Adele will have to get used to it."

So in October, more than two years after she'd graduated high school, without telling her mother, Caroline wrote the college and told them she was coming for the winter semester. When the school replied a few weeks later, her mother intercepted the letter. Caroline came home to find her mother waving it in her face like an accusation. When were you going to tell me about this? she asked. She wept and pleaded, said she would die if Caroline left her. "You never cared what happened to me. I could starve to death and you wouldn't care," she said.

"You won't starve to death."

"I might. I might and you wouldn't even know."

"If you starve to death, believe me, I'll know."

After Christmas, Caroline packed her rusting old convertible, kissed Dottie and Walt good-bye—her mother still wouldn't come out of her room—and drove downstate to Belle Plaine by herself, singing along to the radio. The low beige suburbs gave way to empty fields, trees planted in windrows, miles of red-painted snow fence. She drove to school with the cold air blowing in and a cigarette in her hand as she clutched the wheel.

She had waited and saved, but being on her own was not as easy as she had planned. Belle Plaine was desolate, dirt and corn as far as the eye could see. At night the lights of distant farms were small and bleak and far away. She was able to go days and days without speaking to a single person, and it seemed as if she were cold all the time, her hands and feet. The wind burned her cheeks red. The snow blew across the flat plains with nothing to break its progress until it whipped down the back of her coat, down the back of her blouse, raising bumps on her skin. She walked with her head down in the wind between buildings and the hard mean little snowflakes catching her in hair because she lost her hat in one of the lecture halls the first week of classes and realized she couldn't afford to buy another one.

She was a little older than most of the other students because of the time it had taken to save up her school money. When she arrived at the dormitories in the middle of the year, her new roommate had been using Caroline's bed as a sofa, done up with pillows and scarves, and she was sulky that someone had arrived to take up the space she had previously thought of as her own. Caroline had hoped they would be friends, but that soon seemed unlikely. Her roommate was a lively girl whose social circle consisted entirely of high school friends who'd come downstate with her, a mirror of the world she'd always known and felt comfortable in. At first she seemed unsure of whether or not Caroline qualified as someone to include in her weekend plans, but by the middle of the semester it was clear the roommate regarded her mostly as an inconvenient lump in the bed on the other side of the room. By then Caroline had started retreating to the lounge to read whenever the friends came over with bottles of liquor under their jackets. They drank too much and spent their daddies' money and complained while they did it, and Caroline felt small in the clothes she'd made herself and envied them and hated them.

Her own money ran out with breathtaking speed. She had miscalculated everything. Laundry detergent was expensive, and so were coffee and cigarettes, gasoline and car repairs. Dottie sent five-dollar bills in the mail every once in a while, which Caroline used to buy Sunday night dinner when the cafeteria was closed, and stamps to write home, and change for the pay phone. Instead of concentrating on books and school, Virgil and Shakespeare, history and science and philosophy and economics, as she had always imagined, she spent her class time mentally calculating whether she would have enough money to buy a pack of cigarettes or if she should give up the habit entirely. Worry made it difficult to concentrate, and her grades were middling that first semester, the worst of her life, so much so that she cried when the grade report came, there in the lobby of the dormitory with fifteen girls watching, and she retreated to the bathroom and closed the door to the stall so she could wipe her face in peace, wondering if she hadn't made a terrible mistake. At the end of that first semester, with the farmers plowing the fields and the smell of wet earth seeping into her clothes, she wrote to Dottie to ask if she could borrow a little money. She would pay Dottie back, she said, if she could just have this little bit of help. Dottie sent a money order for five hundred dollars, a gift that Caroline did not have to repay. "Don't mention it again," she wrote. Caroline was so grateful and relieved when the money came that she bought a pack of cigarettes to celebrate and stayed up late, smoking them all, nearly making herself sick.

It was in the middle of her failure and worry that she met David. He was the teaching assistant in her roommate's history class, tall, blue eyed, fierce, and ironic. The roommate introduced David to Caroline outside her classroom, briefly, one afternoon when Caroline went to meet her. This is my teacher, the roommate said. Caroline stuck out her hand for him to shake. His own was cool and firm. "He's brilliant," the roommate said, and though David shook his head, no, of course not, something in the way he smiled seemed important, meaningful. Later Caroline asked the room-mate if she was seeing him, but the roommate only shrugged, said, I can't really talk about it, and left it at that.

In May, after her first semester was over and the roommate went back north for the summer, Caroline moved into a small apartment off campus and went to work as a cashier at a local drugstore. She took a summer class in biology to try to catch up a little but was nauseated at the sight of the fetal pig she was supposed to dissect and had to leave the room. At least she withdrew soon enough to get back some of her fees, she wrote to Dottie. She worked and saved what she could, always surprised that it was so little.

She was working at the pharmacy one afternoon when David came in to buy antacid. No one buying antacid could be trouble. At the checkout counter he recognized her and said, Hello, you're Agnes's friend. Caroline said hello back. David stayed all that afternoon, talking to her between customers, chatting up the other cashier when Caroline was busy. She kept looking at him out of the corner of her eye, the way his hip switched out when he leaned on the counter. He was so sure of himself. I think you want to kiss me, he said, leaning in toward her, and of course she wanted to kiss him. He made her feel small, crouching, a tiny and insignificant thing. He took her to coffee, to dinner. He asked her opinion about the war, had long discussions with her about Johnson's intentions in Southeast Asia, rolling his eyes dramatically if she took a position different from his own. In public places he talked loudly about Catherine the Great's love of horses or the crimes of the Marquis de Sade to see if he could shock and embarrass her, and though she always was shocked and embarrassed, she would feign indifference, because she did not want him to know how much power he had over her.

Above her, that first time, he had said he was surprised. "About what?" she said.

He smiled. "I wouldn't have thought you were still a virgin," he said.

And afterward she was afraid, because she knew she would do anything he asked of her, give up anything, follow him anywhere. She was a slippery new element; she felt suffused with light, phosphorescent. She knew he could see right through her, as if she herself were no longer there.

She read to him from the Romantic poets, Byron, Shelley, afterward in bed, and she knew he was bored, but he indulged her. Later, she would be embarrassed by what must have seemed, to him, a romantic affectation. Those first weeks they stayed together all Saturday night and into Sunday mornings. He slept naked under the sheets and rolled over toward her in the middle of the night to press himself against her hip. In the morning she would make him breakfast and think how things would be if they got married and he moved in, and this would be their life together.

But when the school year started and he had a new classroom full of freshman girls enthralled with him and with their own newfound freedom, he stopped coming around. She looked for his shape on the street, out her window, hoping for a glimpse. She composed elaborate speeches of what she would say when she saw him. She drove past his apartment, but all the curtains were closed, as if he'd known she was coming. She called his apartment late at night to see if a girl would answer, but when she heard his voice on the other end, thick with sleep, she couldn't speak. Later she went by his office on campus, but the secretary said he hadn't been in lately, though she would be sure to tell him she stopped by. On purpose, she left her black cashmere gloves, a Christmas present from

Dottie and Walt, on his desk one day so he would have to return them to her. When he never did, she felt too stupid to ask for them. She was listless, disconnected from things, a ghost of herself moving from room to room in her near empty apartment, her hair unwashed, her teeth covered with grit. If she washed the dirt away, she might disappear, dissolve.

It was the being fooled part that made her bitter, the feeling of not being able to trust her own instincts, of becoming another ridiculous woman, like her mother, who had followed a man to a new country and a new city, taken up an apartment down the street, asked his help with cutting the grass or putting up a shelf or just keeping company, any little excuse to have him step through the door and sit at her table. After a few years, it had stopped being about the person they'd had in common, her father. Caroline wasn't blind. She could see the way her mother's demeanor changed whenever Walt was there, became girlish even, touching his arm or inviting the Dunmores over for supper and making something special, lamb stew or pork chops, because she knew he liked it. How her mother had sometimes been too nice to Dottie, making a concerted effort to praise her home, her clothes, her children, helping her with dinner or baby-sitting or sewing or running errands, because really her mother envied Dottie, the woman whose husband had come back.

In the fall, after Caroline paid her tuition and bought her books, there was so little money left that she had taken to eating once a day and had to give up cigarettes entirely. She lost an alarming amount of weight, enough so that her mother worried and wept over her the one time she managed a visit home. Her homemade clothes hung loose on her, but she was too tired to take them in. One day in October when she stood for too long at her cash register, she fainted, knocking against a display of pain relievers. The manager was so upset that he asked her as delicately as possible if she was in some kind of trouble. When she said it wasn't like that, he looked relieved and gave her an extra ten dollars out of his pocket. Buy yourself a steak dinner, he said, and take the rest of the day off. She walked home to her apartment rubbing the ten-dollar bill between her fingers and thinking what she might buy with it. She thought too that she might like to keep it for a while, just in case, because she liked thinking what she might buy with it. She decided to spend part on groceries and save the rest. She stopped at the grocer's on her way home and bought three apples and a pound of hamburger meat. When she got home she fried up two hamburger patties for herself and ate them straight out of the pan, standing over the stove with a fork. The meat was so greasy and rich in her mouth, she thought she might make herself sick, but afterward she felt better, good enough to sleep through the night for the first time in weeks.

By the end of her second semester, though, a case of shingles had laid her up so long that the last of the money ran out on heat and rent, and she missed her finals, and when she called, her mother said to come home. Just come, Caroline. You can have your old room back and everything will be the same. By then the idea of home was so seductive that she hardly thought about what she would be giving up. She knew only that she would be warm, and she could sleep, and after that she would figure out what to do. She loaded the car as quickly as possible and had not been sorry when she went out and left the keys to her apartment on the counter in the kitchen, along with a note that said she would not be back and the landlord could throw out the furniture or keep it if he wanted.

When Caroline returned home, it was Sam who made it all right for her. He made a point of coming by after classes at Northeastern Illinois University, where he was a sophomore. He kept her company, brought her books he thought she would enjoy, stayed late into the night when she said she did not want to be alone. She rarely went out in those weeks; it was easier to feel like a failure, like a fool, and stay in the house. But his visits let her think about something else. He was kind. At first it was their old familiar friendship she felt, his hopes so apparent on his face, his regard for her so touching that she felt she must protect him from the truth of herself, how broken she felt. He would come over for dinner and Scrabble, helping with the washing up after and chatting with her mother. As always, she knew what he wanted but did not feel capable of giving it to him. But then her feelings toward him started to shift. Her days were long stretches of waiting for him. If he had to work or go to class, she would be impatient, watching for him at the windows, the sight of him walking up the sidewalk. When he was with her, she felt like herself again. She could tease and joke and laugh at herself. It was because Sam was so different from David. He rarely spoke unless it was to say something useful or important, and he never tried to shock her or make her feel small. He was serious and familiar, and everything he said and did was right and good.

One night he asked if he could kiss her, and she said he could. He had leaned in so shyly, with such hesitation, that at first she thought she had imagined the whole thing. His lips were dry and chapped. He had pulled away and taken her hand and did not try to kiss her again, though she would have liked him to. Later she would think it was only the idea of her that had held him back, that he had built her up in his mind as something more than what she really was, more innocent, more worthy of admiration. All that night, while they sat with the blanket on their laps and the creature feature playing in the background and her mother asleep in the other room, she had waited for more, but it didn't come. Not then. It came the next night and the next, when her mother went to bed early and they kissed until their faces were raw. The careful way he'd treated her at first fell away under an onslaught of fumblings on her mother's sofa, her father's portrait near the door looking on the whole enterprise with an expression of benign amusement.

Sam did not ask, at first, what had happened while she was away, but pieces of the story slipped out from time to time—that she had run out of money, that she had been homesick and had trouble making friends. He asked if she had been seeing anyone, and when she said she had, he asked who he'd been and what had happened between them.

"It was nothing," she told Sam. "I didn't even like him that much."

It was true: She didn't miss David at all, didn't wish him back. Still, there were things Sam wanted to know about him. What was his name, how did she meet him, what were the things he said to her? She told him everything, even managing a fairly good imitation of the self-important way he used to talk to her about politics or history. They laughed over the succession of girls who might even then be mooning over him, losing sleep over him, wondering why he didn't return their calls. It became a running joke between the two of them, David's real self fading into the straw-man David they created in his place. But at times she found Sam's interest in all things regarding David a bit disconcerting: Why did he want to know the things David had said to her the day they met, the kind of car he drove, the subjects he taught, whether he was intelligent or not? The more she insisted it was nothing, it had meant nothing to her, the more he wanted to know.

She transferred to Northeastern Illinois, where Sam was a student, so she could live at home while she went to school. Sam was glad to help her, introduce her around. He took the same classes so he could sit with her. Weekends when they should have been studying they would drive out of the city in her convertible, Sam at the wheel, her feet up on the dash, rumbling past the mansions along the lakefront or out into the flat, spread-out suburbs that ringed the city. They drove to Wisconsin, to Indiana, just to have someplace to go. Once he took her all the way to the Mississippi River, the farthest west she had ever been, and they sat on the bluff with the muddy river below them and ate cheese sandwiches and drank coffee in an amicable silence and afterward drove back together, his hand reaching across the seat for hers.

One night, late, he drove her to the Polish cemetery, saying it was a good place for them to be alone. They went in through the front gate and took the meandering road toward the back, where the trees were thicker and the stones were old. There were statues of angels, and tall white stiles, and baskets of stone flowers. It was dark there and very quiet, as if they'd left the city entirely and entered some other country. The cemetery was supposed to be a haunted by a girl in an old-fashioned wedding dress. It had been a favorite of high school boys who wanted to impress one another and their girlfriends, daring themselves to stand among the stones at night, waiting for the girl to appear. She would have thought it would be morbid, but really it was beautiful.

Sam stopped the car and turned off the lights. "It doesn't frighten you?" he asked.

"No," she said. "I don't believe in ghosts."

It was winter then, and cold. His face in that faint light was intent, and it occurred to her that Sam was almost the same age her father had been when he died. It made her feel very old and very young at the same time, as if seeing herself from far away, needing to squint to make out the shape of things clearly. The pressure of his hand pulling her down was light but firm, and she was on her back and his hands were undoing her buttons. The heaviness of him pressed her into the seat. His hands on her, across her belly and breasts, into her hair, as if he would touch her everywhere at once. His hands dug into the soft flesh on the insides of her thighs, enough to leave finger-shaped bruises, and she thought how she would have to hide them from her mother. The pulse of him came through his hands: *now-now, now-now*. He was greedy and damp, beads of sweat in a bright band around his face, and she felt he would tear her apart and crawl around snuffling inside her corpse, and the fury that scraped across her skin and pressed her back into the seat was the fury of love. She reached up and took hold of him by the shoulders and let him rock her into the seat, and when it was over he slumped across her, and she pushed the hair back from his face and smelled the salt of his sweat. He seemed lighter for the moment. His heart was against her heart, and she felt it beat, not *now-now* but *still, still, still.* He sat up and looked at her and beamed, and the weight between them drifted a little and settled. He was beautiful. The smile on him was beautiful. This was when she loved him most, when he was past desire and they could sit together in a human silence without that weight of longing.

"Did I hurt you much?" he asked.

A little, she said. Not too much.

"I suppose that's only natural." He took her face in his hands and kissed her again. She could smell her perfume on his face. He had seemed so pleased that she couldn't tell him the truth.

Afterward, Sam regarded her with a new physicality that was almost startling. If he was shy with her before, afraid to go too far, afterward he was demanding. He needed her all the time, and she liked being needed. They would wait until her mother went to bed and stay up late on the sofa, the possibility of being caught electrifying them even further. He was with her every day, coming to the house in the afternoon and staying all evening, until it was dark, sometimes falling asleep on the sofa in his undershirt with a book open on his face. Caroline would go to bed and get up again, and in the morning he would still be there. Her mother enjoyed having him there and started making more of an effort. If he stayed the night, she would be up early, wearing one of her wigs and putting on her makeup. She made coffee and eggs, asked Sam about school. She started a new job. She caught up with the bills. She would come up behind

Caroline in the kitchen and squeeze her around the arms for no reason at all, murmuring endearments into her hair the way she had when Caroline was small. She took her medication, kept her appointments. It pleased Caroline to see that her mother was starting to come back to herself. Dottie too seemed to take pleasure in the new arrangements and rarely made a fuss if Sam was gone all night, because, after all, she knew where he was. You've made him so happy, she told Caroline. I've never seen him like this.

One afternoon in March, still cold, there was a package waiting for her at the kitchen table when they came in from afternoon classes. It was small, about the size of a book, wrapped in brown paper. Although there was no return address, she recognized the handwriting right away as David's. Her face turned hot. Sam picked it up and held it out for her. "Someone sent you a present."

She wouldn't take it from him. "It could be anything."

"Aren't you going to open it?" he asked.

"Later," she said. "Not now."

"All right," he said, and set it down.

She left it where it was until it was time for supper and she had to set the table. She picked it up and put it in her room on her dresser and tried to forget about it, but it was with her through supper and through the washing up after. David. What did he think he was doing, sending her a package after all this time? She should throw it out. Throw it away and not open it at all. Sam ate the supper her mother put in front of him and complimented her cooking, but she felt him watching, as if she'd done something wrong, and she was nervous and uncomfortable until he left for the night. After the dishes were done, she went back into her room and peeled back the brown paper. Inside was a small cardboard box and taped to the box was a note: "The first time I sent these to you they came back to me. I hope this time they find their way home. I wouldn't want you catching cold on my account. Love, David." Her black cashmere gloves were inside the box. She had left them on purpose, and of course he'd known. He always had to be cleverer than she was. That "Love" he used to sign his name, she knew he didn't mean it. He was teasing her. Still seeing if he could make her blush. Well, he could. She threw out the box and the gloves, too. She didn't want them or any reminder of him. That's it, then, she thought, ripping up the note and the brown paper wrapper and dumping all of it in the trash.

In the morning Sam asked her what had been in the package, and she told him it was only her cashmere gloves, which she'd left at her apartment in Belle Plaine. The landlord had mailed them to her, and wasn't that nice of him? Sam took one of her bare hands and asked why she wasn't wearing them. Weren't her hands going to be cold?

No, she said, I'm not cold. The gloves are at home.

She went to Field's and bought another pair of gloves, and although he never mentioned them again, she could feel him watching her. If she went out with friends, he wanted to know where she was going, or he insisted on coming with her. He wanted to know when she would be home and would call to make sure she was there when she said she would be. He would surprise her at work, at home, catching her around the waist and making her jump inside her skin. He asked again about David, if there was more to it than she had told him. She swore there wasn't, but they stopped joking about him, making up stories about him. Neither of them mentioned David's name at all after that. Like those earlier years when he suffered over her in silence, he thought he was hiding his feelings better than he was. She had to be careful with him. If she had told him the absolute truth, it would not have been any better. In many ways, everything was the same—they still spent all their time together, they still went to the Polish cemetery to be alone—but there was something different about him, something waiting, and she knew it. She made a special effort with his birthday, a surprise dinner for the two of them at the lakeshore with candles and a homemade cake. He had kissed her and thanked her, but he was quiet all evening, and she felt his jealousy tugging at her ankles like a current.

She was working for the library by that time and liked it so much that she decided to get her degree in library science, which would mean an extra year or two of college, but as long as she was working she should be able to manage. Sam liked biology and chemistry, so she tried to encourage him to go into medicine, but he said he hadn't yet made up his mind. She saw him as a scientist, meticulous and thoughtful. He had a terrific memory, a long attention span. When he turned that attention toward her, she always felt as if he lost himself a little, as if he were unaware of anything or anyone else. She liked it, but it could also be frightening.

They talked, in a casual way, about getting married. The war was not so big then, and Sam was safe from the draft because he was in school, but if he got married or became a doctor or a teacher, he could keep his deferment. Then the government started suspending those deferments, and Sam said he wouldn't be surprised if he was drafted when he finished school. Although this thought didn't seem to bother him very much, it made her afraid for him.

In the fall they went to Canada together for a couple of weeks, stopping to see his aunts and uncles and cousins, staying at his uncle Ed's farm on the Lake Erie shore, and getting up early to help with the chores. They had barbecues at the farm, met his cousins and their friends in town for movies or parties. They parked at the lakeshore and sat on the beach. Being back in Canada made Caroline nostalgic. Everything there seemed lighter, more golden. She asked Sam to drive her past the house in Windsor where she had lived with her mother and grandmother before the old lady had died. They parked across the street and sat in the car. It was an old brick house, gabled. The tall windows were capped with a peeling white trim. The house had been split into two apartments in the years since, one upstairs and one down. There were two mailboxes near the door. The front porch had started to sag, and the fir tree in the yard had been cut down. It made her wistful, an emotion she didn't like usually but that now overwhelmed her. She knew if her father had lived, everything would have been different.

The house had the pull of a place she knew well but was forbidden to enter. She thought of her old room, the wallpaper near the bed curling from the time she'd left the window open in a rainstorm, the high ceilings in the downstairs rooms and the dark square on the dining room floor where a rug had once covered the boards. She wanted to see it all again. She wanted to go up to the house, up those sagging steps, knock on the door, and ask to be let in. This used to be my house, she would say, and of course the person who lived there would step back and let her in. How nice it would be to stay here. Maybe she would buy the house. She would get rid of the tenants and replant the tree in the yard, the rosebushes around the front porch, and her grandmother's lace curtains behind the front window. That would make her grandmother happy, if Caroline bought the house and moved home and lived there with her own husband, her own children. It would be so right.

Sam was quiet. His hands were still on the wheel.

"Do you ever think of coming back?" she asked.

"To stay, you mean?"

"You still have a lot of family here. All your aunts and uncles."

He seemed surprised. "Do you think of it?"

"Sure. All the time."

He shook his head. His face pulled forward, bunched together, making him seem like a little boy. She sometimes forgot that he was younger than she was, because he was so tall and broad, and also a year ahead of her in school because of all the time she'd had to take off. Just then, though, he looked very young, petulant even. She wanted to reach out and pinch him. "No, I guess I don't," he said. After another minute, he said it was getting too hot to sit there with no breeze. He started up the car. The old house slid by the windows, grew smaller, and vanished when they turned the corner.

In the fall, without telling her or anyone else, Sam dropped out of school and signed up for the army. His father was disappointed that he wasn't finishing college, his mother furious that he volunteered in the middle of a war, but Caroline was bewildered. It made no sense. She tried to ask him why he'd done it, but he only said it was something he had to do, and he hoped she would understand. She said she didn't. He shrugged and said that was okay, too.

After that he stopped coming around as often. She would see him once or twice a week instead of every day, and he no longer spent the night sleeping on her mother's sofa. When she asked him if something was wrong, if she'd done something to upset him, he would say no, it was nothing, but she knew that wasn't true. He no longer looked at her as if she were the only person in the room.

He left in December, on a bright cold morning with her breath steaming the air and her arms folded across herself to keep warm, her mother watching from the front room. Sam got out of the car and came toward the house to say good-bye to her. Walt was driving that morning, Charley watching from the backseat. Sam said he was sorry they were running so late. She knew he would not try to touch her with his father and brother watching but wished he would anyway. She was waiting for something to happen, something big.

"Got to get going," Sam said.

"Have a good trip," she said. "Be careful." She wanted to sound airy, but her voice came out strangled.

He got back in the car and waved once. Walt drove him away.

At first she expected to hear from him any day. She spent all her spare time at home in case the phone rang, hardly daring to take out the garbage, agonizing whenever she had to leave for work. At the library she would bargain with herself: If I realphabetize the card catalog from A to F, there will be a letter. If I get through the entire day without thinking about him, it will be today.

Those first weeks she sent him letters but didn't know if they reached him. She called the number Dottie gave her, but whoever answered said he wasn't there, not right at the moment, but can I take a message? No, thank you. No message. She had already left half a dozen messages.

People from the neighborhood would stop on the street or in the library to ask her how he was doing, how he liked the army, assuming everything was normal. She said he was fine, that he was learning a lot and making friends. Once she even told a girl they'd known in high school that she was going down to Louisiana to see him that weekend, and then she hid in the house for three days to avoid running into that girl on the street.

Her mother said maybe he'd sent her a letter and it was lost in the mail. Maybe he'd called and they hadn't been home. It was possible. "Give him the benefit of the doubt," her mother said, because she would excuse him anything shy of mass murder. But eventually even her mother started to believe something was wrong. What had Caroline done? Had she said something? Had she belittled him, hurt his feelings? I don't know, Caroline wanted to say. I didn't do anything.

She knew he was safe, or as safe as he could be. She knew this because he wrote to his parents from Louisiana. Once or twice he'd even called.

Dottie would make sure to tell Caroline whatever she heard. He wrote to his father about what he was learning about guns and explosives, the violence and degradation of the army, the alternating exhaustion and exhilaration and boredom. He wrote to his mother that he went for a weekend once at the beach, got the worst sunburn of his life when he fell asleep on the sand, and saw what he thought was a shark fin when he was swimming in the Gulf. Dottie let Caroline read the letters. She would pore over them sitting at the kitchen table in the house where Sam had grown up, Dottie's thin legs jiggling the table so the water glasses trembled, Walt watching the news with Sam's grandfather in the next room. The smell of Jack's pipe smoke filling up the house.

One time Sam mailed Dottie a box of pralines. "He sent these for you," Dottie said. Caroline knew he had not sent them for her, that it was Dottie's way of excusing him, but she had taken them anyway. At home in her room with the door closed, she had opened the box and eaten one of the pralines, its warm taste of burned sugar, and she lay on her bed imagining that he had touched the pieces before he sent them, and it was his hands she was tasting, his fingerprints dissolving in her mouth. She started to feel that he was taking her for granted in ways that only people who have known each other all their lives can do. Maybe it was his idea of punishment, this casual silence, this cutting off of love and history.

She would stop by Dottie's house on her way home from work in the afternoons for coffee and cigarettes. She'd make sure to look her best, rolling her hair around empty Coke cans before leaving the house and wearing her best dresses, her good shoes, so if Dottie or Walt or even Charley noticed how well she looked, they might mention it to Sam. She would have liked to bring a man to the house, a date, but there was no one to bring, no one even to ask. The boys who used to call were all engaged or married or away at school, studying law or medicine or business, or disappeared altogether and turned into rumor. No matter what else they had done, however, the boys had outgrown her long ago.

Every day she announced when she came in that she couldn't stay long, her mother would be worried. "Your mother's going to be worried no matter what. She can share you a little," Dottie said. She would offer coffee, tea if Caroline would rather have that, something to warm her up, say, "Don't you look nice, though? I love that color on you." Caroline would shrug as if her appearance were nothing, an accident.

It was over the letters, smoking one of Dottie's cigarettes, that Caroline first learned that Sam would not be coming home during his leave. Basic training was over, but instead of returning to Chicago, he was going to Houston with a girl he'd met, a student at Rice, to meet her parents. "I hope you don't mind," he wrote Dottie. He thought he might be able to come home after advanced individual training, but he wasn't sure, it would depend on the army. He wrote, "Tell Caroline I'm sorry."

The house smelled of pipe smoke and fried eggs. The sound of applause, a man's voice announcing that some lucky contestant would win *these fabulous prizes!* Jack was watching television in the other room with the volume turned up. He'd lived with Walt and Dottie for years by then and was such a fixture in the house that she rarely thought of him, like a piece of the furniture. She knew Walt didn't like having his father-in-law there and would have asked him to leave long ago, except that Dottie wanted to keep him away from her mother. From what Caroline understood, Jack Farquhar hadn't exactly been the most faithful of husbands.

She tried to imagine Sam in Texas, but she'd never been that far south before. She imagined it hot and brown and dry, the girl a rancher's daughter in a cowboy hat and jeans. Sam didn't say where he'd met her or how long they'd been dating. It didn't matter anyway.

Caroline took a sip of her coffee and doused it with cream and sugar. It was on the bitter side. Dottie didn't always scrub out her pot as well as she could have.

"I don't understand it," Dottie said. She folded the letter back up and put it in its envelope. "I don't know what's gotten into him."

"It's all right. It doesn't matter."

"He shouldn't do this to you."

"It doesn't matter anymore," Caroline said again. She didn't want to cry, not here, where someone might see her and mention it to Sam. The room seemed very hot. From the other room, Jack called out to ask when the noon meal would be ready.

"I'll get to it in a minute," Dottie called back. She took out another cigarette, lit it, and handed it to Caroline. "I think you should forget about him. Sam's made his bed. Forget him and get on with your life, and the hell with everyone else."

Caroline couldn't believe what she was hearing. His own mother was telling her to forget about him. But how could Caroline do that, when Sam was the one who had made everything right for her again?

In the other room, Jack Farquhar laughed at something on the TV. A little tune started playing: "You'll wonder where the yellow went when you brush your teeth with Pepsodent!" He shouted again about his lunch. "Dot?" he called. "You listening?"

"In a minute."

"You said that a minute ago."

Dottie went to the cupboard and opened a can of condensed soup, dumped it in a pot, and added water. The pot clattered on the stove as she stirred it. In the other room, Jack was watching some kind of game show. The buzzer went off to great applause. Dottie pursed her lips and stirred the soup, banging the wooden spoon on the sides of the pot. A little bit splashed out onto the stove, but she didn't bother wiping it up. A game show host was asking, "What's behind door number two?"

"Live your life, Caroline," Dottie said. "You only get one."

At the library, two thirteen-year-old girls came to the circulation desk and said a man exposed himself to them in the biographies. That was what Judy called it, "exposing himself," as if he were having his picture taken. Judy had called the police, but the old man was nowhere to be seen by the time they arrived. She swore up and down it was the same man, but Caroline, who had not been at work that day, told her she was jumping to conclusions. He was a harmless old man, she'd said. It could have been anyone.

Judy said she knew what she knew. "You watch out for him," she said. Caroline told her it was a bad habit, always thinking the worst of people.

But the next time she went into work, when she was standing in the nonfiction stacks, putting her books away, she kept thinking of the way the old man had grinned at her, like a man on a gibbet. She was looking for him to appear. He could be outside, for all she knew, waiting to follow her home. She looked out the windows to the sidewalk, to the delivery trucks and cabs and the newspaperman on the corner hawking the *Trib*, the *Sun-Times*, expecting to see him, his shuffling walk, his small brown teeth. Periodically she told herself she was being ridiculous, but it was thrilling, too. The idea of being watched.

The shelves were dark there, a shelter made of books. The library building was still new, only four years old, more modern and open than the old central library downtown and within walking distance of the two-flat, but it was as familiar to her as any landmark. Caroline had watched the library branch being built. Her last year of high school, she had walked to and from school with her books pressed to her chest, passing the German deli on the corner, the bookstore that sold titles in Hebrew and Polish. On the corner where the A&P used to be, the big backhoes dug the deep hole that would become the library's basement. Then the walls were poured, the tall narrow windows placed so carefully. Walt had been on the work crew that put it together, and if he saw her on the sidewalk, he would call down to her from the roof beams, ask how school was. His white hair made him easy to spot in the crowd of young men bending over their tools. She would call back a hello, feeling how the younger men stopped their work to watch her, feeling the way her skirt brushed against her legs and hips when she walked away.

The week the library opened, her mother had insisted that Caroline go down there to ask about a job. She was graduating high school soon, her mother said, and would need to save up money for college. Mother, who had worked as a nurse for a few months before her marriage, thought library work was refined, dignified, unlike nursing, which meant bedpans and body parts. Except for the year she'd been away at school, Caroline had been at the library ever since.

She was on the lookout for the old man, but when she turned the corner into the history section it was Charley Dunmore she saw, kneeling on the floor with a book open in his hands. His dark hair was mostly in his eyes, so that she wondered how he could see what he was reading. Then he flipped a page over with a slap, and she knew he wasn't reading, not really; it was all an act for her benefit.

In April the news had come that Charley's closest friend, Ralph Zelinsky, had gone missing in action in Vietnam. A littlish kid with a shock of black hair and an uncanny ability to get Charley into hot water, Zel had joined the marines after high school because he was about to be drafted anyway. He and Charley had been inseparable, the kind of boys who would put roadkill in Caroline's car to hear her scream or call the house and tell her mother she'd won the Publishers Clearing House sweepstakes. After Caroline read Zel's name in the paper that morning, she had stopped by to tell Charley how sorry she was. He had been sitting on the front stoop of his mother's house, smoking a cigarette, and didn't look at her when she came up the walk. When she spoke to him, he had only nodded and flicked the end of his cigarette into the wet grass. She asked what he'd heard from Zel's mother, what the marines told the family, where they were looking for him. She would not say out loud what everyone already knew—that Zel was dead but the marines wouldn't say so, not yet.

Nothing, he said. They can't do anything. She wanted to say something that would help him, something that would matter. No, Charley said. Don't say anything. He looked unnaturally bright, as if all the tarnish had been scrubbed off him. It won't help anyway, he said, not if you can't explain it to me, not if you can't tell me what it's all for. What is it for?

I can't tell you. I don't know.

He laughed. That's the first true thing you've said.

When classes let out for the summer, Charley went to Canada to visit his aunts and uncles, and Caroline had thought, had assumed, really, that he would not be coming back.

In the history stacks, Charley did not look up from his book when Caroline approached. He brushed his hair out of his eyes, and Caroline was struck, not for the first time, by the idea that he could be a musician or an actor, someone to talk about and admire. He seemed made to be noticed in ways that other people, herself included, were not.

The old loose wheels on her cart complained on turning the corner. She stopped a few inches from Charley's knee.

He flipped a page. "Did you know that Hitler wanted to be a painter?"

"I did, actually."

"If he'd just gone to art school instead."

"He tried. They wouldn't let him in." She felt her mouth twisting up wryly the way it did whenever she talked to Charley, as if she were always waiting for the punch line. "When did you get back?"

"Yesterday. Did you miss me?"

"I was pining away the whole time." From the other side of the library, she could hear Martha stamping books at the circulation desk. The click of the stamp in the quiet was significant. "I can't talk now," Caroline said.

Charley looked at the books in front of him and picked another one off the shelf. He opened it and scanned the pages. "I should get a job here. This would be a great place to work. All these lonely women."

"All these lonely women are married."

"You're not."

"Thank you. No, I'm not." He thought he was being pretty funny. "They wouldn't hire you anyway. You have to be organized."

"All you have to do is find where the book belongs. I find the number. I put it back." He picked a book off the shelf, looked at it for a second, and put it back. He had not put it in the right spot.

"Don't you have to look for a job or something?" she asked.

"No. I'm taking the summer off. Just lucky, I guess."

"Or lazy."

"That isn't fair. I wasn't criticizing you."

"No. You're just keeping me from working."

He picked up another book. "I'm reading," he said. "I have as much right to be here as anyone." He turned the pages.

"All right," she said. "But don't get me in trouble."

She went down the aisle and put back the book in her hand, a military history of Great Britain. It slid into place as if it had never left. She turned the corner and went into the fiction stacks, leaving Charley sitting on the floor, watching her.

Lady Chatterley's Lover had been in with the automotive manuals again. Earlier she'd seen a couple of younger boys with their heads together, whispering, and when she went past that section later, through volumes on auto body repair and *Transmissions for Everyone*, there it was. The edges of the book were smeared with the collective oil of many hands. Curious boys who didn't have sense enough to be embarrassed for themselves. She had taken the job at the library because her mother said it was the only proper job for a young lady, but her mother didn't know about the teenage boys or the old man who looked down her blouse, and Caroline had no intention of telling her.

She was not especially talented at anything others would recognize as an art, but she was a quick learner and had a knack for organization, for putting things where they needed to go, for finding what needed to be done and doing it efficiently and accurately. She loved the feel of the books, the heft of them in her hands, their spines rounded exactly to fit into a palm, fingers splayed over the cover. The numbers at the bottom of the spine told where the books belonged in the order of things: Poetry and philosophy, gardening and cookery, all had a place in the common knowledge of the universe. It was tedious, methodical work, but after a few weeks Caroline had found that Dewey decimal numbers had a kind of beauty all their own. Some nights when she wasn't sleeping, she would see the numbers in front of her eyes: 917.18. When she was bored or had a little extra time, she would let the books fall open in her hands, and there was always something there she hadn't known before. The spines would be broken at the most interesting parts. She held *Lady Chatterley's Lover* in her hands and once again let it fall open. "What liars poets and everybody were! They made one think one wanted sentiment. When what one supremely wanted was this piercing, consuming, rather awful sensuality." She thought, Rubbish. The word sprang into her head. Where had it come from? It made her sound downright British, and she rather liked it.

She felt Charley over her shoulder and snapped the book shut, but he took it out of her hands. He said, "You know the school board said this was smut."

"This isn't school."

His finger fell to a different page from the one she had been reading. He opened it and read aloud: " 'The sun through the low window sent in a beam that lit up his thighs and slim belly and the erect phallus rising darkish and hot-looking from the little cloud of vivid gold-red hair.' "

"Don't," she said.

"Maybe I should read more." He let the book fall closed again. "You've always been such a good girl. What would your mother think?"

"What would yours? You were reading it, too."

He moved in very close. His eyes were the same color as his brother's, a kind of muddy green, but they were two different shades: the left was more green, the right a little more brown. She'd never noticed that before.

He dropped the book; it fell to the floor. She picked it up. It had landed upside down, and the pages were heavily creased from the fall.

"Look at this," she said. "You ruined it."

"It's not ruined."

"It is. It's all bent."

He stooped and picked up the novel. He smoothed down the pages and closed the cover again. "There," he said. "Good as new."

"But Charley. It's *not*."

He started coming in to see her once or twice a week. She would find him in the fiction stacks, reading aloud from Jacqueline Susann or *Tropic of Cancer*, picking out the choicest bits, reading just a little too loud. Whenever he came in Judy teased her, saying, "The book lover's here," smiling as though she knew something Caroline didn't. She wondered if his visits were his way of making up for his brother. She wondered if he was feeling sorry for her. She couldn't stand the thought that he would pity her, not Charley Dunmore, who didn't pity anyone.

She dreamed about him once, something sweet and potent. His hands on her neck, on her waist, everywhere. When she woke in the morning, she tried to piece it together again, but it slipped away from her. Afterward, when Caroline was bored, when the mildewy smell of old books made her almost ill, when she wanted to throw her cart out the window and watch it shatter on the cement below, she would turn a corner thinking he would be there. She watched the door for him to come in, putting the books away on their shelves, finding the numbers that showed where they belonged, everything in its place, but really she was thinking, Charley could come in that door any minute. Any minute now, he could be here.

Whenever he finally appeared, she wouldn't say any of the things she'd imagined but endured his teasing with a kind of playful exasperation. She knew it was all an act she was putting on but couldn't seem to stop herself. Charley went to great lengths to make her laugh. He called her an old maid, a spinster librarian, but said it so affectionately that she knew he didn't mean a word of it. She hoped he didn't mean a word of it.

She had taken more hours at the library to try to make a little more money over the summer, but something had slipped, something in her started come loose, and her work became sloppy. She read the books for hours when she should have been putting them away. She hid in the stacks to keep the other librarians from asking her for help. More and more she had trouble concentrating, and Martha, the head librarian, took her aside and asked if something was wrong. Why were Caroline's stacks such a mess lately? I'm sorry, Caroline said. I'll work harder. She tried and tried, but the more she decided to buckle down, work harder, the less able she was to concentrate. Her books were everywhere but where they belonged. Martha sighed and said maybe Caroline could sit at the circulation desk for a while, for a change of pace, and she could go back to her stacks later if she felt up to it.

So Caroline was at the front desk checking in the returned books, clicking the stamp in the quiet, the satisfying *chunk-chunk*, when the old man came in again. He smiled at her under his bushy eyebrows and asked where he could find *Leaves of Grass*. She pointed the way to him, Whitman, poetry, 811, but he shook his head and said no, he was an old man with poor eyesight, he would never find it himself. "Could you please take me there, my dear? You're always so good, so helpful." His breath and skin smelled of garlic and onions, faintly of cigarettes, more strongly of something sweetish she couldn't put her finger on. She looked around: Martha and Judy were nowhere to be seen. As always, they had found somewhere else they desperately needed to be.

All right, she said, and set aside her stamp.

He followed her back to the poetry books, to the end of a row of shelves near the microfilm. The whole way she was aware of his eyes on her back. She felt as sorry for him as ever, but she was ashamed thinking of how she had acted the last time and decided she would not give him what he was after, not today. *You're always so good, my dear.* She knew what he meant.

Whitman was up on top. She pointed toward it. "There," she said. Of course he said he couldn't see it, it was too high, and could she get it down for him? She pushed over the kick stool with her foot, stepped on top of it, and reached for the book. The shelf was high, so she had to stretch, and when she did the old man reached out and took the edge of her skirt in his hands, softly, as if she wouldn't be able to tell. He rubbed the fabric between his fingers.

She pulled at her skirt until the cloth came away. "Don't do that," she said.

The old man smiled and showed all of his small brown teeth. He reached out again and very deliberately took the hem of her skirt between his fingers and pulled hard, almost tipping her off balance. He was smiling at her, and his gums and his face were very red. His other hand was fumbling with his trousers. He sighed a little: "Beautiful, beautiful." His voice was eager and heavy. The sound of it nauseated her.

Quickly she stepped down from the kick stool, nearly tripping into him, and he reached out to catch her so she wouldn't fall, and his arms were tight around her and he wasn't feeble at all, but quite strong. She felt her face flush. She pushed against him hard so that he bumped into the shelves and several books toppled to the floor. He caught himself, looking bewildered, as if he'd suddenly woken up from a dream.

She reached up and slapped him, hard, across the face. He stepped away from her and put his hand to the place where her hand had connected. His eyes were wide and blue, clouded and cataracted, but she had wanted to hit him, and it almost felt good. Powerful. She had almost liked it.

She thrust the book into his chest and went down the aisle, nearly running, crossing the lobby and going into the ladies' washroom, where she locked herself in the stall and wept tears that made no sense to her. She was humiliated and sick. She was angry. It was quiet in the washroom except for the overhead fan running and the sound of her sniffling, but she couldn't make herself leave the stall. Women came in and went out again. Eventually she opened the door a crack and, seeing she was alone, stepped out. In the mirror over the sink, her cheeks and eyes were pink with embarrassment. She splashed cool water on her face and patted it dry, arranging her hair with her fingers. She did not want to go out again but had been in the washroom too long already, long enough for someone to notice. She didn't think the old man would still be there, but she couldn't bear to look at him if he was. She should call the police. She should find somewhere else to be, like everyone else.

She opened the door, but he wasn't there. None of the other librarians were visible, so she went back to the circulation desk. She climbed back on her stool and stamped the books in the quiet as if nothing had happened, *chunk-chunk*, but she kept waiting for the old man to reappear. She felt her resolve stiffen, decided that if he said one more word to her, *just one more*, she would call the police. If he came back again, she would tell them everything and have the old man put away for good. A man like that was a menace, a disgrace.

She was keeping such a close eye on her work that she did not see Charley at first when he came in and stood near the desk. "Hello?" he said. He sounded exasperated, as if he'd been forced to repeat himself. The sound of his voice made her jump. She smelled the mint of the gum he was chewing, a strong, sweetish smell. It made her feel a little ill.

"Sorry. You startled me."

"You all right?"

"Fine."

"You look all flushed. Reading those dirty books again?"

"Don't tease me today." She was shivery and hot. The sting of the slap was still in her hand. "Please."

"All right," he said. "Okay, I won't."

"I don't want to talk about it."

"I won't ask. I only came in to say hello."

"Hello, then." She had to admit it: She was glad to see him, his handsome face, the lightness of him. She clicked her stamp and set the book on the pile. "Don't you have work today?" she asked.

"No. I don't have a job, remember?"

"Oh. Right."

"I was in the neighborhood."

"You seem to be in the neighborhood a lot lately." There was a line of small dark hairs across the backs of his hands, a bare spot at the wrists, the same as Sam's hands had been. She thought of Dottie with her pralines. "You're not feeling sorry for me, are you?"

"What made you say that?"

She shook her head. "Your brother."

"My brother is an idiot."

That movie-star smile of his, it was better than coffee. She thought maybe he looked a little like Paul Newman. Paul Newman with dark hair. His chin sharp and dimpled, his irises narrow in the strong light coming in from the window. He looked older. Maybe that was it.

"I thought I might walk you home," he said. "If you wanted."

She still had an hour to go on her shift, but his offer felt like a reprieve, like relief. "That would be fine," she said.

She went into the office to tell Martha she was ill and needed to go home. "I'll be back in the morning, if I'm feeling better."

"Do you have a fever?" Martha asked. "You look so red."

"I think so," Caroline lied. "I don't feel like myself."

"Go home and lie down," Martha said. "Put a wet cloth on your head, and take a couple of aspirin."

"All right," she said. "I'll be sure to do that."

Charley was waiting for her in the lobby, reading the bulletin board announcements for children's story time and notices of lost pets. He held the door for her. Outside he walked in silence, as if he were waiting for her to say something, but it was not uncomfortable, and in fact she felt better almost as soon as they left the library. She looked for the old man outside on the sidewalk, thinking he might be waiting to follow her home, but she didn't see him anywhere. She was very glad Charley was there, just in case.

"Looking for someone?" Charley asked.

"No," she said. "No one."

It was a day of high blue skies, a strong breeze blowing away the hot stillness of summer. They turned and went west toward home. He started to whistle, and she recognized "Paint It Black." Since Sam had left for basic training, Charley was a different person. Without his brother there he seemed more confident, more sure of himself. Even his trips to the library to tease her had an undercurrent of something that had never been there before. She thought maybe it was relief.

"Feel better?" Charley asked.

"I do. Thanks."

"You looked like you needed to get out of there."

"I did."

They stood back to let a group of high school girls pass by. The girls had their cigarettes hidden in their palms, but she could smell the smoke when they went by. She knew the trick, had done it herself when she was younger, thinking she was pretty clever. Later she found out her mother had known the whole time. The smell of cigarettes was unmistakable. The girls laughed when they went past, leaning their heads together to speak low, and Caroline thought maybe they were laughing at her, her frumpy work clothes, the wind whipping her skirt in every direction, sweat on her upper lip and under her arms. But no, they were not bothering with her; she was being paranoid, even mean. She was not herself.

When they went past, the girls looked over their shoulders and smiled at Charley. Charley smiled back at them and said, "Hello, ladies." They laughed at being called "ladies" and kept going, but Caroline could tell they liked the attention of an older boy, a good-looking boy.

Caroline said, "That was rude. What if I was your girlfriend?"

"But you're not."

"They don't know that."

"But you're not." He took her arm, pulled her toward him without breaking stride. It was a long walk from the library to her mother's apartment, but she was glad of him there, the feel of him. It surprised her, how much she liked it.

"If you were my girlfriend," he said, "I wouldn't have talked to them."

"Well"—she smiled—"I suppose you're forgiven, then."

They turned and went into their own neighborhood. She smelled the sauerbraten cooking for supper and the wild raspberries that grew on luxuriant bushes along the alley fence. The raspberries had fallen to the ground weeks ago; a blackbird pecked at the last of the rotten fruit. She thought it was a shame that the raspberries were wasted like that. They were dirty, her mother said, not for human consumption—growing wild like that, in the alley where people put their garbage—and she had forbidden Caroline to touch them long ago. Still, she had often slipped away to pluck some of the berries when they were ripe and burst them on her soft palate, slipping back into the yard before her mother saw. But the berries that year were wasted; she hadn't got to them in time.

They went up the front walk to the door of her mother's flat. The light next to the door was off, and the curtains in the front window were drawn; her mother must have one of her migraines. When the curtains were drawn, it usually meant a bad night.

"You probably shouldn't come in," she said.

"That's all right." It was the first thing he'd said in four blocks.

But he didn't leave, not right away. He was holding her by the elbow, and he leaned in toward her, his face brushing against hers, and caught her mouth. His lips tasted like the gum he'd been chewing. After a minute he stopped, and when she stepped back to look at him, he seemed pleased with himself. She was afraid he would say something awful, but he only asked if he would see her tomorrow.

"I'm working tomorrow."

"So call in sick."

"I can't do that."

"Ah," he said. "Always the good girl."

"I'm not that good."

His hand was damp. He slid it up underneath her coat, furtively, close. Cars went down the street as people came home from their Saturday errands to wash up for supper, but she was barely aware of them. She watched him instead. He looked surprised and happy and secretive, and the smile on his face broadened when he found her bare skin. Under his hand she felt alive, like herself, real and solid, and when he kissed her again she put her arms around his neck and breathed him in and pressed her cheek to the soft place under his ear where the hair stopped growing. He did not remind her of Sam at all, his smell, the feel of him. He was only himself. He took his hand away and said it was time for him to go.

Caroline unlocked her front door and went inside. Her mother was on the couch with her arm over her face. A cup of cold coffee stained with lipstick sat on the floor near the couch, proof that her mother had made something of an effort that day; around her mouth clung a trace of the red lipstick. Through the heavy curtains, a thin trickle of light was visible.

"Don't flip the switch," her mother said automatically. Her voice was low, nearly a whisper, and when she opened her eyes they were thin slits.

Her face was puffy from the migraine, and it made her look very young, almost like a child. "I saw you," she said.

"What are you talking about?"

"On the porch. With Charley." She was frowning. "The way you behave, it's a wonder any man will talk to you."

Caroline slammed the front door shut. The walls of the apartment vibrated, and she could hear Mr. Hartman, upstairs, bang his foot on the floor, his way of telling them to keep it down. She opened the closet and took off her shoes, putting them and her purse in the bottom of the coat closet. Inside, the coats lined up so perfectly, winter coats on the left, lighter coats to the right, their order changed according to the seasons. She couldn't stand the sight of those perfectly organized coats, her mother's need to have everything just so. She slammed the closet door for good measure, and from upstairs came again the answering sound of Mr. Hartman's foot. The hell with him. The hell with you.

But her mother was pressing her hands over her head, in the agony of migraine. She moaned. Caroline was immediately sorry. She wasn't sure what had come over her, but the terrible sound coming from her mother made her anger and impatience drain away. "I'm sorry. I didn't mean it."

"Oh, oh . . ."

"Mother, please. I'm sorry. I'm so sorry, I won't do it again."

After a moment her mother stopped her moaning. She wiped at her face and laid one hand over her eyes, fingers splayed. "Can I get you anything?" Caroline asked. "Something to drink?"

"No," she whispered. "I don't want anything."

Caroline picked up the empty coffee cup and took it into the kitchen. How she hated her mother's loneliness and dependence, the way she relied on Caroline for company. She had lost her husband, but did that mean she was consigned to a lifetime of mourning? There were still men in the world who would have been glad of the company of a woman like Adele Clark.

She brought her mother a cold compress and a cup of tea, but she said she didn't want it. Caroline set it on the floor where her mother could reach it if she changed her mind. She was suddenly exhausted. She wanted to lie down herself. She sat on the coffee table and brushed the hair away from her mother's face. It was thin, getting thinner all the time. "Want me to ring the doctor?" she asked. "He might have something that will help."

"I called this morning. There's some pills waiting at the pharmacy."

"You should have phoned me at work. I would have picked them up on my way." Caroline felt a helplessness that she often felt in regard to her mother, a sense that she was always two steps behind. She wasn't good enough, would never be.

"I didn't want to bother you," her mother said. "You have enough on your mind right now."

"But you look like you're in pain," Caroline said.

"I'll get them. You do so much already. I should be able to get up and fetch my own pills."

"I'll go right now, Mother, just give me a minute to change."

Her mother sat up, her bare legs falling over the edge of the sofa. Her small feet were very white and sickly looking. "No, I'll go," she said. "It will only take a minute, just down the street and back. If I can find my shoes. Are they by the door? I can't see that well."

"No, no, I'll go. Do you need anything else? Is there anything you'd like for supper?"

Her mother lay back down on the sofa. "Whatever you want."

"There's a stew in the fridge I might heat up."

"Whatever you'd like. You work so hard, I don't want to make it any worse."

"Is the stew all right, though?"

"I don't think I can eat anything anyway."

Caroline picked up her purse to go out. The balls of her feet ached. She hadn't yet found a pair of shoes that didn't make her feet ache after working at the library all day. She asked, "Would you like soup instead? Maybe tomato?"

"Oh, yes, that would be lovely." Her mother turned her face back to the couch cushions. "Coming right back?"

She turned the handle. "Of course."

Caroline saw the old man one last time, months later. By then she and Charley were fond and familiar lovers with plans for the future. She was in the grocery, shopping for some bread and apples and a pack of cigarettes, when she turned into the produce section and saw him. He was stealing grapes. His stubby hands were fondling the bunches, and he pulled one off the vine and popped it into his mouth. His red face worked the grape around in his mouth, chewed quickly a couple of times. He swallowed. As she watched, he did it again and again, stuffing in four or five grapes at a time, rolling them around with his tongue. He didn't see her, or if he did, he wasn't interested in her at first. He had stopped coming into the library after she'd slapped him, and for a while she had forgotten about him, but that day he was wearing the same dirty pants, the same nearly vacant, dreamy expression he'd had on his face that day in poetry. He took a handkerchief out of his sleeve, blew his nose into it once, and stuffed it back in his pocket.

He turned and saw her watching him. He took a couple of steps away, then dropped his trousers and showed himself to her, his pink and wrinkled secret.

She looked away, looked at the floor. She should call the police. She should call them right away and report what he had done, what he was doing. But she couldn't imagine explaining it to anyone, much less a police officer. If she closed her eyes, she could pretend that none of it had happened. Because if she went down that road, if anyone knew the truth, they would probably have to know her part in it, too. That she had encouraged him. That she wasn't as innocent in all of this as she looked.

She left the bread and apples and walked out of the store. She went home quickly, almost running, looking behind her, but no one was following.

SEVEN

One time, riding in a car with some friends, Sam saw a kid younger than himself riding a blue Cook County Correctional bus with his face pressed against the glass, looking so sad that he might have been crying. It was winter, and the kid's breath had fogged the window. The bus and Sam's car were going the same speed, and for a minute the kid seemed to hang in midair. He caught Sam's eye. They stared at each other. Then, using his finger, the kid wrote backward on the fogged window, in letters so perfect they were unmistakable: "Fuck You." Sam sped up, leaving the bus behind, and the kid slipped away.

His first day at Fort Polk, Louisiana, it was the kid's face he was seeing when the bus stopped in the yard. It was the same kind of bus, blue with metal grates over the windows. They were already waiting. They pounded the walls of the bus and shouted to the recruits inside: "Wake up, you pussies, wake up! Every swinging dick had better be out here on the count of ten!" Sam took his things and stood on the line where they told him to, and though he heard them say, "Eyes front!" he couldn't resist looking when he heard the sergeant screaming down the line. The next second he was on his knees, and the sergeant was unclenching his fist. "When I say eyes front, you better believe I mean it."

At night in his bunk, awake to the sounds of eighty guys snoring or farting or jerking off, exhausted and homesick, he thought about Caroline, the way her skin looked golden under the mercury lights at night when he took her to the Polish cemetery, the way her mouth opened just a little when he touched her, her mismatched lips—the top one thin, the bottom one full and thick. How he had pulled that lower lip into his mouth. The soft backs of her knees as he moved them apart. He fell asleep thinking of her, and in the morning he woke feeling bruised and exhausted, as if he'd run some kind of race, but he could never remember what his dreams were about or what she'd said to him in them.

He'd loved her since he could remember, since the morning she and her mother arrived in the States, in the middle of an Easter snowstorm. She was at his front door, but he would not say hello. His mother took him by the shoulders and marched him toward the girl at the door because she thought Sam was being rude. Caroline was wearing a red coat, and snow was melting in her hair and on her eyelashes. She had a round face and long, dark eyelashes that threw shadows over her cheeks, which were pink and splotched from the cold. She was not a stranger—he remembered her, barely, from when they lived in Windsor—but it was as if he had never seen her before. He was nine years old and could not have said what the feeling was, but he couldn't speak and he couldn't move and he was afraid to walk toward her. When he was older it became easy to dismiss that emotion as something childish and false, except that it didn't leave him— the girls he dated later were shadowy next to her, pale imitations. He took them out mostly to see if she would be jealous. The fact that she never was didn't mean he couldn't hope.

But that day she seemed so much older than he was, the way she spoke and moved. He had asked if he could take her coat.

"Sure," she said. "Thanks." She stood at the door with the snow melting in her hair, and he loved her terribly from that moment on.

When they were growing up he pined for her in silence, because he would not have known how to put his feelings into words even if he had dared to do so. She always had boys around, smarmy rich kids who drove nice cars and went to expensive private schools. They looked at her, looked *through* her, and he knew what they were after, and he hated them, every one. He found reasons to be around when they picked her up and dropped her off, and he made sure to tell her about the other girls they dated. Sometimes he made her cry. She would beg him to stop, and he would mope in the house for a while, knowing she was angry with him. Eventually those pretty boys graduated and left town, and Caroline, who couldn't afford college at first, was home more often on Friday and Saturday nights, alone. She spent more time with her mother and at work, but still Sam didn't dare tell her how he felt. He felt so helpless with her that sometimes he could not bear to see her or hear anyone say her name. Other times he would bring his girlfriends around to introduce them to her and her mother. Caroline was always polite to them, always gracious, telling them that Sam was like a brother to her, that the girls were lucky to be dating him—no one would treat them better than he would. It gave him hope that really she was thinking about herself, but when he asked if he could take her out, she always said no. Their friendship meant too much to her, she said.

Sometimes he avoided her for weeks, resolving not to see her, not to call, telling himself he was better off without her. He would go out with the guys and horse around, try to meet new girls, strange girls. At first it was a relief to be out of her sight. No, he would think—I don't miss her, I don't need her. But those periods always seemed dreary to him, the girls too dull or too needy or too *something*. He started coming around again as if everything were the same, stopping by to see her at home, at work. She never seemed to notice his weeks or months of brooding, or if she did, she forgave him so completely that he never even had to apologize.

Charley teased him about her, because Charley always had to be the center of attention, even with Caroline. He had the kind of prettyish good looks that girls had always liked to fawn over, very fine long-lashed eyes that they often mistook for sensitive, at least at first, and languid movements that seemed like a dancer's unless he was fighting or fooling around. But men liked him, too; Charley made friends as easily as waking up in the morning. He could be charismatic when he wanted to be. When Charley was eighteen, Sam saw him charm a married woman into the back of their father's Chevy at a drive-in movie, breath steaming the windshield, a glance of flesh out the back window, tantalizingly brief. Sam had caught the train that night rather than sit around waiting for Charley to be done with the girl, cursing his brother the whole way home. He heard later from Charley's friend Zel that the girl's husband had caught them and dragged them out of the car. He would have beaten them both senseless, Zel said, except that Charley talked his way out of it. Neither of them threw a single punch. Zel was laughing the whole time he told the story, but there was a tinge of awe in his voice, too: "You should have seen it. You should have been there, Sammy. Your brother talking to this big guy with his hands out in front of him, like this, and he says, 'She didn't tell me she was married. I'm not a mind reader.' Man." Charley ducked his head while Zel told the story, but he wasn't embarrassed, not really. If he'd been embarrassed, he wouldn't have done it in the first place. Ma always said he should have been a politician or an actor, but Sam knew his brother, and Charley didn't turn on the charm for anyone other than himself, when he wanted to. He wasn't patient or politic enough for the kind of life Ma wanted for him: Sam's brother believed only in his own brand of bullshit.

Next to Charley, Sam always felt a little invisible. Too old. Too serious. He'd never been able to charm anybody into anything.

"Sammy," his brother would say, "there are other girls in the world, you know."

"I know that," Sam would grumble. But for him, there weren't.

When she told him she was going away to school, he was miserable. For weeks before she left, he spent as much time with her as he could, coming by in the evenings and asking if he could help her pack, if she needed anything. But she only smiled and said no, she had everything she needed. She was too happy. He couldn't abide all her happiness. The prospect of a future without her opened up in front of him, gray and empty. The day she left, he was seized with the need to go with her. He should at least drive to Belle Plaine with her. He wanted to be able to find her if she needed him. "We can take turns driving," he said. "I can help you carry all your things."

But she said she could manage. She kissed him on the cheek. "Write me," she told him, "won't you?"

"What should I write?"

"Anything. Whatever's going on with you."

But there would be nothing going on with him while she was gone. She did not come home often. Adele complained to his mother that Caroline must have forgotten her, that she didn't know how a child she'd raised so lovingly could be so unfeeling, and Ma clucked and said it must be very hard on Adele. But Sam hardly felt less abandoned. He imagined what she was doing downstate, whom she was with. He threw himself into school. His college classes were dull but gave him something to keep him occupied, keep his mind off loneliness and jealousy. Out of spite, almost, he started dating someone from his chemistry class, a smart, self-possessed girl named Angela who insisted on paying for her own dinners and movie tickets and who always had to be home by ten o'clock. It lasted only six weeks or so before she put an end to it, saying it wasn't as much fun as she had thought it would be. He saw her later at a restaurant near campus with the chemistry teacher, his hand on the back of her neck, under her hair, and Sam wondered what it was about him that made girls want to run the other way.

Late in the spring, Caroline wrote his mother to ask if Dottie could lend her a little money. While his mother stirred a pot and chopped tomatoes, Sam went through the day's mail and read it out to her. It was something he'd done since he was young and they'd first moved to the States, sitting at the kitchen table and reading letters from his aunts and his grandmother in Canada. That day there was a note from Aunt Bella, something short about Uncle Ed throwing his back out, two bills, and the letter from Caroline. He scanned it quickly, looking for his own name, but she didn't mention him at all. She wrote that she needed a little money to pay some bills, but if Dottie could send just a little, whatever she could afford, Caroline would repay it, every cent. "I don't know who else I can turn to," she wrote. Sam put the letter in his pocket and did not mention it to his mother.

Later that night, alone in his room, he took out the letter and read it again. It was full of so much sorrow that for the first time he felt hopeful. She was not as happy as he had pictured. She was lonely, and she had run out of money. She might have to drop out, come home. He almost hoped she would.

The next morning, though, he went to the post office with five hundred dollars from his bank account. He bought a money order and sent it to her under his mother's signature with a promise that it was a gift she would not need to repay. He imagined her face when she got it, how happy she would be. It pleased him to know that he could do this for her, that her future was in his hands, even if she never knew the truth of it.

The fall was another long stretch without her. She came home only once, for a long weekend, and she looked she so tired and ashen that he wondered if she had come down with something. Ma said Caroline looked as if she had a tapeworm. Sam offered to take her to lunch, but she said she wasn't hungry.

"Thank you, though," she said. "It's funny, how much I've missed you. I didn't think I would miss anything here, but I guess I was wrong."

He chewed that statement over and over. *It's funny, how much I've missed you.* He had wanted to ask her what, exactly, that was supposed to mean, but his courage failed him. He was still wondering when her visit ended and she went back to school.

Then, before Christmas, she was home again. She unpacked her things into her old room at Adele's. Once again Sam found himself spending all his free time there, sitting with her on the sofa, bringing her cups of tea and extra blankets, staying to watch a late movie. She seemed, for the first time, truly glad of his company, not in that little-brother way from before, but grateful and real. If he reached into her lap for her hand, she let him hold it. When their shoulders touched when they sat together on the sofa, she did not move away.

One night when her mother was asleep in the chair and the snow was coming down hard outside, he leaned over and asked if he could kiss her, and her mismatched lips parted in surprise.

"All right," she said.

A hot, peppery smell was coming off her skin and her breath. Her lips were dry, but she licked them once, quickly, before he touched them, and he pulled her toward him so that her arms went around his neck. She was surprisingly hard, because she was so thin then, all collarbone and elbow and chin, but he kissed along her collarbone and up into her hair, and he felt her relax under his hands that moment, on the sofa, with the TV on in the background.

They were happy then. Every day was better than the next. He would get up in the morning wide awake. He was at her house so often and so long that Adele started leaving a blanket and pillow for him on the sofa, in case he fell asleep. He was always looking for ways to touch her or kiss her when her mother wasn't looking. He was always looking for ways they could be alone. He started to make plans. He thought of a motel, but that was too seedy; Caroline would be humiliated at a place that rented by the hour. He thought of something more romantic, taking her away for the weekend, but her mother, who watched her every minute for the first blush of immodesty, would never allow it. Finally he settled on an expensive downtown hotel and a night of dancing, something dressy and preposterous, but he lost his nerve trying to make a reservation for Mr. and Mrs. Dunmore and ended up taking her to the Polish cemetery, where he knew no one would see them. Her hands tightening on his shoulders. He was afraid she would know he'd never done anything like that before. He was afraid of being clumsy with her, of hurting her, and he almost stopped, but her breath was hot against his ear, and the pain he was feeling was so taut, he had thought he could die right there, right in the cemetery with her beneath him, and never ask for anything more.

Like this, she said. *Oh, like this.*

The strange thing was that afterward, after the first time, he felt less control over himself than he had before. He lost whole days thinking about her, imagining the heavy, soft feel of her breasts in his hands, the smell of her skin.

She told him about the teacher—David—because he asked. What did he look like, what kinds of things did they do together? He said it was reprehensible for a teacher to date his student, but she insisted he hadn't been her teacher. She defended him. There was a strange gulping sound in her voice whenever she said his name, a fear almost, a longing that Sam recognized—there was more to the story than what she was telling him. Every time he thought of her with David, he was jealous to the point of rage, and no matter how often she told him that it was nothing, that it was over and she didn't even care anymore, he didn't believe her. How could he? She had always been secretive and sly, always keeping herself closed off from him, telling him what he wanted to hear and keeping the truth for herself. There was a cruelty in her he'd never noticed before.

The package came in the middle of a late winter cold snap. They had just been to class and gone to her mother's for lunch when Sam saw it on the table and picked it up. Wrapped in brown paper, it weighed almost nothing. It did not have a return address, but the postmark was from Belle Plaine, where Caroline had gone away to school. She was wearing a red sweater that day. Red, he'd told her, was his favorite color on her. It made her skin look rosy and her eyes, which were gray, seem brighter. But when he handed her the package and she would not take it, and from the way her eyes had shifted and she was nervous and evasive, he knew she had given her heart away, that there was a piece of her he could never have. It ate at him. David. She was clearly still in touch with him if he was sending her gifts. He started checking her mail after school, stopping by the library unannounced to make sure she was there. When he took her to a movie or to dinner, he scanned the crowd to see if someone was watching them, if someone was paying her just a little bit too much attention. Once, in line for movie tickets, he had thought a man ahead of them was giving her a look and would have started a fight if Caroline hadn't begged him not to. "What's gotten into you?" she said, almost crying. Sometimes he could hardly look at her. She would say she was going out with friends or studying on her own, but he knew she was lying to him the whole time.

Like this. Oh, like this.

He started staying away. He spent less time with her in class or at her mother's. He went out with friends more often. He got a part-time job working with his father in construction after school and on the weekends that kept him away from her. She complained she didn't see him enough anymore. "I'm just busy," he said. He was turning the tables on her, making her anxious and worried. It was as if all the times he'd suffered at her hands had stored up in him, years of hope and humiliation, and now that the situation had changed, he was unleashing his own pain on her. He knew he shouldn't, but he couldn't stop himself. There was something in him that enjoyed hurting her.

In the fall, the president started calling for more military volunteers. Kids Sam had known since high school were being drafted or joining up. It was making Ma nervous. She suggested, not too subtly, that Uncle Jimmy needed people at his auto-body shop in Windsor or that Uncle Ed could always use more hands on the farm. If Sam wanted, either one of them would take him in. Pop told her Sam could make up his own mind about where he would go to work and with whom. "He'll make his choice. It's his and he'll make it. It's his life, Dot, not yours." His mother went very pale. She picked up a coffee cup from the counter and threw it at Pop across the kitchen. It broke against the wall, leaving a gash in the wallpaper as big as Sam's thumb. She looked shocked, as if even she hadn't known she was capable of such a thing. She had never done anything like that before. "It *is* my life," she said. "I'm his *mother*."

Even Caroline got in on the act. On a trip they took to Ontario that last summer, she started talking about moving back to Canada, the two of them, coming back to stay. He couldn't believe she would actually ask him to run. He was so shocked that he didn't know what to say, could barely look at her. He wondered if his mother had put her up to it. He was bored with college by then. Each semester his student deferment was more of a burden to him. Kids his own age or younger, like Charley's friend Zel, were heading to Vietnam while Sam went to the movies and scooped the Loop with his friends on Friday nights. He started to feel like a coward, someone hiding behind the rules. Pop hadn't cowered behind books. More and more, the army seemed to be the place he needed to go, the answer he was looking for. Before Thanksgiving he skipped his morning classes and took a bus to the recruitment office, a storefront affair that smelled of industrial cleaners and burned coffee grounds. He signed on the dotted line and went home and didn't mention it to anyone, not at first, but after a couple of days Charley noticed something was different and said, "What's the matter? You're jumpier than a virgin on her wedding night."

Pop was disappointed that Sam wouldn't be finishing school first, but Ma was furious. She said he couldn't go, she wouldn't allow it. She said he had to go back down to the recruiter's office and tell them it had been a mistake. She said it wasn't possible, it just wasn't possible, he was born in Canada and they shouldn't be able to do that. Pop said, "Benny, be reasonable, we're all Americans now."

"Don't you call me that," she said. "Don't you tell me to be reasonable."

The army recruiter raised an eyebrow when he looked at Sam's paperwork and saw that he was born in Canada. U.S. citizen, naturalized. But Pop always said you couldn't have it both ways. Either you're here or you're there. Pop was a convert to the American religion, like most immigrants. A true believer. It was Pop's idea to move across the border, Pop who took the family to Chicago, full of Poles, Czechs, Croats, Slavs, Germans, Greeks, Jews, Irish, Swedes, Mexicans, southern blacks, a city of immigrants, people looking for familiar faces and familiar languages and creating their former lives block by block. Sometimes whole towns came together, people who'd known one another for ages, and the cooking smells on the street would be the smells they'd always known, and the people who lived next door spoke the language they knew, and they could go their whole lives without meeting a stranger or leaving the neighborhood.

There was no neighborhood for Canadians. They blended. People assumed he had always been an American, so it was easy for Sam to think of himself that way, as a natural-born citizen. To Sam, Canada was only a place he went on yearly trips with his folks, sneaking off with Charley and his cousins to buy the cigarettes Ma wouldn't allow him to smoke. He was only a visitor there, a tourist. Later, at college, he'd heard rumors of people crossing the border to avoid the draft, but they were just stories kids told one another in dorm rooms and in the backs of cars to give themselves a little outlaw thrill.

Caroline had said she wanted to go to back to Canada, for the two of them to go together. She was asking him to dodge the draft. He couldn't believe it.

When he decided to sign up for the army, it was a relief to think that he would be away from her finally, that he would not have to see her every day or talk to her. It calmed him. The fact that she was bewildered by his decision, almost hurt, just sweetened his resolve even more. The day he left, standing outside her house in the blistering cold, her breath rising in the air and her eyes clouding with confusion, made him feel strong and new. He went to the train station almost giddy, thinking about it.

The army was tough, tougher than he would have expected before going to Louisiana. He didn't like taking orders. He thought the drill sergeant was the biggest son of a bitch who ever walked. He did make friends easily, though, and that helped pass the time. When he left home, something in him had changed. He was suddenly outgoing and funny, cracking up the other guys with the kinds of jokes only Charley used to tell. Popes in a boat. A midget walks into a bar. It was fun to pretend to be something he was not. If the guys in his unit could have seen him at home, how he was with his family and with Caroline, they would not have recognized him. But there was no one here to be surprised; as far as they knew, Sam Dunmore had been born easygoing and smart-alecky, the class clown. He shed his familiar self like old clothes that no longer fit.

In the barracks, while they cleaned their rifles or in those few minutes between lights out and sleep, they compared hometowns, compared girlfriends and wives. It was always whose girl was a looker, whose was a dog. They passed around photos. They shared Dear John stories, how so-and-so's girl had ditched him almost as soon as he was drafted, how one guy on leave had caught his fiancée in the sack with the next-door neighbor. Another guy's wife had met him at the bus depot with divorce papers. Sam remembered Caroline's face the day the package arrived, how she said the landlord had sent her gloves. He pictured her with David at the movies, at dinner, in hotel rooms that rented by the hour, and he couldn't write to her. It wasn't a conscious decision—he just went a few weeks without writing her or calling, then a few more, then a few more. She was the source of all his weaknesses, all his humiliations, and if he didn't write to her, he didn't have to remember. "What have I done that you don't answer me?" she wrote. "I hate this silence. I hate being alone." The more worried her letters sounded, the more determined he was not to answer her at all. He was free of her.

When they had a three-day pass, Sam and some buddies decided to drive to Galveston, to the beach. They stayed in a cheap motel off the Strand, four to a room that smelled like mold and cigarette smoke. They went to three or four bars in a row, drinking cheap beer and getting so raucous that they were thrown out. Afterward they walked along the seawall, jostling and jockeying. Teddy James, who'd grown up in Galveston, said the seawall had been built after a massive hurricane wiped out half the city earlier in the century. The Strand had been completely swept away. Thousands died. Sam imagined surging seas and rain, buildings crumbling, people washed out to sea. It didn't seem possible that so much could be destroyed so quickly.

They slept well into the morning, went out again in the afternoon to the beach, hung over and listless. Sam fell asleep on the sand while the others were swimming and woke up hours later, alone and badly sunburned. He squinted at the beach, at the water, but his friends were nowhere in sight. They must have thought they were being pretty funny, leaving him there like that. When he rolled onto his back the sand stung him, and he sat up cursing and sputtering.

"My God," said a voice behind him. "Aren't you a sight. You should get some lotion on that burn and take the heat out."

"Who asked you?" Sam said, shading his eyes in the hot sunlight, but the girl only smiled at him.

Her name was Linda Chesney. She was from Houston. "But don't let that fool you," she said. "I'm actually a nice person." She had just come out of the water, and her long, straight blond hair was dripping over her shoulders and down onto the sand. She was wearing a very small bikini that looked as if it might, at any second, slip down her narrow hips and reveal everything, and Sam hoped it would. She was thin and tall, unlike Caroline, who sometimes ran to plump; also unlike Caroline, she had smallish breasts, a long curving neck, jutting hipbones. She was tanned, but her hair and her eyebrows were bleached so light that they almost disappeared on her skin. White lines on her shoulders showed where she had worn a different bathing suit on some other day. She said she had some lotion he could borrow, if he wanted it.

"Thanks," he said, "but I wouldn't want to put you out."

"Why would it put me out?"

"I don't know. I guess it wouldn't."

"You're trying to be polite," she said. "It won't work on me, I should warn you."

He shrugged, said, "I didn't think it would."

"Oh, yes, you did. You thought if you were polite, I'd think what a nice boy you are. It's more subtle than some cheap line, but the idea is the same."

"All right, all right. Uncle."

She smiled. She was teasing him. She was the kind of girl who would never have spoken to him at home, bossy and flirtatious, sure of the considerable power of her beauty. He liked her immediately.

She asked him where he was stationed.

"What do you mean?"

"The hair."

He ran a hand over his high-and-tight. "I guess it is a little obvious," he said.

When she offered to rub the lotion on his sunburned back, he let her, enjoying the cool lotion, her soft hands. She touched him lightly, so as not to scrape the burn, and when she rubbed the lotion on his neck, her breasts brushed across his shoulder blades. "There," she said when she was finished.

When his buddies came back—Teddy James and Martinez and Danny Shreve—he introduced them to Linda. She was a student at Rice and had come to Galveston with a couple of her girlfriends on spring vacation. The girls laughed and whispered to each other when she pointed them out. She told him their names, but he didn't catch them—none was nearly as beautiful as Linda. He was intrigued by this new person, wanted to know everything about her. It had never occurred to him before that there were women in the world who could be mysterious to him, who could be by their very newness something he would be interested in. Because he'd spent so much time mooning like an idiot over the one girl who didn't want him, he had never taken the time before to seriously consider other girls at all.

Charley was right: There were plenty of other girls in the world besides Caroline Clark.

He asked if he could take her to dinner that night. "I don't know," she said, smiling at him. "Can you?"

He picked her up at her hotel. Through dinner he'd tried to sit, but the sunburn was excruciating, and he couldn't manage to stay still for long. She said that was all right, she wasn't that hungry anyway. They walked along the seawall instead, where Sam told her about the 1900 hurricane. "That's why the seawall is here. In case there's another one."

"Thank you, professor. I never would have guessed. I only *grew up* in Texas—"

"Jesus," he breathed. "You never stop talking, do you."

She laughed. "Sometimes I do. For the right people I do."

"Am I the right people?"

"You could be."

Sam pulled her toward him. He was enjoying this new, bold feeling. He spent the night in her hotel room without the least hint of shame and showed no mortification that she seemed to have had many lovers in the past. Later, when he tried to slip back into his own motel room without waking the others, he tripped over Martinez, who said admiringly that Linda Chesney was the finest thing he'd seen in ten states. "Did you see those legs?" he said. Sam glowed under the praise. He'd never before dated the kind of women who elicited other men's envy.

When he went back to Fort Polk, he wrote her two, three times a week, and she answered all his letters. He told her about his parents, about Charley, about growing up in Chicago, even about Caroline, that she had broken his heart. "I'm so sorry," she wrote. "I guess nice boys do finish last." He could almost hear, in her letters, the musical tilt to her voice when she told him he was being polite to win her over, the way she had laughed at him and made him laugh at himself. He loved that about her— her lightness, her humor. But she was intelligent, too. She was getting her degree in education and planned to teach high school math. Sam wrote her that her classes would be full of teenage boys who would all be madly in love with her. "Of course," she wrote back. "That's the idea."

When basic training was over, he took the bus to Houston to meet her parents instead of going home. Linda had mentioned that her father worked for an oil company, but Sam found out later that in fact he owned a company that manufactured oil drills. The house was in a part of town called River Oaks. The house was a large brick English Tudor with a wide lawn and a blue swimming pool in the backyard. Sam had never known people who had their own pool. When they had dinner and drinks outside, Sam saw that the bottom of the pool had a large *C* done in green tile.

Linda's mother was an elegant woman in early middle age with a blond bouffant and a silk pantsuit. She had the bored, flirtatious manners of a woman who had gone to great lengths to keep her looks and was alarmed to find herself with a beautiful grown-up daughter, like Anne Bancroft in *The Graduate*. Linda took after her father, though, had the same coloring, the same length of bone, except that her father's hair was white now, having faded from its original blond. Linda's mother was asking about his family, his father's work in the construction business—Sam was aware, without having to be told, that his background was not up to their expectations, though they were too nice to say anything—and where his mother's people were from. Sam told them that he had been born in Canada. "I didn't know they could draft Canadians," she said.

"I'm an American citizen. I thought I should volunteer."

"Is that so?" asked Linda's father. "Why would you do a thing like that?"

"I felt like I needed a change," Sam said. "I figured I'd have to go eventually, so better to get it over with now."

"You didn't think you should finish school first?"

"No, sir. I felt that school wasn't offering me much."

"It's hard to go back later on."

"My father said the same thing."

"Your father sounds like a practical man."

"He is," Sam said.

Her mother, changing the subject, asked how Sam and Linda had met. Sam explained about the sunburn, how Linda had offered to help him, how afterward he had asked her to dinner as a way to thank her. He left out the part about spending the night in her room. Linda's mother said it sounded as though Sam were a true gentleman, "a rarity in these days."

"Don't tell him that, Mother," Linda said. "That's his game, being a gentleman. It's all an act."

"Oh," her mother said with the same kind of teasing tone that Linda used herself, "is that so?"

Sam found it a little disquieting, all this female charisma turned on him, but Linda's father just shook his head and offered to pour Sam another drink. "Alcohol," he said, "is the best cure for a woman's wit."

"And a man's," said her mother, sipping her drink. Sam thought she might be a little drunk already. They were all charming and funny. He felt a bit like their straight man, serious and polite to a fault, and by the end of the night they were all pretty well drunk, the three of them taunting one another with stories and jokes that Sam didn't quite follow, as if it were a private language they had invented. They hardly seemed to notice him at times. Sam grew quiet, trying to make certain he didn't say anything rude.

He thought as long as he didn't say much, they wouldn't figure out how uncomfortable he was.

When the visit was over, Sam was transferred to advanced individual training and jump school at Fort Benning, Georgia. It seemed like the ends of the earth. He was heartsick at the thought of being so far away from Linda, and though they made plans for her to visit him in the summer, the wait seemed interminable. He wrote her long letters confessing that he loved her, that he'd never met anyone like her. He nearly embarrassed himself, pouring his heart out like that, but most amazing of all was that she seemed to feel the same way. "I miss you," she wrote. "I've never missed anyone as much as you." He couldn't believe his luck, that a girl like her would even look at him twice, much less write him and call him. She could have had anyone.

By fall they decided to get married. When he was done with jump school, he bought her a ring at a little jewelry store off base and flew to Houston to give it to her, handing it over the minute he was off the plane. She cried there, in the airport, with the flight crew and other passengers watching and applauding, the public spectacle bestowing a kind of blessing on their future.

He never thought he could be so happy, he told her, and it was true— he was.

They went home to Chicago just before Thanksgiving. By then Sam was stationed at Fort Campbell, Kentucky, so Linda flew there to meet him and the two of them took the train north to visit his family. Linda had never ridden the train before, and as they rocketed through small towns and farms and sat in the club car drinking gin, she said it was romantic, the trains, the towns, the cold drink in her hand. "Like a movie," she said. "Like something right out of Hollywood." Outside, Sam could see the farm towns of southern Illinois, the water towers rusting at the seams, empty storefronts, paint peeling on the white farmhouses. There was corn stubble and black dirt and gray sky, a line of cars on the distant highway. He didn't see much romance in it, to be honest. But Linda had never been that far north before, so he decided not to spoil things by contradicting her.

She asked if he wanted another drink.

"No," he said. "Thank you, though."

He didn't feel much like celebrating. In his grip were the letters she'd sent him. Toothbrush, razor. And his underwear, socks, and T-shirts, which had gone to the laundry white and come back dyed green, olive green, camouflage green, because that was how the army gave out its orders: subtle and smug, like an inside joke.

You think something is funny? Come on over here, Private, and tell me what's so goddamn funny now.

He had barely slept the last week; his eyes were burning. Ten days' leave. In ten days he would be back on the train to Fort Campbell, then a transport to Bien Hoa a week after that. Ma was up to a thousand, had convinced herself that he wasn't going, that he wasn't actually going to Vietnam. "You'll be home for Christmas this year," she said. "I know it."

> *Machine-gun shells,*
> *Shotgun shells,*
> *Vietcong and grass,*
> *Take your Merry Christmas*
> *And shove it up your ass!*

He hadn't been home in nearly a year. How much had changed since then, he didn't know, but he felt a familiar anticipation at the thought of sleeping in his own bed, in his own house. At the thought of introducing Linda to his parents, to Charley, even to Caroline. He had not thought of Caroline much since he'd met Linda, hadn't regretted the way things had turned out. His own happiness was so large that it could extend to her as well. If she made Charley happy, if the two of them had found something that worked for them, then he was glad for her and for his brother. He'd never pictured Charley as the one-woman type, but anyone could change. He squeezed Linda tightly around her waist and ordered another drink.

The bartender was watching him. It was the uniform. Olive green, like his skivvies, a camouflage color, but away from the army it had the opposite effect, drawing eyes to him from everywhere.

They were north of Kankakee when Sam saw a man by the tracks. It was quick, just a glimpse, the man not much taller than the dead prairie weeds he stood in, dressed in the kind of green jumper farmers wore, with thick red lips and red, broken-veined cheeks. He spread his hands at his sides, as if in surrender. His lips moved so slowly that Sam could almost make out the words, and then the wind picked the cap up off his head and sent it into the air. It took only a second and they were past, and the man vanished from his sight.

When he was a kid, he had been fascinated by the men who followed the railroad tracks. Sometimes they came to the house in Chicago to ask for something to eat. The house was so close to the Soo Line that passing trains would rattle the pictures on the walls, the windows in their frames. The morning three-twenty came regularly enough that when Sam went away into the army, he had always woken about that time, expecting to hear the sound of the train. Men followed the tracks out of the city and often came to his mother's front door, knocking politely to ask for a little bite to eat, ma'am, please, anything you can spare. Sometimes they were white men with tight, thin mouths who wouldn't speak a word other than "please" or "thank you." Sometimes they were black men with rows of perfectly straight white teeth and thick accents who said they'd come up from Mississippi or Alabama looking for work, but they'd had enough of Chicago and were trying to get home. Sam and his brother would hang back and watch them until Ma told them to quit staring, it wasn't polite. Pop didn't like that she fed the men who came to the door when he wasn't there. He forbade her from letting them in; Ma complied by asking them to eat on the porch. She never turned them away. She gave them meat sandwiches or egg salad or leftover roast and told Sam and Charley that being poor didn't make them bad people. She swore them to secrecy: "Don't tell your father."

Sam was both afraid of those men, because Pop was, and filled with pity for them, and he was proud of Ma for not turning away someone who needed food. He knew the look on their faces, the same look he'd seen on the man by the tracks. It was desperation. He had been shouting at the train, the wind, at all mute, unfeeling things.

"Do you think they'll like me?" Linda asked, and Sam had to ask whom she was talking about.

"Your parents."

"Of course they will," he said. "They'll love you. How could they not?"

She ordered another drink. "I hope so," she said. Sam leaned his head against the window and felt the train carrying him forward, carrying him home.

Pop was there to meet them at the platform when they arrived. The underground tunnels of Union Station made Sam think of being buried alive—the subterranean smell, the rats that scuttled away when anyone approached—but there was still a sense of arrival, of a voyage that at long last had reached some sort of conclusion. Sam saw Pop wave when they stepped off with the bags, his missing fingers evident even from a distance. He offered his hand for Sam to shake. That was something new, shaking hands with his father.

"You've got to be Linda," Pop said, embracing her and kissing her awkwardly on the cheek. Pop didn't look much different, except that his hair was longer than it had been the previous winter and he had gained a little weight. He carried Linda's bags through the cavernous hall of Union Station and out to the car, parked several blocks away. One of Pop's foibles was that he refused to pay to park anywhere in the city of Chicago and would drive around for half an hour looking for a free space. On the ride home, with the three of them sitting together in the front seat, he asked Linda about herself and her studies. He laughed at her jokes, which were all at Sam's expense, and again Sam had the feeling of being the straight man in someone else's comedy show. At home Linda went in first while Pop helped Sam carry the bags. "She's a terrific girl," Pop said. "I can see why you like her."

When they came inside she was talking to Ma, who was standing in the front room in her best clothes and her beauty parlor hair, and although they were smiling and talking easily, Sam felt a strain, a current underneath the pleasantries revealing how much effort his mother was making for Linda's sake. The house had been scrubbed clean, and there were fresh flowers in a cut-glass vase near the door. His mother never had flowers in the house that he remembered. As he took Linda's bags to the bedroom, he thought how awkward it must be for his mother, who thought as much of Caroline as any mother could have, to welcome Linda as if nothing had ever happened.

In the bedroom he and Charley used to share, he put her suitcase on the nearest bed. Linda would be sleeping there alone. Sam would be bunking in the TV room on the old sofa, and Charley would be spending the night on the floor, because their grandfather still had the sofa in the front room. At Linda's parents' house, when he had visited in the spring, Sam had his own room with its own bath. Here Linda would have to share one small bathroom with five other people.

When Sam came back out, Charley was offering her a beer, something she never drank. Sam said he would run to the A&P for some gin instead, but she said no, she would be glad for a beer. "It's so warm here," she said, fanning herself a little with one hand. "I would have thought up north would be colder." Her soft Texas twang seemed incongruous in his mother's living room, amid his mother's cheap but well-kept furniture. He wished he could have rented a hotel for the two of them, but that would have been unthinkable. Out of the question.

When Charley returned from the kitchen with her beer, Linda said how sorry she was to be kicking him out of his room during her visit. "Oh, that's all right," Charley said with an expansive wave. "This way Sammy can keep me company tonight."

"Do you usually need company at night?" She was flirting. Sam felt a pang in his guts, even though he knew it was just her way. She was always flirting with someone. Sam had wanted Charley to like her—had, if he were being honest with himself, wanted his brother to admire the hell out of her—but maybe not this much.

Charley said, "It never hurts." His hair was so long, it was in his eyes. He pushed it back and winked at Sam, as if they were in together on some kind of joke.

The beer he had brought her was in a can. Sam offered to get her a glass from the kitchen, though no one else ever used one.

"No." She waved him off. "It's all right." She popped the top and took a polite sip.

They had supper in the kitchen, extra chairs crammed in, the heat and dampness making the beer cans sweat on the old Formica table. Charley wasn't eating. He drank a beer like everyone else, but his plate was empty.

"Not hungry?" Linda asked.

Charley explained he was having dinner with Caroline, who didn't like to eat alone now that her mother was in the hospital. He waited long enough to be polite, then stood up and went out, saying he would see them all in the morning.

"I didn't realize your brother was such a good-looking boy," Linda said. "He could be in the movies."

"I've always thought so," said Ma. She got up to clear the table.

"What he needs is a job," Gramp said. "He's twenty years old and he's never had to work."

Linda asked Pop about work, where he grew up, the unit he'd served with during the war. Caroline would have been helping Ma with the dishes, but Linda sat where she was, touching Pop's arm and smiling and listening to his stories. Pop clearly enjoyed it. Sam thought she might have been a little tipsy after all that gin she'd drunk on the train, the way she'd looked at his brother. *He could be in the movies.*

His first day at boot, the sergeant had called the enemy "Charlie" and described in various ways what that other Charlie would do to him when he got to Vietnam, because Sam was clearly so soft and useless that he wouldn't last a week in-country. At jump school, his first time, out the plane with the mottled earth below him, the static lines trailing like umbilical cords, he closed his eyes and pictured his brother laughing at him. It was a strange thought, brief and exhilarating, full of a pure kind of malice. And then his chute opened and yanked him upward, and he watched the earth drift toward him. He thought about landing the way he'd been taught, soft on the knees. *Don't you mess up your knees, Private, because out in the bush no one's going to carry you.* Only later did he wonder where it had come from, that image of his brother laughing.

When the dishes were dried, Ma took another beer out of the fridge for herself and offered a second one to Linda, though the first one, still full, was sitting on the table in front of her. Linda said no, thank you, that she had a bit of a headache and she thought she would go to bed early. Sam followed her back to the room, where the twin beds were made up with their familiar blue spreads. Ma had laid out a set of brand-new towels on Charley's bed; she must have bought them especially for Linda's visit. A crucifix hung over the light switch next to the door, a holdover from Ma's Catholic upbringing, heavy polished wood and brass. Linda, whose parents were Methodist, said it was the most gruesome thing she'd ever seen. "I won't be able to sleep with that there," she said.

"Take it down, then."

"I don't want to offend your mother."

"Then I'll take it down." He unhooked the crucifix from the wall and put it in the top drawer of the dresser. "Better?"

"Thank you." She unbuttoned her top button slowly and raised an eyebrow at him. "You could stay. There's a whole extra bed. Seems a shame that it should be empty like that."

"Right. Ma wouldn't have too much of a bird."

She sighed. "I suppose you're right."

Sam kissed her and went out. "Sleep well," he said, and closed the door behind him.

When he went back into the kitchen, Ma was pouring Linda's beer down the sink. "She's a lovely girl. Very beautiful," Ma said. "She seems to have had a lot of advantages." A reproof.

"I suppose that's true. But she works hard in school. She doesn't think the world should be handed to her. She has an academic scholarship at Rice."

"That's good. I'm glad to hear that." Ma threw away the empty can and flicked off the light. "Good night, then, Sammy," she said. In the darkened kitchen, he could no longer see her. "I'm so glad you're home."

Sam wasn't asleep, but when he heard his mother open the door and look inside, he pretended he was. Charley was snoring on the floor, had been most of the night, and sunlight had been coming in the window for at least an hour. Sam didn't want to get up yet. It was close in the TV room, stale, but he kept the pillow over his head against the light, his breathing steady and shallow. The sheets had twisted around his legs and waist like a harness, like something that would hold him up if he fell. She padded in and sat at the end of the sofa, the springs barely compressing underneath her. He didn't move. He wanted her to feel that she was disturbing him, to feel guilty that she woke him too soon.

He could hear her breathing. She touched him on the leg, just there, above the ankle, light as a fly. She touched him again at the back of the knee, again at the elbow, as if taking his measurements to put away for some future use. The sofa shook a little. He kept himself still but felt his resolve stiffen in protest. He wished she would stop, just stop. He wasn't sure what she was after that morning, but he wasn't ready to comply just yet. She waited a minute, then went out again.

He wanted to be asleep. He knew he should sleep, that it would make him feel better. His eyes felt thumbed into their sockets.

He heard his grandfather say something low in the other room, Linda's voice answering. The old man chuckled once. A waft of pipe tobacco. Ma's voice: "Put that match out. You're going to burn the place down one of these days, and then what will happen to you?"

Sam put on some pants and went into the kitchen, where Linda was still laughing at something Gramp had said.

"Morning," Gramp said, and Linda stood up and kissed Sam good morning. Ma was frowning into her oatmeal, but no one else seemed to notice. Making friends with his grandfather would not win Linda any points around here, but she didn't know that yet.

The old man had a teasing streak his mother had never learned to appreciate. She thought he was taking advantage of all of them, herself especially. She had been furious the day he had showed up at their doorstep, only two years after they'd moved to the States. His grandparents hadn't lived together for years by then; Gran had moved in with Uncle Ed and Aunt Bella, and Gramp had been staying by himself on the farm.

Pop was at work that afternoon when Sam heard a car door bang at the curb.

Ma had put her hands on her hips and set her jaw when she saw his old green truck, the bag in his hand. "What do you think you're doing with that?" She didn't open the screen door.

"Staying with you," he said. "Can't a father visit his own daughter?"

Ma didn't say anything, but Sam and Charley were already excited. They got to see their grandfather so rarely. He teased and played with them, let them smoke his pipe when Ma wasn't looking. But Ma wouldn't let him in the house. She said she wanted to talk to Pop. She said there was no room for him, that the boys had the one bedroom and she and Walt had the other, and that was that as far as space went, there was nowhere for him to sleep.

"I can sleep on the chesterfield," he said. "I'm just one old man, won't take up that much space."

"Oh, I know what kind of space you take up."

In the end she stepped back and let him in. "It could be just for a day or two," she muttered, "before he'll tire of it and go home."

But when Pop got home from work, he was livid. He wanted Jack out of the house. Wanted him out *now*. He sent the boys to their room, but they could still hear every word. "You've got no right. You didn't even call first. Just showed up here with your bags and pushed your way in, because you knew Dottie couldn't say no. But this is my house, and I won't have it."

Gramp smiled. "I could always sleep in the truck. I could go park out on the street and live there."

Ma said, "Oh, my God."

"I don't care," said Pop. "I don't care where you live, as long as it's not here."

"I could go stay with Ed and Bell."

"Don't do that," Ma said. "You can't do that to Mother. It's not fair."

"You want to talk about fair, I just want to have a visit with my grandsons."

"You do not, and you know it," Pop said. "You don't have me fooled one minute."

"Don't raise your voice at me. I'm not one of your kids."

"You're sure acting like you are."

"I just want to be in the bosom of my family," said Jack. "You all don't come home as much as you should. So if I want to see my grandsons, I have to come here."

"Just go home," Ma said. "Go back to the farm, and we'll call you. We'll come visit soon, I promise."

"I can't," he said.

"Why not?" Pop demanded. "Why the hell not?"

"I don't have the farm anymore. No point, with you two out here and Jean living with Ed and Bella, and Jimmy with his own place. Don't need all that anymore. I've been living over the Livermores' barn since June."

"Oh, my God," Ma said. "You haven't."

"Cheaper there," said the old man. "I work for my wages, and I don't have to pay for anything except food and clothes. Sold all the furniture, dishes, everything."

"Everything?" Ma asked.

"You're kidding," said Pop.

"Can't stay in that shack all winter, so here I am."

Pop sighed, sat down in his chair. "Why didn't you stay with Jimmy?" he asked. "He would have put you up."

"I'll go," the old man said, standing up, looking angry now. "I'm sure Bella and Ed will do the trick."

Ma slumped in her chair and said, "No. You can stay here for now. You'll have to sleep on the chesterfield."

"Fine as a May day." The old man lit his pipe.

After supper, before the dark outside deepened and closed up, before he bunked down for that first night, Gramp asked Ma for a coffee can, asked Pop where he kept his shovel. He went out to the middle of the gravel drive and started digging. Sam stood in the doorway, in the last of the light, and watched him. His mother came up and watched, too, from behind the screen door. His grandfather's wiry bird-wing arms were strong from years of farmwork, digging cucumbers, chopping wood. After a couple of minutes, he had created a deep hole. He reached into his pocket, took out a big wad of dollar bills, and put them in the coffee can. Sam was shocked to see it; he had never seen so much money, not all at once, not ever. Gramp put the coffee can in the hole, started up the truck, and parked with a front tire over the hole. Then he came back inside. "Can't be too careful," he said. He hid the keys somewhere in the house, someplace only he knew about.

The truck stayed parked there all winter. In the spring, when he left again to go back to the Livermores' farm as the hired man, he took the coffee can but left the hole. Pop filled it in, smoothed the dirt over. "Someone could break a leg," he said.

In the fall, Gramp came back to stay. No one seemed surprised to see him when he arrived with his clothes in two black plastic garbage bags. He sold the old green truck and took up residence in the front room after that, on Dottie's good sofa. Pop refused to build an extra room on the house for him. Don't want him to get too comfortable, Pop said, but it didn't matter—the old man wasn't going anywhere.

There in the kitchen, Sam could hear his grandfather teasing Linda about her accent. "Where's that from, girlie?" he asked. "That voice of yours?"

"Texas," Linda said. "Where's yours from?"

"Aberdeen."

"There's an Aberdeen in Texas," she said. She raised one eyebrow at him, the same look that had made Sam's knees weak that day on the beach. "You sure we aren't related?"

"I don't think so," Gramp said. "Not enough so we couldn't get married, if we wanted."

Ma was standing at the counter, stuffing the turkey. She pulled out the gizzards and dropped them with a *plop* on the counter. "Lord help us," she breathed, and put the turkey in the oven.

The only true war story, Sam's father always told him, is one in which you are not the hero. It is never about what happened, but about the shock of finding yourself alive on the other side of it. It could be funny or it could be dead serious, but if somebody tries to tell you how he blew away the enemy, if the guy shows off his scars and medals, then what he's telling you isn't true.

A story his father told him: how once, coming down through the clouds at fifteen thousand feet and a thousand miles from any kind of land, they came upon a German weather reconnaissance plane, so close, his father said, I could see the color of the pilot's eyes. He looked at us, and we looked at him, and we waved at each other and turned in our different directions, went home.

Sam was young then and didn't understand. "Why didn't you shoot him down, Pop?"

"We were scared. We wanted to go home. Guess he did, too."

His father could not tolerate men who played the hero. Blowhards, attention seekers. Historical revisionists. For instance: Otto Koehler, from next door, telling Sam that if he wasn't ready to kill, he'd never make it over there. Vietnam. These kids, they go over and they're not ready to kill, Otto said, they don't really want to be there, these bleeding-heart hand wringers, they want to play nicey-nice with the natives, and that's when the trouble starts.

That's what he called it—trouble.

"Really?" Sam said, looking away. "How so?"

Otto and his wife had come for Thanksgiving dinner. It was hot inside the house, close and crowded, and even though someone propped open the front door and let in the late fall air, all the windows had steamed. Charley was outside getting a football game going with Otto's two school-age boys, spattering his white pants with mud. Caroline was in the kitchen helping his mother. He had said hello to Caroline when she came in that morning, kissed her cheek, and introduced her to Linda. She'd been polite, even warm, saying she was happy to see him, that she hoped they'd had a good trip. Then she'd disappeared into the kitchen with Ma and Linda. He could hear their voices coming in through the door, rising and falling. He wished he knew what it was they were saying to each other.

Over dinner, Otto cornered Sam. The way he spoke was authoritative—"You'd better be ready to kill or be killed when you get over there"—as if he were initiating Sam into some kind of club. Tall and thick as a chimney, cornering Sam in the living room, he ate sauced meatballs off a plate with his fingers. His breath was heavy with oregano and garlic, and the thick layer of back fat rounding his shoulders and fanning out behind his armpits gave him a hunched, hibernating look. He spent several minutes explaining how he took an eight-man position on Iwo Jima all by himself because a sniper had taken out his entire unit.

"I have the scar to prove it. Here, hold this."

"That's all right."

"No, no, here. You see this?"

There was a small half-moon in the meat of Otto's hairy shin, a pale raised mark like a gouge made with a fingernail. "A bullet right here. Nearly took my leg off. Doctors said I was lucky to still be walking."

Otto's shirt was sticking to his back where he was sweating, a bright red Hawaiian print, loud with leaves and pink and yellow flowers. Sam saw Caroline through the kitchen door. She was at the table, eating off a damp paper plate, a can of beer near her elbow. She picked up a turkey wing and tore off its yellow skin. The bones and her fingers glistened with fat, and she pressed the pad off her thumb against her teeth to suck off the grease.

Otto continued, "Now the thing that happens when they start shooting is this . . ."

Sam waited while he finished chewing.

Pop saved him, waved him over. Sam excused himself and handed Otto back his plate, meatballs rolling precariously across the white paper. Pop looked grim, his mouth set in an ironic line. The ice clinked in his highball glass, which he pinched in the strong place between his thumb and forefinger. The other hand supported the glass from underneath. "Is Otto showing you his Iwo scar?"

"Yeah."

"Don't listen to that old bugger. He told me fifteen years ago he didn't get there until a week after all the fighting was over. He said he was disappointed he missed out."

"So what's the scar from, then?"

"His lawn mower whipped a pebble at him once. He needed two or three stitches. He forgets I was in the yard when it happened. Saw the whole thing." Sam wanted to laugh, but he felt sorry for Otto, an old vet trying to relive glory days that never happened. "If they'd really happened," Pop always said, "he wouldn't want to relive them."

Pop was not the kind of man to pull up his pants legs and show off his scars. He was the first to say there were men who'd seen a lot worse than he had. The bomber units lost men by the dozens. There were men who spent the war in POW camps on the continent, men who disappeared during operations and were never heard from again. He had been lucky, he said. He had lost all or part of seven fingers in the war, not in the crash that took the lives of his crew mates, but to frostbite. When he returned to Ontario, he had retrained his hands slowly, painfully. Ma recalled how he spent hours at the kitchen table learning to hold a knife and fork. She would come downstairs and see him late at night when he should have been asleep, balancing the handles, learning to cut his meat, to bring the spoon to his mouth, until he could eat without dropping the knife or spilling on himself. He couldn't go to college because he'd never been to high school and had trouble finding work on account of his hands. It was hard on a man used to being useful. For months after he came back from the war, Ma told Sam, she would find him in her father's barn with a screwdriver, driving screws into the doorjamb. When he was done, he pulled them out and started over. At first he dropped the tools quite a bit, but eventually he could drive a dozen screws or hammer a dozen nails without dropping anything. He pinched the handle of the hammer between his thumb and first finger, the nail tight in the other hand between the first finger and the second, and drive it in fast and true.

When Sam's grandfather Jack complained that he was splintering the boards in the barn, Pop went out to the woods and drove his nails into the trees.

Eventually, when his hands were stronger, he found work as a press operator at the local newspaper. He loaded rolls of newsprint big enough to crush a man, vats of black ink that coated his skin. It was hard, dirty work, noisy and occasionally dangerous; Pop wasn't the only one missing fingers. Before long, though, he and Ma were able to rent a place of their own in Windsor, not far from Adele, who came for coffee nearly every day, Caroline playing on the kitchen floor with Dottie's pots and pans. Sam was born early the next year, on a day of so much snow that they almost didn't make it to the hospital. Charley followed a little more than two years later, an event Sam did not remember at all. His mother told him how he kissed the pink and squalling baby when she said he must, and afterward he went to Adele and Caroline's house for a few days because Ma needed her sleep.

During the week Pop worked at the newspaper, but he spent his weekends building a house in town on a small lot he bought with his veteran's stipend. He framed up the walls and roof with help from his brothers-in-law but did most of the other work himself, putting up siding and framing windows, installing insulation and Sheetrock, nailing asphalt shingles to the roof. On nice days, Ma took Sam and Charley out to the lot to play while Pop worked on the house. Sam liked to run through the unfinished house and hear his footsteps ring on the plywood floors, echoing in the empty rooms. He played by himself most of the time because Charley was too little then, but sometimes Caroline was there, and they made up elaborate games that usually involved a great deal of running and shouting and Ma asking them to be quiet, for God's sake, they were giving her gray hairs.

One day a man stopped by to watch Pop working on the house, standing in the yard with his hands in his pockets and staring up at the roof. Pop was nailing shingles, overlapping them in a neat pattern. He worked swiftly and with purpose and didn't notice the man there at first.

"Nice job you're doing there," the man said. "Finished all this by yourself?"

"More affordable that way."

"True," the man said. He had a proposition. He was visiting from the States and had been watching Pop work on the house. He owned a construction business in Chicago and was always in need of good people. Americans had an insatiable appetite for new houses in those days after the war. There was more work to go around than people to handle it. If Pop was willing to come to Chicago, the man would give him a job.

That night Pop took the family out to celebrate, a surprise, not telling them where they were going or why. They went to a restaurant and ordered steaks. Pop picked up Ma's hand across the table and kissed it and promised her a diamond ring, and she blushed. "Don't be ridiculous," she said, but she was laughing.

So Pop sold the half-finished house to Jimmy and took the family across the border at the end of that summer. They were sorry to leave the family; Sam's grandmother cried the morning they left, and Aunt Bella promised to visit soon. Adele and Caroline stayed behind at first because Adele was still caring for her elderly mother-in-law, but three years later, when the old woman died, she and Caroline moved, too, to a two-flat down the street from the Dunmores' house in Chicago.

Pop was happy in the States. He came home after dark exhausted and smelling of pine boards, bits of sawdust in his hair and on his clothes, the back of his neck sunburned and raw, but he always had good, steady work—evidence, he said, that they had made the right decision in coming to Chicago. The man who gave Pop the job, Sean Delaney, turned out to have one of the largest and most successful construction companies in the city. He was rich and well connected—he even knew the mayor. Working for Sean Delaney, Pop built whole neighborhoods, blocks rising month by month, here the spine of a staircase, here the skeleton walls. He nailed down drywall, carried loads of roofing shingles on his shoulders. Sam had never seen his father drop anything, not a wrench, a fork, a glass, a pen. Pop could do anything other men could do. More even, as if the strength in his father's hands had been somehow increased by the loss of the fingers.

Pop didn't speak often of the crash and the things that happened to him there. He didn't have to, because his sons were already in awe of him, already mesmerized, from their earliest days, from the time they were old enough to know he was different, by the spaces at the ends of his hands where the rest of his fingers should have been.

In the living room, Otto was coming toward them. He had a new paper plate laden with yellow cake, fissured white frosting. "Yes," he said, as if there had been no interruption, "as long as you're willing to kill or be killed, you'll come out all right." A long silence. He forked a bit of cake into his mouth and then turned to Walt for affirmation. "Isn't that right?"

"Absolutely," Pop said, but only Sam caught the inflection.

The thing he did not tell Pop was that he finally understood, at least a little bit, why a man like Otto Koehler would pull up the leg of his trousers and show off the scar on his shin as if it meant something.

Pop filled two highball glasses, dropped in some cubes of ice, handed the fresh one to Sam, and kept the other for himself. Gin and something else Sam didn't see. The first time Pop had ever poured him a drink. He clinked his glass into Sam's and said, "Praise the Lord and pass the ammunition." He took two long drinks, his Adam's apple bobbing red in the center of his throat, and set it down again. Sam felt something pass between them that he couldn't name, an understanding that was different from that between a father and son. He thought Pop might do something odd, like put a hand on his shoulder, but that had never been his way, and it would have embarrassed both of them to start now. Instead he kneaded the tips of his shortened fingers with the palm of the other hand, working the flesh, keeping it alive.

It was hot in the kitchen, and crowded. The women had congregated to talk privately, the way they always did at these parties, as if the living room where the men gathered were unbearable to them. The table was piled with food: plates of meat and potato pierogi, a cherry pie, a large bag of salted cashews, a dish of pickle slices rolled in cream cheese and stabbed through with toothpicks. They were the kind of random offerings brought to a house in mourning, where someone had died. His mother would freeze most of it and serve it for lunches for the next few weeks, from the look of it. The cashews would be gone in a day or two, once Pop realized they were there. When Sam went into the kitchen, Linda, his mother, and Annie Koehler drifted out again, as if they'd been discussing him and wanted to continue their discussion in private. That left Caroline at the sink washing up, a solitary endeavor and her regular contribution to whatever party his mother was giving, whether it was Thanksgiving dinner or the Fourth of July. She looked up briefly when Sam came in.

"Hi, Sammy," she said. She held out her hand for the glass Sam was holding, and though he wasn't quite finished with his drink yet, he gave it to her. She slipped it into the gray dishwater. "You've lost weight," she said, looking at him sideways. "You look good. Sort of grown up all of a sudden."

She was being polite. They would be polite together, go back to their old familiar friendship, roles they'd known since childhood. He found it comforting, even if it wasn't entirely honest. "That's the army for you," he said. "They really work you to the bone."

"I don't know how you can do that. Jump out of airplanes. I'd be scared to death."

"You get used to it."

"Hmm. I wouldn't think." She set the glass to the side to dry and wiped her hands on a towel. She touched her hair, which was longer than he remembered, loose and straight down her back. She reminded him suddenly of those hippie girls, the ones he'd seen in train stations and bus depots, the ones whose eyes went cold when they saw his uniform. When she pushed her hair back over her shoulder, he could see for a second her mismatched lips and remember the feel of them in his mouth. He felt a momentary stab of grief, not over Caroline herself, but over the emotion she had once evoked in him, all that fine suffering.

She asked him about Vietnam, when he was supposed to be leaving. "A couple of weeks," he said. "The whole division is shipping over early next month."

"Will you have to jump out of planes when you get there?"

"I don't know," he said truthfully enough. "I guess I don't really know what to expect when I get there."

"I hate airplanes. I wish they'd never been invented." It was something he'd heard her say, from time to time, ever since he'd known her. It made her sound like her mother, which had always irritated him. Adele was forever making fatal pronouncements, like she hated airplanes, or winter, or men who wore cologne. She had a tendency to exaggerate and inflate, though he supposed that was natural in someone as brittle as Adele Clark.

He asked how her mother was doing in the hospital. "I was hoping to get to see her while I'm home."

Caroline looked tense. Sam was suddenly sorry he'd brought it up. "She's all right. She doesn't really enjoy having visitors, though. I go once a week, but she doesn't want anyone else to see her there. I think it makes it more real for her if she has company."

"Is the treatment helping at all?"

"I think so. She seems a little better, at least."

"You must miss her."

"I do." Caroline started drying the dishes one by one. She twisted the dishtowel inside the highball glasses, but a few drops of water clung stubbornly to the bottom. "It's your mother I'm worried about, though."

"Ma? Why would you say that?"

"She's been going to church a lot. The Catholic church. I asked her about it. She's praying to the Virgin to stop the war."

"You're kidding."

"She goes every morning to light a candle. I've seen her there some-times."

Sam tried to imagine his mother in church, lighting candles, worrying beads in her hand. She had never been overly religious and had stopped going to the Catholic church when she married his father, though at times a random crucifix would pop up on the walls, an Infant of Prague statue. *There will be a magic show tonight at 1800. You will show the proper respect. Jesus may have died for your sins, but he won't be able to help you here.*

"Your father's worried about her. He'd never tell you, of course. I'm only mentioning it because I know they won't."

"I didn't think it had gotten this bad. She really *believes* this?"

"Go easy on her, Sammy. She's scared for you." She was putting away stacks of clean plates. They rattled together like chattering teeth. "We all are," she said quietly.

"Yes," he said. "I know that." At the sound of his name in her mouth, he felt another tremor of regret, just a shiver. *Sammy.*

But then Linda was coming around the corner with a tall stack of plates in her hand about to tip over, and Sam took them from her.

"Thanks," Linda said. "That was a close one."

Sam put the plates next to the sink, and Caroline started washing them. He thought of the day he met Linda on the beach, the white lines on her shoulders where the sun had not browned her, how he asked if he could take her to dinner that night. *I don't know. Can you?* He had thought, I don't deserve this, I really don't. From that minute on, she'd been his whole world. From that minute on, he'd hardly thought of anything else at all.

EIGHT

There was the time the basement flooded. It was in the fall of 1954, the year they moved to the States, when Caroline was ten. In those days, the apartment in Chicago still had the feel of something temporary, like a place you went on vacation but could always leave when you tired of strangeness and wanted to go home. That week it rained for eight days in a row, the windows slick and damp even on the inside from condensation and cold. When Caroline walked home from school in the afternoons, she had to wade through the flood that, in places, sloshed over the tops of her shoes and splashed her legs under her blue plaid school uniform. The rain made Caroline cold down to her bones, but she had to strip off her muddy shoes and socks before her mother would let her in the house. "Please, Caroline," her mother said with a sigh. "I just cleaned the floor."

It rained so much that the roof at school threatened to collapse and the principal, a hard-faced old Benedictine nun, sent everyone home until it was fixed. Trapped inside by the rain and cold, Caroline and her mother fought over dinner, over schoolwork, over housework, over the fact that Adele made Caroline go to the Catholic girls' school instead of the public school with Sam and Charley. They fought at the slightest provocation, each lashing out at the other for any slight. One time Caroline left a cereal bowl with a little milk in the bottom sitting in the kitchen sink. "With all I have to do, and you can't even help out this little bit," her mother said. "All I do is work and work and work and work, and you never help me. Why couldn't I have had a *good* daughter?" She went crying into the bedroom.

Caroline followed after. "Mama?" she said.

"I wish I were dead," she sobbed. "I wish you had never been born."

Caroline went to the sink and washed out the bowl and put it away, didn't dare turn on the radio set in the living room, did her homework quietly, and went to bed with the light coming in from under her mother's door.

In the morning everything was fine, everything was the same. Her mother in her kerchief and robe, saying, "Do you want some cereal this morning?"

And she said, "Yes, thank you." Oh so good, look how good I am, Mother. Before breakfast was over, they were not speaking again.

After their breakfast Caroline walked over to Sam and Charley's, where Dottie let her listen to soap operas on the radio and made her a little hot chocolate with some kind of peppermint liqueur in it. The hot peppermint in the liquor burned going down and warmed Caroline's fingers and toes, made them feel liquid, as if she were melting. "Don't tell your mother," Dottie said. The two boys came home from school, jealously teasing Caroline because she got to stay home all day, and disappeared into the alley with their friends and private games. They thought their mother's soap operas were junk, but Caroline thought the programs were fascinating. The voices of the men and women on the radio had a hint of an accent, rich and almost foreign sounding, like Audrey Hepburn and Gregory Peck in *Roman Holiday*, which she'd seen three times already. She asked Dottie who the characters were, and what problems they were having, who was married to whom, and Dottie answered all of it as if no one had ever asked her about anything so important before, her face flushed and her hands as animated as a puppeteer's. So-and-so is married to what's-her-face, but what's-her-face is pregnant by Mr. High-and-Mighty. It was so, so interesting. It was so grown up.

When she went home her mother didn't ask where she'd been or what she'd been doing. She seemed to know it all already, and her mother's all-knowingness made Caroline feel very small and young, trapped. She wanted to smash everything in sight, scream the house down.

The fifth day they had a particularly bad fight in the morning. A girl from school had called unexpectedly and included Caroline in her plans to go to a movie, a girl she barely knew but whose company suddenly seemed not only pleasant and natural, but essential, necessary as air. Caroline asked if she could meet the girl at the theater, but her mother thought she should stay in that day, it was raining and cold. "Why do you always need to go out? Young girls shouldn't be out so much. They shouldn't spend so much time away from home."

You don't want me to have any friends. You don't want me to be happy.

She put on her coat and went out, but she was afraid of defying her mother outright, so instead of meeting the girl at the movie, she walked to Dottie's in the rain. Again they listened to stories on the radio while the insides of the windows steamed. She complained to Dottie, though afterward she felt as though she'd betrayed her mother. She listed her hurts one by one: how she couldn't have friends over to the house because her mother was always so tired; she couldn't wear sandals or dresses without sleeves, because her mother said only loose women wore such things. How her mother was nervous about broken things and loud noises, how she flew into a fury if the house wasn't just so. "It isn't fair," she said.

Dottie listened to everything and rubbed Caroline's hands between her own thin ones and said she shouldn't be so hard on her mother, that her mother had had a terrible time of it. "It's an awful thing, being alone," Dottie said. "It makes you do and say things you would never do otherwise."

It was strange to hear Dottie talk about her mother like this. She felt outside herself, as if she had shed an old skin and climbed out wriggling and new, larger than before.

That day she went home reluctantly, dawdled in the alley, stopping to check out pieces of broken toys or the masses of worms that writhed on the pavement because the ground was saturated by too much rain. She wanted to put off going home as long as possible. The flat was too embarrassing, too old, too ugly. The white paint was peeling around the kitchen windows, and the wooden steps that faced the alley were sloped, sliding away from the house, as if they couldn't bear to touch it. In the yard, patches of mud showed through the grass. The metal poles from which the laundry line hung were rusting, tipping over. She wished she could live at Dottie's, where there was a fern basket hanging next to the front door and rosebushes climbing a trellis along one wall. Once, in front of a couple of girls at school, she had even pretended that she really lived at

Dottie's, unlocking Dottie's front door with her own key, waiting inside until the girls were gone to slip out down the alley to her own house.

Caroline went up the steps and opened the door. Inside, her mother was making dinner. The starchy smell of boiled potatoes, the thick brown smell of the meat. "Have a good day? Did you have fun?" she asked. Her tone was light and airy, almost breathless. "Maybe tomorrow, if this rain ever stops, we can go down to the lake and rent a boat for the afternoon, get out a little. A bit of fresh air. Wouldn't that be nice, Car?" she said.

There was a plea in her mother's voice. It occurred to Caroline that she was jealous, that her mother envied the time Caroline spent with Dottie, and this business with the boats was an offering, a net she was throwing out to gather her daughter back in. It seemed another grown-up thrill, this discovery of her mother's weakness, as if she'd caught her out of costume. The rest of that night they were scrupulously polite and considerate, each obeying the terms of the tentative cease-fire. "I would love a day at the lake, Mother, that sounds nice. Thank you."

"You're welcome."

The rain did not let up.

That night the sump pump failed and let the water into the basement, a slow, steady rising while they ate their dinner and slept and got up again. When she woke the apartment was cold and dark, silent the way places are when the hum of electricity is off, the furnace and refrigerator dead. Her ears were ringing: That's what had woken her. Her bedroom seemed cold. She dressed in the gray light and ate dry cornflakes because the milk had turned. Her mother came out later in her robe and babushka, her thin silvery hair poking from underneath the kerchief. "What happened?" she asked.

"Everything's off." Caroline ran her tongue over the roof of her mouth, which was sore and scratched from eating the cereal dry. Her mother looked out the window at the neighbors', where the yellow light in the kitchen was bright and steady.

Her mother went down to the basement to check on the fuse box. The basement was the reason they had rented the apartment, offering storage for the things they'd brought from Ontario. Caroline didn't like the basement, was afraid to turn on the lights to go down the steps, afraid she would disturb whatever things lived down there. The roller washing machine sat in one corner, and there were wires strung across the ceiling from which Mother or Mrs. Hartman would hang the laundry to dry in wet or cold weather. Unpacked boxes left from the move were piled on the floor and in the corners. Anything that didn't have a place to be put away in the upstairs world, such as old photos, winter clothes, Caroline's old toys, stayed in the basement. The basement had two doors—one from the kitchen and one from the backyard, which Mrs. Hartman used—but it had only one small window that let in almost no light, so that when Caroline was forced to go down there to fetch the clean laundry, she had a sense of being buried alive. She wouldn't stay one minute longer than she had to. She'd run up the steps two by two.

Her mother's footsteps were so quiet that it was almost as if she weren't there, as if she were afraid of disturbing someone. The footsteps stopped. She called for Caroline to come help her, a note of fear in her voice.

Her mother was at the bottom of the stairwell, shy of the last step, looking up at her. A little weak daylight from the kitchen window filtered down the steps, catching the top of her mother's blue kerchief and the shine in her eyes, but beyond that the basement was completely black. The air was muffled, sharp and cold, and when the dark perfume of still water reached Caroline's nose, it made her itch.

"Oh," said her mother, and her voice sounded strangled, a noise that made Caroline shiver. It was as if her mother knew there were forces against which no one could muster. For a minute she felt as if her mother might throw herself into the water. "Oh, no."

The water had come up into the cardboard boxes and flooded their things. They were all drowned, all ruined. The boxes had melted around their bottoms, and an old upholstered chair that had once belonged to her father was immersed past its skirts. The washing machine stood white and solid in the corner, an obstacle against which a plastic giraffe floated like an escapee from Noah's Ark. A box holding Christmas decorations had split and spilled its contents into the water, a line of silver garland trailing like a sea anemone, a tentacle waving in an unseen current.

Her mother pulled at her arms. She made small hurt noises in her throat and leaned forward over the water, too far. Caroline came down the steps and took a fistful of her bathrobe.

"Everything's ruined," her mother said.

Her mother took a step down. The cold water covered the last step and her feet went in. The gray paint on the wooden tread had softened, turned slick, and Caroline felt her mother's footing start to give, so she sat back on the stairs and held on to the bathrobe, its fabric stretching between them. Her mother wavered but kept her footing. She didn't seem to notice that her daughter was the one holding her up. "Don't," Caroline whispered. "Don't go."

"How could this have *happened*?"

For a moment Caroline was sure her mother would fall or throw herself in the water, but then she leaned back again and seemed to regain her balance. Caroline did not let go of the robe until she was sure.

Sharply, her mother said, "The photographs."

She took the last step down, and the water came halfway up her shin, the bottom of her bathrobe trailing out behind her in the water. She *slish-slished* her way from the stairs to a box, groped it underwater, moaned, "Oh, no. No, no, no." The label on the side said "*Photos*" in her mother's looping script. Caroline had learned cursive by practicing that slippery *p*, that fearful *o*, for hours at the kitchen table. She could never figure out why her letters weren't as graceful as her mother's. The thick line of the pencil made Caroline's own handwriting look carved in, gouged.

Her mother tried picking it up, but the bottom gave way, and all the pictures poured out and spread across the surface of the water, floating there, and for a terrible few seconds the two of them watched them bobbing on the surface like slivers of ice on a lake. Then they rushed into the flood to rescue the pictures. The water was cold and oily, and Caroline would not let herself think of what else might be floating around in it. She snatched wet photographs and pressed them to her chest, stuffed them in her pockets. Wet, all wet.

Caroline loved the pictures of her parents' wedding day. They had been married in their parish church down the street from the house in which her father had grown up, the same church where Caroline later squirmed between her mother and grandmother on Sundays. In one photo her parents emerged together from the church doors, smiling, her mother looking down at her satin-slippered feet as if she were afraid she might trip. Her mother came only to her father's shoulder, a tiny wisp of a girl. She was thin then and pink cheeked, and even in black and white her face bloomed, the contrast high. Her dark blond hair haloed her face in a mass of pin curls she'd done herself. Her father, wearing a devious grin, was reaching out to shake the hand of someone out of the frame. A white handkerchief poked out from the breast pocket of his coat, and his dark hair dipped in a dramatic wave over his brow. He was handsome and as utterly strange to her as any man on the street might be. The visible sky looked like rain.

In another, taken at her grandmother's house later that day, her mother was nowhere to be seen. Her father, jacket now discarded, shirtsleeves rolled up, stood surrounded by friends. He was laughing, his mouth wide-open to show all his strong white teeth, the shape of them the same as her own years later, round and smooth and straight except for the one place where the bottom two, right in front, overlapped a little. She never asked her mother what he was laughing at, but she imagined it was a joke he told himself, not caring if anyone else thought it was funny or not. In another, after the formal clothes were discarded and the bride and groom were dressed in their traveling suits, they stood together on her grandmother's porch. A haze hung across the photo because a light rain had started, and in the bottom corner of the photo a raindrop could be seen clinging to the camera's lens. Her mother was turned toward her father, looking up, touching his forearm with one hand. He was smiling; he looked roguish, playful. He reached without looking to pull his new bride closer to him so they could run together into the rain. He was looking right at the camera, right at *her*, and she liked to imagine he had known that, years later, she'd be holding the photo and meeting his eyes and trying to guess where, in there, was the beginning of herself.

She had spent hours in her grandmother's house laying out the photos on the floor in rows, trying to re-create the order of events—here the bride arriving at church, here the groom taking her hand, here the two of them getting in the car, driving away for a weekend at a fancy hotel in Windsor before the groom shipped out. The significance of things was always in the order they occurred: For her to be born, her parents had to meet, decide to get married, love. Without those first accidents, nothing else that happened later would mean anything at all.

In the flooded basement, Caroline and her mother splashed around trying to save the wedding pictures, Caroline's baby photos, pictures of relatives whose faces she didn't know, places she had never been, family trips to cabins in nameless woods. They didn't speak. Their hands and heads brushed together, their clothes drank in water like sponges. When her hands and pockets were full, Caroline ran to the stairs, dropped the photos she'd collected, and went back for more. The last ones were the wettest. They hung limply over her fingers like dead fish. Her mother's hands moved swiftly, grabbing at everything.

They took the photos upstairs and spread them out on the kitchen table, the counters, the floor. Many had already started to dry and stuck together so completely that they could not be separated. Her baby photo in the yard with her mother had adhered to the back of a picture of a house she didn't recognize; the house was saved, but she was not. The dog her mother had been given as a child after her own mother had died lost its tail when Caroline touched it. The photos of her parents' wedding day were spread throughout the apartment, disorganized, and she looked for the ones she remembered best, hoping they had been spared, but so many of them had been ruined in the water that the order of events had been obscured. There was her father again, his lively expression, the contour of the nose and chin that looked so much like her own, but the paper that held him together was coming apart. His face came away on her fingers.

Her mother walked through the photos, inspecting the ruins. Caroline followed, trying not to make a sound. The edge of her mother's wet bathrobe stuck to her pale, plump legs. In the living room, her mother found a wedding photo and picked it up, but the paper came apart almost as soon as she touched it, the flowers and the veil, her mother's sister, Dolores, as matron of honor, her father at eighteen, just out of high school, the church, the evidence that there had ever been such a day. The bits of black and gray paper clung to her mother's palms, and she pressed them to her face, spread them across her cheeks, kneeling forward on the carpet with her face to the floor as if she were praying, and a cold sound came out of her, a long keening.

Caroline's palms on her mother's back, the thin robe, the vibration of sorrow making the room seem to shake, and she said, It will be all right, Mother, I promise. I will take care of everything. Mother, please don't. "Mama," she said, "get up, please. See? This one is fine. Some of the pictures are fine." She could not get her mother to come up off her knees.

The keening stopped abruptly, as if her mother had run out of breath, but she would not get up off the floor. She stayed head down against the carpet, her knees tucked under her, pieces of photographs stuck to her skin. She didn't speak. She would not budge. Caroline put her arms around her mother's waist and pulled, but she was too heavy.

"Please," she said. "Please get up. I'll clean them all up, I swear."

Her mother was stiff and still. Caroline pleaded with her, promised anything she could think of, but it was no use. First she ran upstairs to the Hartmans' in her bare feet. She didn't like Mr. Hartman, but he was the nearest person she could think of. She pounded on the Hartmans' kitchen door, but there was no answer. She cupped her hands to look in the window, but the inside of the kitchen was dark, the dishes glinting faintly in the drying rack next to the sink. Her feet were cold and wet. It had started to rain. She shifted from one foot to the other as she knocked and knocked.

Finally she ran downstairs and dialed Dottie's house. Walt answered. For a minute she couldn't speak. The phone amplified the sound of her breathing.

"Hello?"

"You have to come," she said. "My mother won't get off the floor. The pictures are ruined, and she won't get off the floor. She won't talk to me. You have to come right now," she said, and though he said he would be there right away and don't worry, honey, it will be fine, she watched the door, and it seemed to take forever, and the insides of her were screaming, Come *now*, you have to come *right now*.

She knelt beside her mother. "He's coming," she said to her. "He'll be here." Her mother did not look up, did not even seem to notice Caroline was there. Her naked legs stuck out from underneath her robe, and the edges of her white cotton underwear were showing. Her graying hair came out all around her face and stuck up in a hundred different directions.

Walt came in without knocking, out of breath, Dottie behind him. They spoke in low, soothing voices. Dottie put her arms around Caroline's mother and tried to coax her to stand. "Adele," she said. "Adele, get up."

"How long has she been like this?" asked Walt.

"Adele," Dottie said, "you're scaring Caroline."

"A few minutes now. Maybe ten."

"She's awake," Dottie said. "She won't speak to me."

Caroline knelt on the floor. Her mother's eyes were open, but she didn't seem to see. "Please please please please," she begged.

Her mother still would not move. Caroline pulled at her, and suddenly her bathrobe fell open and all of one breast was showing. Caroline threw herself down and covered her. No one should see her like this. Her mother was always careful about how she looked when other people were there. She never let anyone see her without one of her wigs, without a little makeup and a decent dress on. She rarely wore her glasses because she didn't like how she looked in them, only at home where no one but Caroline could see. Caroline would sit on the edge of the bathtub and watch her swipe her face with makeup, a little lipstick and mascara. In the bedroom, in her bra and girdle, her mother would pull different dresses from the closet and ask Caroline which she liked better.

"The red," Caroline would say.

"Yes, that's right," her mother would answer. "You have such a good eye."

With the red dress she put on the brunette wig, though Caroline preferred the blond, the one her mother wore to church. The wigs had names—Ava was the brunette, Doris the blonde. At night when she took them off, she asked Caroline to brush them out, showed her how to arrange the curls and waves with her fingers, and Caroline always did it so carefully, as if the nylon strands were her mother's real hair and any hard tug with the brush would hurt her.

But now her mother lay on the floor nearly naked. Caroline pulled the robe closed, but Dottie took her by the shoulders. "Come on, now," she said. She pulled Caroline off her mother. "Come on. It'll be all right."

Walt knelt and put his arms underneath Adele and picked her up. Her mother's eyes opened. She looked up. "Walter?" she said. "Are you okay?"

"I'm all right. How are you?"

"I'm so tired."

He put her on the bed, and she closed her eyes again and seemed to sleep. Dottie picked the bits of the photos off her face and straightened her robe, the kerchief over her hair, while Caroline told them about the basement and the flood. Walt listened to everything and told her it would be all right, that he would take care of everything. He went down into the basement, and when he came back up he said a leak in the wall had shorted the fuse box, and the sump pump failed when the electricity went out. Caroline didn't know what that meant at the time but knew he would make it right again.

Dottie had her doctor come. He listened to her mother's heart and her breathing, and Caroline decided she didn't like him because he addressed all his questions to Dottie. He left a bottle of pills and said her mother would need to sleep, that he would come back in the morning and check on her.

Caroline sat next to her mother's bed on the chair in the far corner, afraid one moment that her mother would not open her eyes and the next that she would. At one point, her mother looked up and smiled weakly and said she was sorry she'd scared Caroline, that she didn't mean for that to happen, and was everything all right?

"Yes," Caroline said. "Everything's fine."

"I'm so tired. I need to sleep. Will you be all right if I sleep for a little while?"

"I'm okay," Caroline said. When her mother closed her eyes, she sat very still and watched her breathe, made sure her she could see the rise and fall of her mother's ribs. She did not move from her place in the corner for the longest time. She sat so still that her arms and legs and neck felt stiff.

Dottie stayed the rest of the day. She laid an extra blanket across Adele, wrapped the other around Caroline in her chair. Dottie picked up the photographs spread across the house, went through the ruined boxes Walt brought up from the basement, and sorted the things that could be saved from those that could not. She hauled bags of garbage outside, did the laundry, the dishes. She made dinner. The smell of it reached Caroline in her mother's room, and though she was reluctant to leave, she sat at the table and let Dottie cut her some meat loaf and pour ketchup over the top.

"Your mother's going to be fine," she said, but Caroline could tell she didn't entirely believe it herself.

"Are you going to stay here tonight?"

"Yes."

"And you won't leave."

"No. I'll stay here until your mother is better."

"Where are Sam and Charley?"

"They're at home. Their father will stay with them tonight."

Caroline was suddenly starving. She took a bite of food. "Thank you," she said.

Dottie fixed herself a plate and brought Caroline a glass of milk and sat next to her at the table. Caroline drank the milk down fast, hardly stopping to breathe. Her body was suddenly aching for food. She was so glad Dottie was there. Caroline scraped her plate clean, and afterward Dottie made them hot chocolate, but this time there was no peppermint liqueur to put in it.

After dinner Caroline went back into her mother's room to keep watch, but she kept falling asleep. She was frightened her mother would start making that terrible sound again. Although she tried to keep her eyes open, they kept closing on their own.

She woke up in the dark. When she went to use the bathroom, she saw Dottie asleep on top of the blankets in Caroline's room, with a towel thrown over her bare feet. Her mouth was open and she was snoring. Caroline climbed in next to her and pulled the bedspread over the two of them, and only then did she start to feel better, drifting toward sleep in her dark room with Dottie so close that Caroline could smell the shampoo she'd used in her hair.

She felt she should have known about the slow leak of the elements into the basement, the creation of that dark body of water. That her home could be so invaded, that cracks and holes she couldn't see would let the water in, brought on a sense of fear that did not diminish with time. In her dreams, for years afterward, she looked down into water that did not reflect back the light, and she was afraid to put her feet into it, as if something there might grab her and pull her under. She felt the slow rising of the water, the pull and weight of it, the sinking in her belly as the water grew and spread and covered the floor.

From inside Dottie's kitchen, Caroline could see Charley in the yard. It was raining, and despite the grass being wet, he was playing football with the two little Koehler boys, who had come from next door for Thanksgiving dinner. Their names were Max and Alfred, but for the life of her she had never been able to tell who was who. One of them—Max or Alfred—lobbed the football at Charley, who jumped to grab it, but he miscalculated the distance and slammed into the brick wall of the house in midcatch, landing in Dottie's rosebushes. Caroline gasped, but he picked himself up, still holding the ball, and threw it back to the boys at the other end of the yard. When he stood up his good pants were covered, absolutely soaked in mud, smeared with grass and leaves. They would be ruined. Charley never gave a thought to such mundane things as laundry, or rain, or brick walls. He was beautiful and careless, his hair longer even than it had been in the summer and dangling in his eyes, because Walt had said he could wear it as long as he liked if only he would keep going to college.

In four months she had learned to be always aware of him, his presence like a landmark around which she found her way—he is outside, he is inside, he is far away, he is very close. She started to rely on him, the physical fact of him, not in the familiar, almost brotherly way she had relied on Sam, but anxiously, possessively. She always had to be with him, even if he was off with his friends. She could not have said what it was she feared, but she did not like him spending hours playing poker on Sunday nights or hanging out with the large groups of girls that always formed whenever he was around.

She didn't fit in with his friends, not just because she was older, but because they were all like Charley. They were fun and easygoing, and she was not. They had parties at the lake where they drank and smoked, danced with the radio on, and stripped off their clothes and went running into the freezing lake, thinking nothing of it. They shared joints, clothes. They melted into piles around the fire to keep warm, laughing and kissing and groping. Caroline felt like an old woman creeping among them, an old woman with a spinster's job and bills to pay and a mother who needed her. When the others were skinny-dipping, she sat on the cold sand with her arms wrapped around her knees, waiting until it was time to go home. Charley told her she was being too sensitive, that if she would only let herself go, she would have a good time.

"But why do we always have to have all these people around?" Caroline asked. "Why can't we be alone?"

"What do you mean?" he answered. "We're always alone."

She sometimes felt they were speaking different languages. "Alone" to her meant the two of them together. To Charley it meant being away from their families. He was forgetful of her, too. She sometimes got the feeling he wasn't aware of her at all but drifting through some private, thoughtless plane where her presence was accidental, an afterthought. He did care for her—he wouldn't have kept seeing her otherwise—but the more time she spent with him, the more decrepit she felt. She was twenty-three years old and felt as though he were her last chance at happiness.

Charley had always been an outgoing, comical boy, but since he'd come back from Canada in the summer he'd been different somehow. More serious. Not always—he still joked and teased—but there was a steely core in him, a ball of deliberation. She could see it in the set of his jaw when the talk turned to the war, or a flicker of pain across his eyes if someone asked him about Zel, still listed as MIA. She wanted to ask him why he'd come home when he could have stayed in Canada. Like Sam, he'd been naturalized when his parents were, with all its attending privileges and drawbacks. He was failing several classes at the university—he had never been a good student—and if he didn't pass this semester, he would lose his student deferment. One time Caroline asked him, trying not to be too pushy, what he would do if that happened. "I don't know," he said. "I suppose I'll burn that bridge when I come to it." He was ignoring the problem, hoping it would go away. He stopped turning in his papers, stopped going to classes, as if he'd decided it wouldn't do any good anyway. As if he were deliberately trying to get himself drafted. He didn't listen to her protests, her offers of help. There was a desperation in him that made him reckless. She could see it in the moment when he ran into the brick wall of the house, his fingers outstretched to catch the ball, as if nothing that happened to him mattered anymore.

From the far end of the yard, one Koehler boy threw him the ball again, and Charley leaped to catch it with a surprising grace and came down on his knees. Caroline felt a brief pang of jealousy that he got to be outside horsing around while she was in the hot, stuffy kitchen helping Dottie take the turkey, heavy with dressing, out of the oven.

"I'm not sure it's done," Dottie was saying. This was a tragedy, because the guests had already been there for an hour, and the turkey's skin was still pale. She pulled it back to see if the meat was pink. "What do you think? I think maybe it needs another hour."

Caroline looked where the fork pierced the turkey's skin. "I don't know," she said. "It looks all right to me."

Annie Koehler, who a moment before had been sitting at the table eating nuts by the handful, came over to pass judgment. She wore her hair in a large, coarse black beehive that tickled Caroline's nose when she bent over. "Another hour," she decreed.

Dottie sighed. "I knew I should have put it in earlier." They slid the turkey back in the oven.

All these people at the house. It was for Sam's sake, because he would be missing Christmas that year. Caroline went back to peeling potatoes. From the front room, she could hear the men's voices and the high, tinkling sound of Linda Chesney answering. Holding court in the front room. Caroline, carrying the cherry pie she'd made, had met Linda that morning at the front door. Linda was a tall, pale beauty with expensive clothes, a well-sprayed blond bouffant, entitlement in the set of her mouth and eyes, taking in the room and the people in it. The diamond Sam had bought her sparkled on her left hand. Dottie introduced them. Linda chatted easily, said something endearing about how great it was to finally meet her, she'd heard so many nice things, but Caroline could hardly hear for the roaring in her ears. Linda took half a step forward, then stopped. Something had stopped her. Maybe she recognized that an embrace would not have been at all welcome. Either that or the pie in Caroline's hands.

Now Linda came into the kitchen, a blast of cold air as she opened the freezer door and refilled the ice bucket.

"Are you having a good time?" Dottie asked.

"Oh, wonderful," Linda said. She gave Caroline a wide smile. She had very large white teeth, like a horse's. "But I thought your mother was going to be here, too. Sam told me your families were so close."

"My mother isn't well."

"Oh, I'm so sorry." Linda looked embarrassed, and just for that second Caroline felt a kind of triumph. "I hope it's nothing serious."

At the end of the summer, her mother had a nervous breakdown. This was what the doctor called it. Adele had cried for three days straight, deep racking sobs that shook the house and set Caroline's nerves on edge. It started one evening after Caroline was asleep, her mother at the radio listening to the casualty list for the war, the week's dead. Caroline woke at the sound and asked what was wrong, but her mother wouldn't or couldn't say. Through her tears she begged Caroline not to call the doctor, not this time. She had been a nurse; she remembered the poor souls who came to her, drugged and drooling, their unfocused eyes, the way they cried for their mothers. She said the one thing Caroline was not to do was call the doctor. "Promise me. Promise. It will be better in the morning." Caroline wanted to believe her, and promised.

But for two days straight Caroline was up all night because of the crying. She turned off the radio and wouldn't let her mother watch the television or read the paper, but it didn't seem to matter. Her mother wouldn't eat or sleep, either. She sat at the kitchen table, tears dripping off her face.

On the third day Caroline had to go to work. She told her mother to call if she needed anything. "You'll be all right?"

"Yes," she said. "I know you have to go."

Work was a relief. The quiet, the orderliness. When she came home she was thinking of the roast she'd set out to thaw for supper, the potatoes that would need peeling, the beans washed and snapped. She unlocked the front door to the sound of music playing in the other room. The apartment was very still and hot. The windows were all closed. When she opened the kitchen door, her mother was there in her housecoat and robe, head down on the table. The smell of gas was heavy in the room.

She turned off the oven, threw open the windows, shook her mother awake. Adele was groggy and disoriented at first but soon coughed and opened her eyes. Caroline half carried, half dragged her out of the room. Her mother begged Caroline not to tell anyone what had happened. "It was an accident," she said. "I must have bumped the stove when I was cooking." Caroline had called Dr. Scheidler anyway. She was afraid not to.

In private, with her mother weeping in the next room, Dr. Scheidler had asked Caroline what she had seen in the kitchen. She told him how her mother had been making supper and must have turned on the gas and forgotten about it or else bumped the dial on the stove.

Dr. Scheidler said she should seriously consider what had happened— she wasn't doing her mother any favors by pretending it was nothing. He was a former college football player who had turned to medicine after a knee injury, a large and imposing man. "The next time she has an accident, you might not be so lucky. You might be asleep in your bed, and she'll take you with her," he'd said. What would have happened if she'd stopped by Dottie's on the way home, or gone to the store, or simply taken the long way round to enjoy the afternoon?

"No," she admitted. "It wasn't an accident."

She visited her mother in the hospital every week. That first Sunday she had arrived in her best clothes with her hair freshly washed and curled, wearing her pearl earrings, her whitened shoes, hoping not to upset her mother further by some defect in appearance. But the nurses said she was not permitted to have earrings on the ward, or the buckle of the belt around her waist, or her purse with its keys and its nail file. She had to leave these things at the front desk in a little plastic tray and then wait for the nurse to unlock the door for her.

After that first time, she was more careful about what she wore, hoping to demonstrate to the nurses a thoughtfulness for the patients and her mother especially. As a group the nurses were no-nonsense, businesslike, a quality that Caroline felt she lacked. On the days she visited her mother, she waited at the nurses' station while they looked her over, waiting for

one to remark on how careful she was about removing anything dangerous and being disappointed when they didn't. They simply unlocked the
inner door and let her in without comment. It was as useless to be let down
by this as it was to visit at all, but there it was, all the same.

The hospital was clean and white but left her feeling anxious, as if she
were the one who lived there and not her mother. Inside, the seasons
changed by decoration. Halloween pumpkins carved out of construction
paper gave way to brown and orange leaves, turkeys, and cornucopias. She
was permitted to visit with her mother in the common room, usually with
three or four other patients nearby, some with families, some alone.
Sometimes Caroline could hear a patient crying somewhere. There was
always a TV program on in the background, a soap opera, the news. The
other patients on the ward were all women, and though Caroline was
tempted to ask her mother why they were in the hospital, she never
worked up enough courage to ask. Her mother never paid much attention
to them anyway.

She'd visited her mother the day before Thanksgiving, bringing the first
of the two pies she'd baked. Pumpkin was her mother's favorite. Her
mother was listless, barely responding when Caroline gave her the pie or
asked her how she was feeling. She narrowed her eyes at Caroline. "You
know I don't belong in here," she said. "I'm not sick like these others."

"You'll be better soon. Then you can come home."

"You don't know anything."

She wouldn't speak to Caroline after that. Caroline went out to her car
and sat there, not moving, for what seemed like an hour before she felt she
could start the car and drive away.

In Dottie's kitchen, Caroline poured the milk and butter into a bowl to
mash the potatoes. It didn't seem right without her mother there—the
Koehlers and Dunmores, Linda Chesney and herself circling each other
warily. She would have given anything for her mother to be there at that
moment, and still she felt a deep relief knowing her mother was miles
away, that she could not, at any moment, walk in the door and demand
something of Caroline that would be impossible to give.

Through the window she watched Charley tackle a Koehler boy, throw
him to the ground, scramble for the ball. They were both covered in mud,

howling and kicking. She wanted to be out there with them. She wanted to throw herself into the mud and thrash and scream and run.

The morning after the basement flooded, there had been a knock at the door. For a moment Caroline didn't remember what had happened, but the floodwater smell was still in the apartment, and it was still a little too cold. Dottie's arm was across her, heavy, almost suffocating. The knocking grew more insistent. At last Dottie shifted and sat up. Caroline stayed very still and kept her eyes closed. If she acted as though she were asleep just a little bit longer, she wouldn't have to think. She wouldn't have to pretend to be stronger than she was, or good or smart or happy. She could be a bundle of flesh on a bed with no thought other than for her own comfort.

From her warm place in bed, Caroline heard Dottie offer to take the doctor's coat, then the door to the hall closet opening and closing. She pulled the covers over her more tightly, listening to the noises in the apartment. The refrigerator was humming in the kitchen. The furnace turned on, and hot air rushed into the room. Under the door she could see the hall light was on. Walt had fixed it all, just as he said he would.

She felt a little better than the day before, but there was still a cold feeling in her belly when she thought of her mother, of the noises she'd made and how she'd knelt on the floor, seeing and not seeing. Caroline put on her robe and on her way to the bathroom stopped at her mother's room. Through the closed door she could hear the doctor talking but could not make out the words.

In the kitchen, Dottie was clattering the pots and pans in the sink. Last night's supper dishes had sat out unwashed and were crusted over. They smelled sour and greasy and would be nearly impossible to get clean. Dottie wasn't as good a housekeeper as her mother, and Caroline was a little repelled by her now in the morning light, by her mussed hair and the dark circles of mascara under her eyes. When Caroline came to the counter, Dottie put her arm around her and held on a little too long, as if it were Dottie who needed to be comforted instead of the other way around.

Several boxes were stacked near the back door from the day before. Dottie said she would put them back downstairs after the floor had dried.

A handful of photographs, some still damp, some waved and curled, were sitting in the middle of the kitchen table. Caroline pushed them aside. They were spoiled.

The murmur of voices from the other room. "Is she going to have to go to the hospital?" Caroline asked. She couldn't say "my mother."

"I don't know, honey."

Dottie made breakfast, eggs and sausages, and Caroline ate it all and tried not to think about the doctor in the other room or what he might be doing. She was a little afraid of him, as she was of Walt, as she was of all grown-up men. Their loud voices and their rough hands, the space they took up, made her feel very small. She never knew what to say to them or what they would do next. After a minute the doctor came into the kitchen and asked to speak with Dottie. He was older, gray haired, and smiled at Caroline as if to set her at ease, but the tightness in his eyes gave him away. She wanted to order him out of the house, right now, this minute. *Leave us alone. Leave now.* She shot daggers at him with her eyes, but he didn't look at her. She didn't matter.

Dottie wiped her hands on a dishtowel and followed him. They went into Caroline's bedroom. The doctor shut the door so they could speak in private.

When she was sure she was alone, Caroline stood and went over to the boxes stacked by the door. She could not have said why she didn't want anyone to see her looking, only she didn't. The first held some old toys that Dottie had washed and dried and put back in the box: a porcelain-headed doll with drooping eyes, now naked of her frilly dress, a teddy bear whose fur was eroded in patches around his neck and shoulders. It seemed a lot of work for some old things that Caroline wouldn't be playing with anymore. The second box was filled with gold and silver glass balls for the Christmas tree, washed and dried and rewrapped in yesterday's newspaper. She moved the box onto the floor, and there, under it, she found her father's military footlocker, shipped to her mother after her father had died in the war. It was about the size of a small table, with chipped black paint and rusting metal hardware. In big white block letters still visible, the name CLARK was stenciled. It was unlocked.

She and her mother never spoke about her father; it was a subject too painful for either of them. Her mother didn't like to say his name, didn't like to hear him spoken of at all. Her grandmother, on the other hand, had talked about him all the time. In her grandmother's house in Canada, she had felt, always, that her father was preserved in the walls somehow, in the wood and paint and carpet, some kind of residue that would let her know him, despite her mother's efforts to keep the past shut away.

Caroline's mother grew up in rural Essex County, on a poor dairy farm her family had owned until the depression became too severe and the cows died off. Her mother told her her grandfather died a year later, of tuberculosis, in the sanitarium. Her grandmother lived another two years after her husband's death, until she succumbed as well. "Grief," Caroline's mother said, and left it at that, though there was a sense of shame lurking behind her voice that made Caroline think there was more to the story, as if her grandmother had harmed herself. Her mother told her that after that she, only ten years old, went to live with her sister, Dolores, in Windsor. Dolores was already married and had a small baby by then and was glad for the help of a big girl. Adele went to school in town, where she met a handsome boy named Alister Clark. For years Adele lived with her sister and helped with the babies, who came in rapid succession: first the two girls, then the baby, Graham, whom she loved and doted on as much as any child of her own. She would sleep with him in her own bed at night, wrapping herself around him.

When the war started, though, Dolores's husband joined the navy and was sent east; Dolores would follow in a month or so, after the house was sold. Adele and Alister had already been talking about getting married by then, so they had a hurry-up wedding before Dolores left for St. John's, and Adele moved in with Alister and his mother, Vera. Adele missed Graham, especially because her sister was not a very warm person and didn't write often after she moved away. Then, after Caroline was born and Alister was killed in the plane crash, Adele had felt she had no choice but to stay with Vera, who needed her.

Caroline's grandmother could be unapproachable in some ways. She had been an English girl from Dorset when she fell in love with a cavalryman during World War I and afterward always seemed surprised to find herself in Canada, a war bride, a mother, and then a widow. She kept house with formality, served tea every afternoon and God save the king. But she was tender and loving with her son and later with his daughter, to whom she continued to speak of Alister as if he were still alive. If Caroline got in trouble, she'd say, "Your father is always getting himself into scrapes like these." If she did well in school, she'd say, "History is your father's favorite subject, too." Caroline always got a thrill from hearing her say how much she was like her father. It made her feel that even though her father was dead, he would come through Caroline herself, like a radio transmitter, as long as her grandmother was there to listen.

Her grandmother sat up late at night after she thought Caroline and her mother were in bed, speaking to Alister's portrait in words so soft that Caroline doubted she could hear had she been standing right next to her. She had seen how her grandmother looked through her mother's dresser drawers, under the bed, looking for her father's military medals, because she hated that Adele, as his widow, got to keep them. She wanted to put them out where everyone could see them. When her mother found where the old lady had left them, on the mantel or a side table in the front room, she would simply pack them up and take them back to her room and leave them in their velvet-lined cases, moving them to a new place, the back of the closet or the bottom of her underwear drawer, so that her mother-in-law would have to look harder the next time. Her mother didn't think the medals should be displayed for visitors. She thought her mother-in-law's attempts at "shadowbox patriotism" were vulgar, made light of her husband's life and death and her own, still-fresh widowhood. She preferred that such things were held close to the vest, a secret she kept even from herself.

It was after her grandmother died in bed, asleep, peaceful—"the way we all should," her mother said, "if we were so lucky"—that her mother decided to sell the house and move to Chicago, where Walt and Dottie had gone three years prior. They cleared out the house and cleaned it and got it ready to sell. They went through cabinets and closets, sorting clothes and books, dishes, legal papers, cigar boxes that had belonged to her grandfather, piles of shoes that had been out of style since World War I. Her mother was at her best with this kind of task, a purging. She worked swiftly, saving almost nothing unless it had some connection to Alister. She kept his favorite chair, his clothes. Before throwing them away, she went through every scrap of paper to make certain none carried his handwriting, even old bills, credit slips. Everything that didn't went into the trash or was given to the junk man down the road. With each bag or box, Caroline's own past seemed to shrink a little. Her mother went through all the rooms, packing, moving swiftly. If she was unsure whether to keep something, she would ask Caroline, "Do you want this? This little china dog? Do you think I should keep this old silver?" and Caroline would say no, or yes, depending, but really she wanted to save it all. She wanted to keep the house and everything in it exactly as it was. But her mother was determined; she wouldn't hear of it. "The lawyer will be bringing people by starting next week, and I don't want all this old stuff left when they come. Who would want the place like this?" The sweep of her arm seemed to include everything, the walls, the floor, even Caroline herself.

She first saw the footlocker in her grandmother's closet. Her mother was in the kitchen packing up dishes when Caroline went upstairs to the shut-up room where her grandmother had lived. The door complained when she pushed on it. She looked through the drawers, under the bed. She found a photo of her father as a boy in her grandmother's jewelry box, under an old watch without a band. She touched the stockings in the highboy but didn't move them. Her grandmother's black shoes were on the floor next to the bed where she'd left them, their tongues hanging out like old, patient dogs. She opened the closet door and saw the footlocker, the black-painted metal and the white name stenciled across the top, but just then her mother had come up the steps, seen her standing in the closet, and asked why she was dillydallying, we don't have all day, you know, and Caroline had gone to the dressers and started throwing her grandmother's clothes into a box, not stopping to think what should be given away and what she should keep. In the rush, she hadn't thought about the footlocker again.

But in her mother's kitchen, with the doctor and Dottie in the other room, she opened the lid. A musty smell, and something else, like aftershave or shampoo. She had expected the things inside to be a mess, everything jumbled together, but instead the inside of the footlocker was neat, clothes folded carefully, as if nothing had been touched. She took each thing out gingerly, afraid to disturb his presence in each item, each fold of clothing, the creases in his letters. On top there were three dress shirts. A couple of brown stains spread across the collar of the topmost shirt, like rust spots or watermarks. Caroline picked up the shirts and smelled them, but they had the same smell of aftershave and mildew as the rest of the footlocker. Under the shirts she found her father's blue dress uniform, also folded neatly. There was a shaving kit with a rusting zipper; when she opened it and looked inside, there were his razor and nail clippers, still bright against the yellow satin lining inside the case. She touched the edge of the razor that had shaved his face; it was dull and had spots of rust blooming on it, like bloodstains. She zipped it up and put it aside. Under that she found a cake of dried soap. It was cracked and dry, ringed with fissures and crevasses, a petrified piece of earth, but when she picked it up and put it to her nose, she could smell what it was in the footlocker, the earthy, mossy smell of the soap. After all these years it still held the perfume that had been mixed in with the lye. It was round and hard as a hockey puck and had, at one time, some raised letters stamped into its soft surface, but now only the hint of them remained, rubbed into oblivion by her father's hands when he shaved, maybe on that last morning before he headed out to the plane that would take him to Iceland and back, the last morning before he died. Her hand curled around the soap and hid it completely. It fit right in the space her palm made and warmed in her hands.

There were letters there, too, letters from his mother, from her mother. They were tied together with string, and the paper was browned and spotted like the shirts. Also there were letters he had written home to his mother during the war, the name and address written on the front in the same left-slanting hand as on the footlocker itself. On one, the "Mrs." before "Clark" was written with a kind of flourish, the end of the M dipping down and curling around itself like a monkey's tail. There was an exuberance in this that made her feel curious again to know him. Her mother had said he was a jolly person, a joker, but for some reason, looking at her mother and grandmother, she had never believed it, not until she saw his handwriting on the letters. It was as if she were losing him for the first time instead of by degrees, as if she had not lost him every day of her life, but just there, sitting on the floor of the kitchen in her mother's house with the gray fall light out the window.

Her grandmother must have put the letters in the footlocker and forgotten them. Caroline fumbled through the letters, reading. "I have been three times to Ireland this month and am getting tired of that dark beer they serve there. . . . I did not get your last letter, Mother, did you say that your sister was ill? . . . I should be able to make it home in the summer but they say we will miss Christmas again this year, unless the Germans surrender. . . . I'm so excited about the baby, Mother, please take good care of Adele for me and I'll see you soon." This last part thrilled her, because of course the baby was herself.

Under his uniform, almost hidden, was another set of letters, newer, less stained. The handwriting was different, careful, tiny, elegant words written in blue ink on thick stationery. They were addressed to her grandmother. The postmark was from Newfoundland, and the stationery read "The Victoria Inn"; the top envelope had arrived only a few months before her grandmother had died. It said the writer was sorry to learn that Vera had been ill. The writer was so sorry she had often had so many troubles and no one to share them with since Alister was gone, but they must bear it as they always had. It was signed "*Your Rosie.*" The familiarity implied in the signature, the lack of a last name, the floridness of the writing, made Caroline uneasy. She looked through the letters; there were eighteen or twenty of them, going back all of Caroline's life. The first was postmarked only two months after her father's death, asking for any news of him.

The return address read "Rosemary Oram, The Victoria Inn, St. John's, Newfoundland."

She heard the bedroom door open and Dottie's footsteps coming down the hallway. She threw her father's things back in the footlocker, all except the cake of soap and the letters. She put the boxes of toys and ornaments back on top of the footlocker. The cake of soap and the letters she hid under the thick cloth of her robe, between her hip and arm, until she could hide them in her room. Dottie came out and looked at her half-eaten breakfast. "All done?" she asked, and Caroline said she was, thank you, and pushed herself back from the table.

In the other room her mother lay asleep. She smelled her hands. Her father's soap, her father's smell, after all these years.

She could see Charley outside with the Koehler boys while she did the dishes, her hands moving under the soapy surface of the water. There were so many dishes. Charley had changed his clothes before dinner and now wore a pair of white pants that glowed faintly in the twilight, something for her to follow, like a signal. It had stopped raining, and the sky was clearing, a scrim of white clouds and moonlight visible over the tops of the buildings. The two Koehler boys and Charley were climbing the embankment to the Soo Line tracks that ran behind the house, their heads together, laughing about something. Charley had had a little too much to drink that afternoon, and she was thinking she should say something, she should tell someone about this.

Through the kitchen door, she could hear Otto Koehler telling his war stories to Sam, who seemed bored or annoyed, or both. Dottie came in with the platter of sliced turkey, now cold, and wrapped it up for the refrigerator. Afterward she threw open the kitchen window to let out the heat. "Will you feel that air?" she breathed. "We should sit outside."

"It's getting cold."

"It's not that cold," Dottie said. "Anyway, a little fresh air never did anyone any harm."

"You're right."

But after the dishes were done, it was only Caroline who wandered out into the yard to cool off. The wind was picking up, bending the trees and shaking off the last of the dry brown leaves. Inside the house, she could hear the voices of Sam and Walt and Otto, getting louder as they drank more. Annie was calling for Max and Alfred, time to go home, and Linda and Dottie were laughing about something. She had to get out, she had to leave the house. To go somewhere, anywhere.

In the yard, a square of light from the kitchen window fell across the grass, and she slipped away from it, toward the place where she had last seen Charley and the two boys. She had envied their freedom from the chores in the house, the ease they had to pursue their own games and interests. She wondered what that would be like, knowing that the responsibility for things belonged to someone else.

The embankment was steep near the house and damp from the afternoon of rain, and she slipped in the grass as she climbed, wetting her skirt. It clung to her legs with bits of grass and leaves, and her hands were muddy when she reached the top and stood on the tracks. Far down she could see the lights of a train, but it was miles away, still safe. The boys were near a patch of trees, crouched over the tracks, murmuring to each other. They didn't see her at first. As Caroline got closer, she could see they were putting pennies on the tracks for the trains to roll over and flatten. She and Sam had done the same when they were younger. She was surprised to see Charley out here with the two boys, bending over the tracks in the dim light. Charley's white pants fairly glowed. "Look who's here," he said when he saw her. "You're just in time."

"Boys," she said, "your mother's looking for you." The two boys grumbled. Just another minute, they pleaded, until the train comes and flattens the pennies.

Charley had promised them. Once again Caroline felt like the old woman at the party. "All right," she said, knowing it was a bad idea but reluctant to spoil other people's fun. "Just until the train comes."

They waited there in the dark on the tracks, watching the lights grow bigger. At times the lights almost seemed to stop, then crept closer. Charley told the boys to put their hands on the rails to feel the weight of the train, the vibration it made. The boys said they could feel it, oh yes, their voices rising with excitement. The pennies shook slightly, just the slightest wobble. Caroline said they should get down off the tracks now, the train was getting close. "Just another minute," Charley said.

"Come on. It's time."

"Just wait."

"Boys," she said in her best official voice, her librarian's voice, "you get down now. The train's almost here."

The boys got up and slid down the embankment. She could hear the gravel cascading as they went, like an avalanche. Down the tracks, the lights were growing brighter. The pennies shook on the tracks. "Charley, come on."

"In a minute."

"I'm going down now."

"Just another minute."

"We don't have a minute."

The ground was shaking from the weight of the train. She left Charley and slid down the side of the embankment to where the boys were waiting. She reached out for their shoulders, to pull them in close to her. They were small and young under her hands, their heat and scent and sweat like biscuit dough. The younger boy shivered once and looked up at her for reassurance. She couldn't see to the top to tell if Charley had moved—the embankment was over the top of her head. The train's headlights pierced the dark in two long, bright tunnels, and she thought she saw a hand out, waving, somewhere above. The train blew its whistle. "Charley!" she called, but the noise of the train drowned it out so that even Caroline couldn't hear the word, just feel it in her throat, and the train was almost to them, close, and a second later Charley rolled down the side of the embankment and landed at her feet, laughing.

"Did you see that? Did you see?"

He was drunk. He was very drunk, more than she'd thought at first. She suddenly wanted to kick him. He lay on his back, grinning up at her, but his eyes were sad. She recognized the look on his face. It was the same look she'd seen on her mother in the hospital the day before. *You don't know anything*, she'd said.

When the train was well past, Caroline let the boys climb to the top again to retrieve their pennies. They showed Caroline the stretched and flattened disks of copper, and she looked at and exclaimed over them, but she was afraid, she wanted to be back in the house where it was light. She didn't want to be out here with Charley, pretending she was the strong one, the capable one. She was weak and afraid of everything.

Charley pulled himself to his feet. Standing, he was his old familiar self, and he came close to her, until even in the dark she could see his expression. "You don't have to be afraid for me, sweetheart," he said, grinning. "I'm invincible. Superman himself."

"So this is your secret identity?"

"Weren't you fooled?"

"Yes," she said. "You did have me fooled."

She walked behind the boys toward the house. Annie Koehler was standing at the back door, calling her children. "Max! Freddie! Time to go!" she called. The boys ran ahead of her, carrying their pennies in front of them like an offering.

After she found the letters, Caroline hid them and the bar of soap in an old cigar box in a corner of the basement. For the next few weeks, she didn't touch them again. But eventually her mother started to feel better, and Dottie was there less and less, and Caroline started thinking about the letters again and what they might be able to tell her about her father. Afternoons when her mother was at Dottie's or mornings while she still asleep, Caroline would go down into the basement and read the letters and fondle the soap. Down there floorboards and beams were exposed, and it still had a damp underwater feeling, like the belly of a whale. From that distance she was able to contemplate her family and herself in it. From the Victoria Inn, St. John's, Newfoundland, came the first real thing Caroline had ever known about her father.

March 25, 1944

Dear Mrs. Clark,

Perhaps it is strange for you to receive a letter from this part of the world, but I hope you won't mind too much. I called the librarian there in town, who helped me come by your address. I am seeking information regarding a young airman stationed at Gander by the name of Alister Clark who has promised to marry me. Usually once a month or so he has been a visitor here in St. John's at the hotel owned by my father, but I have not heard from him in some time now. He mentioned once that he grew up in Windsor, and I am hoping that you may be a relative of his or may know of another Clark who is. It is not an uncommon name, so I have not had much hope of finding him. If you can, please let me know has something terrible happened, or has he been stationed elsewhere, I would dearly love to know.

Sincerely,

Rosemary Oram

St. John's, Newfoundland

September 1, 1944

Dear Mrs. Clark,

I was terribly upset at receiving your letter as you might imagine, but I cannot say it was a surprise. When I went so long without a word from Alister, which was not his way at all, I had of course feared the worst, but there was always the hope still that it might be a problem with the mail, or a misunderstanding of some kind. The news you sent was the most awful I could imagine. I have had many terrible days, which is why I have not been able to write you before now.

Your letter was so kind and your wish that I might have been your daughter-in-law so tender that I was moved to tears. My own mother has been dead since I was small, and my father often distant and harsh, and with little use of girl children. I could not help but imagine that being part of your family would be a blessing for me. I am sorry if this is all too much for you and perhaps you were just being kind, but I have received little kindness in my life and was so touched, I just had to tell you. I hope you don't mind me writing to you.

Yours,

Rosemary Oram

The handwriting was so small and cramped that Caroline had trouble reading the letters at first, but once unraveled, the words were unmistakable. The audacity of her grandmother's lie astonished her. Caroline thought of her grandmother receiving these letters, hiding them away so that Adele would not have knowledge of them, something of Alister Clark's that was hers alone, something that her mother could not take away and hide in a drawer somewhere, unlike the medals and ribbons. But maybe Caroline was wrong—maybe her grandmother was really trying to spare the woman's feelings, when revealing the truth would be so cruel and pointless. There were many letters, three or four a year at first. Caroline could only imagine what her grandmother sent in reply, but Rosemary Oram continued to write on the friendliest of terms, only with this lie at the center: No mention was made whatsoever of Caroline and Adele, as if they never existed.

The most recent letter had arrived three years before Caroline and her mother moved to the States, just when her grandmother became ill. In it, Rosemary Oram wrote that she had a bit of good news, or at least it was good to her: She was getting married.

He is a kind man, a bachelor. His name is Joe Gilchrest. He comes into the hotel for his evening meals and sometimes for breakfast on Sundays, and over the course of this last year we have struck up a friendship. I told him about Alister and about you, and he agrees that we would both like you to be here for the wedding. I don't know if you would be able to come, but if your health is not too bad, I would be able to send you the money for the train ticket and the ferry boat, as my guest. Please write back and let me know as to the arrangements.

There were no more letters after that, but with the letters Caroline found an old newspaper clipping, yellowed, with the announcement of Miss Rosemary Oram married to Joseph Gilchrest in St. John's in May 1951. The bride wore white organza and carried a bouquet of mums. On the back was a note in the same tiny handwriting: "Wish you had been there. Love, Rosie."

Caroline put the letters, newspaper clipping, and bar of soap back in the cigar box and hid them under some bricks in the corner, but she thought about them all the time. She was curious about Rosemary Oram, what she was like, what was it about her that Caroline's father had loved. She wondered what would have happened if her father had lived, if he might have stayed in Newfoundland and divorced her mother and married Rosemary Oram. He could have had more children. She imagined Rosemary was very tall and dark, elegantly dressed, something like Ava Gardner. She imagined a large and happy family, and she would be the big sister to a gaggle of girls and boys. It was seductive, this dream. Sometimes, on waking, she was filled with such sadness on remembering the truth that she tried to will herself back to sleep, but the dream never picked up where she had left it. She knew she should be angry at her father for her mother's sake but was not. She forgave him and would forgive him still.

She looked up Newfoundland on the map, the city of St. John's, and she went to the library to look for pictures of its long, deep harbor, the narrow, protected mouth that kept it safe from the North Atlantic, Cabot Tower, and Signal Hill. In the photos it was a hilly sea town with colorful wood-frame houses. Icebergs floated past it in the summer, and whales and puffins came to breed offshore. She would like to see it someday, the places where her father had loved this strange woman. She wished she knew what Rosemary looked like so she would know her when she saw her. Her name was Rosemary Gilchrest now, and she might have children of her own.

> *November 15, 1954*
> *Dearest Rosie,*
> *I'm sorry for taking so long in writing back to you. Maybe you thought I disapproved of the wedding, but that wasn't it. I have been sick the last few years. A few years ago I moved to the U.S. to live with my sister, and that disrupted your last letter from reaching me in time to make it to the wedding. I was very sorry to miss it.*
> *Recently I found your letter in with some old papers and was sad to think how long it's been since I've heard from you. I would love to hear about your wedding. I'll bet you were a beautiful bride. Do you have children now? I'll bet you are a wonderful mother. I would love to have a picture of them, and of you, if you don't mind sending one.*
> *Yours,*
> *Vera Clark*

Caroline typed the letter on the machine in her mother's bedroom when her mother was at Dottie's. She was unhappy with the draft but was in a hurry and decided she didn't dare risk a second version. She put it in an envelope, addressed it to Rosemary Gilchrest at the Victoria Inn, St. John's, Newfoundland, and took it to the post office herself. Addressing the envelope made her feel grown up, powerful, and not just because it was the first letter she had ever written. She walked the four blocks to the post office and bought the stamps with her own money, and she licked them and put them in place and dropped the mail in the slot. She felt it *plunk* when it hit the metal bucket under the slot. *There.* On her way back from the post office, she decided to run, and she ran and ran until she thought her heart would explode.

For weeks she watched the mail for a letter written on hotel stationery, tiny handwriting, a Newfoundland postmark. She waited in the house for the mailman, taking the letters that came and checking each one. Only when she was sure would she bring in the mail for her mother. She wondered if Rosemary had moved out of St. John's. Maybe she was angry at Vera for not writing to her sooner.

Winter came, and the lake froze over. Her mother started to feel better, good enough that she found a new job and took some new pills that were helping her sleep, but they didn't speak of the ruined photographs or what had happened that day in the house. It was as if it never occurred. Their first winter in the States, the snow was so heavy in the streets that some days Caroline could barely make the walk to school. The wind coming off the lake was bitter and snapped at her nose and ears, the ends of her fingers.

Caroline had almost forgotten about Rosemary Oram when the letter came. She checked the mailbox on her way into the house, and there it was: She recognized the tiny, elegant handwriting immediately. She pressed the letter close to her belly as if someone might see. Inside the house, she handed the regular bills to her mother and rushed back to her bedroom to open it.

Dearest Vera,

Imagine my surprise receiving a letter from you after all this time. I had thought you were upset about my marriage, and I had some anguished moments wondering if I had offended you, as that was the last thing I wanted. But if you have been ill and moving across the border of course you have been occupied with your own troubles. You wrote as to whether I have children now, and I can tell you yes, there are two, both boys. Joe was in a bit of a hurry to start a family as I am no June bride anymore and he will be forty-two next month. The boys' names are Henry Richard, after Joe's father, and Alister Joseph. I hope the fact that I named one of my children after Alister is all right with you, I wasn't sure how you would feel, but Joe said it was all right with him. Henry is two years old and Alister is three months. I would still like to have a daughter, but whether that is in the cards I don't know. I hope your health has improved since moving to Chicago and you enjoy living with your sister. It must be nice to have some company after living so long alone. We both of us have found some companionship at last, and it makes me glad to know you are well looked after. I hope after this we can resume a regular correspondence, as the lack of your letters has been a great sadness to me.

Your Rosie

Dear Rosie,

I was surprised you named your baby after Alister, but that is all right with me. I hope when he's older you'll tell him about his namesake. We have had a hard winter here, and there has been some weather trouble, including a rain which flooded my sister's basement and ruined all her photographs of her dead husband. She took it very badly, as she has been pining for him since he died and she is not a happy person. Sometimes she is not very nice to me, but I have nowhere else to go. Sometimes I am afraid of her.

Yours,

Vera

Dearest Vera,

I'm sorry to hear your sister is unkind, but perhaps I can offer a treat that will make you feel better. With trains and ferry service improving all the time, Joe and the kids and I would like to take a trip through the States, and we have talked about stopping in Chicago for a few days. Would you be opposed to such a visit? I would love to introduce you to my children and let them know they have a "grandma" in America they have never met. If that is agreeable to you, I will figure a schedule and let you know when we would be likely to be in the area . . .

Your Rosie

Caroline read this last letter sitting in the basement with her mother upstairs talking to the doctor; she could hear their voices through the floorboards. She realized she had made a terrible mistake. She pictured her mother answering the door one day and there would be Rosemary, with her two boys and her husband in tow. She would explain who she was and what she was doing there, and Caroline would have to explain, and it was all too terrible to imagine. A betrayal of the highest order. She had to put an end to it, now, before it went any further.

June 1, 1955

    Dear Mrs. Gilchrest,

    My grandmother is dead. She died a year ago. I'm sorry I lied to you and I'm sorry my father lied and I'm sorry my grandmother lied, I don't know why they did it and I don't know why I did, either, but you can't visit here. My mother doesn't know anything about you. Please do not write here again. I'm sorry.

    Caroline Clark

She wrote this letter in her own handwriting and signed her full name, the twin capital C's like the open mouths of predatory fish waiting to bite, and took the letter to the post office to mail, but this time she did not feel like running. She felt a tremendous sadness—for Rosemary and her mother, for herself—and she was so exhausted that she fell asleep that night in her bed on top of the covers, still wearing her school uniform.

One last time a letter came for her. It was in the same tiny handwriting. "Who are you?" was all it said. Caroline didn't answer it. She kept watch for months afterward—partly in hope, partly in dread—but no other letter from Newfoundland ever came. For years she often wondered about Rosemary Gilchrest and the two boys, Henry and Alister, and she wondered whether Rosemary ever had her baby girl. She imagined herself as that baby, and Rosemary's face bending over her, and though she was ashamed of herself and fearful for her mother, she still wished she could know this other woman, this person her father had loved, as if knowing her would let her know him, too, the real person her father had been instead of the shadow her mother would not let go.

Inside Dottie's kitchen, the light was warm. The Koehlers were gone, having herded the boys next door once again. The half-carved turkey was on the table, and the bread and mayonnaise set out for Walt to make himself a sandwich. In the other room, Jack was asleep with his head against the back of the sofa, and Sam and Linda were sitting on the floor watching TV. The metal clock on the wall, in the shape of a star, said it was only eight-thirty. Walt with his solid presence, so reassuring, so devoid of any drama or artifice, made her ashamed of the wetness of her clothes and the grass stains on her knees and palms from where she had fallen near the train tracks. Despite his urging, she wouldn't sit on Dottie's kitchen chairs. Her hands and face tingled and came back to life in the warmth inside the house. "Where's Charley?" he asked.

"Outside, still. I'm not sure."

"Are you all right?"

"I think so. As good as I'm going to be, I guess."

Walt stood up and put on his coat. "I'll walk you home," he said. When they went out, he put his hand in the small of her back and led her through the door. It felt good to be led. She didn't want to think anything. She wanted to be outside herself. Walt was quiet on the walk. His footsteps on the sidewalk were steady and solid. Inside the houses along the street, people were having dinner, and furnaces were running and letting off steam into the cold air, and the trees bent in the wind. The wind was high now and cold. Leaves blew underfoot.

"Thank you," she said.

"I thought you might like some company."

"You were right."

She thought of all the ways her life could have been different if she'd been smarter, richer, happier. "Did you ever go to St. John's with my father?" she asked. "When you were stationed together during the war?"

"I went once or twice. It was about three hours away by train from the air base. I saw a picture down there. What was it? *Meet Me in St. Louis.* I don't think your father came with me that time. What made you ask about that?"

Another train was going by. She could feel the weight of it when it passed because it was so heavy. She thought about Charley on the tracks, jumping out of the way at the last minute. "I was just thinking how many things about him I don't know. I don't know anything about him at all."

"He was excited about being a father. I remember him talking about that."

"Just think of all the things that would have been different if he'd lived."

"Well," Walt said, but he was quiet. "Maybe nothing would be different. Maybe not so much. Who can tell?"

They walked together silently for a while. Walt was quiet the way Sam was quiet, not wasting words on things that didn't matter. She had always admired that about him. In some ways he was so ordinary that she had taken him for granted, but when they walked together in the rain, she was glad he was there.

At her front porch, he said, "Will you be all right?"

"Yes. Thank you." He squeezed her shoulder once. It was such a tender gesture that she almost threw her arms around him, fell on him, the way she had known girls to do with their fathers. She wanted to be small and unafraid and comforted. Instead, she smiled at him and went inside the house.

In the kitchen, the phone was ringing. She didn't turn on the lights. She stood in the still cold kitchen and listened to the phone ring. She knew it was her mother. She knew she would have some new demand, some new slight to report. She turned and looked behind her, but Walt had already left. She was cold and damp. She couldn't feel her limbs, couldn't move, couldn't see anything in the kitchen, the outline of the stove or refrigerator, nothing that would make the room seem familiar, because everything was dark, as if the cold and wet had made her go blind, and she put her hands out in front of her and touched nothing, touched air. She thought of Charley on the train tracks, her mother at the kitchen table, the money that was never enough, and herself in the middle of it, always trying to keep one step ahead. To be good, to be strong, when others were not. She wondered if goodness, too, could be a kind of madness, a flood that could pull you down, under the water where you couldn't see clearly, and no one would ever know you were there.

NINE

Sam awoke to the sound of someone banging on the front door, demanding to be let in. It was Charley, who had lost his keys. "Ding-dong. Avon calling," his brother shouted. He was laughing, but Sam didn't see what was so funny about it. Three-fifteen in the morning. "Someone open the door," Charley said, pummeling the door with his fist, four hard, fast knocks like a secret code, and in the dark, Sam jumped. Jesus Christ, his brother.

Sam looked out the window. Charley took several steps backward and ran at the door of the house, throwing his shoulder against it like a battering ram. He stumbled off the low concrete stoop and fell into the dead wet grass in the yard, his head flopping backward. His white pants had spots of brown at the knees, as though he'd been praying in the dirt.

Pop was angry. "Go somewhere and sleep it off." His voice, heavy and pained, filled the house. Pop was standing at the door but seemed disembodied, everywhere at once.

"I live here, too," Charley said.

"Not when you're piss drunk, you don't."

"He's going to wake the neighborhood," Ma said.

Linda was standing in the doorway of the bedroom, the light on her face making her eyes look wild. Pop's hand was on the knob of the front door, palm pressed against the metal, almost as if he wanted to turn it but would not. He said he didn't give a damn about the neighbors. His mother in her bathrobe. She wrapped it tightly around herself. "He'll freeze to death."

"It's forty degrees out there. No one freezes to death in forty degrees."

"Walter. Let your son in the house."

His mouth was set. He wouldn't change his mind. "I'll call the cops on him if he doesn't knock it off."

"You wouldn't."

"I would," he said, but then his head sagged and he brushed his hand across his face as if he were wiping away cobwebs. "All right," he said. "Let him in, then." His father went back into the bedroom and closed the door quietly behind him.

Through the window, Sam watched Charley lie down in the grass in the front yard. He was humming to himself loudly enough to hear through the door, a tune that Sam felt he should recognize. Sam saw the Koehlers' kitchen light turn on next door, the curtain pull back.

"Sammy," said his mother, "get him to come inside. Maybe talk to him. You know how he looks up to you."

Sam knew that last part wasn't true, but he pulled on his boots and jeans and went out into the yard. The rain had stopped, but the temperature had dropped sharply since the afternoon, and he rubbed his arms to warm them. His mother stood at the door, her hands holding up the frame like Sampson in the temple, waiting for the house to fall down.

Earlier, after dinner was finished and the guests gone, Charley had gone out to meet some friends. He was always meeting friends, always going somewhere. That night he told Sam he'd won some money in a poker game and needed to collect. When Sam still lived at home, he'd sometimes driven with Charley on those errands, waiting in the car while his brother went into some bar or some strange house. Sam always felt a little uneasy about those trips, as though he should say something to Charley, but he didn't know what to say and doubted it would do any good anyway.

Behind the house the Soo Line train went past, shaking the ground, momentarily drowning out the sound of Charley's singing. When they were kids Charley made a game of naming all the things he could do better than Sam. "I beat you at pinball. I beat you at Ping-Pong and badminton and checkers. I beat you." He recited his list late at night, when their parents were asleep, from his bed on the other side of the room they shared, keeping Sam up late. That irritating voice. "Anything you can do, I can do better. I can do anything better than *you* . . ." Sam would tell him to be quiet, they would get in trouble. If Charley kept going, Sam got up and pummeled his brother under the covers until he cried out or stopped. Then, just as he was about to fall asleep, Charley would start over, adding to the list the items he'd forgotten the first time. "Swimming, drawing, painting, music . . ." He was so proud of himself, so smug.

"For Pete's sake, shut up!" Sam would shout, and their father would come to the door and tell them if they weren't quiet in two seconds, he would make sure neither one of them would speak again for a week.

Charley could goad Sam into things no one else could. If Sam didn't want to go for a swim in the lake, Charley could taunt him into it. If Sam thought it was too dangerous to try to sneak into the drive-in for a late movie, Charley would harass him until he agreed to go. Years ago, it was Charley who discovered their grandfather's .22 rifle in the basement and talked Sam into driving him to an abandoned warehouse, where they used to shoot at cans. Sam was afraid they would be caught, but they never were.

But in the front yard, where Charley was still singing with his head thrown back, Sam was cold and tired and just wanted to go back to bed. He stood over his brother, tried to pick him up by his forearms, but he lost his grip. Charley whooped loudly enough to wake the neighborhood.

"Get up," Sam said. "Ma's a wreck, worrying about you."

"Pop said I had to sleep out here."

"He didn't mean it."

"I think he did."

Sam bent over and got him under the arms, but Charley went limp on purpose, dead weight, grinning his shit-eating grin. Sam got angry and dropped him onto the grass, but Charley fell back and just giggled. Sam thought about insisting, but his brother rolled over and curled up with his knees to his chest. To hell with him. He was old enough to drink, he was old enough to get his own ass in the house or sleep outside with the birds.

When he came back inside, his mother was still standing in the doorway, crying. "Sammy, Sammy," she said, "he has to come in."

"He won't."

"You didn't try hard enough."

"You go pick him up, then."

Sam went back to the sofa in the back room and lay down but never did fall asleep. He heard his mother go to the bedroom and say something to his father, his father's low voice answering. At one point, with the moon coming in the window, Sam stood up and went into the hallway. His father was standing at the door, looking out into the yard, his face bleached and stripped like a skull, the ruined bits of his fingers trailing along the curtains. Outside, the white knees were still there, shining in the moonlight.

The next morning, Ma was gone by the time Sam got up. Charley was snoring on the floor of the TV room with his arm thrown over his face. At some point, someone had let him in. Sam hadn't heard him.

He pictured his mother on her way to church, as Caroline had described, with a doily on her head and a rosary tucked in her purse. Asking the Virgin Mary to stop the war. She had left a note on the kitchen table and eggs and bacon cooling and congealing in the oven.

Pop said he was changing the oil in the car that morning. "I could use a hand," he told Sam. "Would you mind?"

"Sure," Sam said. "Did Ma go to church this morning?"

"I think so," Pop said.

"Caroline said she's praying to stop the war."

"Damned foolishness," said Gramp. A plate of cold eggs sat in front of him on the table. He dumped the tobacco from his pipe into the ashtray, but a little bit spilled onto his breakfast.

"Maybe," Pop said. "But it's her right."

He set aside the last of the breakfast for Charley and ran hot, soapy water to wash the breakfast dishes. One of the men always did the dishes for their mother, either Pop or Sam or Charley. Pop's hands moved in the water.

Linda was in bed and Charley was still asleep on the floor when Sam got out of the shower. He threw his wet towel at his sleeping brother, half covering his face. Charley pushed the towel onto the floor without opening his eyes, rolled over, and started snoring again.

It was cold in the garage, and the sound of the door opening echoed against the houses and two-flats along the street. A long line of clouds was hanging over the lake, but the rest of the sky was a clear, cold blue. Pop was careful about changing the oil every three months, and afterward he washed and waxed the car, too. He always said if you took care of your cars, they'd last longer, and he always took care of his cars. This one, a

1955 green-and-white Chevy Bel-Air, still ran perfectly and didn't have a spot of rust anywhere, even though it had more than a hundred thousand miles on it. Pop had bought it five years earlier and did most of the repair work on it himself, when he could. It was Sam's job to crawl under the car, unscrew the plug, and let the oil drain out into the pan, the heavy sound of it running under their voices.

"What time is your train on Tuesday?" Pop asked.

"Eight-fifteen."

"I'll drive you."

"That's all right. I can take the el."

"No, I'll take you. I want to."

Next door, Otto Koehler came outside with a bag of garbage. Sam hoped he wouldn't see them. Otto walked to where the garbage cans sat along the alley, dumped the bag in, waved, and went back into the house. Across the alley, a small dog Sam didn't recognize ran out into the yard to bark insistently at Otto and, when Otto ignored him, at Walt and Sam.

"Atta boy," Pop said. "Hey, pooch."

"The Falkoffs got a new dog?"

"Falkoffs moved out in March," Pop said. "They got a place in Florida."

"I didn't know that."

"They like it well enough. Your mother talked to Joanie last month."

"You still thinking you want to go to Florida?"

"Sure do. Figure I've got fifteen more years nailing boards before I can manage it."

"That's not too bad."

"No, not too bad."

"Think Ma will want to go?"

"I hope so. Sure would be lonely without her."

When the used oil finished draining, Sam put the plug back in and Pop emptied a new can into the engine. Down the alley, the garbage truck made its weekly rounds, groaning and muttering like some kind of bear. Sirens came close and then passed by. The city was as familiar to him as his own skin, but now he felt like a stranger here, having been away so long. Landmarks in the neighborhood told the story of his whole life: the telephone pole on Belmont where he'd wrecked his first car and broken his nose, the Polish cemetery where he and Caroline had gone to be alone, the bushes beneath the Falkoffs' bathroom window where he and Charley had once waited to glimpse Marley Falkoff undressing for her bath. That day they had seen the side of her breasts through a crack in the window shade. Charley had said they looked like fried eggs.

Pop changed out the oil filter and dropped the hood. "Still have your keys to this beast?"

"Yeah. They're in my pocket."

"That's good."

Pop got out the bucket and filled it, and the two of them washed the car, going slowly over the bumpers, the trim on the hubcaps, the whitewalls, the grille. The water was very cold and Sam's hands went numb, but every inch had to be carefully washed and dried by hand. The wax came next. The garage smelled strongly of soap. For a long time they didn't speak. Work could always substitute for words with his father. "That's a nice job," Pop said finally, looking at the glossy finish. "That's good work there."

"Looks nice," Sam said.

"It's a good car. It'll last another twelve years, I'll bet."

"It might."

Pop gathered up the wet towels and the chamois he used to finish off the waxing job. He was looking across the alley at the little dog, which had stopped barking but sat flapping its short tail on the ground. The dog whimpered once and stood up. Pop tossed it an old rag, which it ran after, tail wagging. "I want you to know," Pop said, "if I wake up tomorrow and the car's gone and you're gone, that will be all right with me."

Sam could feel the keys in his pocket, poking into the soft flesh of his thigh. His hand had gone to them automatically. "Not really."

"I can always get another car."

Sam wasn't sure how to respond. "All right, Pop," he said. He knew he would not take the car; it wasn't even a question. "All right, then. Thanks."

"Just so you know."

Pop took the towels down to the basement, and Sam heard the washing machine start up. Through the garage door window, he could still see the car's glint. His grandfather was in the other room watching the news, and Charley was complaining that his breakfast was cold. "Got to get up earlier, then," Pop said, coming up the basement stairs.

Ma came home with her arms full of groceries, pale but otherwise seeming fine. She said she was planning a roast for supper that night, and carrots because Sam liked them, and was there anything special Sam wanted now, while he was still home? "You can have anything you want." There was still a little cake from the day before. They could have a little cake after supper that night, if he wanted.

"Sounds good," Pop said. He took a bag of groceries from her and started unpacking them into the cupboards, soup cans, sugar, flour. Said it just like that: "Sounds good." Or: "Absolutely." Or: "If you want to take the car and go, that's all right with me." Just like that, as if it weren't anything at all.

Teddy James, who slept in the next bunk, told Sam how he married his high school sweetheart before he reported for induction. This was in the barracks one night before lights out.

"Why?" Sam had asked him, because Teddy was only seventeen.

"So I wouldn't die a virgin," Teddy said.

The other guys in Sam's unit laughed and teased him that he didn't need to get married to get his cherry popped. "You poor kid," Robicheaux said, shaking his head. Robicheaux was a French Canadian and former Legionnaire with two tours in Vietnam under his belt already. The other guys had nicknamed him Bonaparte because he was short and mean, but no one dared say it to his face. "You poor, poor kid," Robicheaux said. "They got you all right. They got you all the way."

"What does that mean?" Teddy said.

"They got you coming and going all right."

Teddy was pissed and would have started a fight, but Sam talked him out of it, and after a few minutes the room was quiet again. Teddy had been sitting in his bunk reading letters from his young wife at home. Sam had seen her picture; she was a pretty little thing, slight, with her hair swept off her head in a grown-up style that made her look even younger than she was. Her wedding dress looked too big for her—Sam thought maybe it was borrowed. Teddy was piss-poor, like so many of the kids Sam met in the army. His dad was a farmer. Sam never saw any politician's kid in the army, no rich boys with good connections. It was something he'd always known, in the abstract—that the world was made for people who already had all the advantages—but somehow, until he'd been in the army a while, he'd never truly believed it.

He watched Teddy polish his boots angrily, almost violently, and then put them away. Later that night, he heard Teddy crying in his bunk but trying to hold it in, so that all Sam heard was the sharp intake of breath and the shake of the springs under him. "Hey, Teddy, hey," Sam whispered, but Teddy didn't answer him, and after a few minutes the shaking stopped.

The next time they had a weekend pass, Teddy didn't report back. No one said where he'd gone, but the staff sergeant came by and packed his personals. There were whispers of an accident or a trip across the border. Rumors, innuendo. Nobody really knew for sure. Robicheaux shook his head at Teddy's empty bunk, talked to it as if Teddy were still in it. "Man, they got you. They got you coming and going," he said. "You poor kid, you never even knew what hit you."

The six o'clock news was all about the big deployment of the 101st from Fort Campbell to Bien Hoa that was starting the next week. Walter Cronkite's voice over pictures of guys in fatigues loading planes, guys in fatigues getting off planes. It was file footage because the deployment hadn't started yet, but Sam couldn't help thinking that they all looked scared.

"Look at that," Charley said. "You're on the news."

"Me and ten thousand other guys."

"Still. I never made the evening news."

"Give it time and they'll draft you."

"Jesus, Sammy," he said. "Thanks a lot."

Charley had been brooding all day, his mood shifting between childish persistence and forced camaraderie. He was trying to talk Sam into going out that night, a little time for just the two of them, couching his real plans in terms of brotherly bonding. Sam knew what he had in mind—target shooting with their grandfather's old .22—but he didn't think it was a good idea. Still, Charley wheedled and demanded like a ten-year-old.

Ma said, "Change the channel, for Pete's sake. I don't want to watch that."

"It's not going to go away when you change the channel," said Pop.

"I know that," she said. "I don't want it on."

Pop got up and changed the channel, but it was still the war. All the channels were showing the same thing, more or less. He turned off the set. "Don't have to have the idiot box on all the time."

"It will be fine," Linda said. She was trying to calm Ma, trying to offer something that would help, though Sam knew nothing would make any difference to his mother. "He'll be careful, and he'll watch his back, and he'll be fine."

"I don't want to talk about it," Ma said.

"It's just a year," Linda said. "A year and he'll be home."

"I don't want to *talk* about it," Ma said. She got up and left the room.

Sam thought at first it was Linda she was angry at, but when he watched his father's face when Ma left the room, he knew the tension in the room was between his parents, some electricity he hadn't been aware of before. As if Ma blamed his father, somehow, for the war, for Sam's decision to join up, everything.

Sam went to the bathroom and splashed water on his face, thinking of the faces on the TV. It was not that he was afraid. He would not call what he was feeling fear, exactly, though that was part of it. Anger and hope and excitement. Almost looking forward to it, to getting it over with, the going part, the getting on with it. He could not have explained this to his mother or Charley or Linda. Pop might understand. He might, if it were something they could talk about. *Praise the Lord and pass the ammunition.*

When they reached the warehouse, Sam turned off the engine and took the six-pack off the front seat. They were in a district of warehouses and factories that used to be bustling, now falling into disuse. A police cruiser strobed down a nearby street with its siren on, loud, louder, then receding. The air smelled like snow. Sam did not want to be there. As usual, he had let Charley talk him into something he didn't want to do. His brother was

232

remarkably persistent: He wore people down until he got his way. It worked on Sam, their parents. As far as he could tell, it was working on Caroline, who didn't know what she had gotten herself into. It was working as they got out of the car and stepped out into the dark parking lot behind the old warehouse, their breath hanging over them in clouds.

You may have brothers and sisters at home, and mommies and daddies and aunties and uncles, but your fellow soldiers are your family from now on. They will put their lives in your hands, and you will put your life in theirs.

Charley was a noise in the dark, a sound of rummaging. He was looking for the rifle in the trunk. In the alley by the warehouse, where they used to have their wars long ago.

You be the German army. You're occupying Paris, from here to the garbage cans. I'm the Fourth Infantry coming in to liberate the city.

No fair. If I'm the Germans, I have to lose.

So I'll lose next time.

There never is a next time. You always have to win.

I do not.

"There it is," Charley said.

Sam could barely see the outline of the rifle in the dark, a slender little gun that was easy to load and didn't recoil much when fired. It had survived the move from Ontario only to rust in a box in the basement. They used to bring it to the warehouse in an old golf bag when they were kids, sneaking it out of the house when Ma wasn't looking. The wooden stock was gouged and pocked, but the muzzle at least was free of rust. Charley must have cleaned it recently.

What will you do to protect your brothers?

Kill! Kill!

The warehouse was surrounded by high hurricane fencing and a gate that had once been padlocked shut but now swung loosely. The windows were dark, some of them shattered by kids. Charley said the city had condemned the warehouse to be torn down, that by the time Sam got back from Vietnam, it would be gone.

Sam dug in the mud with his toe. Was he here, right here, when he heard the shells falling on Bastogne? When he stormed Utah Beach and took a sniper position, tossed his grenades into an enemy bunker?

Hands up, you Nazi pig, I've got you now.

Sammy, Sammy, don't.

Don't cry, Charley, it's just a game.

Charley was rummaging in the trunk for the cartridges. He was making an impressive racket, would make an easy target even in the dark. Sam remembered the long days of running, of push-ups in the yard, the gut punch that first day when the sergeant said, "Eyes front!" He tried to imagine Charley taking orders, Charley marching in lockstep with eighty other guys. In the trunk of the Bel-Air, Charley found the paper bag full of cartridges and handed them to Sam. They knocked dully against one another. Slow, fat snowflakes started to fall, coating their hair and shoulders.

They slipped through the gate, jimmied open the back door, and went inside. It was cavernous, dark. A smell like mice and plaster. At one point the warehouse had housed religious statues, the kinds found in front of churches and Catholic houses all over the city. Virgin Marys, mostly, and Francis of Assisi, sometimes a Jesus, an Infant of Prague. One time they had seen an entire row of Virgins dressed in blue, and Charley said it looked like a lineup of Sam's ex-girlfriends. But that was years ago. The statue factory had gone out of business, and the warehouse had closed.

Now the statues were mostly gone, all except one pockmarked and lopsided Virgin that local boys used for target practice. Charley approached it and placed one empty beer can on its head, one on each upturned hand. The Virgin had lost several of her marble fingers to .22 slugs or BBs, and the cans wobbled unsteadily.

"Age before beauty," Charley said.

"I'm in no hurry."

Charley shrugged and loaded the gun. The click of the bullets sounded hollow, disembodied, inside the warehouse. Charley's face was set, a thing he thought no one ever noticed. How he sometimes had to screw up his courage, how he was often more afraid than he let on. A line pressed into his mouth and eyes, the way he smiled without mirth. In that light, outside the factory walls, Charley looked very young and pale. How he'd looked when Sam had said give it time and he could be drafted, too. Stricken.

Charley put the rifle to his shoulder, aimed down the barrel, and fired.

His first two shots missed, but then the third connected. The can popped off the Virgin Mary's hand and onto the floor with a metallic clang.

"Congratulations."

"Thanks."

Charley picked up the can and set it up again for Sam's turn. The cans glowed faintly orange in the light coming in from outside, some of them still with paper clinging where their labels had been torn off. Sam reloaded. He could have done it with his eyes closed. He remembered Pop telling him that he had learned to do that, once—take a weapon apart and put it back together again blindfolded.

"I hit one at a hundred yards once," Charley said.

"When?"

"A couple of months ago."

"Did anyone see it?"

"I was here by myself."

"Sure you were. From where to where?"

"From here to the statue."

Sam squinted. The statue of the Virgin Mary was in the center of the warehouse floor. "That's not a hundred yards."

"It is."

Sam chambered the first round. "That's a hundred *feet.*"

"It's yards. I'm telling you, I made that shot."

"Are you going to get out of the way?"

Sam fired his first three shots. The cans hadn't moved.

"God, that's got to be embarrassing," Charley said. "You being a trained killer and all."

Sam reloaded. He put the gun to his shoulder again and squeezed the trigger. He hit three in a row, quickly now, *pop-pop!* The cans jumped from their spot as though they'd been frightened. They hit the cement floor of the warehouse, rolled, and lay still. A beautiful shot. The squeeze of the trigger, the minor percussion of the charge exploding, and the sound of the bullet striking home. Beautiful.

Charley missed his next two shots. "This rifle is so old," he said, "it should be in a museum."

"It's not the rifle's fault," Sam said.

Charley missed again. His face pulled in frustration he couldn't hide. "Damn."

Sam hit the next three in a row, *pop-pop-pop*. The cans trembled and fell over. Charley set up again. They made small, angry sounds when he set them down. From this distance, in the faintest light coming in from the windows, Sam couldn't make out his face, couldn't see his expression.

"Three in a row," Charley said. "The army's done a number on you, Uncle Sam."

"If they can do this much for me, they can do it for you, too."

"Yeah, I guess," Charley said. "They did it for Zel."

With his fist Charley knocked first one can out of the Virgin Mary's hands, then the other, then the can on her head. Sam could smell their warm, fermented smell from where he stood. He let the muzzle drop. He didn't want to shoot anymore. He didn't want anything except to go home, and sleep in his own bed, and forget about the war, the draft. Everything.

Charley said maybe they should get back. In case Linda got too lonely. "She's too good for you, you know."

"Don't tell her. She'll find out soon enough."

"I'm sure she knows your shortcomings."

"Yeah, well"—Sam grinned—"Caroline never seemed to mind."

"Nice one."

"I thought so."

They left the warehouse and the cans and the Virgin Mary. Sam threw the .22 in the trunk, the bag of shells behind it. Charley started up the car again and went east, back toward the city. Neither spoke, but people on the sidewalks drew their eyes, and noisy kids went by in cars with the radios turned up, and loud noises went off in the distance.

Signs for south and north. Sam felt Charley look over at him, give a shit-eating grin, and push the turn signal right, south and east, away from Chicago, away from their parents' house on the north side, toward the curving southern tip of the lake toward Gary, Michigan City, Kalamazoo, Battle Creek, Ann Arbor, Detroit. Canada. Home, his mother still called it.

"What do you say?" Charley said. "Five hours—six, tops—and we can be there." He was already in the lane. He was coming up on the right-hand turn.

"Come on," Sam said. "Let's go home. I'm too tired for this shit."

"Who says it's shit?" Charley asked. "Let's go." He seemed very certain he knew what he was doing, but Sam knew he didn't, not really, because what was very simple for Charley was not so simple for him. Sam could see it now, the road trip in the dark, stopping for breakfast in Michigan City or Battle Creek, talking low with his brother over eggs and coffee, leaving his uniform at home and hiding his dog tags under the seat, wearing a hat over his high-and-tight, already looking over his shoulder. The highway through Detroit and over the bridge, over the dark river, the way the customs officer would lean down and look inside the car, the way Sam was sure they would be stopped, detained for some reason that would start out as suspicion and end up as real trouble, and then at the last minute they would be saved, waved through. Over the border and down to the other side.

The look on the recruiting officer's face when he read his papers and saw the city of birth was Windsor, Ontario, the way the man's long, curving eyebrows went up into his forehead like a question mark. *I want you to know, if I wake up tomorrow and the car's gone and you're gone, that will be all right with me.*

"Say the word and we're gone," Charley said.

The turn was coming up. The signal was on. Sam felt a chill fall over everything. In the opposite lane, heading out of the city on a Saturday morning, the cars started turning off their lights, there and there, like eyes flicking shut. Above them, the high-rises blocked out the first of the light. The signal on, the city rising behind them. A car horn sounded in his ear. "Quit screwing around," Sam said. The car behind them swerved and passed them.

Charley would make the turn anyway. It would be like him to do it, keep the joke going long after anyone else thought it was funny, and then, only after Sam descended into angry silence, turn around and go back. Or he might take it all the way, drive the car to Canada no matter what Sam said. He'd done things like that before. Go on, Charley, you do it. I dare you this time. Go on.

But instead Charley turned on the left-hand signal and got in the other lane, slowing down to get behind another car that honked at them as they swerved. He steered the car onto the expressway and went north, toward home.

Two weeks later Sam arrived in Bien Hoa in a C–141, heavy and gray, ponderous, a whale in flight. The plane was full of military cargo: rifles and parachutes, jeeps, ammunition, and Sam in the middle of it, one more piece of machinery, U.S. government property all. His hands and feet were cold from the recycled plane air. They rolled to a stop, and when the engines cut out he still felt as if the vibrations were coursing through his joints. Out the window, the women were bent over in the fields, their white hats like parasols, the bottoms of their pants rolled up to their knees. They didn't even look up when the plane landed. When the doors opened the heat hit his face. It reminded him of the cloth the barber used when his father took him for his first shave at age thirteen. Damp and searing all at once, suffocating. In less than a week he would learn to hate the weather, the heat, the rain, the low, damp skies. The red earth in his hair and on his clothes, under his fingernails, in his mouth. But stepping off the plane that first moment, he was glad of the warmth, a comfort he had not known he was waiting for.

He was in Vietnam three days before he was shot at for the first time. He could hear the bullets zing when they went past, like the sound of someone screaming. In a foxhole as deep as a grave, he woke and saw the moon through a break in the canopy. The jungle was full of noises, birds, insects. Light steps that could be a man's or an animal's. The moon was cold and white, ordinary, familiar. He should have been comforted by the sight, but he wasn't. There should be no moon in a place like this. No stars. No trees. It was not the same earth at all, but someplace else entirely. The surface of the sun. The tail of a comet.

At the end of January, he had been asleep outside the city of Hue when the tracers started. Around him the faces of the other men in his platoon turned green under the tracers' arcs. His platoon leader said it was just the natives celebrating Tet, but as the night wore on and the sound of gunfire got closer, he knew something different was going on. He was unable to sleep, the metal neck of his M-16 going hot and slick under his fingers.

A few weeks later, his platoon leader was killed by friendly fire, a shell of their own mortar, and Sam was made squad leader in his place. He wrote home to his father that he'd gotten the job not because he deserved it, but because it was bad for morale to promote the dead.

In April, walking along a dike, the man in front of him hit a toe popper and lost his leg. Wham, just like that. Walking just behind him, Sam got hit. A big hunk of shrapnel in the meat of his calf. He was on the ground with the red dirt in his mouth, coating his tongue, trying not to scream. Danny Shreve telling him to keep still, goddammit, you're going to make it worse. The medic said his leg might be broken. The pain there was like someone burning a cigar butt into his muscle, but he was oddly buoyant, laughing and joking with the guys while they waited for the dust-off to come, easy breezy, because he was going home at last, a million-dollar wound. They loaded him into the chopper for that beautiful ride, that moment in the air. Lucky son of a bitch. He spent nearly a month in the rear recuperating after the doctors dug the remnant out of his leg, which was not broken after all. Afterward the docs gave him the piece of shrapnel, nearly as big as his thumb, to keep. He ate hot meals and enjoyed the company of the nurses and read his letters from Linda. But as soon as he could carry his pack again, as soon as the flesh closed pink over the muscle, they shipped his ass back to his unit. Son of a bitch. Not so lucky.

In June, he was leading his squad across the beach when they came across a boy crying on the sand and shouting for help; his father was dying. *"Giúp thôi vơi! Giúp thôi vơi!"* Help me! Help me! The boy's face was small and angry.

The sand offered little purchase under their boots. Their packs, with the massive amount of gear they were required to hump, were too heavy. Their footsteps were slow, fingers near triggers. The boy could be VC. You just never knew. They watched him carefully, ready for anything.

The man's muscles had gone stiff, the lids heavy over his eyes. His lips and tongue were already blue. Sam raised an eyelid with his thumb but saw only white. The fisherman was slumped in the bottom of the boat with his head on the gunwale. No sign of what happened to him.

Sam picked the man up under the armpits and tried to lift him out of the boat, but he was too heavy. The sea snake was in the bottom of the boat, still trapped in the net but trying to get away, flapping against the wooden bottom, the silvery scales of fish beneath. The snake was gray with bands of dark across its back and a flat, paddlelike tail. It freed itself from the net and slipped over the side of the boat. Sam stepped back and let it go.

The boy cried, "*Giúp thôi voi!*" A wisp of air escaped the man's throat. His airway was closing; it would be a matter of minutes. Sam held the man's head with both hands because he didn't know what else to do. He had straight soft hair, dark still, no silver in it, like a child's hair. He thought of putting a bullet in the man's brain. End it fast. End it now. But the feel of that fine soft hair, the man's breath in his face strong with fish and garlic, his living breath coming up from him, and Sam knew he wouldn't be able to do it. Not like this.

The boy's hands on Sam's arm were light. "*Thôi xin lôi,*" Sam said. I'm sorry. The boy was insistent. He took his father's hand. The fisherman was missing the tips of two fingers on his right hand, down to the knuckle, old wounds well healed. Sam felt a strange sense that he was not really on a beach in Vietnam but somewhere else entirely, and the breeze came in off the water and hit the back of his neck, red with sunburn, and the water was green, so green, and if he didn't know better, it could have been Lake Michigan on a warm day, the sand getting inside his boots and down into the socks, itching, itching. He thought of his father in the cold woods of Labrador. He'd once asked him what happened to him there, but all Pop had said was, "I survived. That's all."

When the boy wasn't looking, Koch, the medic, gave the fisherman morphine. The man's face relaxed. Sam said he would call for a dust-off, but Koch said they wouldn't get there in time.

When the snake tried to reach the water, one of the guys grabbed his entrenching tool and chopped off its head, quick and slick. The body jumped and writhed. Some of the others joined in, chopping at the snake with their shovels. No one looked at the fisherman. They were waiting for this moment to be over so they could keep going, get this shit over with. All they wanted was rest, food, water. They wanted to go home. They didn't look at the fisherman dying in his boat, or the boy. They didn't look at one another.

Sam waited with the fisherman till the end. The man's breath was like the slow leak of a tire trailing off into silence. The kid was still crying. "*Ba o'i, Ba o'i*," he said. Father, Father.

"Time to go," Sam said.

When they passed the man, still lying in his boat, Sam looked the other way, out toward the sea, to the other small fishing boats floating on that still surface, and he watched the fishermen throw out their nets wide across the water and then gather them in with both hands. The flash of silver fish squirming in their nets.

July, more than six months into his tour. They'd lost half the company, ninety-two men, fighting North Vietnamese Army regulars in a little village up the coast, and two weeks later they were still awaiting replacements that always seemed to come too late. For two weeks they'd been in the bush, chasing a column of NVA farther and farther north, getting mortared at night. Robicheaux had bitten it by then, shot in the back of the head while he was taking a piss along a trail. Danny Shreve had taken a bad hit from a grenade and the word was he'd died on his way to Japan. Sam was tired and hungry all the time, his guts cramped from dysentery he'd caught drinking the native water. He was surprised to find himself still alive. His senses were strangely dulled and heightened at the same time, awake only to gunfire, to trip wires, to the sounds of feet moving and ammo loading and mortars falling. Immune to everything else. He found, suddenly, that he could sleep anywhere, in any conditions, deep, dreamless sleep from which he always woke exhausted and starving.

The log ship was in for the afternoon, bringing supplies and mail, chlorinated water they never drank because it was too heavy to carry. Sam was opening a can of peaches in syrup, his afternoon C-ration, when the lieutenant crossed the paddy toward him and said Sam was supposed to report to the rear.

"What's going on, sir?" Sam asked, but the lieutenant said he didn't know. The log ship was there, waiting for him, propellers cutting through the humid air.

"Get on the bird," said the lieutenant, "and you'll find out when you get there."

LZ Sally, the brigade headquarters, was a dirty little patch of ground northwest of Hue. When the chopper was circling, coming in to land, Sam thought of his father, the look on Pop's face when he had said Sam could take the car. How cool the air had been that morning, how cold his hands. He jumped off the bird and crossed the compound. Someone pointed him toward the chaplain's tent. He took off his helmet and his pack and went inside.

The chaplain told him Charley was dead, that his brother, Charley, had died when the car he was riding in was hit by a train half a world away.

The chaplain was a Catholic priest, thin faced and wearing a uniform that was so clean, it looked unnatural. Sam kept looking at the creases in his pants while he talked, wondered where in the hell he got someone to iron his pants out here. They weren't quite real, the way sleep wasn't real, and home wasn't real. Charley was dead. Even that wasn't real. Outside the tent, a row of helicopters took off, circling the camp slowly, and disappeared over the trees. A sound of distant gunfire. The chaplain sat down and offered Sam something to drink, but he couldn't. His mouth tasted of metal.

"Was he alone in the car?"

"What?"

"Sir, was there anyone else with him in the car?"

"I don't really know, son. I didn't hear that there was."

Charley in the car with the turn signal on, ready to go to Canada. *Say the word, and we're gone.*

Sam was allowed to go home for the funeral. Two weeks' leave. He rode back to the world not in a military plane, but in a commercial jet, surrounded by guys who were done with their tours, who were going home for good, hassling the stewardesses, drinking cold beer. When the wheels left the ground, the cabin was filled with shouts and cheers. Around him guys fell asleep reading or listening to music, but Sam couldn't close his eyes. He couldn't stop looking at the red dirt under his fingernails, picking at it, picking out every little bit. When his fingernails were clean, he got up and went to the lavatory and washed his hands over and over.

Pop was there to meet his plane at O'Hare. He was gray under the eyes. He shook Sam's hand solemnly and offered to carry his duffel. "That's all right, Pop," he said. "I've got it." Sam followed his father out to the parking lot, Pop's shoulders hunched and his hands grasping at nothing, at air. He had aged ten years since Sam had seen him.

Ma threw her arms around his neck and cried until Sam thought she would collapse. "It's all right, Ma," he said, though he couldn't say how. "It will be all right."

It wasn't long before he heard the whole story over and over, how Charley had been coming home from a poker game and had tried to get across the tracks before the train did, how the train had slammed into the driver's side and crushed the Bel-Air so completely that at first the fire department had been unable to determine what kind of car it was or who was inside, until the next morning when Ma, in a panic that Charley still had not come home, started calling around to hospitals and police stations. Caroline was there when the news came—she had been one of the first people Dottie had called when Charley didn't come home. She had passed out right to the floor when he gave her the news, Pop said.

At Charley's funeral, in the Polish cemetery, Sam listened to the minister give the blessing for the dead. It was a hot summer day, and the sound of jetliners overhead obscured the minister's voice. The cemetery was crowded with Charley's friends. Zel's mother was there, some kids whose names Sam didn't even know. At one point he looked at Caroline, who was still and white as stone. Afterward, when he tried to speak to her, she shook her head and moved away from him. The next week she would take her mother out of the hospital, pack up their things, and move back to Ontario.

Ma was a wreck. She didn't eat, didn't sleep. At night when he should have been asleep, Sam heard her walking from the kitchen to the bathroom and back. Sometimes she opened the front door and looked outside in the yard, as if she expected Charley to come home any minute.

After a week Sam returned to Vietnam, but he wasn't sent back to his company, which was in heavy fighting in the A Shau Valley. Instead he was given a transfer to the rear, to LZ Sally, where he typed forms for a colonel who wanted a college boy to do his paperwork. The colonel took a liking to Sam, gave him plum assignments, his own tent where he slept on a cot under mosquito netting, where he never had to pick up his rifle or hear the sound of bullets whizzing over his head. Sam spent the last part of his tour taking daily showers, eating hot meals, drinking Cokes whenever he felt like it. It was a pretty sweet deal, one every guy in the forward units would have given his last C-ration for, and though he was grateful, he couldn't help thinking of the boys he'd known who were still out there, still humping through the bush, just trying to stay alive. He couldn't help thinking of Charley and the train bearing down on him. How afraid his brother had been that night in the warehouse, how hard he had tried not to show it.

In October, getting short, he asked the colonel why he hadn't been sent back to his platoon in the forward areas. The sole surviving son of a family doesn't go to the forward areas, the colonel told him, but some politician from Chicago had got on the horn and requested the transfer sooner than usual, some friend of his father's. "Must be nice to have connections," the colonel said. "Somebody looking out for you."

His last morning in Vietnam, Sam got up early and walked out of the camp toward the trees. His bag was already packed. First there would be a stop in San Francisco, then a plane to Chicago. Pop would meet his plane. In the car, his ruined hands on the wheel, Pop would say nothing, or not much. Ma at the door, waiting; Linda would fly up to meet him a few days later. He was surprised he still had a life to go back to. He was surprised to find himself still breathing.

That day the sun was rising hard and bright, and the birds were breaking into song, but ahead of him the trail was dim. He wondered at the forces in his life that moved him, the things in the world that even now were hidden from him, and he thought he had never been so aware of where he put his feet and hands and the feel of the air in his lungs. He breathed in and out and listened to the quiet, and for that moment he thought he could walk anywhere he wanted; he could just keep walking along the trail, across the fields and forests, over rivers and borders, all the way back to the beginning. How easy it would be to walk into the trees and disappear.

CUSTOMS

1999

TEN

All her life, Dottie had been afraid of water. She had never liked to swim, hated bridges and boats. When Sam wanted to send her and Walt on a Caribbean cruise for their fiftieth anniversary, she refused. Period. Sam said she was being unreasonable, that it was perfectly safe, but on the ship that brought her over the sea as a child, she had leaned over the railing and looked down into the sea and had seen it for what it was, and she didn't want any part of it.

The only one who knew about this fear was Walt, the only person she had ever told. When she started having trouble breathing, when the doctors started to qualify her chances for improvement in terms of prolonging her life for one year, maybe two, she made sure he knew what she wanted. They went to the funeral home together to make the arrangements. Walt shifted in his chair while she bargained with the funeral director, insisting that she be cremated—no ridiculous coffin, no expensive and wasteful embalming. Her one stipulation was that Walt wasn't to dump her ashes over the water. No muddy lake or river for her, no cold sea. She wanted to go to her rest on land. "Somewhere where it's warm," she said. "Somewhere where there are flowers."

He promised to scatter her ashes in the garden behind their house in the city, maybe, or in the park near the fountain where she liked to look at the tulips in the spring. "Whatever you want," he said. "Just not so soon, Benny, all right?"

Not long after that, she started to find him sleeping in the middle of the day, putting off mowing the lawn or working on the car for an afternoon, then two. He was retired, and so what if he wanted a bit of a rest? He'd earned it. The grass would still have to be mowed tomorrow. She found him lying on the sofa in the front room the way Daddy used to, or on their bed with the door half-closed, and she imagined him living in this house alone in a year or two, making his own meals, eating in front of the TV. She was overwhelmed with tenderness toward him. She relished the thought of his mourning, how it gave all their moments together a kind of grace. The arguments of the past drifted away. They would forgive each other their faults. After fifty-six years together, it was the only thing left to do.

But in the fall, not long after his seventy-eighth birthday, he started having trouble getting out of bed, not because he was tired, but because his legs didn't work properly. He had backaches so unbearable, he couldn't sleep at night. A battery of tests revealed a tumor at the base of his spine. The doctor said he didn't know what caused it. Had Walt worked with chemicals, had he spent a lot of time around radios? She remembered him telling her about all those hours during the war sitting on the radio in long-range bombers. It was the best way to keep warm, he'd said. The radio was covered only with some sheets of plywood. The doctor said that could have been the culprit, because you wouldn't believe the radiation those things gave off. No one knew at the time how dangerous it was.

The irony was not lost on Walt: The war, he said, was still trying to kill him after all these years.

He had surgery, chemo. By Christmas he'd lost all his thick white hair. He couldn't eat the dinner Dottie made but did his best to rally, joking that he didn't want to lose his beer belly—it was the only thing he owned that was paid for. In January they found a second tumor, in his kidney. By February he was gone.

At customs they were told to pull to the side for inspection. Around them cars idled, waiting for their turn. Even after all this time it felt like an indignity, having strangers paw through your things. Suspecting you. As though you had a body in the trunk or something. Sam said it was nothing personal. "They're doing their jobs," he said. He took off his glasses and wiped them on his sleeve. "That's all."

"I don't like it."

"You don't have to like it."

In the backseat Katie was reading a book, something foreign that Dottie couldn't pronounce. German or Russian—Dottie could never remember which one her granddaughter was studying. The world was changing so much, she could hardly keep up. The girl was stretched across the backseat with a pillow propped against the door, under her shoulders. Dottie could see her bare feet in the passenger-side mirror, browned across their tops from the summer sun and painted a bloody red. She had quite a sense of style, that girl, something she'd inherited from her mother, though in recent months she'd traded in her mother's Neiman Marcus wardrobe for secondhand jeans, thrift store jackets, a defiant dark smudge of makeup under each eye, as if she were dressing up for a part in a play. Katie looked up from her book to the lines of people at the customs booths, the bridge, the border crossing.

"It looks just like anyplace else," she said.

"Well, we're not really there yet," Dottie said.

Katie went back to her book. She looked sullen and bored. She had been in some kind of trouble earlier in the year—Sam had never told Dottie exactly what happened—but since then he said he had refused to leave her home by herself. With Linda in Europe with her new husband and Jennifer in San Diego, Katie had come with them on this visit. "A forced exile," she had called it. Dottie thought that was a little bit too much but didn't say anything. Sam liked to deal with his girls his own way. In this case, he had decided to ignore Katie and keep driving.

It was moving toward evening, a clear blue day at the beginning of summer, and the border crossing was lined with cars and trucks in both directions. Behind them the skyscrapers of Detroit glowed yellow, and the lights on the bridge winked on for the evening. Dottie was relieved the bridge was behind them. She spent most of the drive from Chicago dreading it, how high it was over the river, how it felt as if you might fly off into the air any second. She closed her eyes and made Sam tell her when they were over land again.

"I don't understand why you're so afraid," he said.

"Just tell me when we get there."

A cloud passed over the sun and the sky went orange around it, and a tug going down the river blew its horn once, loudly. It had been maybe three or four years since Dottie had been to Canada for a visit. Only a six-hour drive, a reasonable distance, not the ends of the earth, but far enough, especially in those months when Walt was sick and she got so tired so easily. She was starting to forget things, too. At first it was nothing serious, misplacing her glasses or pills, but then she'd found a warm gallon of milk in the bottom of the bedroom closet, a month past its expiration date. She took it outside and buried it under the previous night's trash, so Sam or Katie wouldn't see it in the kitchen garbage. The doctors had told her she might start forgetting things, but as months went by and nothing happened, she had stopped believing it. Now she could feel it coming on, a loosening in her mind. A few days ago, she forgot Sam's name. He came in from somewhere, errands or work, and though she knew who he was, a full ten or fifteen minutes must have passed before she could conjure the name, match the graying middle-aged man who looked like his father to the serious little boy he'd been, the young man who'd gone to Vietnam and come back silent and solemn. Sam. You're Sam, she thought at last, watching him take out a casserole to thaw. She was so relieved when she finally remembered it, she nearly cried. He didn't seem to notice anything was wrong, and of course she wouldn't tell him. She didn't want him to worry.

The trip was Sam's idea. He thought it would do her good. Jimmy and Ethel and their three boys would be there, and Adele and Caroline and her husband. Janice and Monty and Ed were driving in from Niagara. "A real family reunion," Sam said. "Everyone wants to see you." Dottie knew they were thinking it might be the last time they all got together. Well, that was all right. There had to be a last time.

Jimmy wrote to tell her of all the people who had asked about her: Bert Mason, now divorced from the English wife; the Livermore twins she'd baby-sat as a teenager; even Bobby Wisniewski. Jimmy had run into Bobby in the hospital parking lot, Bobby on his way out, Jimmy on his way in. Bobby had said, "Tell Dottie I said hello."

Bobby Wisniewski. She felt twenty years old again.

The customs officer came up and tapped on the window. She wore her hair in a long blond ponytail, blindingly white tennis shoes, a uniform too big for her. Her ID tag read "Alison." "She's just a baby," Dottie said.

"That baby could impound the car if she wanted to," said Sam. "Don't say anything foolish."

"What would I say that would be foolish?"

Sam handed their papers through the window and answered the girl's questions about the purpose of their visit (to see family) and the length of their stay (about a week) and then popped the trunk. In the side mirror, as Dottie watched, this Alison opened a suitcase and started taking things out of it. Dottie recognized a pair of her own drawers in the girl's hand.

It took just a minute. The girl—Dottie couldn't think of her in any kind of official capacity—shut the suitcases and closed the trunk, then came around to the side window and handed Sam back their papers. "That was quick," Sam said.

"Quick as a fox," the girl said. He smiled broadly at her. Dottie was embarrassed for him, a girl her age. His divorce from Linda had been final for more than a year, but that didn't mean he had to make a fool of himself.

She kept waiting for things to look familiar, but they didn't, not quite. Buildings were not where she thought they would be or were missing altogether. There were new houses and strip malls and plastic signs in red and yellow neon. The streets she knew when she was young dissolved into dark rivers in a treacherous new country. She didn't recognize street names, didn't feel the rightness of the direction, and as Sam steered the car left, and right, and right again, she felt a ribbon of fear unfurl inside her— they were going the wrong way, they had taken a wrong turn and would end up somewhere they weren't supposed to be. Her heart fluttered in her chest, seemed to stop, and then gave an answering thump.

"Stop the car."

"I'm following Caroline's directions," Sam said. "We'll be there in a minute."

"You should have turned left back there."

"Would you let me drive, please?"

She could see inside the windows of unfamiliar houses that stood where she remembered no houses. She was sure she had never been on this highway before. At one time she had known every building, every intersection, by heart. "I think we're lost," she said.

"Look, here's the turn," Sam said.

They had left town and were in the country on a dark road with no streetlights. She did not recognize the road, didn't see any familiar landmarks. Something about this was wrong. "We're lost," she said. "Stop the car."

She pulled the door handle, and the sounds of the road came flooding into the car. The seat belt held her in place; she couldn't seem to get it off. Then the brakes caught and the door flew open, out of her hands.

Sam rolled to a stop beside the road, gravel crunching under the tires. "What are you doing?" he said. "You want to get yourself killed?" He got out, went around to her side, and slammed her door shut. "If you do that again," he said, his voice low, "I'll leave you here."

He sounded like Daddy, making threats that sounded only half-serious but were deadly meant, and she wondered at how echoes come down through the past, echoes of voices and faces and events, through you, as if you were just a conduit for moving life forward, out of you and into your children. As if there were no freedom in this life at all, just a constant cycling and recycling of the past.

Sam had said she should sell the house. He told her this sitting at the kitchen table one night over Chinese takeout. Plum sauce congealed on her plate as she listened to him. Sam laid out his plans, so practical, so reasonable, lulling her into a sense of disbelief, as if Walt were sitting there, not her middle-aged son. "You know you can't live alone here," he said. "You know what the doctor told you."

There had been many such conversations since Walt had died. She had been resistant, but the resistance left her tired and crabby afterward, a pinched and joyless shell of herself. Still, she refused to give in. She did not want to move, to sell her house. *Her* house. The only house that had ever belonged to her. Why couldn't Sam move in with her? There were lots of reasons, according to Sam. The house wasn't big enough, for one—the girls wouldn't have a place to sleep when they came to visit. It needed new windows, a new roof, tuckpointing that Dottie wasn't sure she could afford. But really she knew the reason was that Sam was worried about her, he didn't want her living alone, as if she were like Katie, always in some kind of trouble, untrustworthy on her own. It irked her, that she, a woman of seventy-six, should be fussed and fretted over like a wayward teenager.

Since the divorce, Sam had taken to calling Dottie at odd hours to chat about some little thing he'd thought or to ask her something—did she need the grass cut, the oil changed on her car?—then hanging up after only a minute or two, embarrassed by loneliness. Dottie had always thought Linda was spoiled, expected a standard of living that Sam hadn't been able to provide, but it seemed as though they had given up, that when things got hard they simply shut down and moved on. That was no way to live your life, she told Sam. He said it wasn't that simple, that marriages were strange countries, stranger inside than out.

That was something she knew as much as anyone.

Finally she gave in and agreed to sell. She would move to the suburbs to live with Sam and Katie, Jennifer's old room cleared of its dolls and its white faux French furniture and made over into an old woman's stale, lonely chamber.

Sam was relieved. It will be all right, Ma, you'll see.

She had forgotten how much work it was to move. A lifetime of accumulated belongings needed to be packed or thrown out or given away. Sam and Katie helped when they had time, but there was still so much she had to do herself. She went through the drawers and closets full of old clothes no one had worn in years, the dolls the girls had played with when they were small, many now missing their hair. Clothes still hung where Walt had left them. His work boots still had mud on them from their last wearing. There were his good shoes in the bottom of the closet, well shined, which she set aside in case Sam wanted them. A single sock, a striped tie she hadn't seen in ten years. She couldn't decide what to get rid of and what to keep.

In an old shoebox she found a bundle of letters she'd sent him during the war, letters from his mother and his brother and sisters, Sam's and Charley's school pictures, a paper bag full of Father's Day cards signed in Katie's and Jen's childish scrawl. In another she found a small, heavy jewel case, the kind that might have contained a pearl necklace or cuff links. Walt's air force medals and insignia, the crowned wing he'd worn on his cap, his silver medal with the oak leaf pin he'd been given for being "Mentioned in Despatches." The bits of metal clattered together in the bottom of the case. Upside down, the white back of a photograph, soft against the faded yellow velvet inside the case. On the back of the photo, in cramped letters barely legible, "All my love." Dottie turned it over. The girl in the photo was black and white—pale face, pale arms and legs, the faintest freckles, hair so thick and dark that it must have been nearly black, dark dress, and dark shoes all against a white building. The sun shining right in her eyes. The girl squinted one eye at the camera, at the long shadow falling there just at her feet. The sign over the door read THE VICTORIA INN. The girl had a kind of slant to her, everything just a little off-kilter either right or left, that suggested a kind of energy—she wasn't standing still to have her picture taken like a prim little thing. It made the white border around the edge of the photo look like a ledge, as though she might be jumping out of the frame at any minute.

How long had the girl been in her house? How long had she lain there, unseen, among Walt's old things?

Dottie closed the box. The photo was still in her hand, and she tried putting it in her pocket, but she didn't like it there. She went around the house looking for a good place to keep it, but nothing would do, nothing seemed like the right place for such a thing; and when she went past Sam at the kitchen table, he put down his coffee and asked what on earth was the matter, why was she circling the house with that look on her face, as if she'd just seen a ghost?

It was dark when they finally reached Caroline's house. Sam was still angry and didn't speak when he pulled into the gravel drive and turned off the engine. The house was out in the country, not far from where Dottie had grown up, an old orchard farmhouse Caroline and her husband had bought in the seventies, in a fit of hopefulness. In those days people were looking to go back to the land, for some more authentic way of life, and Caroline did well with it, turned it into a real success, so much so that after a few years Neil gave up his job at the university and worked the orchard full-time. Caroline still taught poetry part-time in the evenings for fun, and sometimes she'd rent out the spare rooms to her writer friends for a week or a month. "Like an artist's colony," she said. Dottie couldn't imagine having strangers in your house, mooning around all day with their pens scratching across paper. Caroline had published some things herself, poems and stories. Sometimes she sent Dottie copies of them with her letters, but though she was proud of Caroline, the pieces all seemed immensely sad. Not that Dottie had ever professed to be an expert in poetry. She knew what she liked when she saw it.

The porch light went on. Caroline and Neil were in the doorway, calling greetings into the yard. "Hello, hello!" Caroline sang. "You made it!"

"Barely," Sam said.

Dottie got out of the car slowly, went up the front walk. She was tired and felt the need for a bath. Behind her, Katie was getting the bags out of the car. "Just leave those, honey," Caroline called to her. "Neil will get them."

"I guess I have my marching orders," Neil said for Sam's benefit. The camaraderie that sprang up between men in these situations was something Dottie had never understood, but there it was again, immediate, comforting. Pretending their wives oppressed them—a universal language. Lightning bugs were flashing on and off, and behind the house the trees were dark and still as soldiers. The house was foursquare with a large, handsome porch, white with a red front door and red geraniums hanging in baskets from the porch ceiling. It was quaint, a city person's idea of a country house, but then Dottie supposed it would have to be to appeal to Caroline's writer friends enough to get them to spend their money to come. Dottie had been there once or twice before but never overnight. Usually she stayed with Jimmy, but this time when Caroline heard they were coming, she practically begged them to stay with her, all her empty rooms. She never had any children. That would make a person long for company, especially someone like Caroline, who'd never been happy on her own.

When Dottie came up the stairs, Caroline kissed her cheek. She smelled like strawberries, some kind of sweet lotion she'd used on her face and neck. She was wearing a simple red linen sheath that came up tight under the arms and scooped down toward her breasts. Her skin was tanned and smooth, not crepey around the neck like a lot of women her age. The color of the dress made her skin look rosy. She'd lost weight since Dottie had seen her last and had a new set of hard, flat muscles. When she was younger she had been curvy, and Dottie had always thought she would end up fat and matronly, like her mother, but clearly she was fighting it. A lot of women did, these days. Dottie thought she looked exceptionally well.

Caroline stood back to let Dottie inside. "Was it a tiring drive? Did you find it all right?"

"Oh, yes," Dottie said. "Fine, thank you."

"Now she says it's fine," Sam answered, but his voice was good-humored, mild. In front of company, he would not scold her. "In the car, we were lost."

"I never said that. I never said *lost*. It just looked different in the dark, is all."

Neil came up the steps with Dottie's suitcase. He was a lively, uncomplicated man whose interests were mostly in history and politics and his apple orchard. Dottie had thought him foolish at first, with his compost pile in the backyard and his homemade beer and the long ponytail that hung nearly to his waist even when his hair started thinning on top. He'd mellowed over the years, though—or else Dottie had, either one—and they'd come to a kind of understanding. He called her "dear," and she decided not to be offended by it. He did it again on the porch steps. "Excuse me, dear," he said, and she stepped back to make way for him.

In the front room Caroline exclaimed over Katie, how grown up she was, how beautiful she was, like her mother, how tall and elegant. Katie looked annoyed. She didn't like comparisons to her mother or attention brought to her looks, which was probably why she was trying to hide them under all that makeup. Dottie was embarrassed for her.

"The house looks beautiful," she told Caroline. "You've done so much to it since we were here last."

"We have plans for improving it, you know. We're going to turn it into a bed-and-breakfast. We could have people over from Detroit or Hamilton. Even Toronto. There's a woman down the road who's making a fortune with hers."

"Caroline thinks she's going to get her hands on some of that stock market money," Neil said. He came down the stairs shaking his head and smiling. How Dottie missed those moments, those fond, exasperated moments when married couples pretended to be annoyed with each other in front of guests, when a display of true affection would be too intimate. "All those pimply-faced kids taking their companies public. She thinks they're going to spend their money coming here."

"You do have to take those kinds of opportunities when they come," Sam said.

"There," said Caroline.

"I wasn't disagreeing with you," Neil said. He caught Caroline around the waist and talked to her in a low, intimate voice. "You have to learn to be more gracious in front of guests."

Dottie's eyes filled, suddenly, improbably, with unwanted tears. She sat on the sofa and looked out the window, at the baskets of geraniums on the porch, so no one would see.

"Who wasn't being gracious?" Caroline said.

After Charley died, there were the clothes to go through, the shoes, the high school yearbooks, the record albums. At first Dottie said she would do it, but when a few weeks passed, then a couple of months, Walt did it himself. He got rid of it all. Dottie was angry, thinking he might have saved something for her, he might have kept one piece of clothing, one scrap of paper, something of Charley's for her to keep.

She started sleeping in Charley's bed after the accident, refusing to change the sheets. She could still smell him on the pillow, the slightly spicy smell of the aftershave he had used lingering at first; but weeks and weeks went by and the smell of him started to fade, replaced by her own dusty, worn-out smell. Walt said it was ridiculous, that it was time for her to make her peace with Charley's death. But how could she? How could she close her eyes at night and see him under the wheels of the train? Walt was the ridiculous one. How could he get up in the morning, how could he breathe, knowing what had happened? They moved through the house in separate directions, at different times, grief making strangers of them.

One day when she was out, Walt took the sheets off the bed, washed them, and put them back. She was furious. She pressed Charley's pillow to her face, but it smelled like detergent and the warm inside of the dryer.

Charley was gone. She marched into the kitchen and told Walt he was heartless. "That's not true," he said quietly. "You know that's not true." Oh, but it was. She had never seen him as clearly as she did then, the lines of his face and the empty look in his eyes. Those gruesome hands. She had believed all his promises: *I'm not going to fool around with your heart.*

The cup flew across the kitchen, and Dottie could still see the daisy painted on its side, yellow with an orange center, the colors blurring together like a spinning sun. Then hitting the far wall of the kitchen, and in breaking, the cup turned into chunks of porcelain and powder and spread out over the table and the floor and the countertops. In the drywall, a gash in the yellow paint: A piece of the cup had lodged itself there when it broke, like a crooked tooth.

"Jesus Christ!" Walt said. "What the hell did you do that for?"

But Dottie was already out of the kitchen, out of the house, and running into the yard, down to the street. The half-moon was just starting to come up, blood-red over the city. She wanted Walt to suffer the way she was suffering. She wanted him to shout, to cry, to do anything at all that might tell her that he, too, was filled with pain, that she and the boys were everything to him, that somewhere in that head and heart was a life that was without compromise. Instead he was unruffled, reasonable, and, she couldn't help feeling, untouchable.

She walked down Belmont toward the lake. At a certain point on the horizon, the lanes vanished into a single point. The land here was so flat that over the tops of the buildings she could see the skyscrapers down-town, the blocks of houses and apartments, the brown life of the city. She felt the world split and sawed apart like a puzzle, dividing into grids that got smaller and smaller until even the tiniest inch of ground was marked and numbered, spread open and exposed to a sky that seemed never to end. She should never have agreed to move here. She should never have had any children, so she would never have any to lose.

She looked back in the direction she'd come, and thought, I don't have to go back. Not if I really don't want to.

What did she want?

The moon grew lighter as it rose in the sky, as if it were being scrubbed clean. She turned around and went back toward the house. It was late, the sidewalks were mostly deserted and the businesses shut up for the night, and she put her head down and didn't look at anyone. She had too much to do still to be walking around in the dark by herself. She would go back inside as if nothing had happened. Walt would say something safe and reasonable, talk about work or something he wanted to do around the house or compliment her on dinner, and they would go on, and Dottie would forgive him for not being what she wanted him to be. She would try to remember how often she had been grateful for the calm weather of his temper, how she knew he was the one who would never take chances with her heart, but she would wish he would, just once, just to prove he still had one.

When she came in the back door, Walt and Daddy were in the other room, talking about the war. Walt said he was certain that Johnson would keep things small, not let their boys get into things too deep, Daddy grunting in reply, which could have been argument or agreement. Standing alone in the kitchen, eavesdropping on her husband, she heard at last the sorrow in Walt's voice, a note that was audible to her alone.

She was sorry she had thrown the cup. She was sorry it broke.

Eventually Sam came home from Vietnam and Dottie moved back into the room with Walt, but there was always this little ball of fear and loneliness at the center, as if she and Walt were both waiting for the bomb to drop. It was still with them when the girls were born, at Christmases and birthdays. When the doctors told Dottie about the spot on her lung, it was almost a relief. At last they knew from which direction the disaster was coming. They found a new forgiveness, a renewed appreciation for each other. They spent their days at the lakeshore or at the museum, going for lunch afterward like a couple of kids on a date. They went dancing at nightclubs they had always meant to visit. They drove to the Grand Canyon and stood on the rim, looking at the layers of earth uncovered by the river. They were giddy and funny and generous with each other. It reminded Dottie of the war years when Walt could come home only for a week at a time, a few days here and there, when the possibility of danger made every decision seem more important.

They wrote their will. Dottie picked out the music she wanted played at her funeral and the Bible readings she wanted read, and she put her jewelry in little plastic bags with labels so Walt would know which pieces went to Jen, which to Katie, which to Caroline. Everything was done.

In the end, Walt ruined all her plans. He went first.

In the morning Jimmy took her for a drive, hanging his cigarette out the window so the smoke wouldn't bother her. He talked a steady stream of news from people they had both known, stopping to fill in the details of marriages, children, deaths. Dottie remembered only about half of them and wondered when her brother had acquired such a good memory, but then he had lived here nearly all his life, while she had moved away, started over among strangers in a strange place. He was talking, she knew, to keep the silence at bay, the uneasy silence of people who had once known each other well.

When he first appeared at the door that morning, she was certain, for a moment, that she was looking at her father. The same shock of white hair, the same droll expression. Even the clothes seemed the same, loose over his body, as if bought for someone else. It hadn't been that long since she'd seen him, just a few years, but the change was startling. She almost thought he was the one who was ill. Then his family was behind him, calling greetings as they came in the door. When he kissed her cheek, she could smell the cigarettes on him and would have given all the remaining days of her life to have one.

He said they should go for a ride, get away, just the two of them, out to see the old places while the kids had a chance to visit.

The countryside was as flat as she remembered, but clusters of new houses squatted close to the earth where she expected to see nothing but fields, and for a minute she felt again the rising panic of being lost. Then Jimmy slowed the car to a stiff crawl, and the horizon flew into clear relief again when she realized that this was the way to Mother and Daddy's old place and that the patch of grass and gray green stone Jimmy stopped in front of was the very spot. The house was gone, its timbers stripped away and the barn in back collapsed like a faulty lung, but there was a faint outline of the yard, slowly being taken over by fields, and the foundation was still there, a deep hole in the ground, and the concrete steps that had led up to the front porch. A crunching of sparse gravel marked the place where the driveway used to be. They got out of the car and walked over to the foundation. They leaned down, looked in, and saw it was filled with the detritus of farm life—tractor parts, barbed wire, wooden fence posts weathered past usefulness, an old chair with torn, unfamiliar cloth upholstery.

"My God," she said. "Will you look at that. Mother must be rolling over in her grave."

Mother had died in the spring of 1973. Dottie and Bella had gone through Mother's clothes one by one, but none was fit for her to be buried in. For years Mother never wore anything but a housecoat, the thin kind with the zipper in the front so Bella could get it on and off when she needed. Anything more than four or five years old was too big, because Mother had grown so thin after she became ill. Her plump arms and legs and breasts had deflated and sagged. Finally Bella gave the undertaker her own best dress, something she'd treasured, so that Mother could be buried in something nice. Afterward they went back into Mother's room to clean up. Dottie was folding an old skirt when she felt something heavy. At first she thought there was something in the pocket, but then she felt along until she found it, hard and round: a coin, sewn into the hem. She tore the threads. It was a silver crown with a portrait of a jowly old Queen Victoria, heavy and tarnished, so that only the queen's odd little coronet was clearly visible. They went back through the clothes, feeling along the hems of old slips and slacks and dresses for telltale bulges and ripples. It was like a treasure hunt. They found bills and coins sewn into the hems of dresses, curtains, pillowcases. Some of the coins were old and tarnished, the bills soft at the creases. Dottie unfolded them and spread them out on the mattress. She touched the coins but did not pick them up. There were so many. It added up to about three hundred dollars face value, a fortune to someone like Mother. Dottie wished she had spent it, gone out and bought herself something frivolous, a new dress, a fancy hat, anything.

Daddy came in and saw the money there. He picked up the bills and folded them neatly, scooped up the coins. "Must have been saving up for a rainy day," he said, and put the money in his pocket.

In front of what was left of the old house, Jimmy took her by the arm and they walked down the road a ways, along the gravel shoulder. Sometimes, through a break in the trees, she could see the blue green lip of Lake Erie on the horizon. She was thinking of her sister. Bella didn't last long without Mother. She told Dottie that with Mother gone, there was hardly a reason for her to get up in the morning. Four years after they buried Mother, she told Ed she wasn't feeling well one afternoon, lay down for a short nap, and never got up again.

Jimmy had stopped walking but still held her arm. "Look at this, Dot. Guess where we are now?" Dottie saw again the old farmhouse and the white barn with the cupola, the matching tractor garage. It was Ed and Bella's old farm. She hadn't recognized it at first because there were houses built up all around it, but of course this was the same place. She almost expected to see the red farm truck Ed had kept parked in back and a cluster of Chinese geese guarding the front walk, but Ed had retired a few years back and moved to the countryside outside Niagara Falls to be closer to Janice. Now there was only an old Cadillac parked in the grass and no animals in sight. Patches of brown showed in the yard and the paint was peeling on the garage, but otherwise everything seemed in good repair. From the road she could see the open back door to the tractor garage, the stairs up to the little room where Bobby Wisniewski used to sleep when he worked for Ed and Bella, but the stairs were blocked with a rusted lawn mower and a roll of snow fence.

"Do you believe that?" Jimmy said, flicking his cigarette ash on the ground. "No one farms the place anymore. The house is still here, but the land was sold off about ten years ago. Built all those houses right up to it."

"Ed's father would be furious."

"You got that right. So would Daddy. He would have loved to get his hands on that place." And Dottie turned away, knowing it was Jimmy himself who had most wanted it, who had done the figures and made the plans that all came to nothing when the land got too expensive, who had watched it parceled up and foundations sunk and the frames raised one by one. He had taken her here to see the end of everything he had wanted.

When he got back in the car, Jimmy asked brightly, "Where to now? Should I take you into town for an ice cream? It'll be just like we're kids again."

"I'm feeling kind of tired. Maybe we should go home." Funny how "home" had become, in a pinch, Caroline's house, no place she had ever lived, while the home she remembered, the one she returned to in her thoughts again and again, had been swallowed up by the earth. Jimmy started up the car to head back. The only sound was the buzz of the road underneath the tires.

Bobby had moved away in the fall of 1944, following the call for factory workers, better pay, a pension. He packed his clothes in a couple of old burlap feed bags and came down the stairs from his little room over the tractor garage. Somehow Dottie made sure to be there when he was going. He stood on the porch with his bag in his hand, waiting for Ed to come out and give him a ride to town, his white blond hair sticking up in all directions while the wind blew it around. A few errant snow flakes got caught in it and melted with his body heat. Dottie watched him from the kitchen window while she helped Bella clean up the lunch dishes. She opened the front door and said, "You can wait in the house if you want. Don't want you to catch your death."

"Thanks," he said. "You're too kind."

He sat at the kitchen table in his coat and boots, his hand still wrapped around the burlap sack as if one of the women might try to take it from him, his eyes searching the next room for any sign of Ed.

"In a hurry?" Dottie said. "You'll be out of here soon enough."

"Looks that way," Bobby said. "Will you be sorry to see me go?"

"Not in the least."

She was already pregnant with Sam then, five months. She was starting to show, a slight bump that pushed out the fronts of her dresses. From the other room she heard a child's voice, Janice playing with her blocks on the living room floor. Bella went in to check on her, and Dottie went back to washing. She kept her face to the wall over the sink, listening to her own breath in the silence. After a minute she said, "So. Had enough of farm life, then?"

"Pretty much. Ford's hiring a lot of new people. Thought I might see what I could do there."

"I'm sure you'll do well."

She wished Ed would come. The only sound was the muffled clink of dishes under water. "How's that husband of yours, Mrs. Dunmore?"

"Fine, thanks."

"Happy to hear it."

"His fingers are healing up nicely. He's starting a new job. He's got plans for renting us a house, and then we'll be moving into town ourselves."

"That's good news."

"You're right. It is."

"You be sure to look me up when you get there."

Dottie laughed. The dishes clinked underwater. "Oh, I'll do that all right," she said. "That's the first thing I'm going to do."

Bobby sighed. "You won't forgive me still. I haven't had a kind word from you in I don't know how long."

She wouldn't look at him, she decided. She would not look at him. Where on earth was Bella? "You're wrong," she said. "I don't blame you. It was my fault entirely." She could see him out of the corner of her eye. Sitting at the edge of the table with all his belongings in two burlap sacks, he looked like a little boy. Like a runaway. She almost felt sorry for him.

Bella came back with a stack of towels and wiped the last of her glasses with one of them. Outside, the snow beat against the windows as though it wanted admittance to the house. Dottie said, "So, Bobby, where do you think you're heading to?"

"Windsor. If I have trouble finding work, I may go as far as Toronto."

"Not Detroit? Not back home—where was it—Ohio?"

"Canada is home now," he said. "I like it here."

"Well," Dottie said as Ed came in and put on his coat, "I wish you the best, then."

"You too, Mrs. Dunmore. Say good-bye to Walt for me." He picked up his bag and followed Ed out the door. A few snowflakes came in when the men went out. Dottie turned away and didn't watch him go.

Neil was snoring again, and Dottie heard Sam turn over in bed when she flipped on the light in the kitchen and sat at the table. She had woken up afraid because she didn't remember where she was. There was a solitude to four A.M. that she liked, a contentment with herself that had always made the middle of the night feel like a good place to be, but these days that was tempered by a fear of sleeping, of drifting off, and a feeling like falling. She spied Caroline's cigarettes and lighter on the table and lit one and took a long, slow puff, feeling the heat work through her, warming her lungs and limbs, and for a minute she felt she could breathe again.

On the table, under the salt and pepper shakers, she saw the phone book. The thin pages stuck together as if they were glued; they wouldn't yield until she slipped a fingernail underneath each one and flipped it, carefully, Wagner turning to Wilson. He was in the book. Wisniewski, R. He lived on the county road, not five miles away. He hadn't gone very far. She was filled with a sudden, compulsive urge to see him, just to see what he looked like. She didn't really want to talk to him or spend any time with him, just see how he, too, had changed over the years, if the face was anything like the one she remembered. It was a silly schoolgirl impulse, she knew, of a kind she hadn't had in a long time.

Five A.M., and still too early. She put on her coat and sneakers and made her way toward the door with Sam's car keys in her hands. Open, shut, quietly as possible. The cool morning air, a faint blue tinge to the sky. She should not be going, but if she did this quickly and quietly, she might get home before anyone woke up.

A noise behind her, the door opening.

"Ma, what do you think you're doing out here?" Sam said. He rushed down the stairs and took her by the elbow, steered her back into the house. Over breakfast, Sam said, "Where is it you wanted to go? You know all you have to do is ask."

But how could she ask him this—to drive her past the house of a man she hadn't seen in fifty years, not to walk up and knock on the door, just to sit in the car and see if she could get a look at him? Something that seemed perfectly all right to do on her own seemed ridiculous if she needed to bring another person into it. She felt again the rage of being old, of her body falling out from under her like a beach under the onslaught of a hurricane. "Forget it," she said. "Never mind."

"Don't be like that, Ma. Just tell me what you need. I'll be happy to help you."

"No," she said. She saw his look. She knew what he thought. She had secrets of her own to keep. There were things about her no one ever needed to know, not even now, when she forget so many other things that bore remembering. "Really. I'm all right."

In the afternoon, she and Caroline went to see Adele at her assisted-living apartment in town. "Don't expect too much when you see it," she told Dottie. "It's too depressing for words." But when they got there, Dottie thought nothing could be further from the truth. Adele's apartment was in a low building shaped like a horseshoe, with walls of bright glass windows. There was a huge floral arrangement in the lobby that looked as if it belonged in an expensive hotel, and a well-dressed woman behind the front desk took their names and pointed them toward the elevator. They rode up to the second floor with soft music playing. When they got off on Adele's floor, a long hallway with expensive carpets and another large floral arrangement made Dottie remember a time Walt had taken her for a weekend at the Palmer House in Chicago, where they stayed in bed until well after ten and ordered room service all weekend.

Adele greeted them at the door with kisses. She'd put on a nice dress and some makeup, and Dottie had to say she looked well. On the table inside, she'd set out tea and cookies. The apartment was small, an L-shaped room with a kitchenette at one end and a sofa and TV near the window where you could almost see the river. A bed at the far end of the room was covered with a pink satin spread that looked as though it belonged in a little girl's room, but the color was cheerful and Dottie could see why Adele had chosen it. A small hallway leading from the front door to the kitchen had doors for a bathroom and a storage closet. In every room there were red buttons to call a nurse if she needed one, but as far as Dottie could tell, Adele was doing just fine—better, in fact, than she had been the last time Dottie had seen her, at Walt's funeral in the winter. She had been a mess then, worse off than Dottie herself; she had nearly fainted in the parking lot on her way into the funeral home. Neil and Sam practically had to carry her inside.

In this new place, though, she seemed calm, more like herself. She smiled and chatted and said how glad she was to see them. For years she'd been a nervous, unhappy woman, and their friendship had, in a way, relied on that unhappiness—Adele was the one person who always needed her, a balm in that time when her life centered around boys, boys with their war games, their sports, their dirt. It was nice to have a woman there to talk to. If Adele complained then, Dottie was happy to listen, and after Adele went back to Canada, Dottie had felt the absence like a missing tooth. They wrote and called, but it was not the same.

They had coffee and cake and a little bit of news about a man down the hall whom Adele had begun seeing, an old bachelor who enjoyed taking her to dinner or a show. She was taking some new pills that were helping tremendously, and she had even started playing bridge and bingo with some of the ladies in the building. She seemed happier than Dottie had seen her in a long time. She was forming a life for herself here. If Adele wanted, someone else would do her shopping for her, pick up her medication. It was a pleasant small place to grow old in.

As they were leaving, Caroline straightened Adele's pale blond wig and said she'd see her mother again tomorrow. When the door closed she pulled on Dottie's arm and said, "You see. You see what I mean about this place."

"I don't know. I think it's pretty nice."

"Oh, no. It's awful."

Dottie nodded, but she thought no such thing.

She had meant to lie down for a while after they got to Caroline's, but in the afternoon, late, she took a pack of Caroline's cigarettes and her lighter, put them in her pants pocket, and went outside. Neil and Sam were out for the afternoon, playing a round of golf, though it looked like rain. Katie had gone into town with her cousins. Caroline said she would be outside if Dottie needed her. She was there now, in a ridiculous long flowered dress that made her look like a hippie, her hair loose over her shoulders. She was kneeling on the ground by her roses, hands in the dirt. It made Dottie's back ache just to look at her.

Dottie slipped out the side door and went down the driveway into the yard, under the trees. Then she turned and started walking down the road's gravel shoulder, past houses and schools and farms, revising her mental map of landmarks. Her feet started to hurt because she wasn't used to so much exercise, but she was pleasantly surprised to find that she didn't have trouble breathing if she took her time. Every once in a while she took out a fresh cigarette, lit it, and breathed in as deeply as she could, liking the way the smoke made her feel more awake. Sam didn't let her smoke and would have been furious if he'd found out.

The house was a little ways up on the edge of town in a newer development. The trees there were only about as tall as she was, and without shade the sun was bright and hot. She stopped on the sidewalk across the street. The house was neat and large, with boxes of wisteria in front of the windows and a large garden of hydrangeas under the windows. Bobby didn't live here alone, though she didn't know why she'd thought he would. In the upstairs window she could see someone had attached colored plastic flowers, large pink and orange daisies that would give a kind of stained-glass pattern to the room on the other side, the kind of thing a little girl would do. She remembered the day Bobby had picked up her little niece, Janice, and tickled her belly, saying he liked kids and wanted to have a bunch of his own someday. In her head he was still a young man, tall and thin with laughing eyes.

She stood on the sidewalk outside the address she'd found in the phone book and thought about knocking on the front door, introducing herself. Walt would have said she was being ridiculous. But this part of her had never had anything to do with him. Maybe he would disagree—maybe he would say it had everything to do with him. Walt had never known Bobby as anything other than a friend of the family, one of a string of hired hands who passed through town without making much of a mark on anyone. There was this thing, then—the part she had kept for herself, all these years.

As she stood across the street, watching, a man came out the front door and walked toward her. He wore tan slacks and a blue shirt that bulged a little over his belly and large aviator-style eyeglasses that darkened in the bright sun, but the white hair looked almost the same, sticking up in all directions. She was thinking of his hands around her waist. She was almost going to introduce herself when he spoke to her and asked if she was all right. "Is there something I can help you with?" His voice was bland and meant to be comforting, easy to digest as baby food, not at all as thrilling and dark as it had been the day she had seen him in the garage. She was already wishing she hadn't come. "Is there someone I can call for you?" he asked. "Somewhere you need to be?"

"No, thank you. I was only out for a walk."

"We don't get many walkers through here. Are you visiting someone?"

"Yes. My daughter lives down the road. I was just on my way back there."

"Can I give you a lift?"

"No, thank you." She took a step back, a step away. She was hurt that he had not recognized her after all. It was nothing that mattered except for the feeling inside herself that she had once been young, that she had wanted someone and been wanted in return. Now there was nothing but the memory, like old glue in an album after the photo has fallen away. Really, she hadn't missed it that much. She turned and started walking back.

After she found the photograph of the girl, Dottie had kept it in her wallet, under her driver's license. She would take out the girl's picture at odd times, like while waiting in line at the grocery store or under the dryer at the hairdresser's, and look at it once again, trying to guess the location of the photo, the girl's name. It must have been during the war, she decided. It was most likely in Canada, but it could have been Great Britain or Ireland as well. Who was she? What was it about her that had made Walt keep her picture all these years?

Jennifer—Sam and Linda's older girl—had seen her looking at it once. This was in May, when Jen and Brian had been home from San Diego. "Who's that, Gran?" she'd asked, looking over Dottie's shoulder. "She's pretty."

"Peggy Mason." How easily this lie came out. "She was a friend of mine from school. You think she's pretty?"

"Don't you?"

"Hmm. I didn't notice, I suppose."

Jennifer was a quiet, serious girl, like her father, without any of her mother's and sister's blond southern beauty. She had Sam's dark hair and green eyes, the furrow between the brows that showed she was annoyed or upset or both. She'd had that look on her face a lot recently. She and Brian were living together in San Diego but pretending they weren't to keep the family out of their business. It seemed a lot of work, these secrets. Dottie told her she needed to move home if she and Brian were thinking of kids, that having grandparents or at least an aunt to baby-sit made all the difference in the world when you were a new mom with a little one underfoot, and oh, she said, if Granny hadn't been there to help her take care of Sam those first few months, in those years after the war while Grandpa was working so much, she didn't know what she would have done.

"We're not talking about kids yet," she said. "We're not even married."

"You shouldn't wait too long, you know. You're not getting any younger."

"Hey, thanks," Jennifer said. She was quiet for a while. She frowned at her hands and said, "I can't believe you lived with your parents after you got married."

"It was the best we could do at the time. And anyway, I would have been living alone if we'd had our own house, and being alone is not such a good thing." She paused. "You need to come home, you know. Your father worries about you."

Jennifer, she realized, looked like Dottie herself at that age. Strange to see her own face on her granddaughter's body, except the face was rounder, maybe, Linda's genes moving things around a bit. Dottie's own face had slowly sunk into something she no longer recognized, an old lady's face, Mother's face from long ago. Poor Mother, living her life under Daddy's thumb. She had deserved some kind of life of her own, some joy, something to look forward to, or at least some happiness to look back on. Maybe she did have that; maybe she found her own. Who was Dottie to say for sure that she didn't? A mystery to her, in the end. All the people she'd loved had been mysterious to her in their own ways— Mother and Daddy, Bella and Jimmy, Walt, Sam and Charley, Adele and Caroline—as much as she was to them, she supposed.

Jennifer patted Dottie's thin, old hand and asked if she could get her a cup of tea. A good girl. Walt would have liked to see his grandchildren all grown up and starting families of their own, to see through to the end what the two of them had started in the Anglican church so many years ago. Maybe Jennifer would be getting married soon, and Dottie would look forward to that, but after that there was just bad health and a slow sinking away, the way it had happened to her mother, her mind going and her body crumbling underneath her. She remembered Janice as a baby, a headful of red curly hair, a round red smile. She remembered Daddy sitting on the porch at Ed and Bella's, brushing Janice's hair, careful not to snarl it, and how the baby had closed her eyes and swayed under Daddy's hands, getting drowsy with the rhythm of the brushstrokes. When was that? Where had that come from? She remembered Mother on the day Charley was christened, taking the baby from Dottie and blessing him under her breath in the heavy brogue she carried all her life. She remembered the day Sam came home from Vietnam, so thin he seemed almost as if he might blow away, and how she and Walt had tried not to look at the red scars on his legs and the hollows under his eyes.

She remembered the day Bobby Wisniewski kissed her in the tractor garage, how quickly he had pulled her to him, how light her dress was, how her whole body had pressed up against him, knees to breasts, and the silky feel of the hair on the back of his neck, and the cotton of his shirt under her hands when she pushed him back, pushed him away, and still somewhere under her skin she could feel the place where he had grabbed her wrist and held her, and though she couldn't remember the exact color of his eyes anymore, she could conjure up that smile he gave her, the two front teeth too close. He had made her afraid—but was it the way he looked at her or the way she looked back at him that had filled her with so much terror?

She looked Jennifer up and down, tried to remember when she got so tall. She was grown up. "You're living with him."

"You're not supposed to know about that."

"You think you know what you're doing?"

"I love Brian. He loves me. What else is there?"

Dottie smirked. Here was her grown-up granddaughter, thinking she knew about love. Thinking all her choices would be easy ones, that her heart would always lead her where she needed to go. Thinking that love was something magical and mysterious that descends from somewhere *out there*, something thrust upon you against your will, instead of a choice that has to be made again and again, every day, each day of your life.

She had put the photo of the girl back in her wallet. Even Walt Dunmore had kept his little secrets, after all.

ELEVEN

Caroline was working in her garden, picking sawflies off the leaves of her rosebushes, when Dottie vanished from the house. She pinched their fat green bodies between her fingers and dropped them in an empty jar that still smelled faintly of peanut butter. How she hated those worms. She hated the sight of them in her rosebushes, the way they ate the flesh off the leaves, leaving only a skeleton, the thicker veins and the stem. The worms writhed over one another in the bottom of the can. It was early in the summer, and the rosebushes would die if she didn't get the sawflies off them. She dropped another one in the can and thought, There.

Dottie was inside having a rest. That morning she had been impatient, sitting in front of her plate of eggs for a moment before getting up again, looking through the cabinets, opening the refrigerator as if she were searching for something. "Do you need something?" Caroline asked. "What are you looking for?"

"Nothing," Dottie said.

She asked if Dottie wanted to come out and enjoy the day, get some sun and air, but Dottie shrugged and said she was tired, and Caroline knew she would wait until she was alone and then have a cigarette.

That morning the two of them visited her mother, a prospect that always made Caroline wretched afterward. She could never help thinking how sad it was, her mother in that one small room alone. Why was she the only one who saw it? Neil said her mother was doing well there, all things considered. She was dating a man there and getting out more. She was seeing a wonderful therapist, living on a small pension she'd earned as a secretary in a doctor's office. She's better off, Neil said. She needs to have a life of her own. But Neil didn't understand that her mother needed her, and Caroline couldn't quite get over the feeling that she had abandoned her mother there, to fend for herself.

Caroline dropped another worm in the jar. Disgusting. The bottom of the jar was already covered with them. Neil didn't want her using pesticides on the garden, so she had to remove the worms by hand. Before Sam and Katie and Dottie arrived, she had taken extra care with cleaning the house, with the shopping and cooking. She made her own strawberry jam. In the room she'd chosen for Sam, she put a candle next to the bed, made sure he had the best sheets. She had seen them all in February at Walt's funeral, but they'd never stayed with her before. She didn't know why she was nervous about it, only that she wanted to make a good impression. She took pride in her house, her orchard. Neil said it wasn't as if the queen were coming to stay, and Caroline had told him, You don't understand, it's a matter of principle.

When they pulled into the drive the evening before, though, Sam had looked annoyed at being there, his brows furrowed, frowning at the house she'd cleaned so carefully. Caroline had been surprised at how frail Dottie looked, how stooped she'd become just in the few months since Walt had died. Her granddaughter had helped her in the house. Katie. She was grown now, a college student, artful in the way Caroline's poetry students were artful. She had her mother's coloring, but her face and eyes looked like Charley's. Caroline had almost been dizzy, looking at her. Later she and Katie had talked poetry for a while, comparing notes. Katie didn't know that Caroline had published a book earlier in the year, and she asked to see it. Caroline said she would give her a signed copy, which seemed to impress the girl a good deal. She watched Katie go up the stairs to bed and thought, I could have been your mother. I could have been, just for a minute. Another dizzying thought.

She reached into the rosebush and felt around, her fingers snagging on thorns and bleeding a little. She was so used to the feeling by then that she hardly noticed. She thought of it as fertilizer anyway, a bit of herself poured into the roses. The flowers were large when they bloomed, perfectly pink and as big around as her hand. She'd clipped some last week and brought them to Lainie Rogers, the young woman across the road—a girl, really—one morning after Caroline heard her arguing with her husband. They'd been slamming doors, shouting at each other so loudly that she had heard every word clearly across the distance that separated their two houses. They'd shouted, and the walls shook and something broke, something glass, but it didn't sound as though he'd touched her, so Caroline hadn't interfered. Later that morning, after the boy had left for work, she'd gone over. Lainie had colored when Caroline gave her the flowers in a vase and said she looked as if she could use a little pick-me-up. She'd touched the roses to her face. She was a serious little thing, a born-again Christian. Lainie had taken the roses and put them on the table in her front window, and Caroline could still see them there from across the yard. They lived five days in that water. Then they started to drop, and by the end the petals were on the tabletop. Still, five days.

She was proud of her flowers; she had a way with them. It was something she had come to later in life, after she met Neil and got married and had a house of her own. Begonias with tiny red blossoms, white campanula with lemon-drop centers, purple hydrangeas the size of bowling balls. Tulips and daffodils in the spring, marigolds in the summer and fall to keep the rabbits away from the garden. The flowers grew in a carpet all the way around the foundation of the house, and along the border of the drive, and in an old tire in the front yard. They grew in the sunlit windows of the kitchen and in boxes outside the front windows and in hanging baskets by the front door. And not just flowers, but all kinds of plants, spider plants and ferns, jade plants with juicy leaves, ficus that threatened to take over the living room. Caroline knew what would grow where and how to care for it just so, coaxing out of clippings or bulbs or seeds the beginning of life.

Her talent with plants, as it turned out, also extended to apple trees. She found the orchard herself one afternoon driving out of Harrow after a visit to her mother. It was in disrepair, the apples malformed and sour and rotting on the ground, but Caroline saw potential in the rows of trees and the farmhouse and the tire swing in the yard. She thought about raising children there, what a beautiful place it would be to grow up. She and Neil in the fall up on ladders picking apples by the hundreds. She managed to save up a little money from her teaching job, and Neil, who was a tenured professor then, put down a little more. They spent a fortune on seedlings, long afternoons putting them in the ground by hand. They decided to raise the plants organically, without pesticides—Neil's contribution to the endeavor. They read up on soil pH and covered the ground with powdered oyster shells to reduce acidity. They set traps for codling moths and apple maggots. After three or four years, the trees started bearing well. They took the apples into town and made enough profit that Neil quit his job to tend the orchard full-time. He loved it— working out of doors, the earth that got in the crevices of his fingers, the red ripe fruit on the branches in the fall. They did not make a lot of money at it—Caroline kept her job teaching poetry classes at the college, just to make certain the bills were always paid—but she loved the sight of the orchard as she drove up the road, the long rows of trees, the fermenting cider smell the ground gave off in the fall. She was content, as much as anyone could be.

In the yard, Caroline could feel the back of her neck starting to burn, and when she touched her fingers there the skin was warm. She set the jar of worms on the ground by the rosebushes, went up the stairs into the cool dark house, where the TV was on loud still. She took a bit of leftover chicken out of the fridge to make herself some lunch and called to Dottie to see if she wanted any. Maybe a cold sandwich of some kind. That would suit her. "Dot?" she called. "Dottie?" No answer.

When Caroline went out to work in the garden, Dottie was sitting on the sofa in her old slacks and a nylon blouse with a sweating can of beer in her hand. Since then the channel had been changed to the nature station. Caroline leaned over and turned down the volume, then flipped the darn thing off completely. The house was utterly silent. Dottie was not in the bathroom. She was not upstairs lying down. Caroline went downstairs and looked in the basement, but she was not there, either.

Maybe she was out in the yard. Maybe she was just down the road a little ways and Caroline could catch up to her and it would still be all right.

Caroline went up the stairs and out the door. The backyard was empty. The front held only her jar of squirming sawflies. She went out to the road and stood squinting down the center line, but no Dottie.

She went across the road to the Rogerses' front door and knocked. The girl came to the window with her robe on, her hair still damp from the shower, a slightly alarmed look on her round face. Caroline asked if she'd seen Dottie walking away someplace, maybe down the road? "I stepped out for a moment, and when I came back in she wasn't there," Caroline said. "She hasn't been well lately."

"How long do you think you were outside?"

"Ten minutes. Fifteen. It wasn't long." It was longer than that, but she did not want anyone to know she had neglected Dottie. It might have been half an hour. It might even have been an hour. She had really not been paying attention, thinking Dottie was safe in the house, that she had never done anything like this before and there was no reason for her to start now. The girl said she hadn't seen her, but she would help look, just give her a minute to change.

Caroline was angry at herself for not being more careful. Dottie had not been herself since Walt died. His sickness came up so fast and was over so quickly that it was all Dottie could do just to make things comfortable for him at the end. Before the last of the funeral roasts came out of the freezer, she would sometimes forget whom she was talking to, mistaking Caroline for Jean, or Bella, or even Adele. She would tell Caroline two or three times in the course of one conversation that Sam wanted her to sell the house. After she moved in with Sam and Katie, she seemed to perk up a bit from the company. But from one minute to the next, you couldn't tell what she might do.

Outside Caroline went up and down the road, looking for a familiar gray head. How could one old woman disappear so quickly? She called over to Jimmy's and left a message. Lainie Rogers came out with her wet hair tied up, wearing shorts and a pink T-shirt. She went east down the road, calling, "Dottie! Dottie! Where are you?" Caroline went in the opposite direction, squinting at the roads. How far could an old lady get on her own, just walking, on a hot afternoon, the sun beating down on everything? She would get dehydrated; she would get hit by a car; she would pass out from heatstroke and that would be the end of her.

Down the road she could hear Lainie shouting. "Dottie!" called the girl. "Dottie! You need to come home. Everyone's worried about you, so come out now, okay?" Like a game of hide-and-seek. Like when Caroline and Sam and Charley were small and Dottie and her mother were young together. They relied on each other then. When they were young, they were as close as sisters, Dottie tall then and graceful, and so sure of herself, and Caroline had remembered thinking that if she were a man, if she were Walt, she would have been in love with Dottie, too. Playing with the children in the yard. Dottie hiding her face in her hands, counting to ten, calling out, "olli-olli-oxen-free! Ready or not, here I come!" She and Sam and Charley too eager to hide quietly; they had been so easy to find then, giggling behind shrubs. It was the being found part that was fun for them, more than the hiding. Dottie had sent them into the bushes and around corners and said: You hide, and I'll find you, I promise.

Caroline was pregnant the day Charley was killed on the railroad tracks. This was a thing she had never spoken out loud, not to her mother, not to Dottie, not to anyone. She had made the appointment the week before, choosing a doctor she had never been to before, giving her name to the receptionist as Mrs. Dunmore. The nurse congratulated her when she came in with the news. Caroline felt dizzy, thought she would be sick. The nurse told her to lie back for a minute and she would bring her some juice. When she went out the door of the examination room, Caroline put on her coat and purse and slipped out of the office.

At the library, she spent the afternoon reading as much as she could. It seemed an impossible thing. She couldn't imagine telling Charley, couldn't imagine telling her mother. Her mother would insist she and Charley get married, but Caroline couldn't picture it at all. Charley was not the marrying kind—she had known this about him from the beginning. She didn't want to marry him, no matter what her mother said. She had gone to him out of desperation, out of a sense of loneliness and loss, and Charley probably knew it. He had his own problems. His failing grades, his fear of being drafted, his increasingly desperate behavior. Still, when he put his arm around her and pulled her to him, she knew she didn't want to leave. She was afraid of losing herself, of disappearing altogether.

She couldn't tell him about the baby. Not then. Soon, perhaps.

The night he died, Dottie called to find out if Charley was there with Caroline, and when she said he wasn't she walked the four blocks to Dottie's house to wait until Charley came home. She was there when the police came and gave them the news, fainted right away when they told about the car and the train that smashed into it. The next morning she started to bleed. She bled through the funeral, through that terrible day in the Polish cemetery when they put Charley in the ground. She was bleeding when Sam, home from Vietnam, tried to tell her how sorry he was. She bled out her fear and hope and sadness, and when the bleeding stopped she went to the hospital, checked her mother out, and moved them both back to Canada.

It was nearly two years later that she met Neil. Caroline was taking poetry classes at the university in the evenings to finish up her degree. Neil was in the class with her, the only man. She was drawn to him immediately, his sureness, his steady calm. He said he was taking the class because he was bored, because he needed something to keep him sharp. History, he said, is only about lives already lived. He said he had lived nearly thirty years by then and wanted to know when his history would begin. By the end of the year, they were married.

Spurred on by Neil and by the instructor, Caroline started taking her poetry seriously, sending out pieces for publication, even placing one now and again in a journal or magazine. They lived in Windsor for a while with her mother, who was being helped along by a therapist whom she saw at Neil's expense. Adele had found a new job, was sleeping through the night. But when the children they wanted didn't come after two years, then three, then four, they started to wonder if something was wrong. They measured their lovemaking out in smaller and smaller doses until it was only once a month, at precisely the right moment. Caroline went to the doctor for blood tests, exam after exam. Nothing seemed to be wrong, only she wasn't pregnant. Neil thought the stress of caring for her mother might be too much for her, but even after Adele moved out they still didn't have any children. After five years they stopped hoping. Caroline found the orchard and threw herself into that instead, and Neil, as if sensing an opportunity, followed suit. He was patient and kind with her, but she always knew it was a disappointment to him and a frustration that the doctors had never been able to give them a reason. He was an excellent uncle to his brother's kids, an eager baby-sitter. She never told him about the earlier pregnancy. She thought it would hurt him too much to know. She taught her classes and tended her gardens, let herself be a mother to her students, to Lainie Rogers across the street, a favorite aunt, a confidante, a friend. Unlike her own mother, who had always needed so much, Caroline gave back to everyone she met. In some ways it was better. In some ways, she came to believe, it was for the best.

Dottie did not come home all that afternoon. When Neil and Sam came home, she told them what had happened, omitting the length of time she had been outside. She had been worried that Sam would be angry, but he said he didn't blame her, that his mother had been acting strangely lately. "Did I tell you she opened the car door on the way here?" Sam told her. "Just a mile or so down the road. She tried to get out while the car was moving. The seat belt was the only thing that kept her from jumping into the road. I was furious. She could have gotten herself killed."

Neil said he would take the car and drive the roads while Caroline and Sam and Lainie checked the orchard. Later, Jimmy and Ethel arrived to help look for her, and Janice and Monty, as soon as they got Caroline's phone messages. All afternoon and into the evening they tromped through rows of apple trees, calling, "Dottie! Dottie!" No one wanted to come inside after it was dark, so she got them all flashlights from the house so they could keep looking. Neil stayed in the house, saying someone needed to be there in case Dottie came back.

Caroline walked out into the orchard in the dark. She could hear footsteps swishing through the grass, and here and there the branches were low and brushed against her face, the hard little nubs of the early apples. The light from her flashlight didn't illuminate much beyond the patch of ground ahead of her feet. The voices of the others seemed disembodied, almost ghostly, and Caroline remembered the story of the girl's ghost in the Polish cemetery, walking among the stones in her wedding dress, how the high school boys took their girlfriends there to scare them. How long ago that seemed, yet part of her felt as though it were just a day or two ago. Part of her still remembered what it had been like to be the girl who had lain below Sam in the cemetery, oblivious, sure that those moments were the beginning of something instead of the end.

Eventually they wandered back to the house in twos and threes, giving up for the night at last. They had missed supper, a beautiful rack of lamb Caroline had bought especially. Instead she heated some frozen pizzas and set them on the table for everyone to help themselves while they waited. They were all afraid to leave. They were afraid to go to sleep, though it was starting to get late, as if wakefulness would be a talisman against disaster.

The police came to the house, asking if she had a photograph of Dottie. "Something recent," said the older of the two. Caroline was nervous with them in the house—it made the day more real. She pulled out the photo album and flipped through it quickly. Dottie had sent her photos of the girls from time to time, or Sam and Linda, family snapshots, since Caroline was practically family. But in those pictures Dottie was only a slippered foot near the Christmas tree, a partial head of gray hair behind Sam at Thanksgiving dinner. Dottie didn't like having her picture taken; whenever the camera came out, she would wave the picture taker away. But there must be one of her somewhere.

Caroline went upstairs to Dottie's bedroom. Dottie's suitcase and purse were next to the bed, her nightgown from that morning lying on top of the clothes, unfolded. The lingering smell of cigarettes. She went into Dottie's purse. The best, most recent picture might be her driver's license photo. She pulled out her wallet. It was crammed with old things: a prayer card from Walt's funeral, school pictures of the girls. She found the driver's license and pulled it out.

Beneath the driver's license was an old picture Caroline had not seen before: all freckled girl in a dark dress, sitting on a bench in front of a building covered in peeling white paint. The sign over the door read THE VICTORIA INN. She turned the photo over. On the back, in tiny, meticulous handwriting, was written "All my love." Caroline knew right away who the girl was, where it was taken. She had looked for such a photo many years ago but had never found one. She put the photo on the bedside table and went back into the kitchen with Dottie's driver's license.

In the front room, the policemen said they would call if they found out anything new. Jimmy and Ethel said they should be getting home, and Janice and Monty stretched and said it was late, they would get some sleep and be back in the morning. Lainie apologized and said she should be getting home as well; her husband was probably anxious for her, wondering where she was.

Eventually Neil went to bed as well. Katie was anxious and worried, afraid to sleep, but Sam promised he would wake her if he found out anything new, so she went upstairs to bed. It was touching, their concern for each other, the way Katie dropped a kiss on her father's gray head before she left the room. How she would have liked to see someone do that for Neil.

Afterward Caroline and Sam sat with the television on, checking the news. Soon Sam's head dropped forward on his chest, and Caroline covered him with the quilt from the back of the sofa, and then she turned off the lights and went up to bed herself, but she didn't close her eyes, couldn't sleep at all.

A few years earlier, Caroline and her mother had flown to Newfoundland to see her mother's older sister, Dolores. Dolores had moved to St. John's with her husband and children before Caroline was born. She was elderly then, and Caroline had never met her before. Her mother planned the trip, but Caroline was thinking of the Victoria Inn, and Rosemary Oram, or Gilchrest, if that's what she was still called. The two boys. She might never get another chance to go.

Neil had elected not to come, so it was just Caroline and her mother on the plane that day, Toronto to Halifax to St. John's. It was getting dark, and below them the North Atlantic was calm and gray. Her mother poked her every once in a while to point out spots of white below, floating on the ocean. Caroline leaned out the window to look—she had never seen an iceberg before. From the air they were tiny specks hardly worth looking at.

Dolores's house was in a newer development on the edge of the city, the rooms mostly empty now that her husband was dead and her girls had moved to the mainland with their husbands. Only the son, Graham, had stayed with her. Graham was a slight man with thin gray hair that had once been blond. Her aunt was a larger version of her mother, older, squatter. There was something familiar about her, and Caroline felt at ease almost immediately. She was disappointed that her aunt did not live nearer the city center, where she imagined the Victoria Inn would have been, but she did try looking up the name in the phone book when they first arrived. No Victoria Inn. No Rosemary Oram, or Gilchrest, in St. John's. Maybe she had given up the business after her marriage. Maybe she had moved to the mainland, like so many Newfoundlanders.

One afternoon they decided to go out, see a little of the surrounding areas. There was a small fishing village up the coast where the whale-watching boats went out in good weather, her cousin told her. If she wanted something touristy. It was June and good season for whales. They drove out to the little hotel near the harbor where Graham said they could buy tickets. Inside, the walls were covered with glossy *National Geographic*–style photographs of whales and icebergs and seabirds, promises of sights to come.

The man behind the counter asked if he could help them.

"Is this a good place to see the whales?"

"Sure is. We're going out in about half an hour."

"Are there a lot of them?"

"Tons. We saw some earlier today. A large pod, maybe twelve or fifteen of them."

He had the Newfoundland accent she'd noticed from her cousin, Irish with a drop of Canadian thrown in for good measure. He was handsome, a bit younger than her, maybe in his forties still, but his skin was ruddy from being outside. She smiled at him. Her mother was exclaiming over the pictures, how much they cost. Caroline paid for two tickets.

From behind the counter, someone called his name. "Alister," said a woman's voice, "can you give me a hand here?"

Caroline could see a little into the kitchen in back, where a pretty gray-haired woman who might have been his mother was trying to move a large bag of flour into a storage room. Alister struggled to help her, and for a moment they both disappeared. Caroline didn't get a good look at the woman's face, but she knew her anyway.

There were several others already on the boat when they got on, and her mother talked about what kinds of whales they might see, and puffins, and kittiwakes. But Caroline was watching Alister. He introduced himself and his older brother, Henry, who was piloting the boat while Alister ran the tour. There were only a few people on the boat that afternoon. Out of the harbor, the boat rocked gently on the waves. The clear blue sky gave over to a little haze offshore, and it was colder away from the harbor. There were small islands nearby where puffins were nesting. Henry slowed the boat while Alister pointed out their burrows. "The real good watching is just a little farther," he said. The wind whipped his hair back and tinged his skin pink. She decided he was very handsome.

They saw their backs first, the smooth gray black of their flesh, and then the spray they blew in the air. The other passengers started talking excitedly when Henry turned the boat toward the pod and cut the engines. When Caroline saw that the current was carrying them closer, she was tense and excited. How big they were, how slow and beautiful. They came so close to the boat that she could see their tiny liquid eyes when they rolled over and slapped the water with their fins. She leaned over to look at them and felt Alister's hand on her back. "Don't fall in," he said.

"What kind are they?"

"Humpback. Watch them dive. You can see where they get their name." One of the whales surfaced, humped its spine, and dove down, and the great tail came up out of the water and down again, slipping under the boat, and she could feel the weight of it under the surface of the water.

"Are you all right?" Alister asked.

"I'm fine. I'll be fine."

"You look green."

"Just give me a minute and I'll be all right," she said. She grabbed the railing and held on, and the boat rocked there a little more, back and forth. The horizon wavered. The older brother started up the engine. They circled the island where the puffins nested, watched them skim awkwardly over the water, their funny little feet just inches from the surface. After a while they turned back, and Caroline felt a little ill until she saw the harbor coming back into view.

As they got off the boat, Alister took her hand to make sure she didn't slip. "Thanks," she said. "That was fun."

"Was it?" he asked. "I didn't think you liked it."

"No. I enjoyed it very much."

"I'm glad. Watch your step now."

She asked her mother to wait, just wait for her one second, she had to ask something. She went inside the office. The pretty gray-haired woman was behind the counter, taking money for tickets for the next boat out. She was elderly now, but still vigorous. The other customers went outside to wait, leaving Caroline alone. She tried to muster her courage, but she was nervous, excited, as if she were meeting a long-lost relative, one whose absence had been particularly painful to her. She didn't know quite what to say. Instead she removed one of the expensive souvenir photos off the wall, a large, framed picture of a humpback's tail against a white iceberg. She took it to the counter.

"Ah," the woman said. "This is a nice one."

"I thought I'd buy it for my mother. She enjoyed the boat so much today."

"Aren't you thoughtful. That will be a nice gift," the woman said. She took Caroline's money and gave her change. "Would you like me to wrap it up for you? I have some paper here."

"That would be great. Thanks."

The woman wrapped the photo and frame in three layers of tissue. "Where are you visiting from?"

"Windsor. But I grew up in the States, actually."

"Where about?" the woman asked. She taped the ends of the tissue paper together and slid the picture in a bag.

"Chicago."

"Oh, Chicago. I always wanted to go there."

"You should sometime."

"Yes, well," the woman said. "Maybe sometime. But I'm getting too old for much travel, I'm afraid." She rubbed her hands together. They were chapped and spotted, the hands of someone used to doing hard work, and suddenly Caroline was ashamed of her presence. This woman, the one who had once loved her father, who had expected him to come back from the war and marry her, was a person who had spent her life in hard work, had probably never even been away from Newfoundland. She had her sons and her business. She didn't need Caroline showing up on her doorstep, reminding her of old lies, old hurts. "Thank you," Caroline said, and took the bag from her. "It's a lovely photo."

"Come back anytime," the woman said, then turned around and went back into the kitchen.

TWELVE

Sam and Neil were coming back from their golf game, not yet out of the car, when Caroline told them that Ma had disappeared. Sam thought of the highway, his mother stumbling in front of someone's tires. She had started having trouble in new situations, strange locations. She misplaced her false teeth. She wandered off in the grocery store. Once, not long after Sam moved her in with him and Katie, she had given him a narrow-eyed look and said, "You thought that was pretty clever, didn't you? Keeping her from me all this time."

Sam had thought she was talking about Katie, but that wasn't it. "Who, Ma?" he'd asked.

"You know who," she'd said, but he didn't.

It was a hot day. Ma might be lost and she might not, but wherever she was she was on foot, and that meant she'd been gone a while.

Sam followed Katie out into the orchard to look for Ma. His daughter was wearing clunky-looking black sandals, impractical for the mud and brush and leaves underfoot, but she said she didn't care, didn't have time to change her shoes. She was anxious, calling, "Gran? . . . Gran? Are you out here?" It reminded Sam of when she was a child and brought home a stray cat to feed, crying when it wouldn't stay in the cardboard box she fixed up for its bed. She was more tenderhearted than she liked to let on. Sam worried about her. She was more vulnerable than Jennifer, who had her mother's strength, her mother's ability to put things aside once she was done with them. Katie was more like him. She bruised easily but hated to show her bruises. Since the divorce Jennifer was managing all right, but Katie, who was twenty that year, was taking it hard. She blamed her mother. She hated her mother's new husband, Phil, and wouldn't go visit them in Paris when school let out, even when Linda sent her the ticket. She made herself look sloppy because she knew it irritated her mother. She was drinking a lot, Sam knew—he could smell it on her when she came in at night. Then there was that business in March. Sam had come home early from work and seen not one but *two* different men slipping out the back door when he'd walked in. She'd said they had only been drinking, but Sam knew that wasn't the whole story. He'd kept a close eye on Katie after that, wouldn't leave her alone for a minute. She groused and grumbled, but it was all he could do not to tie her to a chair so he could keep an eye on her all the time.

Together they went slowly through the trees, calling for Ma, looking for anything resembling a person, a slip of cloth, a footprint. He reached the creek and walked alongside it. He was afraid at any moment he would see a familiar white head, a familiar shape, floating in the water, but he kept walking and didn't see anything but brush and dead leaves, bits of metal and string, once the smelly carcass of a dead skunk rotting along the bank. No sign of his mother.

He was tired and thirsty—he'd had a beer after the golf game, but that was hours ago. It was hot, getting hotter every minute.

From somewhere he could hear Caroline, calling, "Dottie! Where are you?" He could see her through the apple trees, her hair falling loose around her ears and her cheeks. When they'd arrived the day before, he'd been struck by the fact that Caroline, at fifty-five, was more beautiful than she had been at twenty. At a time when most women started to run to fat, Caroline was in the best shape he'd ever seen her, muscular and athletic, tanned from working in her garden. The little lines around her eyes gave them depth, and there was a wryness in her expression as she greeted them that night, a twist to her mismatched lips. He found himself wanting to rub his thumb across them, to wipe that look from her face. "It's good to see you," he'd said.

"And you," she'd said. "Divorce agrees with you, I see."

He'd laughed. They were still friends, after all.

In the orchard, it was getting dark. Caroline said they should come inside, she was going to call the police, but Katie said she couldn't go back to the house, not with Gran still missing, she couldn't just sit around and wait; so Caroline brought them flashlights, and they kept moving slowly through the woods and fields. The stars came out, but there was no moon. It was very dark. Ma could be anywhere. The longer they looked, the more certain he felt that they would not find her, that she would never be found.

It was after midnight when they went back to the house to talk to the police. They stayed up to watch the news, waiting for a mention of Dottie Dunmore, age seventy-six, missing since this afternoon, but none came. "What good is calling the police if they don't send out alerts?" Caroline said. She was blaming herself, but it wasn't her fault—it could have just as easily happened at home as here.

Sam dozed a little in the chair. When he woke it was dark, and Caroline had gone up to bed. He stood and went to the windows. He sat, got up again. He knew there was nothing he could do until the morning, but every minute Ma was gone, he knew there was less and less chance of finding her, or at least finding her safe. Even if they did find her, at this point he feared for her health. Charley was long dead and Pop was dead and Linda had removed herself from him, finally, and he found that now, the prospect of losing his mother as well made him afraid. It was something entirely different from what he'd felt in Vietnam with the bullets going past his ears, or in those days when Linda had threatened to leave and everything he ever thought he wanted started to unravel. This felt like losing himself.

Sam and Linda were married less than a year after his tour in Vietnam ended. They held the ceremony at his parents' church, with a party thrown by her folks afterward at the Drake Hotel. He was uncomfortable in his tuxedo and around his in-laws' friends and relatives, the pyramids of shrimp and the expensive champagne, but when he danced with Linda that night, when her arms went around his neck, he couldn't believe his own luck.

Linda had finished her degree at Rice by then, and despite the fact that she hated being so far from her family, they decided to stay in Chicago. Sam knew he could not move away from his mother. She was fragile after Charley died, cruel one minute and hysterical the next. The fact that they were all hurting didn't seem to register with her—she lived inside her pain like a room full of mirrors, reflecting it back at herself.

Linda didn't like the winters, fought with his mother. They were both stubborn, had particular ideas about how to do things, and those ideas were often at odds.

Linda taught in the public high school in one of the nearby suburbs, and Sam went to work for his father while he went to night school to finish up his degree on the GI Bill. When Jennifer was born after less than a year, though, Sam gave up hope of finishing college and went to work with Pop full-time. Linda stayed home. She had not been quite ready for mother-hood, not yet, and Jennifer was a demanding baby, colicky and clinging, the worst combination, because she screamed bloody murder whenever Linda held her, and she screamed even worse if she was down. With her own mother so far away and Dottie so distraught about Charley, Linda was alone with the baby most of the day. It made her resentful. They retreated from each other, grew intensely private, talked only of the baby or the bills or the repairs that needed to be done. They pretended it was normal, that everyone's marriage was like that.

When Jennifer started school, Linda went back to work as an editor at a textbook company. She worked long hours, made good money. More than ten years after they were married, they were surprised to find out Linda was pregnant again. Katie was born that fall. Linda decided to keep her job, a decision they argued over for months. She said she enjoyed the work because it made her feel useful. Sam began to suspect there was more to it than that. He grew to dread the stories she told at the end of the day, the people in her office, the men she met there. He started to harbor suspicions, to be jealous when one co-worker or another came to the forefront of her stories. If she worked late, he accused her of the most terrible things. If she attended a conference in a faraway city, he would call at strange hours to see if a man would answer. He couldn't help remembering the day they'd met at the beach, how effortlessly she had invited him back to her hotel room. She withered under his accusations, cried and threw things at him. Sometimes she disappeared for days and days, which upset the girls. Sam felt so foolish. He didn't understand why she would do this to him, when he loved her so much.

Once, when Sam was certain she was sleeping with someone from work, he followed her to a restaurant, and then to a hotel, and sat in the car outside the entrance to see when she arrived and when she left, but he fell asleep in the car and missed her when she came out. When he woke, her car was gone.

He couldn't bear to think of the men she saw, putting their hands on her. He was miserable, and he was making her miserable. She told Sam later, when they were in the middle of their most hurtful phase, that she had done it mostly because she was tired of him suspecting her. "If I'm going to be accused anyway of doing something wrong," she'd said, "I might as well get to enjoy myself first."

The divorce was her idea. She said there was no point to it anymore. The girls were grown. Jennifer had moved to San Diego with that boyfriend of hers. Katie would be a junior at Loyola that fall. Linda's latest had turned into more than a fling—he was leaving his wife, he wanted to get married again right away. Linda had inherited some money from her father and decided to go to Paris, something she'd always wanted to do but had given up when she married Sam. She said it would be best if they went their separate ways.

He didn't want her to leave. He admitted his jealousy had driven this wedge between them—it had made him crazy. But it seemed like stubbornness, like arrogance, she said, to assume that they could fix the things that were wrong. Sam hadn't thought so. He would have fixed anything, changed anything, if only she had stayed.

In the morning he went out again to look for his mother, taking his cell phone with him just in case news came to the house. Neil said he would call if he heard anything. Sam walked toward the lake. In this direction at least there was a cool breeze coming in from the shore. Walking made him feel better and burned off the last of his sleeplessness. Essex County was still mostly farmland, and flat. Ma had grown up here. She'd told him stories about it when he was younger, about the chickens and hogs they'd kept, the Jersey cow her father had for milk, how her father had kept her out of school when she was thirteen to stay home and help with the chores. His mother—cooker of roasts, mender of pants, washer of dishes, a wife, a mother, a daughter, a grandmother—was out there alone in the world because he had not been watching.

He walked down to the shore of Lake Erie, down the stone steps, and stood on the hot sand, the hot boulders. The lake stretched to the horizon. It had once been too polluted to swim in, someone had told him, but Caroline said it was coming back now, the government was cleaning it up. He took off his shoes and stood in the water. His feet were hot; the cold water felt good on them.

He heard someone behind him, a voice from the cliff above.

"I thought I'd find you here," Caroline said.

"Were you looking for me?"

"I was. I thought maybe you'd like some company."

"I would."

She took off her shoes, waded into water that lapped around her ankles. The rocks were slippery.

"Careful," he said.

"I won't fall."

"I just don't want to have to come in after you."

"Would you come in after me?"

"I suppose I'd have to."

Sam crossed the boulders toward her. Her skin in this light was very brown and looked soft. He remembered the soft backs of her knees, the way they felt under his hands when he moved them apart. He sat next to her with his feet in the water. She was looking out to the horizon, at the place where the water met the sky.

"I heard Katie say Linda's remarried already."

"That's right. In the winter."

"She didn't waste much time."

"She had plans long before the papers were signed."

"So I gathered."

Sam grinned. "You never liked her, did you."

Caroline looked as if she were hesitating, but then she smiled. "No," she said. "I never did."

"Aha. The truth comes out."

"Well, how was I supposed to feel?"

"Jealous, after all this time." He was enjoying the feeling of teasing her. "I never would have thought it."

"*Me* jealous? You're one to talk."

Sam didn't know what to say. He thought of the look on Linda's face the night she had said there was no point in her being faithful if he was going to suspect her anyway. How tired she had looked, how small and lonely, not the beautiful, vibrant girl he'd met that day on the beach. They had been in the kitchen, music on in the background, something of Katie's featuring several loud guitars. The driving noise seemed like a warning, the beating of his heart. He had known all along that it was coming to an end, but he still dreaded the moment of unveiling, the terrible moment of honesty they had avoided for so long. "You never believed in me," she'd said. "It was like you wanted me to hurt you. You *wanted* it to end." How much that suspicion had cost him. How hard it had been to let go of fear and jealousy, even after all that time.

Sam and Caroline sat on boulders and watched some kids playing up the beach. They were jumping from some rocks into the water, splashing, shrieking in delight. Their mother shaded her eyes with one hand to watch them, and she said something Sam couldn't hear, probably an admonishment to be more careful, that there were stones under the surface where they couldn't see.

There were others on the beach. A young woman in a black bathing suit floated on her back near shore. A golden retriever flung itself into the water after a stick, which was thrown by a young man in shorts with a large tattoo on his upper arm.

Farther up the beach, he saw her, the white-haired woman wading into the water up to her waist. She was walking slowly out into the lake, her hands in front of her, her pants dark from where they were soaking in the water. She swayed, said something Sam couldn't hear, but it didn't matter, he was already running down the beach toward her, toward his mother in the water, and he was pulling her back to shore. "Ma," he said. "Ma, it's me!"

She looked up when he approached her. There were scratches on her chin, as if she'd fallen, and she'd lost her glasses somewhere, so that she squinted at him. "It's you," she said.

Sam wondered if they should take her to the hospital. She could have hypothermia, dehydration.

"My God, you scared us," he said. "We didn't know where to look for you."

"I'm not going to the hospital. I'm fine. I just got lost."

"You were more than lost," Sam said.

"No hospital," she said. "I just need to rest."

Sam called Neil to bring the car. Ma was shivering from the cold water despite the heat of the day. They went up the steps, away from the beach, and Ma walked slowly, her breath running out, her hands out in front of her. She was so weak that he worried she might collapse on him, might stop breathing any second. Finally he picked her up and carried her up the steps to where the car was waiting. She was as light, almost, as a child. She did not complain. He could smell the hot sour smell of her breath and see the watery color of her eyes. Without her glasses she looked younger, more fragile, as if she had shed some essential piece of armor.

At the house, Caroline went into the kitchen to make Ma a cup of tea while Sam helped her change her clothes and drew a bath. She sat on the bed patiently, letting him minister to her, and this was how he knew how frightened she was, because normally she would never let him help her. He took off her shoes and socks. Her feet were swollen and gray from so much walking. He took them between his hands and rubbed them. They were cold, despite the summer heat.

"Oh, that's good," she said as they warmed.

He put her in the bath himself. It was shocking to see his mother's naked body, her pink, papery skin, her flattened breasts and light downy hair. He closed his eyes, turned away, and when Caroline took his arm and said she would help Dottie with her bath, Sam was only too grateful to let her do so. He went out and shut the door. In his mother's room, he sat on the bed. The air smelled like cigarette smoke. He would have been angry about it, except that the damage was already done. He decided not to say anything.

On the table next to the bed there was an old snapshot of a girl standing in the sun in front of a sign that read THE VICTORIA INN, squinting at the camera. Sam picked it up. He tried to guess who it was—Aunt Bella? No, she'd looked like Ma. Someone he'd never seen before. On the back was written, in small, elegant handwriting, "All my love."

Ma was standing above him in Caroline's bathrobe, her hair wrapped in a towel. She was looking at the picture in his hand, Caroline in the doorway behind her.

"Who is this, Ma?" he asked.

"I don't know," she said. "I never met her."

It had been in with Walt's things, Ma said. After he died. With his medals and insignia. "I don't know who she is," Ma said again. She looked at Sam with an intensity that bordered on anger—at his father, Sam thought, or at herself for trusting him. "Your father, he certainly knew how to keep a secret."

"No, no," Caroline said. "It isn't his. It belonged to my father. He must have kept it after my father died. All this time he had it. I never would have guessed." She held up the photo and turned it over. "Her name is Rosemary Oram. My father was engaged to her during the war. Of course, she didn't know he was already married. My mother still doesn't know a thing about it."

"Your father?" Ma asked. "Are you sure?"

"I'm positive. I even met her once. She still looks just like this, or did."

Ma stood up and went down the stairs and out into the yard with the blanket wrapped around her. Sam followed her. He was thinking about Alister Clark, Caroline's father, a man he'd never met and knew only from his father's stories. He had been a good navigator, a good friend. A funny man, a joker. Pop had always been a little bit sad talking about Al Clark. As if he blamed himself for what had happened. As if he'd known that with just a little more luck, out there in the bush, Al could have lived, and everything would have been different.

Ma was out at the orchard, the rows of trees with their young green fruit, the branches waving in the slight breeze that had started to come up. "Your father never mentioned the photo. He never told me about the girl. I thought, since it was with his things, that the photograph had belonged to him."

"But Pop wasn't like that."

"Oh," she said, looking at him sidelong, "you'd be surprised at the secrets people can keep."

For a moment Sam was expecting to see her changed, but there she was all the same, the same old Ma, tired and cranky. She was safe for now. Still, he felt the weight of what was coming. Someday, probably someday soon, she would die. It was there, just ahead of him. There would come a time when he would wake up in the morning and she would be gone, just as Pop was. It seemed too awful to contemplate. Yet there was a relief hovering just behind his fear, a sense of release and of the completion of something imperfect and beautiful.

"I liked having a swim," she said. "It was so refreshing."

"It certainly was," Sam said, and suggested maybe it was time for bed.

They showed their papers at the border. This time the border agent was a kid with a pimply face and sleeves that were too short. He looked at their papers, then leaned down to look inside the car. Katie was reading in the back, her feet propped up against the window. Ma with her eyes closed, afraid of the bridge. "Do you remember," Ma was saying, "when we moved to the States? Do you remember that day?"

They had sold the unfinished house that Pop had been building, most of the furniture. That morning they said good-bye to Sam's grandparents, to Uncle Jimmy and Aunt Bella, to Adele and Caroline, and drove away from the Lake Erie shore in Pop's secondhand car. Sam in the backseat, wearing his cowboy hat, singing, "Happy trails to you, until we meet again . . ." Charley on Ma's lap, trying to reach for the car keys. Sam had wanted to know if they were going to be cowboys.

"Yes, of course," Pop said. "All Americans are cowboys."

"Walt. Don't tease him."

She was laughing. When they went over the bridge, she had rolled her window down and put out her hands and laughed.

"You were happy that day," Sam said. "That's what I remember."

The border agent waved them through. Sam aimed the car up the incline toward the bridge, the sun behind them, the wind coming up, blowing the air clean, a bright day, Detroit glinting, steam rising from factory smokestacks, the highway pointing west. Up the bridge, nosing the car toward the sky. Ma kept her eyes closed. "Tell me when it's over," she said.

"Gran," said Katie, "there's nothing to be afraid of."

"Easy for you to say." There was something teasing in her voice. The old Ma.

Sam rolled down the window and put out his hand, felt the air pushing against it. The wind felt good on his hands and his face.

"Close that window!" Ma said, but she was smiling, and then her eyes opened. She told Sam to drive with both hands on the wheel, thank you, but she wasn't angry, she was laughing. The three of them were laughing. They were high on the bridge with the river below, high up like flying, like flying through the air with a watch and a sextant and a celestial point to guide you, and he thought, This is how you measure great distances; this is how you find your way across the earth.

I am most ⋯ ⋯ssociation of
Canada, esp⋯ ⋯ss Hamilton.
Many thank⋯ ⋯Gander Public
Library; Da⋯ ⋯ntic Aviation
Museum; F⋯ ⋯Worrall; Nhai
Tran and V⋯ ⋯tion. Thanks
to Robert l⋯ ⋯eying camps
and the R(⋯ ⋯e Michener-
Copernicus ⋯ ⋯sistance.

For their ⋯ ⋯nk Conroy,
Ethan Cani⋯ ⋯, Marilynne
Robinson, (⋯ ⋯o my editor,
Gillian Blak⋯ ⋯mble thanks
for your faith⋯ ⋯ also to Kate
Lee, Marisa ⋯ ⋯ssistance.

Thanks to ⋯ ⋯Dougherty,
Saundra Cra⋯ ⋯d, John and
Marilyn Hel⋯ ⋯y, the Ayers
family, the K⋯ ⋯y Eppinger,
Michelle Fal⋯ ⋯ogers, Alex
Ruskell, Sara⋯ ⋯rley, as well
as all my frie⋯ ⋯pport were
priceless.

Finally, tha⋯ ⋯gs possible.

A NOTE ON THE AUTHOR

Rebecca Johns was born in Libertyville, Illinois. She has worked for
publications such as *Life* magazine and *Woman's Day*, and her articles have
appeared in *Cosmopolitan*, *Mademoiselle*, *Self*, and *Seventeen*. She is a recent
graduate of the Iowa Writers' Workshop and received the Michener-
Copernicus Award for this, her first novel.